# UNDYING

AMIE KAUFMAN AND MEAGAN SPOONER

HYPERION

Los Angeles    New York

First Edition, January 2019
10 9 8 7 6 5 4 3 2 1
FAC-020093-18334
Printed in the United States of America

This book is set in Jenson Recut/Fontspring; Adobe Jenson Pro, Andale Mono,
Futura LT Pro/Monotype
Designed by Mary Claire Cruz

Library of Congress Cataloging-in-Publication Data
Names: Kaufman, Amie, author. • Spooner, Meagan, author.
Title: Undying : an Unearthed novel / by Amie Kaufman and Meagan Spooner.
Description: First edition. • Los Angeles ; New York : Hyperion, 2019. • Summary: "Trapped
aboard the Undying's ancient spaceship and reeling from what they've learned there, scavenger
Mia and academic Jules are plunged into a desperate race to warn their home planet of the
danger humanity's greed has unleashed"— Provided by publisher.
Identifiers: LCCN 2018039040 • ISBN 9781484755563 (hardcover)
Subjects: • CYAC: Science fiction. • Extraterrestrial beings—Fiction. •
Space flight—Fiction. • Technology—Fiction. • Love—Fiction.
Classification: LCC PZ7.K1642 Unb 2019 • DDC [Fic]—dc23
LC record available at https://lccn.loc.gov/2018039040

Reinforced binding

Visit www.hyperionteens.com

SUSTAINABLE FORESTRY INITIATIVE  Certified Sourcing
www.sfiprogram.org
SFI-00993

THIS LABEL APPLIES TO TEXT STOCK

*We love to tell stories.*
*We're so grateful for those who read them.*
*So, Reader, this book is dedicated to you.*

Dear Reader,

You know what we love about sequels? Meeting beloved characters again, exploring new parts of a well-traveled world, learning how all the little clues add up in the end. You know what we *don't* love about sequels?

Trying to remember what on Earth (or Gaia!) happened in book one.

So we decided we'd help you out with a lightning-quick recap of *Unearthed*, because we wrote these books to have fun and to *be* fun, and wandering around confused for half a novel is no fun at all. (Plus, after the cliffhanger in book one, we figured we owed it to you.)

If you haven't figured it out yet, here be spoilers for *Unearthed* . . .

We meet our main characters on the surface of a planet named Gaia, in a far-distant solar system discovered after receiving instructions for building a portal from a long-dead alien race called the Undying. Earth is in dire need of relief, and after the failure of a massive colonization attempt, scientists believe that the Undying hold the only key to saving our planet from ourselves.

Jules Addison is the privileged son of the Oxford professor who first decoded the aliens' message and urged the world to take notice. When Dr. Addison changed his mind, however, after discovering evidence that the Undying might not be the harmless benefactors they seemed to be, the world turned on him. Jules has made his way to Gaia in order to find proof that his father is right.

Amelia Radcliffe is a scavenger who grew up taking care of her sister, in direct violation of one-child laws. When her sister gets in over her head with a sketchy nightclub, Mia must raise the money to buy back her contract. So she signs up with a professional low-life named Mink and is smuggled to Gaia's surface in order to scavenge as many valuable bits of tech as she can.

A scavenger and an academic. Of course, they end up forced to work together. Despite their drastically different upbringings, they learn to respect one another. And as they navigate a series of deadly traps, leading them to another portal deep in the heart of the Gaian temple, they start to fall for each other.

The portal transports them to the southern pole of Gaia, where they discover a vast ship locked in ice. Military forces from the International Alliance, a global coalition of world governments, have beaten them there and Jules and Mia are in for a shock: The woman who recruited Mia is the same woman who recruited Jules, and she lied to both of them about her identity. Jules's mission was all a setup to lead Mink and her forces to the prize at the heart of the maze: the Undying ship.

While Mink forces our heroes to activate the ship and send it back to Earth, Mia and Jules try to find a way to stop her for fear that Jules's father was right all along and the Undying technology is dangerous after all. When they fail, they stay on board as the ship launches, determined to find a way to stop the ship before it reaches Earth.

A series of power surges on the ship bring them running in time to discover a corridor full of portals, all activating so that an Undying invasion force can step through.

Think a Trojan Horse, only instead of a dozen crafty ancient Greeks, it's full of aliens.

Or is it? Because in the final pages of the book, Jules and Mia get a shock even worse than the realization that the Undying aren't extinct, and that they're coming for Earth. They watch as one of the Undying soldiers removes a helmet and reveals a human face.

Dun dun duuuun!

So, without further ado, we bring you to an ancient crystalline spaceship in orbit around Earth. We zoom in on a particular deck, and a specific corridor, and a little dark crawlspace beneath it. We'll leave you there, and wish you happy reading! Hopefully you have as much fun reading this book as we did writing it.

1

JULES

THE DARKNESS IS CLOSE AND STILL, AND ABSOLUTE. MIA IS NEARBY—
I can feel her body heat, a gentle warmth along one side. In the
quiet, our ragged breaths are as harsh as a siren's wail.

And then Mia shatters the thick, eerie silence: "Screw it, I can't
do this in the dark—Jules, turn your watch on, will you?"

Despite the fear coursing through me, I find myself smothering
a smile as I fumble at my wrist for the LED. A week hiding aboard
an occupied alien spaceship, and she's the one thing I can count on
to feel familiar. Safe. Like home.

Most of our devices are dead, with no access to the sun to
recharge, but my wrist unit charges kinetically—something I'm
increasingly grateful for each day. The idea of existing this way in
utter darkness is too terrifying to contemplate long.

The pale blue light spills out from the watch screen. Mia appears
out of the darkness like a ghost, her face framed by her choppy
black and pink and blue hair, skin white beneath her freckles. She's
got her multi-tool out, and with a wan little smile at me, she goes

1

back to work, trying to pry the bolts off an access cover to the narrow passageway we're in. The glint of the crystalline stone lining the shaft plays tricks on my vision, masquerading as glittering eyes in the gloom.

The hinge on the cover gives a tiny creak of protest as she finally succeeds. Easing the cover aside and letting it dangle from one hinge, Mia reveals the opportunity we've been searching for: a chance to get ahead of the Undying aliens that came pouring through the portals on this ship a week ago.

• • •

The passageway we're using is actually a cavity *between* the walls of the ship. We found these hidden spaces by crawling up into the ventilation system to hide in those first frenzied minutes after the ship took off, and the Undying emerged from the portals along the long hallway we'd discovered. We wriggled through the vents on knees and elbows—we still do, occasionally—until we found the hatches leading down inside the walls.

Thick metal doors are recessed along the hallways at regular intervals, ready to snap shut and seal off any one section in case of a hull breach. The vents have impressive shutter systems, no doubt designed to lock down automatically at the first sign of a change in air pressure. As Mia said when she discovered the first set of auto-doors, the Undying are *seriously* spacefaring. They make the ships we used to reach Gaia look like a kid's toy rocket set.

The Undying wasted no time in grid-searching the ship, hundreds of sets of boots stomping down the hallways, voices echoing over each other so that the individual words were impossible to make out. They know humans launched the ship—all their traps were designed to make sure we did, after all.

What they didn't know was that there were two of us still on board.

They would have found Hansen's body in one of the corridors, where we had no choice but to leave him after one of the

International Alliance soldiers shot him. Even as they were drag-ging him away to dispose of him, Mia still had his blood under her fingernails, from where she tried to stanch his wounds.

I wonder what they made of him. Of us, that we killed one another in the middle of an extraordinary discovery like this.

So Mia and I hid first in the vents, and then in the walls when we found them, and now, after a week on the run, we know our territory. We even have a home base of sorts. We call it the Junction—a slightly wider spot where six different walls meet in a star-shaped intersection, and there's room to sit, wedged in side by side. We have neighbors on just one side there—a pair of Undying who call each other Atlanta and Dex—and if we hold perfectly still and they stand in the right place, we can listen in on their conversations, and catch a glimpse of them through the vent. And when they're out of their room, on shift, we can talk quietly our-selves without risk of being overheard.

But we've been too busy just surviving to *do* anything—to hunt for answers, to take action. We haven't been able to figure out how—or why—they've managed to look so much like us, only that they're *not* us, and the resemblance only goes skin-deep. We haven't even been able to figure out what they want with Earth, except that they intend to take it from us.

Whatever that means, neither of us particularly likes the sound of it.

All we need is a single chance to contact Earth. We may not know why they're here, but if we can warn humanity that the mas-sive ship in orbit *isn't* empty, as they believe, there's a chance the cavalry will arrive before the Undying discover we're here.

Of course, as Mia pointed out, the IA's equally as likely to sim-ply blow the ship out of the sky. But I prefer to hope for the best. To trust that they wouldn't destroy their last chance to discover technology that could save Earth from its rapid decline and dwin-dling resources.

The access panel Mia's been working on opens up into the

corner of a small chamber habitually occupied by a single Undying worker, whose movements we started tracking two days ago. As best we can tell, this Undying drone seems to think it necessary to take at least two breaks an hour. There's a slacker in every bunch, and we're counting on ours today. We've heard enough one-sided conversations through the wall that we know he's outfitted with one of the clever little headsets most of the Undying on the ship wear, composed of a small metal piece that folds over one ear and a slim strip of glass that folds out over one eye.

If these headsets are like phones for the Undying, then maybe— just *maybe*—we can find a way to use one to call home.

Without wasting a moment of this latest break, we climb down into the small room where our target works, crossing our fingers this is one of his longer absences. I catch Mia as she lets herself drop after me, feet-first. She rests in my arms for a moment, almost nose-to-nose with me, and our eyes meet. My heart speeds, even as I try to remind myself this is hardly the time.

She's kissed me twice since we met.

Once was to get me to follow her through the portal inside the temple. The second time was right before we thought we were going to die.

Since then, we've never been apart for more than half an hour. We've curled up together to sleep, we've wedged ourselves in together to eavesdrop in the narrow passageways, but neither of us has made a move toward another kiss. Me, because I'm too damned awkward to know if it would be welcome outside an emergency— nothing like a survival scenario with someone who's had to politely turn you down—and her, because . . . well, if I knew, this would be easier. Maybe it only occurs to her when we're in a life-and-death situation.

Then again, one could make a convincing argument that death's pretty close, and every moment we're aboard this ship is an emergency.

*I wonder if I could convince her of that.*

I set her down, and she doesn't linger, crossing over to the door to stand by it and keep watch, ready to give me as much warning as she can. I turn for the workstation, which thankfully didn't retract into the wall when its operator left—but then my gaze is caught by the window.

For the first time since I left it, I can see Earth.

I can make out the mostly golden-brown shapes of North and South America, wreathed in white wisps of cloud. Somewhere down there is Mia's little sister, Evie, lost in the huge sprawl of the two continents. Some green still clings to the bulge of the south, but the coastal deserts in the north are slowly creeping in toward each other.

It's a paler brown than the rusty red of Gaia. In the short time I was there, I grew quickly accustomed to the barren beauty of the alien planet. I thought I'd die there, at the hands of scavvers, or crushed in a temple trap when my wits let me down, or simply when my breather ran out. Or, over those last few days, at the hands of the IA—of Charlotte, or Mink, or whatever our double-crossing puppet master's really called.

And after that, I thought I'd die sabotaging this ship, or when that failed, when it came through the portal and self-destructed in an attack on Earth. Now we're stranded. Compared to being stuck on Gaia, we're so close to home it's like we're standing on the front porch. But without a way to get to the surface, we might as well still be on the other side of the galaxy. And expecting, every day, to be caught and most likely killed.

*Mehercule, no wonder I'm tired.*

My cousin Neal's down there too, on the green teardrop of England, hidden around the curve of the globe. Maybe my father too, somewhere in the heart of Prague.

A loud, dull thud nearly sends me sprinting back toward the dubious safety of the ventilation shaft. Mia, at my side, retreats several steps. A spattering of scrapes and a second, smaller clang, and I see a glitter of something metallic drift past the window—the sound came from outside the ship, not inside.

At the Junction, we're too far in the interior of the ship to have heard this—but here, on its outer edge, we can hear the sound of Earth's satellites colliding with the ship's hull, bouncing off as a cloud of debris to drift forever into space, or else return home in an arc of fire as falling stars.

Trying to regain my composure, I grab the headset, hook the curve of the metal over my ear, and position the glass lens over my right eye. I can still see the room beyond it, but after an instant, a line of glowing white text appears, projected in front of me and superimposed over the view.

COMMAND/QUERY?

"Is it working?" Mia whispers.

"It's working," I murmur, trying to keep my voice calm. "And Mia—it's in English."

She meets my eyes, strangely overwritten in my vision by the text in the headset. Her gaze is wide, confused, frightened—but I've got no way to comfort her, and no answers to provide.

Abruptly, she stiffens, her gaze going past me toward the exit. "Quick, he's coming back!"

My heart leaps, and I yank the headset off my head. But when I go to replace it on the workstation, I find my fingers refuse to obey me.

"What're you doing?" Mia hisses.

"We need this." I'm frozen, all the more so now that I can make out what Mia heard a second before: footsteps approaching down the corridor. "We can't just leave it."

"We steal it, they know we exist." Mia's fingers curl around my wrist, squeezing, and under her hand my own relaxes.

"Perfututi," I mumble, and let the thing go.

I'm about to whirl around and race back to the vent in the wall when I see the headset wobble. My stomach seizes. In my haste, I've dropped it down on the edge of the workstation. It teeters, and as Mia and I both lunge for it, it slips off the corner of the desk and drops.

The approaching footsteps falter as the sound of shattering glass echoes through the crystal-lined room. Then they break into a run.

2

AMELIA

**FOR A MOMENT JULES AND I CLASH AT THE VENT ENTRANCE, AND** it takes me two long, precious heartbeats to realize we're both trying to get the other to go first into the vent. I abandon my efforts and clamber up him like he's a tree, then press myself in against the interior wall as tightly as I can so Jules can squeeze in past me.

His long limbs barely fit, and he makes so much noise when he moves that it sounds to my ears like the drummer in a band has taken up residence inside the walls, but so far no one's noticed us. I lean over after him, with barely enough room to turn and replace the hatch behind us.

I grab for Jules's ankle and squeeze, warning him not to move. Reminding myself not to hold my breath, I watch while the worker falters halfway to the console, then bends down to retrieve the headset. Heart pounding, ears straining, I wait.

Then comes a gusty sigh and a muttered word I don't know,

though I certainly recognize its tone. A tap of fingers on controls, and then a voice: "Screen repair request, shifting it yourways for recyc now."

The worker's footsteps start moving again, but we're both frozen when a crackly voice bleats tinnily in the small room. Until now, he's always spoken to the others through his headset—this is the first time we've heard them use a communications system built into the ship.

"Sirsly?" The voice is more annoyed than professional. "That's two you've lixo'd since we shifted."

"Don't give me hassle, it's just the screen," protests Slacker, coming to a halt only a meter or so from the hatch, which I'm still holding in place. I have a brief flash of panic that "recyc" is somehow the vent we're hiding in, but then he pulls a drawer-like receptacle out of the wall and places the headset in it. "It still works, just cracked-like."

"Hold up your send, someone's using the transit."

Slacker sighs, starting back toward his console. "Broken piece of lixo ship," he mutters.

I can still see the drawer if I crane my neck. The ship has a built-in delivery system, not unlike the old vacuum tubes they used to use in banks and post offices on Earth. It's how we've been stealing food—if you can call the flavorless, rubbery white protein cubes *food*—intercepting deliveries to individual rooms and stations.

Abruptly, I realize he's sending his headset down that way. And there are precious few seconds before he hits the button that'll send it zooming away.

"Don't move," I breathe, watching the boots intently as I ease forward, keeping the hatch clutched in one hand.

Jules goes rigid under my fingers, choking a protest. I squeeze his leg to reassure him, all too aware there's nothing he can do to stop me without getting us both caught. We've wasted a week waiting for someone on Earth to notice the ship in orbit isn't empty—this is our first chance to take action, rather than waiting to be rescued. I *won't* let it slip away because I'm scared.

I slide out of the tunnel, lowering myself down and carefully placing one foot and then the other, my eyes on the Undying worker the whole while.

For an instant, I'm standing only a few meters away from him, looking at his back as he gazes down at the console, waiting for permission to proceed. It's the closest either of us have been to the Undying since they arrived. I can't see his face, but from the back he could be any normal Earth boy, right down to the impatient drumming of his fingertips against the console. His skin is a rich, dark brown, and his hair falls to his shoulders in tousled waves that remind me of Evie's. My whole body shrinks from the idea of this ancient alien menace masquerading as something so familiar.

It's so easy to forget they're not human. Like us. But when I look at this thing, all I can think of are those first few frantic moments after the Undying portals first activated. Jules and I hid, terrified of the bulbous-looking heads and jet-black suits, and got the shock of our lives when one of them took off its helmet to reveal it wore a human face underneath.

A few hours of watching them march about the ship from our ventilation shaft, and Jules whispered, "They're human—they may be different, but maybe we can just *talk* to them? Find out how and why they're here, explain who we are?"

The suggestion made every hair on the back of my neck lift and prickle, but he'd squeezed my hand and looked at me with those big, brown, Jules-sweet eyes, and for a moment I was ready to lead us out of hiding, to throw ourselves on the mercy of these ancient beings. And then one of them slipped on a patch of melted snow from the ship's resting place on Gaia, and fell into a bit of exposed rock wall.

With a cry he fell, clutching his leg—and a spray of bright blue blood spattered across the wall opposite.

Jules had frozen, his hand suddenly ice-cold in mine.

Whatever these things are, they're *not* human. They're nothing like us. And if they catch us, there will be no mercy.

Now, looking at one of them standing casually at his workstation, it's somehow even worse than if they'd remained bulbous-headed mysteries.

My hands are steady, though, as they slide the drawer back open and retrieve the headset.

I'm retreating slowly back toward the hatch, clutching my prize, when the intercom crackles again with the all clear. He'll sit once he sends it, and I'll be well within his peripheral vision. I almost stumble in my haste, grabbing at the edge of the ventilation shaft and withdrawing into its cramped confines like a hermit crab scuttling back into its shell. He turns to hit the button, and I pull the hatch into place with a tiny clang that sounds in time with the whoosh of moving air just above us in the wall.

Neither of us moves for several long, tortured heartbeats. Slacker eases back down onto his bench, and with a sigh, bends over the console. The ship has none of the fancy tech the Undying wear and use as they go about their day, and they rarely seem to use much of the built-in technology that to us seems so advanced. But, without his headset, Slacker's working like someone forced to switch from digital back to analog.

We wait a few more minutes, Jules's body still stiff with panic and outrage. Then, as silently as we can, we slip away into the walls once more.

● ● ●

"Of all the foolish, impulsive risks—" Jules's whisper is infuriated once we emerge into the Junction.

"Shut up!" I retort, scowling. "It worked, didn't it?" It's exactly what we needed: a chance to get a step ahead of these alien beings for once, and maybe even find a way home, all without them ever knowing we've stolen anything, because the headset was on its way to be recycled.

"Mehercule, every time I think I know just how stubborn and reckless you are, you go and pull something—"

"I don't want to die up here, Jules!" I gulp for breath, trying to stop my voice shaking. "And if I do, I want to go out fighting, not hunted down like a couple of rats in the wall."

Jules runs a hand over his face, features glinting with perspiration in the pale blue light of the wrist unit. "Let me see the headset," he says resignedly.

The request is a peace offering, and I respond with one of my own as I hand over the stolen headset. "You wanted more time with it to see if we can call home. Don't say I never get you anything pretty."

Jules's lips press together as he carefully inspects the headset. "Don't ever buy me a birthday present," he mutters. Then his eyes flick up to meet mine, and his lips relax into a little smile.

I grin at him and then fold myself into the edge of the meager space in the Junction, to make room for him at my side. My heart is still racing, and every tiny sound—not uncommon, inside the walls of an ancient spaceship—makes me jump. The close call is enough to make *me* snap, but I force myself to at least *seem* calm for Jules's sake.

A quick look at his wrist screen tells me we've got a little less than an hour before our neighbors, Atlanta and Dex, finish their shifts and return to their cabin. An hour to talk.

Jules finishes his inspection by slipping the headset into place, which makes it come to life again. "The screen's cracked," he reports, his visible eye distant as the hidden one focuses on the glass. "But I can still see most of what's on it."

Triumphant, I rummage around in the shadows beneath the pipe that carries water throughout the ship. My fingers locate the remains of breakfast, a block of sponge-like cubes the size of my palm. I break it apart and bite into a cube, putting the rest aside for Jules. He's bigger than me, and eats more, and when he goes off into one of his scholar fits of intensive study, he always comes out ravenous. And every time, he's surprised by how hungry he is.

"What is it saying?" I ask, all too aware that he'll forget I'm even there, in the midst of his intellectual exploration.

Jules shakes his head. "It's—hard to say. It's like it's interfacing with my brain waves somehow, reading my mind . . . every little distracted thought I have, it tries to run with."

"Maybe that's why it's in English, not glyphs." I lean to the side, but I'd have to press my face to Jules's to see anything on the glass, and I abandon the attempt. "It reads your mind and translates itself into the language you speak most easily."

"Maybe." Jules's voice sounds troubled, but it's clear he has no better explanation. "I can't get it to give me anything about communication, except to other headsets. Nothing about transmitting to a nearby planet."

"What about a map of the ship?" I suggest, chewing, trying not to let my disappointment out in my voice. We have time—Jules may yet figure out how to use the headset to signal Earth to come get us. *And, you know, stop the Undying, but maybe rescue us first.*

"A map of the ship isn't exactly going to tell us what they're doing here, what they want with Earth."

"But it might show us if there's a communications center we could use to talk to Earth. Or at least how to stay hidden a while longer." Although I know he wants to get home as badly as I do—and he knows finding a way to send a message is key to that—he does keep circling around to his old research instincts. He keeps wondering what the Undying plan to do, trying to understand them like the academic he is.

What I need him to remember is that it doesn't *matter* what the Undying are doing here, because even if we knew, we couldn't do anything about it unless we could send a message home.

Jules sighs. "I'll try to find a map."

And then he's gone. I leave him to it, leaning back against the wall, ignoring the now-familiar ache its angled surface brings to my shoulders. I'm wearing his wrist unit right now, and by its light I survey the objects scattered about our hideout.

To anyone else, our supplies would seem pathetically few. A shallow cup improvised from a piece of waterproof mesh cut from one of their discarded jumpsuits, stretched across a frame made from crumpled foil from the food blocks, catches water that drips from a tiny hole we've cut in the pipe. The rest of the uniform fabric, gathered up to serve as a blanket. My multi-tool, the only thing we have to cut, harvest, craft what we need.

Not much, when you think about the fact that these bits of junk are the only weapons we have to defend ourselves against a clearly hostile army. But each object represents a victory, some risk or gambit made to secure it. And we've had precious few of those.

Unless you call staying alive—and undetected—for this long a victory.

*Which I do, dammit.*

Our only advantage is that the Undying don't know we're aboard their ship. They're not careless, but they also don't have any guards posted in every corridor like they might if they suspected foul play. Still, the ship is getting busier by the day, with more Undying coming through the portals all the time.

The portals are a mystery to us—we know they lead from one place to another, that the Undying can choose those locations, and build them the size of a spaceship, or of a regular door . . . but we don't know how they do any of it. Twice, we've tried to sneak into that corridor full of portals to see if there was any way to use them to get home, but both times the whole place was chaotic with activity. There's no way to get to them unseen.

Jules's body is warm against mine. The air on the ship is several degrees lower than comfortable room temperature, although it doesn't seem to bother the Undying. The chill combined with the confines of the Junction keep us in close quarters. But as much as I wish I could stretch out, spread my arms as wide as I can and take a deep breath, I'm grateful for the cramped space.

Because I'm not sure if I'd have the guts to snuggle up to Jules if there was more room.

He's so absorbed in learning how to use the headset that I can watch him openly. He's a mess, his clothes sweat-stained and grimy, with a noticeable scent I wish I could call "masculine" rather than "gross as hell"—but then, I'm just as bedraggled and unwashed as he is. You don't get to shower when you're a stowaway.

He looks tired, and that muscle ticking in his jaw means he's holding tension there. I wonder if he'd even notice if I touched him—touched him more, I mean. He's barely looked at me in the last few days.

Which is as it should be. We're probably going to die—we've both accepted that, in our own separate ways, I think. But if there's a chance to get a signal to Earth, we owe it to our families on Earth to try. I owe it to Evie. Even if she stays indentured to the club where she works for the rest of her life, it has to be better than what these aliens would have in store for her. Whatever the Undying are planning, the fact that they went to such enormous trouble to trick all of humanity suggests it's not going to be a fiesta for the people we love.

With the weight of that on our shoulders, the last thing either of us should be thinking about is—

A clang makes us both jump, and my heart leaps into my throat. Voices from the wall at my back give us a source for the sound, and when another clang reverberates through the stone, I recognize it as the slam of the sliding door to the room on the other side of the vent at our feet.

Fumbling in my haste, I hide the blue glow of the wrist unit against my leg until I can turn it off, and Jules wriggles a strip of rubber from my boots down into place over the leak in the pipe. How much they can hear on their side, we don't know, but the last thing we need is a maintenance crew coming through here looking for a leaky pipe.

The headset clinks as Jules sets it down. I see the glitter of his eyes in the darkness as they search for mine, and I know why he's uneasy. From the first moment they arrived, the Undying have operated with clockwork precision. Not once has anyone missed a shift or arrived late.

Today, Atlanta and Dex are early.

**3**

**JULES**

"Aw, come on, Peaches, don't give me hassle." That's Dex, as two pairs of footsteps walk into the crew quarters on the other side of the wall.

"What kind of lixo's *peaches?*" That's Atlanta, sounding seriously unimpressed.

Mia and I exchange a wordless glance, then slowly ease down onto our sides, so we can watch through the vent at floor level—we're invisible in the dark, but if we get the right angle we can see most of the neat little room, with its two bunks and tiny closet.

"Peaches are food," Dex says, unpeeling the top half of his jumpsuit to reveal the undershirt below, giving me a glimpse of a tattoo as he knots the arms of the thing around his waist. He *looks* no older than we are, and neither does Atlanta. They look like teenagers—but all I can see when I look at them is that spray of blue blood, and for all I know he could be centuries older.

I glance at Mia again, and by the furrow in her brow, I know she's noticed the tattoo as well. It's one thing for these aliens to have done something to themselves—surgery, some kind of hallucinogenic projection—to look human. But for them to sport *tattoos* is an attention to detail that turns my blood to ice.

The Undying pair are still talking. "I searched it," Dex protests. "You're named for Atlanta, where they used to grow plants called peaches. *Peaches* is an endearment in proto-speak."

"Did I do something to endear myself to you?" she asks pointedly, words punctuated by a thump as she throws herself down onto her bunk.

"Not this cycle," he admits, sinking down opposite, just his shins and feet visible from our vent. "But I live in hope. Can we talk on this?"

"There's nothing to talk on," she snaps. The two of them squabble like siblings, exchanging barbs and little insults as often as they share affectionate jokes, but they've never outright fought before. Dex is easygoing and Atlanta's more formal, but it's clear they've known each other a long time. Maybe they grew up together. Wherever the hell they grew up. *If* they even grew up—to assume they had anything like a human childhood is to fall straight back into the trap of thinking they're like us.

They're both tall, around my height, and built on slender lines, though they're wiry and strong rather than delicate. They both have the same light brown skin and black hair, though hers is sleeker and smooth, his thicker and curlier. They both keep it long enough to braid it back from their faces neatly.

"Slow it, Peaches." His tone is conciliatory. "I pledge, I only think it's worth thinking on requesting another destin. We can have our pick."

*Destin*, my mind echoes, turning over furiously. As in *destiny*? I find myself hoping against hope that they're about to tell us what they're all doing here, and what they want with Earth.

"We're taking Prime-One, okay? I didn't get us to top roster to take some lixo know-seeking destin." She sighs. "Have you seen what the world looks like down there? There's more desert and smog than blue and green, the whole thing's gonna be lixo soon . . . we gotta shift downwards, Dex. The sooner we get rid of them down there, the better."

"I compren." Dex's voice is quiet. "And we will shift. I just—"

Atlanta's voice sharpens. "What is this, Dex? You scared? You never been scared before."

"Yeh, and I'm not scared now," he says calmly. "And I'm not trying to give you hassle. All I'm saying is there's a lot we don't compren yet. You and I hold on, the first teams down to the surface are going to send beno data thisways. Give it a little time, and maybe we'll know Prime-One isn't as beno as we think. Maybe some more important destin comes ourways, and that's when you and I step up."

I can feel Mia's shallow breaths where she's pressed against my front. With her head tucked under my chin as we lie on our sides, we can share the view through the vent.

Atlanta huffs, unconvinced. "You can make anything sound beno."

Dex laughs. "That's why all the boys look myways," he agrees.

Atlanta gives a massive sigh and folds her hands behind her head. "I want to shift *now*, Dex. What use is all our training if we only sit up here watching their television stories and reading their internets?"

"There'll be action," he says. "I pledge, there'll be action for every single pair aboard this ship by the time we're done, and every single person below."

"Don't start on about the protos again," she groans, halfheartedly tossing a piece of dirty laundry at him.

He pushes up to his feet, and his boots approach her bunk. "Let's get something to eat," he suggests.

She grumbles a reply. "We *could* be eating planetside, if we'd shifted already." But even though she protests, she's swinging her legs off the bed, and taking his hand so he can pull her up.

"Regular food will taste like lixo once we've eaten planetside," he replies cheerfully. "So we might as well eat up before we learn what the beno stuff's like." He's already untying the sleeves of his jumpsuit from around his waist as they prepare to leave. "We'll hit the bridge after, learn what the new data is," he suggests, as they make their way through the door. "We'll make clear we're up for the challenge, okay? Whether we go Prime-One or not—our assignment will be beno."

She pauses in the doorway, looking into his eyes, searching. "And you *do* want a beno destin?" she says quietly.

"I pledge," he says, herding her out into the hall. "We'll get this done. They've had their chance with this planet."

The door clangs shut behind them.

Mia and I lie in silence for half a minute, processing what we've heard and waiting to make sure they're good and gone. Then she starts to move, so I sit up to give her room.

"Holy *shit*." She flicks on the wrist unit, face pale in the light. "Jules, did you—"

"Yeah. *Destin*—like *destination*? For a mission of some kind? *Lixo* is Portuguese, and in Portuguese it's *destino*. Not to mention it's similar in French, Italian, Spanish—"

"Jules!" Mia's voice is urgent, a quick reminder to bring myself back to the point.

"Right." When the academic fog lifts, I'm left with the same horror that has Mia trembling, horror that makes my heart begin to pound. "They're sending Undying troops down to Earth with recon assignments—that's how they're learning about us. They're actually down there, *right now*, hidden in plain sight."

"That's why they've made themselves look human." Mia's voice is shaking.

"And why they speak English and other Earth languages." A memory strikes me, leaves me cold. "Centuries ago countries would send specially trained spies to other countries to blend in among the population, and they'd only be allowed to speak the enemy country's language from the time they were children. That's why they're speaking like us now."

"Do you think they know?" Mia's voice is shaking. "Down there on Earth—that there are aliens among them, things that look human but aren't? Do they know we're being invaded?"

"If they knew," I reply grimly, "they'd have found a way to attack the ship by now."

"But the Undying look exactly like us, so no one will try to stop them. They could be setting bombs to go off, or infiltrating various governments, or taking hostages, or . . . or . . ."

I know she's thinking about her sister, Evie. I know, because my first thought was for my father, and for the first time I'm actually *relieved* he's in detention at IA Headquarters in Prague. Maybe he'll be safe there. But there are other people I care about who have no such protection. My friends, the rest of my family.

I reach out and take her hand, and she wastes no time tangling her fingers in mine and squeezing. We touch each other so much now that there aren't many moments like this, moments of conscious choice. It should feel like nothing, a common thing. But for me at least, the choice makes it electric.

Then her grip falters, and I look up to find her nibbling her lower lip, fear making way for something else. As I watch, her eyes light with that fire I've come to admire—and fear—so much. That fire that means she's about to suggest something insane. "Wait—Jules. If they're sending Undying forces to blend in among the people down there, that means they've got some way of getting from the ship to the surface and back."

And suddenly I know what she's realized. "They've got shuttles." I straighten so quickly I bang my head on the wall that slants in toward the ceiling of the Junction. But I don't care, because for the first time, there's hope. "If we can figure out where they are . . ."

"That's our way off this ship." Mia grabs for the headset and presses it into my hands.

I hesitate, fingers curling around the band of the headset. "But, Mia, they'll spot us if we try to steal a ship—and we don't even know how to fly it. Neither of us are pilots, and even if we were, these are alien ships, and—"

Mia makes a wordless sound of frustration. "We'll figure it out as we go, Jules, we always have! We'll tackle the next problem once we've solved the first one."

I gaze at her, at that terrifying light in her eyes, and know that if I take this first step, she'll start running with me until I can't stop either of us as we rush headlong off a cliff.

"Put on the headset, Oxford."

Her hand on my arm is warm, and familiar, and grounding.

I put on the headset.

4

AMELIA

JULES MUTTERS SOMETHING UNDER HIS BREATH, A LEVEL OF IRRITATION there that even our increasingly frequent brushes with death don't inspire. His body next to mine is rigid with effort as he tries to navigate the Undying's headset system. It's been hours, but my gentle suggestions that he take a break have gone unnoticed. I did insist at one point on taking over, but no sooner did I put the thing on than the whole display flashed with blinding, searing lines of scattered text, bringing with them an equally searing headache.

"It's like an advanced prosthetic leg or something, controlled by nerve impulses, but for the whole brain." Jules's explanation was almost apologetic as he took the headset back from me. "It just takes practice."

I've got no problem admitting that Jules is smarter than I am, at least when it comes to the kind of precision thinking these contraptions require. Still, my voice was a little sullen as I muttered, "I don't suppose the idea of a keyboard ever occurred to these aliens."

A shift in the muscles rigid against my side draws my eye back to him, and I notice there's sweat gathering at his temple and along his collarbone. I know we need this information, and I know he's got to keep working, but before I can stop myself, I reach out to wrap my fingers around his wrist.

"Easy, Oxford," I murmur, when he jumps at my touch.

Jules flips the glass over his eye up so that he can blink and refocus on me in the blue glow of his watch. "How long was I in there?"

"Long enough," I tell him. "Take a break, eat something. Tell me what you've found."

Jules reaches automatically for one of the sponge-like food cubes, easing his arm away from me again so he can point the display of the watch toward the map we've scratched into the wall of the Junction, copied from the images Jules is getting from the headset. "I was right about this being the shuttle bay," he announces, gesturing at a large open area at the opposite end of the ship.

I raise an eyebrow. "Why don't you sound more pleased?"

"Because I still haven't found a single thing about how to actually *fly* one of the shuttles." Jules squishes the rest of his food cube between thumb and forefinger with a little grimace, as though it's taste he's objecting to rather than lack of success in his research.

Staring at the map, such as it is, I wish we could actually get a look at the shuttle bay in person. But there's Undying personnel everywhere, and no ventilation bulkheads to hide in around the shuttle bay—which makes sense. You wouldn't want your ventilation system connected to a room that opens out into space.

"Maybe we don't have to fly it," I say finally. "Maybe we can sneak on board one of them. Stow away, like we are now."

"Maybe." Jules's voice is dubious, and for once I don't disagree. It's one thing to hide on a ship the size of a small skyscraper. It's another to hide on a shuttle the size of someone's bedroom. "Maybe we can use their own tactics against them. Blend in with them like they're blending in on Earth. If we could get our hands on a couple of those suits . . ."

He trails off, carefully not looking at me, and I know why. I rise up onto my knees with a grimace. "We haven't seen a single one of them under six feet tall. Even if we could steal matching outfits, I'd look like a kid wearing one of her mom's pantsuits."

Jules stifles a laugh, the sound cutting through the bands of tension around my heart like a knife through butter. "You paint quite the mental picture."

I grin a weary grin at him, but it fades before I can get the next words out. "But you could go."

Jules's smile vanishes too. It takes every ounce of my willpower not to show how terrifying that idea is to me, because I know he'd refuse if he saw me frightened. If I can't get out of here alive, knowing Jules had gotten away would be the next best thing. But then I'd be here alone.

"Don't be stupid," Jules says finally, whisper rising hoarsely.

"If you could get away, you'd be able to warn someone at the IA about the Undying. They could hurry preparations on the shuttle and be here in no time. Or don't you think I could survive that long on my own?"

He doesn't rise to the bait. "We go together. We both go, or we both stay."

"Jules, don't be—"

"Would you go alone and leave me?"

*Yes.* The word rings clear and bright in my mind, hovering on my lips. But my mouth won't move, and I curse my sudden—and uncharacteristic—inability to lie.

Jules's eyes gleam. "I thought not. Besides, going alone would probably draw almost as much attention as going with you."

"Why?"

"They go everywhere in twos—you haven't noticed?"

Frowning, I think back to the Undying we've watched all over the ship. "But Slacker . . ." Even as I raise the objection, I'm realizing what Jules is talking about.

"The support staff, I suppose you might call them, don't go in pairs. The engineers and what-have-you. But the . . . the soldiers, I guess, or spies? The ones like Atlanta and Dex, the young-looking ones going down to Earth's surface? They're all partnered, and they go everywhere together."

My heart's sinking a little, because somewhere in the back of my mind the beginnings of a worst-case-scenario plan had started to form. Hijacking, with Jules and me against one of the Undying, *might* work with the element of surprise. But if the soldier-spies are always in pairs, then we'd have to take two of them out at once, and if they've got half the combat training their bearing suggests, our advantage would drop to nil.

Jules pushes the headset back on his forehead and lets out a long, gusty sigh. "I wish Neal were here."

"Neal?"

"My cousin. My best friend, really. He's been obsessed with aeronautics since he was a kid." His eyes lower as he fidgets at a hangnail, his brow lightly furrowed. "He'd figure out how to fly one of their shuttles in a heartbeat. And he'd be doing barrel rolls all the way down."

I can tell by his tone how much the guy he's talking about must mean to him. Jules does wonder and absentmindedness a lot better than he does soft, or emotional, but it's right there in his voice. And in the back of my mind, the reminder that I don't even know this basic fact about him: who his family is, his best friend. In some ways we're as close as two people can be. In others, we're strangers.

I push that thought away. "Too bad he's not here."

"You'll meet him," Jules says, shooting me a quick grin. "You and he will get along swimmingly. And my father's going to love you. He'll talk a lot of mathematics at you, but . . ." He trails off at the expression on my face. "What?"

His words are ringing in my ears. *His father's going to love me? The street rat his genius son dragged home?* Jules has always lived in some sort of fantasy world just slightly left of reality, with his academic ideals and his optimism, but this is a whole new level of delusional. But he looks so genuinely puzzled by my expression that my sarcastic retort dies on my lips.

He really believes there's some kind of future for the two of us. Assuming the world doesn't end.

"Jules," I say softly. "I'm not what you'd call Oxford material. Evie and I aren't made for the places you come from. And that's okay. I like us the way we are."

"I like you the way you are too," he protests.

He doesn't get it. He can't see how impossible it would be for me, trying to fit into his charmed life. He doesn't understand that against that backdrop, even he'd start to see me differently. More like the way he saw me back on Gaia, when we first met. Scavenger. Thief. Uneducated, unethical, money-grubbing trash. Not that he'd ever say it to my face, but it'd be there. We'd stop being on the same team.

And I don't want to be there when that happens.

Something about my face, or my silence, makes Jules lean forward and reach for my hand. His is warm, and his fingers feel certain and strong as they wrap around mine. "Mia," he murmurs, when my gaze starts to slide away from his. "These days there's not much left I'm sure of. But I promise you, there's nothing that could—"

He lets go of my hand with a surprised yelp. I'm reeling back too, because a jolt of electricity surged through our joined hands like a static shock, though neither of us moved.

For a moment we just stare at each other, baffled, until Jules twitches again, stifling an oath. Though I didn't feel the second shock, he clearly did.

Heartbeat quickening a little, I inch closer. "Are you okay?"

"I think it's the headset doing it. It doesn't hurt, it was just—" He bites the words off with a faint frown.

"Shocking?" I finish for him, my voice dry. "Gotta say, I'd rather have my phone. Even on its strongest setting the vibrate doesn't . . ."

But my voice trails off as realization strikes, and a new urgency settles in. "Put the headset on!"

He gives me a startled look, but catches my meaning quickly and settles the earpiece in place, the cracked glass sliding over his right eye. His head lifts immediately, eyes meeting mine. He says nothing, but the distant look that falls across his face tells me I was right: The tingle was a silent alert, just like the vibration on a cell phone.

He listens—or watches, maybe—I don't know whether it's the screen or the earpiece that he's paying attention to. His expression grows increasingly troubled, until he pulls the headset down again with a mute look at me.

"Well?"

"I don't know, everything's gone dead. I can't control it anymore, it's just . . . like someone's switched it off."

He flips the glass up and meets my eyes. In a flash of recognition, I know exactly what conclusion he's reached—because I've reached it too.

"They know someone's been accessing their database," I whisper, as if I might make the words true if I spoke any louder. "Someone who's not one of them."

"It was probably the repeated searches for piloting instructions," Jules replies, reaching up to pull the headset off. He folds it carefully, tucking it away as calmly as a professor might stow a pair of reading glasses. "It was a risk we had to take, but these Undying have been training their whole lives for this—they don't need to look for instructions."

"But they can't know we're stowed away." My voice has a bit of an edge—now I *want* my words to be true. "They'll think it's someone from Earth, right? A remote hack of some kind. We're still hidden. The Junction's still safe."

And in that moment, as if my words were a summoning spell, the corridors of the Junction light up with a glaring red laser grid, sharp lines dissecting every angle. I scramble frantically into Jules, but he's trying to climb my way—the grid is closing in on us from every direction.

An instant later it traces across each of our bodies in half a dozen places. Red lines radiate from Jules's shoulders, his lanky, bent legs, his hand. And when he turns wide eyes on me, a red dot appears in the center of his forehead. Like a sniper's scope out of an action film. My heart seizes.

*They know we're here.*

• • •

We haven't slept in forty-nine hours. Every time we think we've found a nook or cranny the Undying don't know about, it's only a matter of time before we hear the stomp of their boots or the metallic screech of a nearby hatch being torn off. And a matter of minutes, not hours. It's like they've got a way to see through the very walls themselves, some way to come straight for us every time.

I've got myself wedged in at the top of a ventilation shaft, my back over a thirty-meter drop, my shoulders against the wall and my boots braced against the corner. Their laser grid doesn't cover this spot, and for good reason—only a fool would hover at the top of a deadly fall. A fool, or someone desperate enough that the height is less frightening than the alternatives.

Jules is leaning back against my legs, dozing. I don't think he was aware of leaning against me—he'd have pulled away if he was, trying to take off some of the pressure of staying in this position. He has it harder than I do, anyway. His height makes traversing the wall cavities and crawlspaces agony, and he hasn't been able to stretch out properly in days.

My eyelids are drooping. With a swift intake of breath, I go from head to toe, tensing each muscle group and relaxing it again, focusing on physical sensations to keep myself awake.

I've done this before, in Chicago. Once, I ran into a scavver gang sitting on enough food to feed a platoon, and I set up a diversion a block over to lure some of them away. They were stupid enough that they all took off after the sound of someone shouting for help—an ancient digital recorder I found in a looted pawn shop—and I walked right into their empty camp, helping myself to their rations and some of their more portable loot as well. But I got greedy and stayed too long, and they came back before I could get clear. I spent a day and a half curled up inside an old chest freezer eating cold canned peas until they moved on.

A sound interrupts my thoughts, and I jolt awake without even realizing that memory had started to become dream. My heart pounding, I wait until my mind identifies the sound as a distant fan turning on somewhere. I check the wrist unit. Twenty-two minutes since we stopped.

Jules's body gives a jerk, sending my heart rate skyward again. I squeeze his shoulder, and his eyes flash at me in the dark. Hurriedly he pulls himself away from my legs, but when he speaks it's not an apology. "The headset buzzed me," he whispers hoarsely.

I want to tell him to ignore it. They know we're here now, so any message they send through the headset is one they don't mind us intercepting. They could even be sending false messages, bait to lure us out from the walls. But it's also the only window we have through to the Undying's network of communication, and if they've turned the system back on . . . we need to know what they're saying.

I squeeze his shoulder again, and he settles the headset into place.

I'm bracing myself for a long silence while he's gone, gone even more than he is when he's asleep—but he pulls the headset off after only a few moments, looking at it with confusion.

"What happened?" I whisper.

"Just one sentence," he replies. "'Abandon departure schedule, all surface teams to shift immediately.' And that's it—it's still not responding to me at all, and the screen's still dead."

I'm so tired my mind is sluggish. "The ones like Atlanta and Dex, the soldiers—they're all going down to Earth now?"

"Seems that way."

"They've been chasing us for days—why are they just now moving up the schedule?"

Without warning the duct stretching out before us comes to life with bright red lines. I grab for Jules, but he's seen them too, and with a jerk he pulls his long legs back out of the way, shoving in close against me. There's only a few centimeters between him and the edge of the laser grid, but it's enough. We wait, hearts pounding, as silent as if the lasers might somehow hear us if we moved—until the place goes dark again.

I squeeze Jules's shoulder, and when I creep ahead along the horizontal shaft, he follows me silently, no questions. If he's the master of the headset, I'm the one keeping us alive and on the move in these tunnels.

The shaft we're in runs at floor level along one of the upper decks of the ship, and we've gotten no more than a few meters before running footsteps make us freeze. Too often, that sound has meant a hasty retreat for us, and another mad scramble for a hiding place. But this time, the boots go racing past, followed and joined by more and more, until there's a veritable stampede.

Once the crowd has passed, I whisper, "We've got to get to one of those shuttles if we're going to get off this ship."

"And what, ask if we can hitchhike?" I catch the glitter of his eyes in the gloom, and I want to smile—he sounds like me, burying his exhaustion and fear under sarcasm. But we're both too tired to smile. "Even if we could get aboard one unseen, we've got no hope of learning to pilot an alien landing craft made by a species tens of thousands of years ahead of us."

"We have to try!" I stop at an intersection, and grab Jules's ankle to tell him to do the same. There's just enough room for him to ease to one side and rest for a moment. "Maybe we can find a pair of suits as a disguise, like we talked about."

Jules's eyes fall, and I know he's looking at my legs, outstretched and interlocking with his—and ending a good foot shorter than his do. I'd look like a child in one of their suits. It might fool them for a moment or two, but not long enough to locate the shuttle bay from the memory of our map, find a shuttle, and sneak—or talk—our way on board.

I force myself to let go of the tension holding me upright and just lie down where I am, forehead pillowed on my crossed arms. *Think, Mia. You've done this before. How do you steal something from a group with vastly superior numbers and organization?*

*Chicago. The tape recorder.*

"We need a diversion." I'm speaking slowly, not bothering to think first—at this point, any idea is better than nothing. "A way to lure some of them away, get their suits, and then take their places on the shuttle. Do you think you can talk like them? Imitate the way we've heard Dex and Atlanta talking?"

Jules is eyeing me askance, an expression I recognize as a dim relative of the surprise and skepticism he displayed when I first proposed stealing one of our rival scavver gang's skimmer bikes back on Gaia when we first met. "I think so. As long as I don't have to make any fancy speeches. But we don't know enough about them to blend in for long."

I've got my mouth open to go on, but I'm saved from trying to plan any further by a clang and a narrow, bright beam of light several meters ahead of us. A voice, distorted by echoes, rises in query, answered by a second, more muffled voice. They're at the far end of our shaft. They've found us.

Jules mutters one of his Latin oaths and ducks down the other branch of the intersection, with me on his heels. Literally—I almost get a boot to the face in my haste to follow him.

"How do they keep finding us?" he puffs, but I'm so winded I can't reply in anything more than a gasp for breath.

It's a few more minutes before he stops abruptly, body stiffening. Quickly, he wedges himself in sideways and pulls the headset off his neck. "God, we're such idiots—the headset, Mia."

"Shit." My heart's sinking. *How did I miss that? I guess two days of sleep deprivation slows me down.* "They must be like cell phones, they've got some kind of tracker or positioning chip. And since they know someone's been accessing their database . . ."

Grimly, Jules draws his arm back, hurling the thing as far from him as he can. It skitters along the vent as we head in the opposite direction.

"What now?" he murmurs, looking across at me by the dim light of his wrist unit. "I know that look on your face. What terrible idea am I going to go along with now?"

"We keep on with the plan. We catch a couple of these surface operatives on the way to the launch bay, pull them off to investigate, and then get their suits."

Jules's face is grave, eyes going distant as he summons up the image of that scrawled map. This time, he doesn't bother arguing the hopelessness of the situation. Either he's finally convinced it's worth a try, or he just thinks we're so screwed that we might as well go down swinging. "The best place will be somewhere near the bay itself, to make sure we get foot soldiers with suits, and not ship staff."

I take a breath, thanking whatever gods or universal forces might be listening that Jules has that freakish memory. "I'll follow you."

• • •

We refine the plan, such as it is, on the move. We leave the headset behind—the fact that they came after us even after the network was turned off tells us that the positioning chip must still be functional. And we don't want a welcoming committee when we reach our destination.

We're sidling through the wall cavities again until we reach a small chamber off one of the main corridors that houses a bunch of unidentifiable equipment. To me, it looks for all the world like a water heater closet.

We're forced to wait there for the right opportunity. Pairs of Undying rush past at irregular intervals, but we need a single pair alone, and ones who haven't started putting on their suits yet. Half those running past have them tied round their waists like mechanics' jumpsuits.

Jules and I are both starting to fidget restlessly when two sets of footsteps prick my ear after a long silence. I touch Jules's arm, and we ease the door open a crack in time to see two forms eclipse the light from the corridor as they pass.

I'm shifting my weight to move when Jules's hand comes to rest against my back. The sudden warmth of the touch is what halts me—we've been communicating by a squeeze here, a nudge there, for so long now that I ought to be used to it, but this touch lingers.

I glance over my shoulder to find Jules close, his brows drawn in and his lips set. "Are you sure about this? Couldn't we both—"

"I'm faster than you are." It's not a boast—it's simple truth, and something Jules has had plenty of opportunity to observe over the past weeks. "I can lose them again—I swear to you I can."

And in that moment, I *am* sure. I'm not lying, and I'm not exaggerating—I'm quick and I'm small, and I've been training for this my whole career as a scavenger. I turn the rest of the way around and take Jules by the arms, trying to look as stern as I can when tilting my head back to look up at him.

"We'll only be split up for a few minutes. Stash one of the suits here, put on the other, and find us a ride out of here. I'll be back before you're done sweet-talking the Undying into letting us stow away. You've got the more dangerous task than me—you have to make them think you're one of them. I just have to run."

Jules scans my face for a heartbeat, then draws me in. I'd forgotten how different his arms feel this way, as opposed to when he's just got one around me for warmth as we huddle in our hiding places.

*No, that's a lie*—I haven't forgotten at all. I've been trying not to think about it.

"I don't like this," he says quietly.

I try out a smile, my heart racing a little more quickly. "Me neither. But it's either this or keep running and hiding until—until this is over, one way or another." I don't want to say the words. I *can't* say the words. But they're there in my mind, as real and vivid as if I had said them: *Until Earth falls.*

Jules drops his head, forehead touching mine. I long to tip my face up, seek out his lips just a breath away from mine. For a moment I nearly do, and my head must have moved a fraction in the darkness, because I feel his hands slide farther along my back in response.

Suddenly all the time we've spent together on this ship feels like such a waste. I could've asked for more—I could've taken advantage of that time, of our closeness, to explore this fragile connection between us. Odds are we're not both going to make it off this ship, and when Jules goes back to his real life on Earth, I want him to remember . . . I want him to remember how I felt about him. Not what I thought of his crackpot ideas, or how I teased him for his optimism, or how I shot down his well-meaning—but naïve— attempts to make room for me in his life.

I want him to remember how I *felt*. And I don't know how to show him that. A kiss could never be enough.

"I have to go now." I draw back, forcing myself to concentrate. "This might be our best chance, and they're nearly at the end of the . . ."

"Be careful." Jules lets go of my hand, flexing his now-empty fingers in the space between us.

"You too." I ease the door open again, just enough to lean out and check on the progress of our targets. Then I pause, in spite of myself and my urgency. "If I'm not—stall them, but don't blow your cover if . . . One of us has to make it to Earth."

This time, Jules doesn't try to fight me. His mouth tightens, and he says nothing, but he gives a tiny nod.

If I had time, I'd tell him I'm not being noble and brave about anything—if I had time, I'd tell him I'm terrified at the thought of being left behind. Instead, I sacrifice one more second to look at him, and then slip out into the corridor.

I take a few quick, sharp breaths to get my blood pumping, and then break into a run. Hearing my footsteps, the Undying pair ahead of me pause, their flight suits draped over their arms and flopping as they go. When one of them looks back, I stop short as if surprised to see them there in my path.

For a long moment, we stare at each other along the length of the corridor.

They're male and female, each as tall as Atlanta and Dex, though aside from their height they couldn't be more different. The young woman's hair is shaved close to her head, exactly the same light brown as her skin, while the boy's reddish-brown curls are gathered into a knot at the crown of his skull, thick and coarse.

The boy's mouth falls open. "Is that—is that a proto?"

The girl's eyes widen. "She's the one they're after!"

In a split second, they both drop their suits and break into a sprint. They're faster than I expected, freakishly fast, and a curse tumbles out of my mouth as I nearly slip in my haste to turn back and run the other way. I can't spare a glance for the utility closet where Jules stands concealed, and race past it, blood singing in my ears.

When I reach the opposite end of the hall, I ricochet off the wall as I make a ninety-degree turn. I catch a flash out of my peripheral vision, beyond my pursuers, and get the briefest glimpse of a figure stooping to carefully retrieve the fallen suits, then vanishing again into the shadows.

Heart surging with triumph, I pour all my focus into running.

I planned my path the best I could ahead of time, with information from Jules's nearly photographic memory of the maps the headset revealed, and with what we've cobbled together on our expeditions through the walls and ventilation systems. Another right will bring me back toward the shuttle bay, and then a left will take me back toward the living quarters. Where there's a knee-high vent standing open and ready for me to slide in, grab the hatch cover, and pull it shut before my pursuers have rounded the corner.

I skid around, eyes already dropped for the hatch—and then all the air goes out of my chest as I slam face-first into a dead-end wall. Reeling back, gasping for air, I stare at the blank wall for half a second too long before I realize: I'm not where I thought I was. The path was wrong, or I miscalculated—either way, the result is the same.

I'm lost.

Blindly—the sound of quick, efficient breath and pounding boots just around the corner—I choose a direction and take off.

*I'm sorry, Jules. Please, please, be strong enough to leave without me.*

**JULES**

THE SHUTTLE BAY IS BUZZING WITH ACTIVITY, UNDYING WORKERS AND soldiers striding across the open spaces, readying shuttles, calling orders, and hauling gear. The room is massive, on a scale that makes my head spin. It's a feeling almost like vertigo after spending the last week crammed inside a long series of too-small spaces. The bay's large size requires support, and ribs of that metallic stone curve upward to meet in the ceiling like buttresses supporting the weight of a cathedral. If cathedrals shimmered with iridescent power, and looked down over an alien invasion force.

From above, this place would look like a sprawling ants' nest, with suited soldiers scurrying in every direction. Everyone's moving with purpose, and my steps falter for a moment on the threshold.

I'm in one of those suits too—like Earth's astronauts, the Undying wear them in transit down to the surface, in case of hull breach, I guess. They're jet-black, the helmets strangely bulbous, the faceplates opaque unless you're up close. The last time I saw someone dressed like this, Mia and I were hiding, watching the first of the Undying step through the portals, minutes after launch. Last time, we were braced to see the helmets come off and reveal some nightmarish alien creature, with tentacles for a face or teeth like knives.

Somehow, seeing them reveal human faces was even worse.

There's comfortable padding inside my helmet, cradling my head like Neal's motorcycle helmets do, and I'm glad it conceals my features, because I know I'm gawking. There are just so *many* of them. At least half aren't in their helmets yet, and with a slow blink, I realize that every single one of them looks to be around my age.

The Undying invasion forces, whatever they've done to camouflage themselves as human, are all masquerading as teenagers. Why?

Is this their first mistake, a misunderstanding about humans, or are they hoping to be underestimated, to go unnoticed?

I'm forced to sidestep a group hurrying in through the door, and try to quell the rising panic constricting my chest.

*I'm about the right height,* I tell myself. *There's no reason I won't blend in.* I'm glad I told Mia to wear her helmet, though—of all the sea of faces I can see surrounding me, I'm realizing abruptly that not one of them is as pale as hers. They range from the darkest of browns to a light tan, but she's unquestionably the whitest girl on the ship, as well as the shortest.

The second suit and helmet are waiting back in the utility room where Mia will—I hope against hope—collect them, but in the meantime her absence means I'm the only one in this huge, high-ceilinged hangar without a partner by my side. I'm desperately hoping the crowd of bodies around me will conceal the fact that I'm alone.

As if I wasn't feeling her absence keenly enough already.

And that's when I see them. Atlanta and Dex, our unwitting neighbors, walking together across the middle of the hangar, helmets under their arms, steps in unison. I've never gotten to see them like this, only in glimpses and flashes from behind the ventilation cover in their room. They've both got their hair pinned up to fit underneath their helmets, and they're deep in conversation about something. Debating about their *destin*? Perhaps. I lift my chin a little to keep track of them, and a few moments later, they come to a halt beside a shuttle that's about ten back in the queue for launch. Dex climbs up the step to the entryway, hanging on to the door frame as he scans the surrounding area.

I realize what he's doing in the same instant my feet start moving. He's looking for the rest of their crew. Some of the shuttles hold two, but most hold four, and the one he's hanging off is definitely one of the latter. Without working earpieces, he and Atlanta have no way to check in to find out where the other half of their crew is. Or perhaps even who they are.

Which means there's no reason *they* can't be *me*.

My throat's tight, and my hands are tingling as I make my way past the scrambling soldiers, practicing my first words in my head. I speak nine languages and a further six dialects. I've been listening to the Undying for days. If anyone can imitate their accents and their lexicon, it's me.

If only telling myself that would stop me feeling like I'm about to throw up in my helmet.

My legs are moving anyway, and I stride up to the pair like I mean business, causing both their heads to turn my way.

"Atlanta?" I ask, pointing a finger at her, leaning back from my vowels to keep them sharp, making it a question. "Dex?"

"Yeh?" Atlanta says, speaking slowly.

I throw my hands up like I'm praising the lord that I've found them. "Talk about hassle. My partner'll be thisways any minute."

Neither of them immediately expresses the relief and understanding I'm fishing for. Dex remains in the doorway, watching me, and Atlanta blinks slowly.

"Who are you?"

I know what Mia would do. She'd lean in, she'd completely commit. *Deus, I wish I was Mia right now.*

"I'm Jules," I say, contriving to sound like this is just a little bit obvious, and I'm surprised they haven't already been briefed. I think I'm better sticking to my own name—from what I've observed, theirs are mainly traditional human names, but shortened, as in Dex's case, or things or places, as in Atlanta's.

"We're not waiting on you," says Atlanta, with her customary bluntness. She'll be the harder sell, I know that.

"I compren," I agree. "But it's all shuffled now, yeh? I was told to meet up with Prime-One." I'm praying that Atlanta got her way, and that she and Dex got the *beno destin* she'd been hoping for.

Atlanta's still squinting at me. I know I'm close enough for her to see through my faceplate, so I keep my expression serious. "What destin you got?"

"Prime-Two," I answer, wishing I had Mia's glibness.

Atlanta's squint turns to a frown. "Prime-Two's on the flipside of the planet down there, Jules, why you landing on Europe with us?"

*Europe,* I think, my heart throwing in an extra beat. Where home is. Where Neal is. *Where my father is.* I scramble for words. "We *were* Prime-Two, but in the shuffle someone else got it." I throw every ounce of irritation and frustration I have into my voice, channeling the tutors back at Oxford when forced to deal with undergrads—the ultimate indignity. "Now we're support for Prime-One, like they think we can't all handle the destin we got first time round."

But before she can interrogate me further, Dex peers down from his place above us in the doorway to the shuttle. "I don't see *us,*" he points out, though he sounds slightly more friendly. "Where's your partner?"

I roll my eyes. "She's coming. I pledge, I told her to check her suit again, but no, and now the piece-of-lixo seal . . ." I wave one hand in a what-can-you-do type gesture, because while I'm fairly sure a seal would be part of even an alien spacesuit, I certainly don't know what would go wrong with it.

Atlanta shakes her head. "We're shifting with Keats and Nakry," she insists.

I shrug. "I'm pretty sure they're already mostways to planetside, they got shuffled too—they're the ones that got Prime-Two."

Exactly what I'm going to do if Keats and Nakry show up before Mia does, I have no idea.

The pair of them exchange a long look, and some kind of unspoken communication—he tilts his head slightly, she lifts her brow. For all Atlanta's outward bluster, they're deciding together whether they need to go seek clarification from someone higher up the tree.

"Sirsly," I say, wishing I were half as good at bluffing as I am at getting these sharp vowel sounds and truncated words right. "It's beno. You're Dex"—I point first at him, then swing my finger across—"and you're Atlanta. Those are the names I got. It's all hassle, all day long without the—" I'm about to say "headsets," when I realize I have no idea what the Undying call them. So I tap my finger to the temple where the glass would rest instead. "I pledge, you're my new destin."

They exchange another long look, as I wonder how much slang is too much. My chest is still tight, and I know my words are tumbling out too fast, and my palms are sweating, and I still have no idea where Mia is, or how long she'll be. But I can't push the two of them—even I, in all my inexperience, can sense that. If I press too hard, the bluff will fail.

I have their names. Double-checking the instructions would mean trekking around the ship in search of an authority figure, without their headsets. I just need to wait this out.

Dex speaks casually, tucking a stray strand of hair back into place. "You from the Cortes squadron, Jules?"

One heartbeat stretches to an eternity. Is he trying to figure out why he doesn't know my face, or is this a trap? Does the Cortes squadron exist?

"Yeh," I say, pushing all my metaphorical chips to the center of the table. Betting on Cortes existing at all. On it being a place I might have trained without meeting them.

Atlanta huffs. "Well, your training better match up with ours," she says, frustration evident. "If this goes to lixo because—"

"It won't," I tell her, too quickly. "We're dying to get planetside. We're your backup, we'll take your lead. We're ready. This is what we've lived until now to do." I'm parroting her own enthusiasm back at her, the readiness I've heard her talk about to Dex a dozen times, and her shoulders drop, relaxing just a fraction.

Then Dex's voice sounds from above us again. "Forget the destin, the *launch* is gonna go to lixo if your partner doesn't show up."

I glance across at the line, and my heart, which had only restarted a couple of beats before, speeds up to double time. We're not tenth in the queue anymore.

We're fourth, and Mia's nowhere to be seen.

There's a gap between our shuttle and the one in front, and Dex braces against the door frame with both hands as it suddenly lurches forward—it's on some sort of conveyor belt, and Atlanta and I keep pace, walking along beside it. Ahead, I can see the first shuttle in the queue—alongside four other shuttles from the heads of four other queues—move forward into the airlock.

Once all five shuttles are in position, the airlock doors close behind them. In a moment the outer doors will open, and the five shuttles will launch. Then the airlock will repressurize, and the inner doors will open to admit the next five.

We're third in the queue.

"Where's your partner?" Atlanta says again, and I crane my neck, looking at the entrance through which I'm desperately hoping I'll see Mia appear.

*Trust me, Atlanta, I'm more worried than you are.*

"She'll be here," I say. "No hassle."

*Hopefully she'll be here before Keats and Nakry show up.*

"What do we do if she doesn't show?" Dex says from the

doorway, anxious. "We've got our launch slot, we can't just give it up. We could land mostways across the planet from our site, if we don't get out on time."

Atlanta's mouth firms to a thin line. "If she doesn't show, then us three go," she replies. "I'm not gonna miss the landing site we prepped for. We fought for this destin, and I'm not losing it."

The shuttle abruptly shifts again, trundling along its own length, as another five disappear into the airlock.

We're second in the queue.

*Perfututi, Mia, what do I do?*

I abandon that question as quickly as I ask it, because I know Mia's answer—I climb into the shuttle and I go, and I try to bluff them until I can get away from them and warn somebody. Because our families are down there, because billions of people are down there, and all of them outweigh one girl left behind in orbit. But just because I know what answer she'd give doesn't mean I like it.

Because she's just one girl against billions to them—but not to me.

Dex pulls on his helmet, and Atlanta climbs up onto the step beside him to check the seals at the back, then dons her own.

"Jules," she calls. "We gotta strap in, we're next."

My heart's hammering. I'm staring at the entrance, the voice in my head chanting a rhythmic command, over and over, lost for anything else to do. *Hurry, Mia. Hurry, Mia. Hurry, Mia.*

I try for a slow breath, to convince my body for even a few seconds that everything's all right. To force myself to *think*. But this isn't a water polo match, this isn't a final exam, and my body's having none of it. My head's pounding.

"Jules," Atlanta calls again, impatient, then ducks into the shuttle to take her seat.

*I can't do this. I can't leave her.*

"Jules," Dex says, gentler, still on the steps. "We have orders. Prime-One—we can't risk that destin. I compren you want to share it with your partner—I wouldn't want to do this anyways but with Atlanta—but this is bigger than any one of us."

It's like he's echoing my own thoughts.

I force myself to take one step backward toward the shuttle.

*One girl left behind in orbit.*

*Warn Earth, and maybe they can get to her before the Undying do.*

*One girl left behind.*

*Mia . . . I don't think I can do this.*

And then I see her. One figure in a suit, shorter than everyone else, racing in through the door and stopping short, helmeted head swinging around as she hunts for me in the crowd.

"There she is," I tell Dex, even as I raise my hand to catch her attention. "Strap in, she's coming thisways."

I don't want Dex to see how short she is, but a moment later he's inside, and I'm jumping, waving. I can tell the instant she spots me. She shoves past a group of ground crew in jumpsuits to race toward me. She's so obviously smaller than everyone around her, but she's moving so quickly, and amid so much chaos, that nobody has the chance to do anything about it. I see a few heads turn, I see the moment when they realize something's not quite right, but before any of them can reach out, she's past.

I can see her grin through her faceplate as she reaches me, and I reach out to grab her hand, squeezing tight. She squeezes right back, eyes a little wild, though whether it's at the near miss or the chase she just provoked, I don't know.

"Atlanta and Dex are inside," I tell her, nodding to the shuttle, keeping my accent up. "They're the ones we were ordered to join. Our destin."

"I compren," she says simply, picking up on my reminder to use their slang without skipping a beat. She hurries up the steps, eager to get out of sight.

I climb up into the shuttle after her, and I turn to reach up for the door, grabbing the thick handle on the inside and preparing to tug it down.

That's when I spot a pair of Undying running straight toward us, one waving urgently. I know without question that they're Keats and Nakry, the pair we're replacing.

I yank at the handle, slamming the door shut behind me.

The interior of the shuttle is small, not much larger than a private vehicle at home. Atlanta and Dex are strapped into the two front seats, and she must be the pilot, because she's running her hands over controls that glimmer on the dashboard before her.

Mia and I throw ourselves into the seats behind Atlanta and Dex, trying not to look baffled by the configuration of restraints and straps. I yank the harness down over my shoulders, fumbling until I find the place to click it home.

"Dex?" Atlanta barks, as a jolt tells me we're moving up into the airlock, the conveyor belt shuffling us forward.

"Beno," he says, as a shield slides down to cover the front windscreen, and protect us on reentry.

"Jules?" she says.

"Beno," I choke out, pressing my foot against Mia's, then shoving it back into the padded groove cut in the base of my seat for it, to keep it from moving as we're jostled around. Deus, we're about to take this tiny thing all the way through Earth's atmosphere, to land who-knows-where, with two Undying who'll do who-knows-what once they figure out who we are.

"Other girl," she snaps.

"Mia," she supplies, following my lead in giving her own name. "Beno."

"Launch sequence," Atlanta says, all business, flipping another switch and running her finger over a dial that lights up in response. A panel pulses expectantly, and Atlanta places her palm against it until it gives a pleasant chime of acceptance. I glance at Mia, who's watching me, grim-faced. If we'd tried to steal a shuttle, we wouldn't have gotten past the palm scanner.

"Here we go, Peaches," Dex says, low and excited.

Mia's eyes are still on mine. "Onward, if you dare," I murmur.

It's the last line of the Undying broadcast. It's the challenge they issued us, that led to everything that's happened. It's the way Mia and I have operated since the moment we met.

And maybe it's my voice, or my choice of words, or maybe it's just instinct, but that's the moment Dex leans forward in his seat, straining at his straps, and twisting to try and get a better look at us both.

And just for an instant, he sees Mia's noticeably smaller frame strapped into her seat, her face, clearly white and freckled even through her faceplate, completely unfamiliar.

His eyes widen, and his mouth opens like he's been punched in the gut, forced to suck in a quick breath of air. And then the whole shuttle gives a teeth-rattling jolt, and he's forced back into position.

"Here we go," Atlanta says, a kind of grim pleasure in her tone. "Ours for the taking. Brace in three, two, one . . ."

6

AMELIA

**THE FORCE OF THE LAUNCH THROWS US ALL BACK AGAINST OUR SEATS.**
My internal organs are trying to shove their way out around my
spine, and all I can think is how glad I am I haven't eaten much
of anything in the last two days, or I'd be upchucking all the way
from here to Earth. When I close my eyes, I can feel tears pooling,
cold and unfeeling, along my lashes.

And then it all stops.

This isn't like the rocket launch that got me up through the
Gaia portal and to that space station—the initial force came from
the launch bay we just left behind, some kind of rail system or
slingshot that pushed this spacecraft out into the black. No shuddering, gut-wrenching vibrations, no crushing weight of G-forces
compressing your lungs. And this time I'm not hidden away in
cargo, lost in blackness, blinded to the experience of going up into
space.

I can hear my breath, strangely artificial in the confines of my helmet, and yet quivering and unsteady with adrenaline. I open my eyes, and something flickers past my vision, making me jerk away until my gaze focuses.

It's a teardrop, floating just beyond my eyes.

My arms rise, and automatically I try to pull them down again, my body struggling to understand why my shoulders have to work to stay in my seat, and as a faint blue glow appears at the edge of the viewscreen ahead, upside down, I'm flailing for the armrests, trying desperately to find something to hold on to.

Then my mind catches up with my instincts, and I remember I'm strapped down, that I'm not falling, that this is weightlessness. This is space.

Unable to resist, I lean forward until I can see out a little triangular viewport to my left. All I can see is stars. More stars than I've ever imagined, more stars even than I could see on Gaia, which had the darkest, blackest nights I'd ever known. My breathing quickens until a touch at my elbow drags my eyes away from the view.

Jules is watching me, his face difficult to read behind his helmet. He can only brush the edge of my arm with his fingertips from where he sits, but I can read his worry in the tautness of his frame as he strains to reach me. But as soon as he sees my face, the taut muscles relax and let his arms float as carelessly as mine are.

*I never got to see this, the first time.*

Jules did, though. Still, his face doesn't wear a smile like mine. Little jets kick in at intervals around the exterior of the craft, tilting us at an angle, intensifying the glow of light still out of view. But it's enough to see his face. His head turns forward, and I know what he would say, if we could risk speaking.

*Dex.*

My mind plays the moment over and over. The intense gaze, the stiffening body, the flash of recognition mixed with confusion and horror. He saw us. I don't know if it was my voice that gave us away, or my height or face, or if something Jules said had raised his suspicions already, but he *saw* us. He knows we're not Undying.

And he hasn't said a word.

"We're right on target," comes Atlanta's voice, tinny and artificial, but crystal clear within my helmet—we must be miked, with speakers in the helmets, wirelessly connected to each other. "Trajectory at ninety-nine point eight—hah! And you said we'd be scrambling to readjust."

Dex shifts, and I stiffen, but he's only reaching out to tap at some display I can't read from back here. "The lixo heap does a better job at launches than I guessed."

I glance at Jules, who's listening and staring as intently as I am, and wearing an expression of such bafflement I'd laugh if I wasn't so frightened. I can't think what will happen to us once they're secure enough in their "trajectory" to deal with stowaways.

*Is there an airlock on this thing?*

An image flashes before me: two spacesuited bodies, spinning out of control, surrounded by inky darkness and stars, just a breath away from each other but without a way to close that distance.

I choke on my own breath as I try to bury that image. *Don't even think it.*

In front of us, the spacesuit on the right moves, helmet twisting a fraction. "Okay back there, Mia?" Dex's voice is mild.

For a moment, I can't speak—a genial question about my well-being was not what I expected. "Yeah." I clear my throat. "Yeh. Beno." I want to look at Jules, but with Dex eyeing me sidelong, I can't risk it.

Was I wrong? Had I mistaken something else for recognition? Except that Jules saw it too, I know he did.

Abruptly, the thoughts that had been suppressed by the sheer strangeness of spaceflight kick into overdrive. I don't know how long we've got until we get far enough into the atmosphere for the weightlessness to vanish—long enough for me to get out of my seat, incapacitate the other two somehow, and get back? But even if I could, we've got no idea how much of the controls are automated. We can't hijack a spaceship we don't know how to fly.

*Hijack,* my mind repeats. I could threaten one of them—they're close, as close as me and Jules, and if someone held a gun to his head I'd do anything they asked. I don't have a gun, but I do have . . .

*Damn, damn, DAMN.* I do have my multi-tool. I made sure to shove it carefully in the waistband of my pants before I pulled on the suit, because I didn't want to leave it behind on the Undying ship. And now I'm all zipped and buckled up with no way of retrieving it.

Even an idiot would notice me stripping down right behind them in order to retrieve a knife—and these two are no idiots.

The little exterior jets are still rotating the craft, and abruptly the source of the glow out front swings into view, completely interrupting my scramble for a solution.

Earth.

Dazzled, my eyes can only drink it in, this glorious blue-and-white arc bisecting the screen. Fantastic landscapes of sculpted cloud glow in the sunlight behind us, casting shadows upon the oceans below. Like shapes coalescing out of the fog, the outlines of a continent show through the gaps, but in the strangest moment of confusion, I cannot for the life of me tell which continent it is. Earth looks nothing like the maps we memorize in school, with their neat, consistent outlines and conveniently colored countries and states. All I can see is a coastline. *Somewhere down there,* I think giddily, *some kid is making a sand castle.*

"This is really it." Atlanta's voice, usually so quick and decisive and bright, is soft now. So soft the microphones struggle to pick it up, delivering it amid a burst of white noise. "We're really going planetside."

I hear Dex's intake of breath, and my own heart seizes. He's going to tell her what he saw. He even shifts, helmet tilting as he looks back at us again. "It doesn't really look like the pics, does it?"

"It looks enough like them," replies Atlanta more firmly this time. "The protos have no idea. No idea what they got." Her voice sharpens, the warmth draining from it. "No idea what's coming."

"We made it," Dex agrees. "It's gonna be beno, Peaches."

His voice is so warm I feel sick. They have such affection for each other, these two soldiers in the army come to wrest our planet from us. And they look no older than we are, despite the enormity of what they're doing.

At first I thought it was just something to do with their appearance—as I hurried through the shuttle bay, my first thought was that they all looked like teenagers because that was the image they copied when they altered themselves to look like us. But now . . . the way they speak, with bravado and fear all at once, the way they move, the affection between them—they *act* like teenagers, albeit exceptional ones.

It was easy to think of them as enemies when we were crouching inside the walls, eavesdropping, stealing food when we could. It's a lot harder now, watching Dex reach out and brush Atlanta's arm in exactly the way Jules tried to touch me.

"Oh chill, look—it's a storm!" Dex's voice is quick with boyish excitement, and he gestures at a seemingly stationary spiral of clouds hovering over a cobalt expanse of sea.

Atlanta's body jerks as she twists to follow the line of his hand, gasping in delight. "Clouds! I can't believe how easy they are to see—water vapor! On Hestia you can be mostways to the middle of an electrical storm and not know it until your suit kicks out."

But as she's speaking, Dex's other hand moves, smooth with stealth, toward a control on the panel before them. A tiny touch, that's all—but an indicator light winks out on the panel.

Atlanta's leaning back again, tipping her helmet our way and asking cheerfully, "Did Cortes do surface training on Hestia?"

It takes me a moment to realize the question's directed at us. I have no idea what Cortes is, aside from some vague memory of history class in fourth grade, and somehow I doubt that's what this invader from an ancient alien race is talking about.

I glance at Jules, only to see him wide-eyed and frozen, mouth half-open. He recognizes the question, but doesn't know how to answer.

"Don't hassle them, Peaches," replies Dex, as lightly as ever, his hand gliding over the controls, fingers stealthily touching a few more buttons. "Not everybody wants to chatter while fulfilling their life's purpose."

Jules's mouth closes, and I hear him exhale—loud enough for the mics to pick it up. His eyes meet mine, and he lifts both eyebrows in a helpless shrug of an expression.

If it were any other situation, if the boy in the front seat wasn't an alien wearing a human face—I'd think Dex was *covering* for us.

The arc of Earth's horizon is gone, above the edge of the viewscreen now, giving us a rectangular cutout of sea, cloud, and land. It's even more impossible to tell now what part of the planet we're seeing. The colors seem strangely muted, and as I narrow my eyes in an attempt to clear my vision, I realize my arms aren't floating anymore. They've settled gently back against the armrests, and the rest of my body is no longer pressed against the harness but rather cradled once more in the embrace of the seat.

The landscape below is tinted a rosy orange now, and it's not until I lean out to look through the side port again that I realize *everything* is that same pinky-tangerine color, and that the stars have vanished. It's not that the Earth is glowing red—we're in the atmosphere, and it's burning.

The drag pushes us down into our seats all the more, the plasma outside glowing hotter and hotter until, with an innocuous little beep at the console, some automatic system kicks in and all the windows go black. Some kind of heat shield, I hope—I'm trying not to think about it, but I can feel sweat pooling at my throat.

*You're imagining the heat*, I tell myself furiously. *If you could actually feel it, you'd be dead.*

The pressure against my body keeps growing, long past the point of normal gravity, until drawing a simple breath is an effort, and my vision starts to sparkle warningly. My peripheral vision starts to narrow, and when I realize I can't see Jules anymore, even out of the corner of my eye, I lose even the ability to breathe.

"Brace for chute deployment," comes a voice through my helmet. In the crush of G-forces and the jolting and shuddering of the craft, I can't tell who's speaking.

I only have a moment to drag in a little air before my harness grabs me by the shoulders and yanks me backward. The heat shielding has vanished, and through the screen I see a wild jumble of colors and shapes zigzagging every which way. Someone gurgles something—maybe it's me—and then the shifting scenery settles a little. We're swinging side to side, the horizon tipping one way and then the other. I see a city in the far distance, nothing more than a jagged skyline at the edge of a distant expanse of ocean. Trees, or a plain, below. Clouds. Sky.

The Undying seem more irritated by the violence of reentry than utterly destroyed, like I feel. Atlanta's the first to speak, and she gives a gusty sigh and mutters, "Only think, this is how they all made planetfall just a couple hundred years ago. Primitive."

Dex chuckles, though his voice is a little shaky and he's slower to move, uncurling his hands from the armrests. "Primitive but tough, our founders."

Atlanta snorts, and when she answers, her voice is much darker. "Gods, compared to the protos."

Dex doesn't answer. Nor does he turn and look at us. But as we dangle from the parachute, basking in the sudden calm, he's far more tense than Atlanta—she just seems eager. Excited, like a kid on Christmas morning.

Until she stiffens, examining something on their dashboard. "Dex—Dex, this is all wrong. We're off course."

Dex makes a good show of alarm, but I saw his surreptitious use of the controls. If we're off course, he's the one who made it happen. "Sirsly? This lixo shuttle—it must have something wrong with one of the thrusters."

Atlanta's poring over the dashboard, movements frantic. "We've gotta do something—"

"The chute's already out," Dex protests, flashing her a helpless look. "We'll land where we land. If we're off course, we'll find a way to shift to our assignment." He pauses, watching her stricken face. "I pledge, Peaches. We'll make it."

The horizon swells slowly against the view screen, like a line of water rising in a fish tank, until I can no longer see the sky. There are mountains all around, but different from anything I've seen—bulbous, swollen stone instead of the sharp, crisp peaks in the Rocky Desert back home, or the gentle rolls of the Blue Ridge Mountains. I'm half expecting a burst of panic from Atlanta or Dex, for surely this can't be a safe place to land—and then the soft green of a valley comes into view.

Choking back my panic, hoping none of it was audible over the mics, I watch the ground rushing up toward us with rising certainty that this is going to *hurt.*

*We're going home,* I tell myself, chanting the words over and over in my mind. More often than not over the past few weeks, I thought I'd never get to say those words again. I try as hard as I can to concentrate on that.

And then we slam into the earth with all the force of a truck hitting a rock wall.

**JULES**

WE ALL SIT PERFECTLY STILL FOR A LONG MOMENT, SHOCKED BY THE force of the impact. I can still feel it reverberating up and down my spine, the pain running through my jaw where my teeth clashed together.

All is quiet, except for a soft pinging noise, as the shuttle cools around us.

Atlanta's the first one to speak. "Let's shift. Quick-like, we need to compren where we are and shift to Prime-One."

And then it's a flurry of movement. I fumble for my straps, hauling them off over my shoulders, and beside me Mia's moving with the same urgency. She squeezes between our two seats, yanking the release on the hatch behind us. As soon as there's room, I rise from my seat too, trying to block Dex and Atlanta's view of her slender, too-small frame.

But Dex *knows*. I saw the moment he knew. And so did Mia. Why he hasn't said anything I don't know, but there's no way his silence can last. In a moment we'll all be outside the shuttle—in a valley, as best I could tell through the window.

The greens look European to me, remind me of home—we may be off course, but I think we're still on the continent they intended to land on. And as soon as we're all standing on that green grass, Dex and Atlanta are going to get a clear look at Mia, and there'll be no hiding what she is. There'll be no hiding what I am either, as soon as they try for an extended conversation.

Mia's out the hatch, and I clamber through after her. We both turn, making our way around the curve of the small shuttle, putting a little distance between us and the others as they climb out, keeping her behind me.

Dex is through next, and he glances in our direction, then back at Atlanta, who's following him.

She, however, doesn't spare us a glance. She reaches up to flick the releases on her helmet, yanking it off and tossing it casually back through the hatch. It clatters against the inside of the shuttle as she takes two steps, and folds to her knees, ripping off her gloves so she can press her bare hands to the ground.

"Grass!" Her voice sounds like a prayer.

Dex sounds wry, taking his helmet off more slowly, taking out his hairpins so that his braid can fall back down his neck again. "You seen a plant before, Peaches."

"Yeh, in a *lab*, or on a grow-ship," she retorts, reaching up to undo her hair as well now the helmets are unnecessary. "Not the same."

I glance over my shoulder at Mia, saying a little prayer of my own that when we make eye contact, she's going to look like a girl with an idea.

Do we try to get away from Dex and Atlanta? Do we try to bring them with us? Given that we just crash-landed in an alien spaceship, it won't be hard to convince the local police to call in the International Alliance, and then this whole invasion will be their problem. But if we *did* have Atlanta and Dex with us, they'd yield up physical evidence even a small-time country doctor could unravel pretty damn quickly. They might look like us, but the resemblance is only skin-deep. Mehercule, they bleed *blue*.

Atlanta's on her feet again, peeling out of her suit to reveal simple clothes beneath, different from the jumpsuits we've seen the Undying wear up on the ship. This is a pair of navy blue pants, sturdy brown boots, a lighter blue T-shirt, and a brown jacket. They're not particularly fashionable, but they could pass for regular clothes most places on the planet. They did mention watching our TV, studying our internet—these outfits must be the fruits of their labors.

"The grav's what we expected," she says, giving her arms an experimental swing, as if testing out her ease of movement. "Trained just right." I can hear her grin in her voice. "It's gonna give the olders ten kinds of hassle, when it's time for them to shift here."

"Tragedy," Dex says, dry. He's peeling out of his suit as well, revealing different shades of brown and blue, a shirt buttoned over an undershirt. He turns to shove both suits in through the hatch.

When I meet her eyes, Mia lifts her hand, jerking her thumb over her shoulder, suggesting we put some distance between us and the two aliens. And I know she's right. We can prove what we need to without Dex and Atlanta, as soon as we get to the authorities. The two of them are bigger than us and stronger than us, and if it comes down to it, I don't doubt they could outmatch us. If we stick with them, more likely than not we won't make it to the authorities at all.

"Suits," Atlanta says, glancing our way.

This is about to go badly wrong. They're going to get a look at our faces, at our clothes, but if we refuse . . . and for all we know, they'll have a way to track us if we keep the suits on. Not to mention there's *definitely* no way we could outrun them if we were encumbered by spacesuits.

Slowly, I reach up and release the catches on either side of my helmet. I lift it off my head, the warmth of the sun kissing my skin. There's a hint of a breeze, something I haven't felt in what seems like a lifetime, and just for an instant it's bliss.

Then I begin to peel out of my suit, and behind me, Mia's doing the same. She passes hers forward, keeping me between herself and the others, taking another step back around the curve of the little spaceship. Dex takes our gear, turning to lean in through the hatch and settle them on the floor inside the shuttle.

My heart's thumping madly. It's time to make our move—to run, to hope they're not armed. But before I have time to even turn away, Atlanta's speaking.

"What's that?" Her voice is sharp.

As one, we all turn in the direction she points. A dirt road curves around the edge of the valley, some distance away, and along it a convoy of all-terrain vehicles is raising a cloud of dust.

"Land-based transports," Dex says. "Incredibly inefficient."

It's not their efficiency that's worrying Atlanta. "Are they coming thisways?"

A flash of hope leaps inside me, and I lean to one side to see around the Undying better. Could we possibly be that lucky?

But Dex is shaking his head. "It's only a road. They're not coming thisways. Nobody saw us. We're just one more piece of lixo falling from the sky."

I realize with a start that that's how the Undying scouts have been getting down. Everyone knows that pieces of the old comms arrays fall from the heavens on a daily basis. When you're not in the midst of the city lights, you see them arcing across the sky at night, like shooting stars. They're from a time orbital tech wasn't regulated, and a lot of very questionable workmanship ended up circling the Earth.

Now, it's all falling down. And the Undying shuttles are posing as just a few more pieces of junk each day.

Atlanta studies the road, then nods, satisfied for the moment that the vehicles aren't turning our way. She swivels toward us, and I see the instant that she registers something's not right.

"What the . . ." Her voice trails away, and she's gawping at us like a fish out of water, her mouth open—closed—open again, like she's gasping for air. "Dex, they're *protos*. How—"

She looks across at him, and that's when we realize that he's not looking at the three of us. Instead, he's turned back toward the cars. "The transports are off-road. They *are* coming thisways."

All our heads snap around, and he's right. The convoy has turned our way, bumping over the grass toward us at speed.

They're military vehicles.

Atlanta responds first. "Dex, the destruct! Hit the button!" An urgent wave of her hand takes in the ship.

That must be how they're stopping people from finding the shuttles, once they're down.

Dex springs to life, tossing his helmet in through the hatch after the rest of our gear and yanking a plate off the smooth outside of the hull, revealing two dials and a red button beneath them. The button's protected by a clear hatch, presumably indicating it shouldn't be pressed accidentally.

A voice rings out over a loudspeaker. "Fora del vehicle! Aixequeu les mans!"

I recognize the language as Catalan and realize we must be somewhere along the mountains in Catalonia. *Perfututi*. It *would* be one of the languages I don't speak. But when the man repeats the order in Spanish, a wild desire to laugh strikes me, as I comply with the command. *Step away from the* vehicle? *Mehercule, it's a bleeding spaceship!*

"He says they're armed," I lie. "He says hands up."

Beside me, Mia raises her hands. "Never thought I'd be glad to have someone tell me to do *that*," she mutters, and I grin. The authorities will handle Atlanta and Dex, and all we have to do is tell someone in charge about the Trojan spaceship in orbit over our heads. The impending invasion will be the IA's problem—and whatever the Undying's plan is, it clearly hinges upon stealth. If we expose them, then surely . . . *surely* the IA can stop them.

The all-terrain vehicles—there are four of them—pull up in a semicircle before us. The troops inside wear the black of International Alliance forces. The front doors of each vehicle fly open so the soldiers can use them for cover, sighting us down the length of their rifles through the open front windows. Turns out I wasn't lying.

*Deus, they're* very *armed.*

I glance across at Dex and Atlanta, who both have their hands above their heads, their expressions blank. *What was their briefing for a situation like this?*

I can see the man with the megaphone now. He's in his forties, with a black mustache and a no-nonsense expression. Perhaps he saw me translating, because he speaks again. "Hablas español?"

"Hablo español, pero hablan inglés," I explain, raising my voice to make myself heard.

He switches across to accented but flawless English. "All debris crash sites are the jurisdiction of the International Alliance." I'd recognize him as IA even if he hadn't just announced his faction—linguistics training is paramount for their forces, and even the soldiers are multilingual. "What are you doing here?"

We've been desperately fighting and hoping for the chance to explain to the authorities, but now, I find myself paralyzed. Where does one even begin answering a question like that? The story is so long, so unbelievable, that there's no way I could hope to make a ground-level IA officer understand me. *Well, it all began when my father came up with an alternate theory on the translation of the Undying broadcast . . .*

I try a different tack. "The answer to that is incredibly complex, sir. We need to speak to someone senior within the IA as a matter of urgency." Someone who'd know who I am—and that I was on Gaia.

He inclines his head. "Captain Mateo Abrantes," he says. "IA."

His tone isn't friendly. "And you'll go through the proper channels like any other trespasser."

I pause, trying to figure out how to say, *No, I mean someone* way *more senior,* when Mia takes her turn.

"We have an IA contact, a handler," she says. "Our recruiter. We need to speak to her. It's a matter of life or death."

I eye Mia sidelong—the use of "her" gives me an idea of where she's heading, and I'm not sure I like it. But if there's one person within the IA who *knows* she and I have just come from the surface of Gaia, and that our story needs to be taken seriously . . .

Abrantes raises his brows. "Your contact's name, por favor?"

"Mink," she says.

"Charlotte," I say, at exactly the same moment.

My heart sinks, as his brows go even higher. He's not buying it. We can't even get our stories straight on our contact's name. And truth be told, her name isn't Mink *or* Charlotte, the woman who recruited Mia as a scavenger, and me to play the unwitting bloodhound and lead her people through the temple to the ship that's now orbiting the planet. Truth be told, we have no idea what her real name is.

Atlanta's recovered, and at just the wrong moment. "We were only fooling."

Captain Abrantes switches his attention to her. "With this?" His nod takes in the shuttle behind us.

Atlanta nods. "We don't want to give anyone hassle. We saw it fall, we thought it'd be lixo from a satellite, but it's real." Her eyes are wide, her tone panicked. She has serious game.

This girl knows how to act. And though her English is sharply accented, so is his. And *lixo* is a word originally from Spanish, or Portuguese, or probably even Catalan, come to that.

I see the moment that he starts to buy it.

The moment that her version of events starts to sound more reasonable than ours. The moment it starts to slip away, our chance of convincing anyone with the power to stop the Undying that our planet is in danger.

"This is serious business," he says. "This is *not* a place for children."

"Yes!" The words burst out of me—I can't help myself. "Yes, Captain Abrantes, it *is* serious business. This shuttle is from the ship in orbit. *They* are from the ship in orbit." I'm jabbing a finger at Atlanta and Dex. "We have to—"

He cuts me off with a gesture, and the soldier beside him twitches his gun to indicate I should keep my hands still. "They're just kids," Abrantes says, looking Atlanta and Dex up and down. "And the IA operatives on Gaia's surface verified that the ship was empty before launching it through the portal to Earth."

"Except for us," Mia breaks in. "*We* were on that ship, Captain Abrantes—how else do you explain this spacecraft landing in the middle of a field?"

Abrantes glances at the shuttle, which is still pinging and cooling after its descent through the atmosphere. "Space junk," he says, although his voice carries the barest hint of uncertainty. "There's been a lot more of it since the ship arrived. It's knocking other satellites out of their orbits."

"Does this look like a satellite to you?" I ask softly. "It has a parachute, for god's sake!"

Abrantes's brow lowers a little, and his eyes flick between the four of us.

Sensing, perhaps, that belief is starting to swing back toward me and Mia, Dex steps forward. "We're very, very sorry, sir—we shouldn't have come to spy the crash site. We pledge we'll never do it again."

Abrantes sighs and gestures to the soldiers, two of whom stow their weapons and move forward, reaching for restraints to take us into custody.

*No. I'm not letting this happen. We didn't survive all that time in hiding, survive all of Gaia, just to get home and have no one believe us.*

Desperation flares, and in that moment, I abandon everything I'd do—and I do what Mia would do.

"My name is Jules Addison," I blurt, voice cracking with intensity. Out of the corner of my eye I see Mia's gaze jerk toward me, surprise stiffening her shoulders. "I was recruited by the IA to go to Gaia and lead them to the ship that's now in orbit. If nothing else, you *have* to report to your superiors that you have Dr. Elliott Addison's son in your custody."

The soldiers hesitate, and I feel their eyes on me. I look like my father—I always have. But for my lighter skin and the difference in our ages, we could be brothers. And my father's face is one of the most well-known in the world, following his humiliation at the hands of those who doubted the warnings he tried to give.

After a long, *long* silence, Abrantes lets out his breath in a sigh. "It certainly doesn't look like a satellite, and you certainly do look like . . . Either way, we'll be keeping you in our custody until we receive orders on what to do with you."

It's there. Doubt. I see it in the shift of his eyes as he looks at the shuttle's parachute, in the uncertain glance at the four teenagers before him. And that's all we need—for him to report our arrest to someone who *does* know that I was on Gaia. Someone who knows there could be some truth to what we're saying.

We keep our hands up as the soldiers with the guns approach. I can see Dex eyeing what must be the self-destruct settings out the corner of his eye—he must want badly to incinerate the shuttle, rather than leave it for these soldiers to crawl all over. But the controls are out of his reach. There's no way he'd get to them before someone stopped him, probably with considerable force.

He must draw the same conclusion. His expression is blank.

My gaze slides from him to Atlanta, and there's poison waiting for me in her eyes. I can't imagine IA detention played any part in their plans, whatever they were.

The four of us let them wrap zip ties around our wrists and pat us down, but despite the restraints, despite their rough handling,

I can't help but feel a wisp of relief wash over me, like a cool breeze on a still, hot summer day. As soon as someone more senior than Abrantes looks at our situation, someone who knows about Charlotte's operation on Gaia and that we were there, they'll know we're telling the truth. Or they'll know enough to take a closer look at the ship in orbit.

It's only a matter of time now, and we've done our part. The authorities will know what we know, and the burden of stopping all this will be on *their* shoulders, not ours. Mia and I are safe. And soon—so soon I can almost feel his arms encircling me in one of his massive hugs—I'll see my father again.

We're home.

8

AMELIA

FOR ONCE, I DON'T MIND BEING GRILLED BY UNIFORMED OFFICERS.
Or being poked and prodded by a medical examiner, the inside
of my cheek swabbed, my fingerprints taken. For once, I have
absolutely nothing to hide. Not that I haven't done anything
wrong—I'm a criminal by every definition of the word—but my
crimes are nothing compared to the intel we've brought back to
warn our race that we're all in danger.

My heart lightens with every detail I give them: being captured
by the IA's secret-ops division under Mink's command amid the
ice back on Gaia, how the Undying ship took off with us on board,
the moment we realized it was a Trojan Horse, the plan we half
uncovered involving aliens masquerading as human teenagers. Less
than twenty-four hours ago, I thought I would die on an alien ship
in orbit around a world that would never know what was coming
for them.

Now—now they have a chance.

*And I have a chance to go home.*

The relief is so profound that I don't even feel the flicker of sick dread at the thought of trying to sort out what to do about me and Jules. Right now, I'm invincible, and there's nothing we can't solve.

Jules is waiting for me by the time the uniformed soldier escorts me back to what looks like a holding cell, little more than three concrete walls and a fourth, transparent glass wall that allows for observation from the hallway. He leaps to his feet as we come into view along the corridor, and stands rigid as the guard swipes a card through a slot and opens the door. The guard ushers me through and into the cell, his movements jerky—a quick glance tells me his eyes are a little wild, the details of the story I told the officials leaving him more than a little shaken.

*Good,* I think, with great satisfaction. *You should be freaking terrified. Welcome to my life.*

When the glass door goes whooshing closed behind me, Jules's eyes are waiting for mine.

Those eyes tell me everything. There's a light in them I haven't seen since we were first setting foot inside the temple on Gaia, what feels like years ago. My hope recognizes his, and in a rush I move toward him, and his hands curl around mine.

"Are you okay?" he whispers.

Smiling has been an effort for so long that the feel of my lips curving uncontrollably is like sun on my face after a month in shadow. "I am now. You?"

He gives a light grimace, and lifts one arm to show his wristwatch. "They took my SIM card," he replies. "But at least all my pictures are still on here. And I don't know where my journal is—I think it ended up back in the shuttle with my suit."

I glance around the bare cell. "Where are Atlanta and Dex?"

"I haven't seen them since they split us all up."

I snort. "It's an age-old interrogation technique. Divide and conquer. See if we all tell the same story."

Jules's grin is like air, and I soak it in. "It won't matter what story they tell. The IA guys swabbed your cheek too, right? Checked your DNA to ID you?" His eyebrows lift.

I nod, and in this moment I know exactly why he's asking. "Somewhere, they're doing exactly the same to Dex and Atlanta. So they've seen what we saw, right? The blue blood's probably just the beginning, there'll be signs all over the place that they're not what they seem on the surface. Do aliens even have DNA? Whoever checks them will be in for a shock."

"I'm sure it'll take some time to process them, but . . ." Jules's fingers tighten around my hands, and he steps closer so he can press his forehead to mine. "Mehercule," he breathes. "This is real, right? I'm not dreaming?"

My own heart's asking the same question, barely daring to believe, because the weight of terror and exhaustion and hopelessness has been so great that I almost don't know how to let it go. I almost don't *want* to, for fear it could somehow come back and find me again. But I squeeze his fingers in return and whisper, "We made it, Jules."

He takes half a step closer, and instantly the gentle warmth of relief shifts, an awareness of his body shifting against mine surfacing like a long-submerged ship from beneath the waves. He lifts his head from mine, but only so he can drop it to murmur in my ear. "My father," he says firmly, in a voice that brooks no opposition, "is going to love you."

I can't argue with him. I don't want to, not anymore. We're just a couple of teenagers again—the weight of saving the world is back where it ought to be, with the governments and the armies and the world's greatest minds. Finally, *finally*, we're just us. And—especially as his hand slides around to the small of my back and pulls me close—I'm not saying a single word to shatter that.

But then another sound does it for me. The sound of someone clearing his throat startles us apart, like—well, like a couple of teenagers caught on the verge of making out.

A man stands just beyond the glass wall of the cell, watching us with the polite air of someone waiting for his opportunity to interrupt. Though he wears an ordinary—if expensive-looking—suit, rather than a uniform, he holds himself with the confident rigidity of a soldier. He's not particularly tall or muscular, and his features are finely sculpted, almost feminine in their delicacy. Impeccably trimmed black hair and well-shaped eyebrows match a pair of intense black eyes, which are currently fixed on us.

"Good afternoon," he says with exaggerated civility. He speaks with the faintest trace of an accent, though I don't know what kind. "I am Daniel De Luca, IA Security Director for Europe."

Jules's arm goes rigid, but when I glance his way, his face is eager rather than daunted. He squeezes my hand in reassurance. "My name is Jules Addison," he says. "This is Amelia Radcliffe."

"Yes, so I've been told." De Luca smiles an even, attractive smile. "Forgive my tardiness—it took some time to verify that you were, indeed, who you said you were. How are you? You've eaten?"

"We're fine." Jules takes a quick breath. "You can skip the pleasantries, Mr. De Luca—"

"*Director* De Luca." The interruption is gentle, even friendly, but absolutely firm.

"Yes, of course." Jules doesn't sound chastened—if anything, he sounds encouraged.

Something about the Director's manner sets off alarm bells in my head, but whatever it is, Jules isn't picking up on it. He's just eager, impatient even—excited by the fact that someone so senior's been alerted to the situation.

*Steady, Mia.* The voice in my head has the tiniest trace of a British accent, and if I wasn't so busy trying to order my thoughts, I'd be amused that my attempt to comfort myself sounds like Jules. *You've been dodging death and doom so long that you're just looking for problems.*

"Director De Luca," Jules echoes, conciliatory. "Please let us know if there's anything else we can tell you. I know this whole thing sounds completely mad, and I know there'll be a lot of people who don't believe us, but you've no idea what a relief it is to know we've finally gotten someone's attention."

"You certainly do have my attention," De Luca agrees. "I also have the advantage of being privy to information my colleagues do not have. Information the International Alliance has spent a great deal of effort and resources to keep from the general public."

My misgivings vanish entirely. That info he has—it's got to be data from Gaia about the ship up in orbit. Maybe it's even whatever the doctors found when examining Atlanta's and Dex's DNA. It's not that he doubts us, he's just not happy about the news we came bearing. I can't blame him for that.

I hold my tongue—better for Jules to do the talking, given how precise and genteel the guy's speech is. I'd just piss him off. But finally someone with the security clearance to know about Mink, to know about what happened with us on Gaia, to actually *do* something is here. IA Security Director for the whole of *Europe*.

Jules senses it too, for his voice quickens. "Then you believe us? About Dex and Atlanta, about the invasion? You know about Charlotte's—Mink's—mission on Gaia, and that we really did come through the portal with the ship?"

De Luca's dark eyes are intent, for all his features are relaxed. "I don't have to believe you—I *know* you were on Gaia, Mr. Addison." His gaze flickers toward me with a faint lift of his eyebrow. I probably wasn't mentioned very prominently in whatever report Mink made—I was just one of dozens of scavengers she planted on Gaia to trick Jules into leading them to the portal ship.

Jules lets out his breath, the tension in his shoulders finally easing, so that he nearly sags where he stands. "Then you have to listen to us, Mr. D—Director. The ship in orbit is *not* empty. It's not inert or benign. It's full of Undying, and they want Earth."

It sounds outrageous, said out loud. But the Director merely considers Jules thoughtfully, as if sizing him up in some way. "Certainly, you must have come from the ship—how else would you find yourself here, rather than on Gaia, where our operatives left you? And there are quite a few details that seem to corroborate your story."

My spine straightens, that hope still flickering through me as bright and warm as a fire. Trickles of doubt keep trying to stem the flames, but I ignore them. *He may be a creepy international government official, but he's what we've got.*

De Luca continues: "Strangely patterned signals that seem to come from the engines of the ship in orbit. Sightings of what looks to be some kind of UFO crash-landing in the middle of the Gulf of Mexico. Exactly the sort of thing you'd expect to see if aliens were about to descend upon Earth from on high, as you claim."

*As you claim.*

The words ring in my ears. My heart is pounding even as it threatens to sink. "Then you *know* we're telling the truth," I blurt, forgetting to let Jules do the talking. "Please tell us you guys are doing something about it already—tracking the incoming shuttles, or—or alerting the various governments that something's coming?"

"It's interesting, though," remarks De Luca, undoing the button on his suit jacket so that he can slip his hands into his pockets. "Despite the apparent fluctuations in the orbital ship's engines, its course hasn't altered, as it would if it were being piloted. The bogey that went down in the Gulf was conveniently of such a small size that all efforts to recover it have failed, so our technicians cannot study it."

I can't help it—I glance at Jules, whose lips are pressed tight together, face stricken. He didn't get it before, but he gets it now.

*No. This is some sort of sick joke.*

De Luca's gaze shifts from Jules to me. "All together, and with your nigh-miraculous return with the ship through the portal bearing tales of ancient beings from across the galaxy, they certainly paint a picture of an alien invasion. Straight out of Hollywood, one might say. The conspiracy theorists are going wild about it online, and some of them are even trying to connect it to Dr. Addison's own theories. But individually, each one of these incidents is so easily disproven as to be laughable."

I can feel the hope draining away, and I can't help but try to cling to it. "Listen, Director, you *know* we were on that ship, you *know* we came through from the portal to Gaia, you *know* we got here to the surface again in one of their shuttles. You have two of them in a holding cell somewhere—all you have to do is look beneath the surface, you'll *see* they're not human!"

The man's head bobs, as if in agreement, though when he speaks it's a question. "What you have to understand, Miss Radcliffe, is that the ship's retrieval has created a very . . . delicate situation for the IA. Every country in the world wants a piece of the technology it promises, and some are ready to press their claim by any means necessary. The last thing we need is a couple of wild-eyed teenagers throwing gasoline on the simmering coals. Do you *want* to be the cause of the next world war?"

I blink my eyes, trying to keep myself from crying out of sheer frustration. "The next world war is already *here*, Director, but the enemy's up there." I point toward the ceiling—not as dramatic a gesture when we're inside, but it's all I've got. "What possible reason could we have to make something like this up?"

De Luca smiles at me, giving me the distinctly unpleasant feeling that I've just asked the question he was waiting for me to ask. His eyes shift back toward Jules. "Tell me—Mr. Addison, why did you agree to go to Gaia in the first place?"

Jules's eyes narrow. "To prove my father's theories about the dangers of adopting Undying technology too quickly."

De Luca nods again. "And you, Miss Radcliffe?"

I say nothing, all too aware that I look like a sullen child. But all my past experiences dealing with the authorities have come screaming back to me, and I know what Jules does not—that once someone in charge has made up their mind about you, anything you say will only make them more convinced they're right.

And with a sickening, twisting sense of dread, I'm realizing: *He doesn't believe us at all.*

My hope, such a roaring fire moments ago, flickers out like the last guttering efforts of a burned-out candle.

De Luca smiles again as my silence draws out. "I'll tell you, then. You signed on with our undercover agent for simple profit. Quite an undertaking for someone your age—either you have a remarkably developed sense of greed, or you need that money for something else. Or some*one* else."

My heart stutters, a painful throb in my chest.

*Evie. No, he can't know. No one knows I have a sister—I've spent years making sure the records connecting me with my illegal sister have been purged in every database there is.*

But the gleam in De Luca's eye tells me he knows *exactly* what I needed that money for. My hand stretches toward Jules—or maybe he reaches for me—and the warmth of his fingers in mine is all that keeps me on my feet.

"So," De Luca says briskly. "The two of you form a team on Gaia's surface, and lead us to the ship currently in orbit. Rather than remain in IA custody on Gaia, you escape and stow away on board. Neither of you received the prize you went to Gaia to obtain—Mr. Addison, there was no convenient artifact or inscription elaborating on the many dangers of an extinct race's leftover technology. And Miss Radcliffe, clearly, is not in possession of any valuable artifacts or tech to sell on the black market. So, what are two criminal teenagers to do?"

Stomach churning, vision sparking with moisture, I can't help but watch Director De Luca speak—he's so convincing, so calm, that for a moment I almost believe the story he's spinning.

"It seems to me that returning to Earth with tales of an alien invasion would create exactly the kind of public panic necessary to win people to Dr. Addison's cause. And this, certainly, would've gone down in history as one of the most elaborate hoaxes ever perpetrated against the world—a story worth a fortune to anyone willing to buy the rights. Certainly enough to pay for the release of one Evelyn Radcliffe."

"No." The word is barely a whisper, hoarse and strangled. My lips refuse to cooperate, though, and I can't do anything other than repeat that same syllable. "No . . . no—"

"You're making a huge mistake, De Luca," Jules interrupts, suddenly fierce where he was calm and conciliatory. "Please. *Please.* We're not asking for fame, we're not even asking to be released— we'll sign whatever you want, anything to say we won't profit from this in any way. But you have to know, everyone has to know— they're coming for us. They're already here."

De Luca's face doesn't even shift.

"The cheek swabs!" I blurt. "Wait until the DNA results come back. You have to—they won't even have DNA to identify them, they're not human."

De Luca's brow lowers, and suddenly his suave, urbane face flickers for an instant, and I see something far darker, more vicious, beneath it. "That's enough, Miss Radcliffe. Both of you." And then he's his usual, calm self again. His hands slide back out of his pockets, and his long fingers deftly slip the button of his jacket back through the buttonhole. "You know, we actually were beginning to grow concerned about the accumulation of events of seemingly extraterrestrial origin."

He turns, ready to stride back down the corridor out of sight, but then pauses. "I don't know how you did it. Perhaps the other two arrested with you were accomplices on the ground to help sim- ulate UFOs and radio signals—I don't know. I don't care. What matters is that your arrival, your inventive stories, are all the con- firmation we needed. The ship's arrival in orbit marks the most crucial era for the IA in the last fifty years—the two of you are nothing more than a distraction." His voice is taut, and the last words he speaks sound anything but cordial: "Good day."

And he's gone, leaving us in silence.

**9**

JULES

**Neither of us has spoken in six hours.**

There aren't any words—not even between the two of us, who've been through so much together—to fill the gaping, gutted hole where hope once lived. The sheer relief of that hope, so profound and transformative, after such a long, grueling crucible of fear and sleepless toil and despair . . . my mind had filled with a million images in just those few moments.

Images of the world coming together to combat the threat in orbit, of the Undying banished from our planet once and for all. Of a world at peace, finally.

But more immediately, my mind summoned images of calling Neal to come bail us out of jail. Of having a hot shower. Of walking to the shops for a pie, or riding on Neal's souped-up bike, of calling my dad in IA detention. Of seeing my dad *released* from detention, of seeing his reputation restored, of seeing his face crease with an absentminded smile as I put a mug of tea down at his elbow while he worked at his desk.

Of introducing him to Mia. Of showing her my home. Of telling her that I want her with me, no matter what, that if she's not "Oxford material" then neither am I, and we'll go wherever the hell she wants to go as long as we go together.

An infinite universe of possibilities—and in a few words, Director De Luca has thrown us both straight back down into a terrible purgatory of helplessness.

I've slept fitfully, on and off, and I think Mia has too. She's been curled in on herself since the director left—the news that these people know about her sister, whose very existence is a contravention of "one child" policies, has hollowed her out.

There's no way we can ask if they've done anything with the information about Evie—mentioning her at all would tell them they've found the leverage they need from now on. But I know whatever Mia's imagining—and her world has been dark enough for her to imagine some pretty horrendous things—must be running through her head on repeat.

I keep thinking of the laughing young girl I saw on Mia's phone back on Gaia, of their identical smiles. I'm afraid for my father, even more so now that I've had a moment of thinking his ordeal was over, but I have no doubt he's safe. These people might be ruthless in their pursuit of their goals, but they're not stupid. They won't harm their leading expert on the Undying. But there's no such guarantee for a solitary American girl on the other side of the Atlantic. The IA's reach spans the globe—there's no one they can't find if they really want to.

"Mia," I murmur, looking down at the trays of rice and beans beside us, delivered some time ago by a disinterested guard. My voice is thick and hoarse with disuse. "Will you eat something?"

She's leaning against my side, and tilts her head up to look at me, eyes shadowed. "I know," she murmurs. Our two trays hold feasts compared to what we had aboard the Undying ship, but are somehow infinitely less appetizing. I keep thinking longingly of the chicken and porcini mushroom dinner I made Mia our first night together on Gaia. "I know I should. But . . ."

But she can't, and I certainly can't make her. It's hard to imagine getting anything down, with the sick knot in the bottom of my stomach.

We're in limbo, back where we started—a couple of kids that no one believes. We're back to being the only protos, as Atlanta and Dex would say, on the planet to understand how close we all are to utter extinction.

And here we are, with nothing we can do to prove the truth of our words.

*It's not purgatory*, I think, watching Mia's shoulders quake with suppressed emotion and feeling my heart shatter all over again. *This is hell.*

As if my mind doesn't want to cope with the enormity of that— and I can't blame it—it drags me elsewhere. To a smaller issue. *I'd walk over hot coals for a shower right now.*

I'm still in the same khakis I wore on Gaia, and it's been weeks. I must smell horrendous. They're filthy, torn and crusted with dirt and sweat, and I know I need a shave. My face prickles with stubble.

The only change in scenery we've been allowed since we were brought to the cell has been two heavily guarded trips to the bathroom each. And last time I went, when I tried to wash my face in the sink, my escort pointed his gun at me.

Mia slides down to settle on the ground and rest her head on my thigh for a pillow, one arm slung over her face, because of course they've declined to turn down the lights at any point.

There's a camera in one corner of the cell, and though there's no convenient little red light to tell us it's recording or transmitting, I have no doubt they're watching our every move. Mia knows too— that she curls up in my lap regardless is a tiny flicker of warmth.

Surely at some point, even if they don't release us, they'll move us to better quarters. Perhaps then there'll be a chance that we can do *something* to get out, or to get away. Maybe they'll actually check those DNA tests eventually, or we can find some other proof, or supporters who believe us, and turn the tide before the Undying can accomplish whatever they've snuck among us to do.

I'm roused from that brief fantasy by the sound of footsteps.

*Is it time for another meal already?*

But then the last thing I'm expecting to see appears outside the glass—it's Dex and Atlanta, under the same kind of friendly escort as we've been enjoying so far. They both look tired and sullen—Dex has his head down, his braid out now, hair hanging around his face—but I can see the light of triumph in Atlanta's eyes. Facing toward me and away from her armed guard, she permits herself just the tiniest smirk.

Then the glass door is opened, rousing Mia, and the two of them are pushed inside. They take up positions facing us, leaning against the wall at the opposite end of our little cell, seating themselves with their legs stretched out.

For a long moment, we stare at each other across the empty space of the room. A million questions and accusations fly through my thoughts, so crowded I can't make sense of any of them.

"Well?" I say finally, and I can hear how belligerent it sounds.

"Well what?" Dex's eyes on us are cool, but there's a spark in them—whereas Atlanta's are full of ill-concealed hostility.

"Who are you?" Mia blurts, before I can try to form a coherent sentence. "Your people—what do you want with Earth?"

Atlanta holds up her hands, placating, palms out. "We don't want hassle," she says. "We just want to go homewards. This was a piece of lixo idea. I pledge, we ever get out, I'm gonna shift back to school and stay there."

Mia splutters in response, and I lay a hand on her arm. When she looks my way, I lift my chin, indicating the dark pinhole of a camera in the corner of the cell.

Whether Dex and Atlanta recognize it or not, they're too smart not to assume we're being watched. They're still playing the part of the repentant pranksters, and why not? All they have to do is hold on. Even though nobody here ever bloody says *lixo* or *I pledge*, unless they're declaring allegiance to their bloody country.

And it's working. The very fact that they've been brought back here, to be kept with the other "teens" tells me there's no lingering suspicion on the part of the IA. As De Luca pointed out, they could very well be our co-conspirators in the elaborate hoax De Luca sketched out for us.

Everyone on Earth has *known*, ever since the Undying broadcast first reached us, that we were dealing with an extinct race. The idea that they could not only be alive, but wearing human faces and plotting to take our home for themselves, is ludicrous. It sounds ludicrous to *me*, and I'm living it.

I wouldn't believe us either.

It's one more blow in a long, steady beatdown—so much so that I barely feel it land.

Mia's tone is sharp. "If you're such terrible kids, why hasn't someone called your parents already?"

Atlanta smiles, rueful. "We don't have parents," she replies with the ease of prior rehearsal. "Orphans, yeh?" Her veneer of woefulness is a slap in the face.

I clench my jaw to make myself stay silent. She's playing to the camera mounted above us, and if Mia can't trip her up, I know I certainly can't.

I slide my gaze across to Dex instead. He meets my eyes for a moment, then looks away. *I wish I knew what to make of him.* He knew who we were—what we were—on the way down in the shuttle. Certainly he had every opportunity to figure it out or confirm his suspicions after we landed. And yet he was silent.

Does that mean he could be an ally?

I wish I could make my mind stop searching for hope. I wish I could make it go quiet, let me rest. But my mind chases the question in circles, around and around and around . . .

Eventually I must've fallen asleep, because I wake to a sharp pain in my neck, which has lolled to one side for too long, and the sound of a guard's voice.

"You're wanted," he says roughly, not making eye contact with either of us, but rather studying our legs where they're stretched out in front of us. *Not promising, when no one wants to meet your eyes.*

Dex straightens where he'd been leaning against the wall next to Atlanta, who's stretching out her limbs one at a time as if warming up for some sort of marathon—*Do aliens sleep?*—but the guard takes a step back, eyes flicking across them nervously. "Not you two, the others." His gesture is for Mia and me.

Despite De Luca's dismissal, the guard is still nervous around the Undying teens—still watching them, still looking as though he's seen something he wishes he hadn't.

*Maybe it isn't hopeless after all.* The thought is tiny and quiet and part of me tries to drown it out. But the rest of me clings to the idea, holding it close and sheltering it like a fledgling bird. *Maybe we aren't the only ones who see what they really are.*

Mia and I climb stiffly to our feet, and we're escorted down a pair of unremarkable, anonymous hallways, brightly lit but otherwise featureless.

The room we're headed for contains a long metal table flanked by six chairs, three down either side. Three of the walls are a pale gray, and the fourth finishes at waist height, with a sheet of some transparent—and no doubt practically bombproof—material sealing it the rest of the way. Down one wall a series of pages are tacked up, a sequence of meaningless letters—some kind of code, I guess. I glance at the window, fingering my watch, and then when I look back at the pages, they snap into focus. AGCT. I recognize those letters.

It *is* code: DNA code.

And there are four printouts—one for each of us? I straighten, moving my arm so I can surreptitiously photograph the pages, one after the other. Maybe, just *maybe*, these pages are Atlanta's and

Dex's results. Which means they do *have* something like DNA, enough to pass a cursory glance, but no one's processed these results thoroughly enough to see the reality. If they had, there'd be alarm bells going off everywhere about the two blatantly non-human entities sitting in our cell.

This is a language I never learned. To me, it's a seemingly randomized list of endless combinations of those four letters. But if I could somehow smuggle these results out, maybe I could get them to someone back at Oxford who could analyze them. *Maybe.*

Mia and I wordlessly take a couple of chairs, settling in to face that window by unspoken agreement, so we can see what's coming. On another table at the far end of the room are the few belongings we had with us when we were taken into custody, laid out like clues in a murder mystery. A few empty wrappers from the Undying sponge rations. Mia's multi-tool. My journal. Under the table I find Mia's hand and squeeze it. She squeezes back.

De Luca appears first, on the other side of the window. His mouth is moving but I can't hear anything. The transparent wall is soundproof. I glance at Mia, who's watching him intently, and my heart swells with admiration. Even now, even exhausted, she's still gathering data, still desperately trying to figure out how to get these people to listen to us. I know she's terrified of what they might do to Evie if she gets on the wrong side of them, but she's not letting it stop her.

Suddenly her lips peel back into a snarl. "You!"

My gaze snaps across. There's a woman outside, and she—

*Mehercule.*

It's Charlotte Stapleton, the IA operative who recruited me to go to Gaia in the first place, pretending to work for Global Energy Solutions, a ruse so sophisticated that she created an entire corporate front—she hired my cousin Neal for an internship, just to impress me with her imaginary company's resources. If I haven't lost track of time, he was supposed to start the thing this week.

Mia knew her as Mink, and I think I prefer that name—I've no doubt both *Mink* and *Charlotte* are fictitious, but the former seems more fitting.

Mink knew that with my father in IA detention after his outburst to try and warn the public about the Undying, there was no way I would voluntarily lead anyone from the International Alliance through Gaia's mysteries. I didn't trust them to share what they found, to preserve the learning, to interpret it properly. I knew they were too desperate for the power sources they might find there. I must have heard it a thousand times—one small piece of Undying tech was enough to power the fresh water plant for the whole of Los Angeles, and send power up the grid to what's left of the west coast. Imagine what else we could find.

She counted on the fact that I'd search for evidence to confirm my father's theories only if I didn't know I was being followed—if I thought I was on my own. She seeded the planet with scavengers to give me the impression that more than one company had found a way to smuggle people through the portal to Gaia, that I'd need to hurry if I wanted to get to that evidence before the scavengers did.

She sent me to meet with a nonexistent party, and then watched to see what I would do when I thought I was alone and unobserved. She was sure I'd lead her to the tech she needed. Except Mia found me first, which wasn't part of Mink's plan.

Only once we were well inside the temple did she send her hired guns to find me. A group led by Liz, who's dead now—we've seen firsthand what Mink does with people she doesn't need anymore.

This is the woman who realized how I felt about Mia and forced me to decode the operation of the ancient ship with Mia's life as collateral. The woman who launched the damn thing, despite my desperate warnings.

Now, Mink walks into the room alongside De Luca, with Captain Abrantes bringing up the rear.

*Brilliant. Now we've got the IA's European security, ground forces, and . . . skullduggery represented in the same room.*

And the interesting thing is that the air is singing with tension—it's in every line of their bodies.

But though Mink has been utterly ruthless every moment I've known her, she's never been stupid. She may be our last hope—even though I wouldn't trust her for a second.

"You have to convince them that we're telling the truth." The words are out before I choose them.

Mink turns her gaze toward me, brows lifting slightly, but she doesn't get a chance to respond before De Luca speaks.

"She doesn't *have* to do anything, Mr. Addison."

*What is it with this guy and making sure he enforces every possible subtle nuance around rank? Insecure much?*

Mia speaks. "Why are we all back here? I thought the two of us were liars, out to cause trouble and get rich."

*Good question, Mia. This is a lot of attention for two kids they've already dismissed.*

Captain Abrantes folds his arms. "You are both more than that. There's a massive alien ship in orbit, and until the IA has analyzed and divided the technological advancements onboard, you are a danger."

I glance across at Mink, hoping she'll join the conversation, but she's still studying Mia and me more intently than she ever has.

Mia nods. "So everybody wants a piece of the shiny new thing. What else is new?"

De Luca's brow lowers disapprovingly. "World governments are not the same as scavengers, Miss Radcliffe." He pronounces *scavengers* with careful articulation, as though he doesn't want his mouth to come into contact with the word a second longer than it must.

Mink leans against the wall at her back, folding her arms casually—though the sharpness of her gaze is anything but casual. "But she's right. Everybody does want a piece of it."

De Luca exhales, nostrils flaring. "Had the ship not been placed in orbit so precipitously, the IA would have been in a better position to anticipate the response of the major players in this game."

Mink's expression is stony.

*Oho. There's tension here indeed. All is not well between our captors.*

I glance sidelong at Mia, whose expression is speculative—she hasn't missed the friction between the various branches of the IA represented before us. I can almost hear her thoughts turning over, searching for a way to turn them against one another and to our advantage. But finally Mink's joined the conversation, and I can't waste the chance.

"Look," I say. "Do you accept that Mia and I were on Gaia?"

Mink and De Luca nod. "If nothing else, the data there in Mr. Addison's journal confirms you were on the surface," De Luca says, tilting his head toward the motley array of belongings on the far table.

"And do you accept that the ship that is causing so much trouble now came through the portal, and that Mia and I took a shuttle from it down to the surface?"

They both nod again.

I turn my attention to Abrantes. "And, Captain, you found the two of us beside that shuttle, which was clearly *not* just another downed satellite, along with two others, correct?"

"Yes," he says, gaze flicking warily toward his two superiors. "Your accomplices on the ground, to help you perpetrate the hoax."

Mia snorts. "You were there within minutes of us hitting the ground. How could they possibly have joined us? You'd have found some trace of their approach, a car or bikes nearby."

Director De Luca's reply is smooth. "You are correct, Miss Radcliffe. It is far more likely that they came with you from Gaia. That they were scavengers."

Mia turns to Mink. "Look," she pleads. "Just take a look at them. You hired everyone on the surface of Gaia, right? As part of tricking Jules into helping you? You'll know they're not scavengers."

Mink's reply is an age in coming. "Show them to me," she says eventually.

My heart's beginning to beat harder, relief threatening to tumble loose and flow through me, however much I try to suppress it. *Fool me once*, I think furiously. But I can't help it. Mink might have used us unforgivably, but I certainly don't doubt her competence. She knows who she put on that planet.

More important, she knows who she *didn't* put on that planet.

With an irritated twitch of his mouth, the Director walks over to a blank pad fastened to the wall beside the door. His thumbprint brings it to life, and he taps in a couple of commands. The wall to our right lights up—it's a screen—and it's running a live feed of our detention cell.

Dex and Atlanta are still in much the same positions as we left them. He has his head bowed, and she's murmuring something in his ear. There's no audio on this feed, but that doesn't mean there's not a microphone somewhere in the cell, picking up everything we've been saying.

Mink studies them for a full minute, until Atlanta turns her head again, giving the camera—or one of them, for I'm realizing now there must be many—a front-on view of her face. Mink is still staring at the screen when she speaks. "I didn't hire them."

"No," I say. "You didn't. Because they're *Undying*."

Mink's sharp eyes flick back toward me. "The only people aboard that ship when it traveled to Earth were you and Amelia Radcliffe—I know that for a fact. We had agents in every part of the ship right up until its launch."

"That's because there are portals on board the ship—it's a Trojan Horse. Dex and Atlanta—those two—they came through with hundreds of others *after* the ship went through the portal to orbit Earth."

Mink's eyes stay on me, and though there's no flash of horror or understanding to tell me she believes me, she's not denying it either. I can almost see her thinking, in an eerie echo of the way I can sometimes see Mia thinking—both their minds work at light speed, calculating every angle of a situation.

"They certainly weren't on Gaia," Mink says finally, her tone even. "Perhaps Abrantes was mistaken, and there was more time between the craft's landing and when his men arrived."

Captain Abrantes starts to bristle, his eyebrows drawing in and face tightening, but before he can protest aloud, De Luca kills the feed. "Or," he says smoothly, turning to Mink, "you didn't have as tight a control over transport to and from Gaia as we were led to believe."

Mink's gaze is subzero. "I did."

He lifts his hands as if to indicate his helplessness. "The evidence says otherwise."

"Look," I try. "I am begging you to at least *consider* this. The people in that cell are part of the first wave of an invasion. They *are* Undying. The ship above us is full of them. We have to ready ourselves."

Abrantes, spine still stiff with indignation, leans forward. "The Undying have been extinct for centuries. Millennia. How do you explain away the gap of time between the construction of the Gaian temples and this so-called invasion? Do you really think a civilization with that kind of technology would wait fifty thousand years for humans to rise to dominance on this planet before invading?"

I open my mouth, but I've got no ready reply to that one. For all that we spent a week aboard that ship, eavesdropping on the Undying soldiers, Mia and I have no answers. If anything, all that we saw and heard only raised more questions.

My eyes skitter sideways, seeking Mia's, but she's not looking at me. She's watching Mink, her face still and set—stubborn, like that look she gets when she's preparing to fight me on something. Except that she's quiet now, not fighting at all. And that's enough to kick my dread up into high gear.

Finally De Luca steps forward. "It's a clever story," he says in that calm, cool voice like stainless steel. "But until the International Alliance has allocated the ship's resources among the world's nations, and overseen the process, we can't risk dissension from anyone high profile enough to cause further agitation."

"High profile?" I echo stupidly.

"You are the son of the world's leading expert on the Undying," De Luca replies, raising one eyebrow.

"And why listen to Jules, any more than they listened to his father?" Mia speaks, but her voice is soft. Furious—but resigned.

"It will be better all round if you stay here," De Luca says smoothly.

"For how long?" I ask, my heart sinking.

"Until the situation is resolved," he says simply.

"You can't hold us indefinitely," I protest. "We have rights."

Abrantes shakes his head. "In the currently escalated security situation, we can."

"But that kind of arrangement is for times of *war*," I protest. I read up on this stuff after my father was arrested and confined at IA Headquarters in Prague.

De Luca's smooth expression is all faux regret. "And we are rapidly approaching just such a situation," he says. "The IA is the only thing standing between that ship in orbit and all-out war between the countries who want it. And we can use whatever means necessary to ensure your cooperation." His eyes flick over toward Mia, who stiffens, eyes burning with fury.

"Leave my sister out of this," she snarls. "She's just a kid."

Mink has been watching this in silence, and her gaze lingers on Mia for a moment longer before she finally speaks again, her tone sharp. "I don't recognize those teenagers in the cell. And I am completely confident I controlled the flow of traffic to and from Gaia."

De Luca shoots her a *Really, still this?* look. "Operative, if you were able to smuggle your crews—including Mr. Addison and Miss

Radcliffe here—to Gaia under the noses of the IA crews manning the scientific vessels, then who is to say someone else could not have done the same to you?"

She shakes her head. "We need to take this to Prague." For once, Mink's voice carries with it some heat—she does *not* like De Luca.

And De Luca's expression as he looks back at her is just as unfriendly. "So Dr. Addison can find a way to twist it to suit his version of the truth?" He waves a hand in a regretful, mock-helpless gesture. "I wish I could assist."

Mink fixes him with a stare that's all cold fury. I've seen this woman shoot someone between the eyes and then calmly go about her day. If she was looking at me like that, I'd be running. "I can petition to have all the prisoners released into my custody and bring them to Prague myself. You don't have the authority to prevent me."

"Petition whomever you like," says De Luca mildly. "And when the decision comes back in two months, feel free to come and collect them yourself."

*Two months?* The words land like a physical blow, leaving me winded and groping for support. We can't be stuck here for two months—whatever the Undying are planning, it'll surely be too late to stop them. We'll be watching an alien takeover of our planet from the inside of a jail cell.

*Just like my dad.*

As if he senses my thoughts—or the mounting tension between the head of security and the covert operative—Abrantes calls for a pair of guards with the press of a button on his earpiece, then addresses us. "Mr. Addison, Miss Radcliffe, the guards will escort you back to your quarters now."

I start to rise from my chair, but Mia leaps from hers and strides across to Mink, getting up in her face. "Mink, you *know* what's happening. You have to do something!"

In the most intimate gesture I've ever seen from her, Mink rests both her hands on Mia's shoulders, gazing down at her. "You're not helping your cause, kid," she says quietly.

And Mia, uncharacteristically, falls completely silent. For once, I *want* her impulsive outrage, I *want* her headlong rush to act and speak without weighing the possible outcomes. I *want* her to be Mia. But she just stands there, wide-eyed and blinking at Mink.

I don't know what to say. I don't know how to stop this. A pair of guards enter, preparing to escort Mia and me back to our cells. De Luca just stands there, watching us with that cool stare, utterly unperturbed by anything we've said.

This man is going to be single-handedly responsible for the overthrow of humanity.

And there's nothing we can do to stop him.

## 10

## AMELIA

As the guards walk us back to our cell, I can't help but think of the crash course in overwhelming an armed opponent I received from Javier, one of the mercenaries who followed Jules and me through the temple on Gaia. There are only two guards, and they don't seem half as well-trained as the operatives Mink brought with her to Gaia's surface. But even if I could wrest the gun away from one of them—and even if I could pull the trigger—the second one could use Jules as a hostage, or even kill him.

And assuming I could get control, we're still in the middle of a detention facility whose floor plan we don't know, full of IA operatives and staff, with countless locked doors between us and freedom. Not to mention, killing someone here would make us fugitives and criminals forever, even if I had the stomach for it.

Mink's gaze, intense as it met mine, has left me shaken—and burning with curiosity, because there's a slim outline of pressure in the front pocket of my jacket. She slipped something to me, while she had me by the shoulders. But I can't risk a look until the guards are gone.

The cell door whooshes closed behind us and the guards retreat without another word. The seething frustration and fury in Jules's expression is slowly giving way to a blank-eyed hopelessness, and he barely glances at Atlanta and Dex, who are almost exactly where they were when we were escorted out.

"If I could just get to a phone," Jules mutters, shoving his hands deep into his pockets, defeat in every line of his body. "Or get the SIM card for my watch back. I could call Neal, see if he could get word to my dad, tell him what we know. Tell him that I'm okay." His lips twist. "For a given value of okay. It's been so long, I know what he must be thinking."

"And I could call Evie. Tell her to get out of town, hide somewhere until this is over." I cast a long look at our cellmates, using it as cover to glance at the camera in the corner. Once I'm sure I've got its position memorized, I sigh and say in a clear voice, "There's nothing for it but to wait. Come here—it'll be okay."

The look Jules flashes me would be funny, under other circumstances. I can almost read his thoughts: Me, suggesting we wait and see how it plays out, is about as likely as us sprouting wings and flying out of this joint. He actually looks a little wary as he redirects his pacing strides to bring him to me.

I turn, making sure my back is to the camera, and pull Jules into a loose embrace. Between our bodies, I slide a hand up to retrieve the rectangular object Mink slipped into my pocket. I drop my forehead like I'm leaning it against Jules's shoulder, and inspect the bit of plastic.

My breath catches. It's a keycard.

Jules, hearing my intake of breath, starts to draw back. I tighten the arm still wrapped around him, and he freezes, glancing down at the card in my hands. It's the same type of card the guards have been using to pass through the doors as they escort us around the base. Jules's eyes widen as he looks back up at me. Swiftly, I slip the card back into my pocket and let him go.

"How?" Jules breathes.

"Mink."

"You stole it from her?"

I'd take offense at the skepticism in his voice, except that it's *Mink*, and I doubt the most skilled pickpocket in the world could fool her. "She slipped it to me. On purpose."

The reply leaves him speechless, his brows drawn in. I turn and lean back against the wall. Atlanta and Dex are watching us still, though they didn't see the keycard. Dex's expression is hard to read, but Atlanta's is clear enough. Her eyes are narrowed and not at all friendly.

"It's a trap," Jules says softly. "It's Mink. The cameras will see us and we'll be caught immediately."

"Normally I'd agree, but why bother?" I keep my voice to a whisper, barely above a breath. "We're arrested already. They're not going to kill us or move us for trying to escape, they'll just bring us back here. What does she get out of that?"

"Nothing good."

Mia shrugs. "They were at one another's throats in there. Maybe she's just trying to discredit De Luca for that power play? Who cares *why*, so long as it gets us out?"

"Or she's bypassing the whole petition thing and taking us for herself, and she'll be waiting for us with her own team of armed guards when we stroll out through the gate. We'll just be trading one jail cell for another."

"Maybe—but Jules, it's either trust her or rot here while aliens take over our planet." She glances over her shoulder at Atlanta and Dex, who are watching us even though our voices are too low to be overheard.

Jules shakes his head, expression grim. "Don't forget this is the woman who manipulated us both into being her pawns from the moment we left Earth."

"I remember." My voice is taut, and Jules's expression flickers with a faint, apologetic smile. "But do we have a choice?"

He glances at our cellmates and then back. "If we break out, we'll be fugitives. All hope of convincing anyone we're telling the truth will be gone."

"Jules, we literally handed them two aliens and they still don't believe us. No one's going to—no one in the IA, anyway." My stomach is in knots, hating the words I'm saying, hating everything about this. Part of me wants to give up—to just sit here in this cell, with Jules, while the world burns. I draw a shaking breath. "We thought we were done—but we're not. We have to keep fighting."

Jules gazes at me, his face like a mirror reflecting my own exhaustion back at me. "What can we possibly do?"

I swallow. "I don't know. Maybe we could get to Prague, maybe even disguise ourselves some way and get in to see your father." I bite my lip to keep from adding, *One more time.* Because he actually does have a chance of seeing his family before . . . before whatever the Undying are planning actually happens.

*I'll never see Evie again.*

Jules is gazing at me distantly, like he *wants* to listen to me, and isn't letting himself. I focus on him, trying to put the mental image of my baby sister far, far at the back of my mind. "Jules, think. We're in Spain, right? How far is that from Prague?"

"I think we're in Catalonia, actually—most of the guards here are speaking Catalan. They're very different languages, although they share a lot of the same roots, just as Spanish and French—"

Ordinarily he's irresistible when he goes off on one of his linguistic or historical tangents. This time, I speak swiftly to head him off. "How *far*, Jules?"

Jules's brow furrows, his eyes going distant as he performs his mental calculations. "I'm not sure. Maybe fifteen hundred kilometers, as the crow flies. We could be there in a couple days if we had a car. Do you know how to hotwire one?"

I raise an eyebrow, amused by his assumption that I'm well-versed in everything criminal. "If I could, do you know how to *drive* one?"

He blinks. "Don't you? The skimmer bike on Gaia—"

"Not the same thing." As much as I hate to disabuse him of the notion that I can do everything, I don't much like the idea of careening across Europe in a stolen car with no idea what I'm doing. Before we can take this increasingly implausible idea any further, Jules's head lifts abruptly, and he touches my arm. Following his gaze, I meet Atlanta's eyes, which are fixed on us so intently I feel a shiver run down my spine. They're on the opposite side of the cell, and Jules and I have been speaking far too quietly for them to hear—and yet I'd swear that the look in her eye was recognition and understanding.

Dex pushes away from the wall, swinging his arms and pacing slowly. His steps have a measured deliberation that chills my blood—he moves like a predator. "You two are pretty close-like, huh?"

Jules stiffens at my side, and I lean sideways to nudge him unobtrusively before he can say anything idealistic and provocative and, well, Jules-ish. Atlanta and Dex have hardly spoken since we were captured, and if I can get one of them to say something that conflicts with the tale they told our wardens, it might be enough to raise doubts about their origins. Maybe they'd redo the cheek swab, or even take a blood sample—there's no way they can fake having the right color blood.

*Right?*

Hell, if his reflexes weren't so much better than mine, I'd try just punching him in the nose. Instead, I play for time, try to draw out a response from him that's somehow wrong.

"We got close, working together on Gaia." I tilt my head and flash a wan, tired smile their way. "Like you guys did, right?"

Dex smiles back, though the expression doesn't reach his eyes.

"We raised up together, we've always been close-like. Think they'll let us out for exercise? Primitive system." That last is muttered partially under his breath. He's busy pulling off his shirt, uncovering his dark blue undershirt and a tattoo that spreads across the rounded curve of his shoulder. It's gorgeous work, the blue and green and violet arms of a galaxy swirling toward a glowing center. But it's so human I could tear my hair out with frustration.

Their façades are so flawless—except they aren't, not really, because Jules and I can see all the little ways in which they're just *not quite right*. But short of seeing them bleed blue, all anyone else will see is a couple of teenagers. Maybe a little odd, maybe a little off-putting. But human.

Too thrown to continue, I turn away. I stop upon seeing Jules's face, though—his skin has gone ashen, and his eyes are fixed on Dex. The other boy seems unaffected by Jules's stare, but Atlanta's eyes narrow and flicker between the two of them.

Taking Jules by the arm, I pull him back to our corner and lower my voice again. "What's going on?"

"His arm," mumbles Jules in a strangled voice.

I glance back at them. Dex has dropped to the floor and started doing a series of pushups, except that his hands are balled into fists instead of flat on the floor. The tattoo is oddly three-dimensional in the harsh glare of the fluorescent lights overhead. "What about it?"

"Nautilus." The word is almost inaudible.

I blink at him. "Jules, it's a galaxy. A lot of spiral galaxies line up with that Fibonacci thing."

But Jules's gaze is fixed, his face transformed. "And what about how he *saw* us before launch and didn't say anything?"

I know why Jules wants this to be true. To connect this alien with his theory that someone in the long, long history of the Undying race felt some human empathy for the inhabitants of the planet they planned to invade. That they planted the symbol in the original broadcast to warn us, that the spirals like nautilus shells carved into the temple walls were messages from a long-dead ally.

I know why he wants to think that we might find living proof of that theory in Dex, to think that the spiral shape hidden in his tattoo means we're not alone.

He wants it, because he needs to think there's still hope.

I sigh, making a show of stretching out my shoulders as I duck my head and whisper back, "Those symbols in the temple are fifty thousand years old. You think the guy who carved those spirals to warn us about the Undying's plan is still alive, and sharing a cell with us in Cat-landia?"

"Catalonia." Correcting me seems to restore him somewhat, for he looks a bit less like someone's just walked over his grave. "And no, although who knows what their life span is like, I guess nothing's impossible. But it's too much of a coincidence."

"For a member of a spacefaring civilization to have a galaxy tattoo?" I let my breath out and shake my head. "Forget the tattoo. We need to focus on busting out of this joint."

Before I can continue, the distant clank of a door brings all our heads swinging toward the glass wall. Footsteps sound soon after, and a guard appears with a stack of trays. It's the same one from earlier, the one who seemed nervous—and he still does, his eyes lingering on the Undying teens as he approaches. He checks to make sure we're all far enough from the glass before swiping his keycard, and he doesn't take his eyes off of Atlanta and Dex.

*Maybe he sees what we see. Human, but then again, not so very human after all. Just . . . off, ever so slightly. Like they're computer generated, not quite real, though you couldn't tell someone exactly why.*

The guard sets the four trays on the floor and straightens slowly, still watching the Undying. Atlanta follows the movement, and after meeting his gaze for a few seconds, jerks forward in a feint with a hiss of air between her teeth. It's a tiny movement, but it nonetheless sends the guard scrambling backward, hitting the far

wall of the corridor and fumbling for the sidearm at his belt. Seeing that Atlanta's still standing in place, he straightens and swipes
the door closed again, his hand still resting on the grip of the gun.

Atlanta's grinning, finding amusement in his fear, but Dex isn't
laughing. He's watching the guard, and his brows are drawn in. If
he were human—properly human, like me and Jules—I'd say he
felt *sorry* for the man.

We don't speak again, dividing up the four trays and retreating
to our opposite ends of the cell to eat. It's not until we're mostly
done that Dex, quicker to eat than the rest of us, tosses his empty
tray aside with a clatter of plastic and leans back against the wall.

"Do the numbers 3-0-0 and the letters *C* and *S* mean anything
to you?" The question is almost pleasant, warmed with mild curiosity. When I look up, he's got a small, food-stained scrap of paper
held between his fingertips. He's keeping his hand low, out of sight
of the cameras.

They must have passed the paper back and forth while we were
distracted by our food, as Atlanta doesn't look surprised by the
question—she's watching us for any sign of comprehension.

Jules gazes across the cell at him and then gets to his feet. He
steps slowly and deliberately—no sudden movements—toward
Dex, who rises effortlessly to meet him. The boy grasps his hand,
placing the paper in it, then sits again, watching Jules expectantly.

Jules throws him an intent look, but it's brief, and then he's striding quickly back toward me. Wordlessly, he hands me the paper,
which bears the handwritten message *300CS*. There's a slight gap
between the numbers and the letters that could be a space—or just
an anomaly of handwriting. It certainly doesn't mean anything to
me, but Jules suddenly stiffens.

"What?" I breathe the word as softly as I can.

"Charlotte Stapleton. C. S."

*It's from Mink?* She couldn't speak privately during our interrogation, and I don't think she walked into that room expecting to slip
me her keycard. There was a fifty-fifty chance the note would've

ended up on one of our trays. She must've thought it was a gamble worth taking, since it wouldn't mean anything to Dex or Atlanta.

It's another set of instructions. The start of another path to walk. A new maze.

"I'm getting really tired of puzzles," I whisper.

Jules huffs a quick breath, amused but not quite a laugh, his eyes warming a little as he glances at me. "I know the feeling."

"A password, maybe? If there's a door somewhere that doesn't open for the keycard and needs a numeric code?"

Jules furrows his brow, inspecting the paper again, turning it over in his hands. "Even low-security passcodes have four numerals, not three. And this is the IA."

"Maybe there's more to it. She's basically a spy, right? Maybe it's in invisible ink or whatever."

Jules glances at me, his lips twitching. "You watch too many movies, Mia." But nevertheless, he holds the paper up to the fluorescent light, which does nothing but illuminate a translucent section of the paper stained by grease. Perhaps someone will see him do it on the camera, but it's clearly just a piece of paper. No doubt they'll think he had it in his pocket.

Then he flicks the LED on his wrist unit on, and tries holding the paper over the display. He sighs, and moves to turn it off again—and freezes as I seize his arm.

"Wait." I move his other hand a little, then rotate his wrist so we can see the display. It reads 2:49 a.m. I can feel the muscle in his forearm contract as he sees it too. I don't have to explain—we've been solving far more complex riddles for weeks, and he's even better at it than I am.

"We don't know it's a time."

"If it is, we have eleven minutes."

Jules lowers his arm, keeping his voice to a whisper. "Until what? She comes riding to our rescue?"

I glance over at the two Undying, watching us like they can hear every word. A chilling thought flickers to life—maybe they *can* hear every word. A human wouldn't be able to, but the whole reason we're here is because they're *not* human at all. Maybe they're just pretending not to hear us for the sake of the cameras.

My gaze lifts to that pinhole in the corner, and then suddenly the meaning of Mink's message clicks into place. "Jules—the reason we can't just use the card she slipped us and walk out of here is because the second we go near that door, they'll see us on the cameras and catch us again."

"You think she's telling us she'll shut off the cameras then?" Jules doesn't look over at the camera, though I see a muscle stand out in his neck with the effort of fighting that natural instinct. "It's too risky. We've no idea that's what she meant. And no idea if she actually means to help."

"What's our alternative?" I reach for his wrist again. 2:50 a.m. A part of me feels sick for what I'm about to say, especially because the likelihood of us even getting to Prague, much less getting into IA Headquarters, is so low it hurts. But I say it anyway. "You could see your father in just a couple days."

Jules's jaw clenches. He crumples up the paper and stuffs it into his pocket. Casually he gets to his feet, as if just stretching his legs, but I recognize the new sense of purpose there. He casts me a sidelong look. "That's dirty pool, using my dad."

"Do I ever play fair?"

Jules grins, and seeing his smile again is like feeling the sun on my face. He's been through so much these past weeks, getting him to smile is a victory all its own.

Though we've got less than ten minutes left, the time seems to creep by with aching slowness. We've got no preparations to make, no gear to assemble or plans to finalize—our plan extends no further than "get through the door and reach the end of the corridor." I can feel our fellow captives' eyes following us as we move, stretching our legs and venting what nervous energy we can without raising suspicions. We want them to stay where they are—if we're quick, we can swipe the card, get outside, and then lock them in behind us before they catch on.

Still, I'm at Jules's side when his wrist unit reads 2:59 a.m., and I can't help but join him in watching it, counting the seconds, and waiting.

3:00 a.m.

As one, we look up at the corner where the little black pinhole remains unchanged. There's no convenient indicator light to turn off, no mechanical whirring down or telltale beep. If we're wrong about Mink's message—or about her intentions toward us—then half a dozen armed guards are going to be swarming down that corridor seconds after we open the door.

I slip the card from my pocket into my palm, and catch Jules's eye. He checks his watch one more time, then nods at me. I swipe the card through as quietly as I can, heart pounding—either it won't work, or it's going to be a headlong rush to get through and lock the door again before the Undying have time for their freakish reflexes to kick in.

The door whooshes open, and Jules rushes us both through. My hand's shaking as I reach back again, aiming for the card reader, and for a moment it looks like I'm about to miss it—and then the beep of a successful read sends the door slamming back into place.

Almost.

When the door stops in its track, Jules and I look up to find Atlanta and Dex in the doorway, Dex casually keeping the door open with one foot, Atlanta standing uncomfortably close, arms crossed, cold eyes unblinking as they fix on us.

I can't think, pinned under that icy stare. My whole body freezes, and when Jules's hand curls around my arm—for support, or comfort, I don't know—I realize I'm shaking.

"Back away." For a moment, I don't recognize the speaker. Jules's voice is hard, slick with fear and fury, and inch by inch, he's moving between me and Atlanta. And in this moment, I don't have it in me to stop him. "They think you're regular kids right now. Run with us, and they'll *definitely* look at your DNA samples—the whole world will know you're not humans like us, and you and your friends won't be able to hide anymore."

Dex's voice is just as slick, but there's no trace of fear in it. "We're shifting with you." His eyes fix on Jules's face, and I wonder if Jules feels the alien weight of it like I feel Atlanta's. "You know this world—you'll make sure we reach our destin."

I finally get my heart going again and find my voice. "We're not doing anything to help you. And we're certainly not letting you out."

Atlanta's lip curls, and she mutters in distaste, "Protos. You're every part as smug and self-serving as history says."

"*We're* self-serving?" Jules's face darkens a few shades, and I have to stifle the urge to grab his arm in case he swings. "You're trying to destroy our world."

Atlanta's expression doesn't flicker. "Destroy it? We're *saving* it."

"Why would we let you out?" Jules nudges me behind him a little more, and for a moment I think he's responding to my rather cowardly attempt to use him as a shield—until I realize he's nudging me back from the door. Perhaps he thinks he can kick Dex's foot free, slam it shut.

"If you don't," Atlanta counters, "I pledge we'll set up such a fuss and hassle to wake every proto on the base."

*Shit.*

"Why do you keep calling us that?" I snap, my temper unravelling. I had no idea they could hear our plans so clearly.

"Protos?" Atlanta's lips twist. "Proto-human."

The hairs on my neck lift, the chill in her voice making me want to shiver. "We *are* human. This is our planet. We belong here."

"*We* are human—the new humans, the new masters of Earth. You're just what came before."

"You're Undying," I spit.

"I'm sure Neanderthal hunters thought they were the rulers of their world—but would you entrust this planet to them now?" Atlanta smiles her chilly smile. "We are *beyond* you. We are the future of this world."

Fury and fear together rise up like bile, and I hiss, "They're going to see you. A few shuttles, sure, you can hide as space junk. But enough of you to invade our whole planet? They're going to see you, and stop you."

Atlanta just continues smiling that metallic, not-quite-right smile. "We won't need more than a few," she says, her voice as sharp and threatening as a knife. She doesn't elaborate, but the smugness on her face suggests there's far more to their plan than just sneaking a few operatives onto Earth's surface.

While I'm fumbling for a response, Jules straightens at my side. "Fine. You can come."

My voice bursts out of me before I can stop it. "What? Jules—"

"Trust me." Jules murmurs the words—though the Undying can no doubt overhear, his tone is still intimate and soft, like a whisper. When I look at him, his eyes aren't on Atlanta and her fierce gaze and clenched fists, but rather on Dex's face, unreadable and calm.

I seize Jules's wrist and turn it. We've lost four minutes. Glancing up, I spot cameras at regular intervals along our path. "I really hope Mink's on our side," I whisper, and turn to lead the others down the corridor.

11

JULES

**ALL THE LONG, BLANK HALLS IN THIS PLACE LOOK EXACTLY THE SAME.**
I have no sense of where we are, and worse, no sense of where the
exit is.

It's like this whole facility was built to disorient the visitor, and
perhaps it was. Each hallway shares the same smooth floor, the
same featureless walls. There's not so much as a number on a doorway, let alone a helpful location map with a cheery little You Are
Here! indicator.

We have to swipe Mink's card twice more in the first two minutes to make our way through security checkpoints, heavy sliding
doors that would've been impassable otherwise.

There are only two things on our side. First, it's a little after
three in the morning, and though in a place like this there are certainly people still on duty, nobody is roaming the corridors. And
secondly, the cameras are down, thanks to Mink. They must be, or
someone would have raised the alarm by now.

I know from Mia's grim expression that she's worried—the

cameras aren't our only concern. Surely in a situation like this, protocol dictates that somebody should check the prisoners are where they're supposed to be.

With a swift intake of breath, Mia halts, gazing down a branching corridor. At first I can't tell what's grabbed her attention, but when she whispers a quick "Give me one second," and slips down the hallway, I recognize the interview room where we witnessed Mink and De Luca's showdown. When she returns, she's tucking something into her waistband and sidling up to me. Only once Atlanta and Dex have returned their attention to the issue of escape do I glance sidelong at her—she slips something to me wordlessly. I can tell by feel that it's my journal. I shove it down into a cargo pocket and raise an eyebrow at her.

She lifts the edge of her shirt a little, just enough to show me the handle of her multi-tool. "I modified this myself," she whispers, voice half defensive, half triumphant. "It's been to the other side of the universe and back. I'm not leaving it behind now."

Before I can reply, a noise echoes down the corridor, stopping us dead in our tracks. It's Director De Luca shouting at the top of his voice. I catch a snatch of a few words—*don't want to hear a goddamn*—and then the rest of it is lost, just noise again.

*I guess he knows something's wrong.*

The door to the room where he must be opens with a smooth hiss, and Mia collides with my chest as she backs abruptly around the corner. Wordlessly, the four of us—a team at least in this— duck back down the way we came. Which looks exactly the same as every other corridor. This is hopeless.

But we haven't made it much farther when Atlanta abruptly stops, pointing at a fire extinguisher next to a doorway.

"We saw that when we were shifting inward," she says, completely confident.

Mia lifts her brows, and I share her skepticism.

"I expect they have more than one fire extinguisher," I offer.

Atlanta shakes her head firmly. "No, was that one. Got a

scratch." She points to a minute little half-moon chip in the cylinder's smooth red paint.

My own brows shoot up. How could she possibly have spotted *that* while being hustled in? But Dex is nodding when I glance across at him.

"She says it, she's right, I pledge," he tells us in a low, urgent whisper.

I know we have no choice but to trust her, but I don't.

*Dex, on the other hand . . .*

Slowly, the evidence is beginning to add up. The tattoo. I'm sure his finger traced the spiral of it, pausing as he pulled his shirt off to exercise. The way he looked at us on the shuttle, before we launched. The moment in which he could have said something to his partner about the stowaways on board, and didn't.

And when he handed over the piece of paper from his tray— *300CS*—he squeezed my hand a moment longer than he needed to. Caught my gaze with a stare more urgent than the gesture required. I have an inkling this is what he wanted to convey: *Trust me.*

I know what Mia would say. And her healthy skepticism of literally everyone and everything around her is what kept us alive on Gaia. But Dex is the only hope I have left now, and if I lose that . . . No. No, there's *something* deeper going on here, I have to believe it.

I *choose* to believe it.

I squeeze Mia's hand, and together we turn to follow the Undying.

Atlanta seems to have her bearings now, and she leads confidently. It's slow going—we duck into doorways and back around corners over and over, because in these clothes nobody's mistaking us for anything but what we are, if we come face-to-face with the soldiers hurrying along the hallways. Once, we pile into an empty meeting room, standing together in the darkened corner of it, so close I can hear the Undying's breath—while several pairs of boots pound past us, purposeful. Is that purpose to do with us?

But as soon as we're out and moving again, there's another checkpoint ahead. And this one I *do* recognize. So does Mia. Her hand flies out to grab my forearm and squeeze, at the sight of it. This door is different, thicker and heavier. The way out.

"Let's hope Mink's pass is still working," Mia mutters, gripping it tightly as she jogs toward the door.

It will still be night outside. If they don't realize we had the means to leave, we could make some distance, even on foot, before they—

The door slides open, a fraction of a second before Mia reaches it. A trio of soldiers stands just on the other side, returning from some patrol. For a moment, everything stops.

Mia is frozen just a few steps from the uniformed soldiers. I'm a few paces behind her, with Dex and Atlanta to one side. The first two soldiers, a man and a woman, stop at the sight of us, and the third only halts when he bumps into his comrade's back—the phone he was staring at falls from his hand and clatters to the floor.

Before I can do more than register the trouble we're in, Atlanta's moving, barely more than a blur in my peripheral vision. In an instant, she closes the distance between her and the soldiers, taking one of them down in one swift sweep of her leg. Dex is with her half a second later, and as the first soldier's partner reaches for the rifle at her side, Dex grabs it and slams the butt of the rifle into her face. She staggers back and falls, clutching at her nose.

All I can see after that is a flash of surprised terror in the face of the man who dropped his phone, and then both Atlanta and Dex are on top of him. They move so quickly I can't even see what they do to him—but he's down within the space of a single breath. Dex retrieves the rifle he'd grabbed from one of the soldiers and slings its strap over his chest, while Atlanta returns to the still-conscious form of its wielder, considers her state speculatively, and then gives her a swift kick to knock her out.

Mia, who flung herself to one side when the Undying team

rushed the soldiers, is still pressed against the wall, her eyes wide, her face white. I'm not doing much better, my vision blurring with the impossibility of what I've just witnessed.

*They're not human.*

Even though I knew that before—even though I'd *seen* them bleed blue, impossibly alien—I'm not sure I entirely believed it, deep down on a subconscious level, until now.

Catching Mia's gaze as it swings toward me, I find myself wishing I could summon even an ounce of bravery to reassure her. But all I feel is terror sweeping through me. All I want to do is run.

"Stop!" The shout is hoarse, and it comes from behind us. "Stop, I'll shoot!"

We all freeze. Instinctively I lift my hands, and glance over my shoulder.

There's a uniformed guard behind us in the corridor, pointing his sidearm straight at us. Summoned by the commotion, no doubt. His hands are shaking a little, the barrel jigging up and down as he swings it in a slow arc, as though to demonstrate he has complete coverage. Nearby, Mia's got her hands up too, and slowly Dex and Atlanta comply as well. Dex has the rifle, but it's dangling just out of easy reach, too far away when there's a gun pointed at his face.

"Please," I say, but I don't know how that sentence finishes. *Let us go? Shoot them?* I'd take either, right now.

The guard takes two steps forward, and I realize who it is. It's the same guy who's been bringing us our meals. The same one who's been watching us nervously since we arrived. He's had time to study us. And maybe that can help us, now.

"You have to let us go," I try, soft.

"I can't," he says, still hoarse. He's gripping his gun so tightly, I'm scared his trigger finger will tighten as well. His eyes flick down to the crumpled forms of his fellow soldiers on the floor at our feet, his Adam's apple bobbing as he registers the sight of blood.

Mia speaks beside me. "You have to." She doesn't sound nervous, though a second ago there was utter horror in her expression.

There's no shake to her voice. She sounds as calm as if she were issuing an order she has every right to give.

The guard's eyes are so wide I can see their whites. He has to clear his throat before he speaks, his gun swinging around to point at her. It takes everything I have not to do something stupid. Not to grab her and yank her behind me, as if I could protect her from a weapon like that.

But she's not focusing on me right now. She's staring at the man holding her at gunpoint. "You saw the shuttle," she says, quiet and calm. "That's not space junk. You know something's not right here." She tilts her head at Dex and Atlanta, keeping her hands still. "You know something's not right with *them*."

The gun drifts across toward Dex and Atlanta. He's listening to her, but he's certainly not ready to lower it.

"The cameras are off," she says, still calm. "That's because we're meant to leave. Not officially, they can't do that—but someone up there wants us to get out and stop what's about to happen. It also means nobody's going to see, when you lower your gun and let us go."

"The stuff they're saying online about all this . . . it's insane." He shakes his head, but it doesn't seem to put her off.

"You need to let us go now," she says quietly. "This is what's meant to happen."

He gazes at her then, and I don't know what passes between them. She doesn't blink, doesn't waver, but instead lets him see every ounce of her conviction. She knows that some part of him, deep inside, a part that operates on instinct, is deciding whether to trust her.

I don't know how she projects such calm, such purpose, in a moment like this. I do know that all the years I spent growing up—in classrooms, at black tie college dinners, in the damn water polo pool—she spent on the streets, learning how to bluff, how to keep herself intact. All of it practice for this one moment in which she has to talk our way out of here.

Because if she can—no exaggeration—perhaps she'll save the world. At the very least, she'll keep a glimmer of hope alive. And right now, that glimmer, that spark, is everything.

Suddenly the air goes out of him, and he lowers his gun.

She nods, as though he's pleased her, then turns away to swipe Mink's card across the security pad again. The door slides back open and the four of us turn to run through it. The skin between my shoulder blades is twitching, waiting for a bullet, but ten seconds later the door hums closed.

We're outside, alone, in the night air.

My gaze sweeps the compound we find ourselves in. It's dimly lit—still not observed by cameras, I hope—and surrounded by a chain-link fence. This place really is in the middle of nowhere. To get here, we followed a rough trail that wound its way along the length of the valley, not another building in sight.

The whole of the compound is inside that fence. Beyond the lights I know all we'll find is a swath of grassland, mountains rising on either side. No easy way to escape, but in the darkness . . . maybe there's some way we can lose Atlanta and Dex. Replays of the way they took out three armed soldiers between one breath and another flash in front of my eyes like afterimages burned into my retinas.

*We've got to get away from them.*

Atlanta draws a breath as if to speak, then goes quiet. She lifts a hand, and when I follow where she points, I can make out what must be the vehicle pool. There are rows of cars and trucks under a sheltering roof, which is supported by a thick column at each corner.

But it's not the vehicle pool that's caught her attention. It's the truck near the front of it. A huge flatbed, with our shuttle strapped onto the back of it, a tangle of cords flung over it like a nest of overgrown vines. The truck's engine is still running, a low, bass rumble that rolls across the compound. And when it shuts off, the silence is keen.

As my eyes adjust to the dark, they tell me there are three or four IA personnel over there, doing some kind of shuffle with the cars, moving this one forward and that one backward, presumably trying to access one they need that isn't in the front row.

Mia's voice is barely more than a breath. "Those cars—" she begins.

But she gets no further. An urgent siren starts up, blasting its wail across the yard, and one by one, the floodlights begin to turn on with a soft *boom, boom, boom.* They're mounted along the roof of the buildings and the edge of the fence.

We press ourselves back into the sliver of shadow at the edge of the building, as the vehicle personnel go running past us to report for duty.

This time, Mia has to shout to be heard over the sirens. "The keys must still be in those cars," she yells.

I blink at her, then remember our discussion earlier. That we could be in Prague in a couple of days, if we could . . . "We can't drive it," I shout back.

But she's already grabbing my hand and tugging me away from the shelter of the building. "We'll have to ram the fence to get out. Hitting things is kinda the goal there. It's not like I *learned* to drive, but I know where the gas pedal is."

"Let's shift," Dex shouts, and he and Atlanta are running past us, straight out into the light.

Mia hauls on my hand, and then we're just a step behind them. Part of me wants to veer off, to let Dex and Atlanta escape without us, because I don't want to spend a second longer in their company than we have to. But if we do that, we'll almost certainly be caught again and put back in that cell, and this time they'll make sure we don't escape.

Dex runs straight past the first row of cars and into the shadows, but Atlanta pulls up short, thumping the hood of one of the jeeps the officers were moving when the alarms sounded.

"This one," she barks. "You, proto-girl, drive it, compren?"

I doubt Mia's in the mood to take orders from Atlanta, but she doesn't waste time stopping to argue. Instead, she leaps into the driver's seat, finds the keys still in the ignition, and starts up its engine. I grab the huge bull bar bolted onto the front, using it to swing myself around toward the passenger side.

But Atlanta doesn't move as I throw myself into the passenger seat, just standing there with her hands resting on the hood to stop us from driving away.

"Get out of the way!" Mia screams.

For a moment, I think this could be our chance. We could drive away and leave Dex and Atlanta behind—to be caught and imprisoned again by the IA, or to destroy the entire base with their superhuman combat abilities, I don't much care in this moment.

But Atlanta still doesn't move, standing in the path of the jeep. She's staring back into the dark, to where Dex disappeared.

"I swear, I will run you down," Mia shouts, her fingers wrapping around the hand brake. Her fingers are shaking, though, and her eyes are wild, and I know her too well to believe her. Despite everything we've witnessed, I don't think she could actually run Atlanta over in cold blood. She wouldn't be Mia if she could.

We're stuck waiting for Dex.

The sirens are wailing louder, a second joining the first in a dissonant counterpoint.

*Perfututi, we have to get out of here.*

Then there's a sudden scramble behind us, and Dex is throwing himself into the backseat of the jeep, his arms full of something I can't make out in the dark. Three quick strides, and Atlanta's in beside him.

Mia hits the accelerator, and the car shoots forward. She yanks the wheel to the left, and we arc around to head straight for the chain-link fence. "Get down," she barks, so loud her voice cracks.

I double over and twist sideways to get my body below the level of the windshield, and Mia folds herself down beside me, her foot still jammed on the pedal.

The seconds tick by, stretching forever, and I begin to think we must somehow have turned, somehow veered away. Then there's an almighty crash, a high-pitched noise. And there's a hurricane all around us, something whirling over my head, a shudder passing through the car that rattles every bone in my body.

And we're through the fence, tearing out across the open grassland, the car bumping over tussocks, fishtailing wildly as Mia wrestles the wheel for control, without giving up an ounce of speed.

"Veer left," Dex yells from the back seat. "Left, mountainwards."

"There's no way through them," I shout back. "There's no pass, we'll be trapped against the cliffs."

"Shift left," he yells again.

Mia looks across at me in the dark. In this moment, I can't afford to believe any of the signs I've been interpreting to mean that Dex might be, even in some small way, on our side. In this moment, I'm just trying not to die.

And I believe he is too.

"Left," I say, and she swings the wheel.

There's no way to see what's ahead of us by the faint starlight, but I know there are mountains, cliffs, looming somewhere before us now. We daren't turn on the headlights, even if we knew where to find the switch.

"Well?" Mia demands, without turning her head, the wind grabbing at her words. "What now, what's *left*?"

"Fifteen seconds," Dex says.

"Fifteen seconds until what?"

"Ten seconds." His voice is grim.

I don't bother asking, because there's nothing I can do in the next ten seconds, whatever's coming. Instead, I just count silently down in my head, as Mia finally takes her foot off the accelerator, and finds the brake, slowing us to a halt. I can see the shadowed cliffs in front of us now.

Mia turns her head to look back at the two of them, and past them, to the compound.

I twist as well, searching for any sign of pursuit. There are lights running all over the place, uneven, as though people are carrying them. They're mobilizing.

"What—" says Mia.

"Now," says Dex, at the same moment.

And a bright orange ball of flame blossoms up from the facility behind us. An explosion, huge. The boom reaches us a moment later, a physical force.

"What the hell?" I shout.

"The shuttle," Atlanta says calmly. "It's not designed to be detonated near vehicles like that. Fuel."

*Of course.* As the IA were taking us out of the shuttle, I watched Dex weigh up whether or not he could hit that ignition switch just outside the door. He must have run back to do it just now.

"There could have been people near that thing," I hear myself say.

"Yeh." Dex's voice is calm. "I hope not."

"Doesn't matter," Atlanta says, dismissive. "Keep them busy, they won't have time to hassle us."

"Not for long," I point out.

"Slow them down," Dex says.

"So now," Mia says slowly, "we need to give them a reason to think they can stop chasing."

Atlanta nods, finally looking like she approves of some aspect of Mia. "The vehicle," she says. "Out, now."

Mia and I exchange a glance. I don't know what Atlanta's planning now, but as one, we dive out of the vehicle. Atlanta's hauling a rock toward the driver's side, and Dex is fiddling with a small handheld device he must've retrieved from the shuttle. He's also got something metallic slung over his shoulder, but just now, I'm too busy imagining how loud the gunshots will be as the IA forces catch up to us.

Atlanta shouts something I can't make out, and then Dex is slapping the device onto the hood of the jeep and she's dropping the rock onto the accelerator pedal. Mia and I scramble away as the jeep peels off, tires spinning, toward the cliffs out there in the dark.

Together we all watch in silence as it speeds into the night, completely vanishing from view, though the sound of the engine travels back to us, still audible over the faint sirens coming from behind.

And then it strikes the base of the cliff with a massive gust of smoke and fire, the boom shattering the night. Mia gives an inarticulate cry, instinctively shrinking against me as I fling my arms around her, as much for my comfort as hers. I look at Dex, whose eyes are calm and cold, and suddenly I'm not so sure he's an ally after all. That device he put on the car—he planned that explosion, I'm sure of it. He and Atlanta acted as one unit, so in sync they barely needed words.

"Thisways," says Atlanta, pointing along the valley.

They're just far enough away that if we ran for it now, we might be able to elude them in the dark. Even with their training and their strength—we'd stand a chance. I take a step backward, feeling Mia tense with understanding and readiness in my arms.

Then Dex reaches for something behind his back. At some point—when he went to destroy the shuttle, I'm guessing—he exchanged the rifle for a more manageable handgun. Now, he pulls it from his waistband and fixes its barrel on us. His hand doesn't waver.

"Thisways," Atlanta repeats, her voice expectant.

At my side, Mia gulps a shaky breath. I squeeze her shoulders before releasing her, and slowly—our movements careful, our hands raised—we do as our new captors command.

12

AMELIA

**THE FRENCH BORDER CROSSING STATION IS LITTLE MORE THAN A PAIR** of officials in a gatehouse with a few floodlights, but it's as impassable as a prison gate. None of us have passports with us, and even if we did, it's been hours since we busted out of IA custody. Our names—and probably our faces too—are bound to be on some kind of watch list.

Not to mention the fact that we're driving a stolen car.

Technically it's the second car we've stolen in a few hours, the first one now smoldering at the base of a cliff. This one we found at a gas station—*gasolinera*, apparently—after the first car we broke into turned out to be too modern to hotwire, with a fancy computer regulating its ignition. It took several tense moments of explanation, Dex's stolen gun still trained on us, to convince our captors that we needed to find a *crappier* car. Now we're in an old, broken-down junker of a station wagon—which is fine by me, because we don't want to attract attention anyway.

I'm hoping the IA is too busy sorting through the wreckage at the bottom of that cliff to send someone after us, but it won't take long for them to realize there aren't any bodies there. And not long after that to think of looking for other recent car thefts. It was a risk, crashing our original transport, but it was worth it. Drive away at top speed in a car, someone's going to chase you. Send that car up in a ball of flames, and you buy yourself some time to get away on foot, in the dark, before they realize you're not smoldering somewhere in the wreckage.

Turns out driving isn't all that complicated—but driving knowing that the guy sitting behind you has a gun pointed at the back of your seat?

Much harder.

A handful of other cars are stopped on this side of the border. A couple are outfitted with roof racks with kayaks, bicycles, and other unidentifiable outdoor gear, and I'd lay good odds that the drivers are sleeping inside until morning. The IA guys talked about a heightened state of security, so there might be people here who didn't realize they'd need to have papers to get through a usually lax border crossing.

It's not like there's a fence along the whole border—we could make the crossing on foot by heading out into the farmland nearby, but that would mean leaving behind our only means of transport, and we'd be in the middle of nowhere without a ride.

Evie and I used to have this plan to go to Europe one day once she was free from her contract, and we'd spent hours researching how we'd make it work. We planned to rent a cheap car in Barcelona and then drive until we hit Amsterdam, sleeping in the back whenever we couldn't afford a hostel.

My heart twinges painfully at the sight of others doing what we'd planned. I suppose we never will now. Either I'll be in jail or the world will end, and either way, not a lot of room for road trips there. Evie hasn't heard from me in weeks now—as far as she knows, I'm still on Gaia. As far as she knows, I never even made it to Gaia. She could think I'm dead.

And if she doesn't—then it's because the IA have taken her, detained her, and now they'll never let her go so long as Jules and I are on the run.

I swallow the stabbing in my heart at that thought, and focus.

I pull the car off the road to join the others. The crunch of the gravel under the tires is the only sound that's interrupted the silence for at least an hour. In the rearview mirror I can see Atlanta, whose eyes are scanning the darkness as if she can see through it. Her expression suggests she's not pleased with what she sees.

I cut the engine, and we all sit in silence for a few seconds, listening to the metal ping erratically as it cools.

Behind me, Dex lets out his breath in a long, steady exhale. "You two are sirsly resourceful." He sounds impressed.

Atlanta, when she speaks, does not. "You," she says, nudging at Jules's seat with her knee, "how far are we from Prague?"

"My name is Jules," says Jules. His voice is quiet and even, but I can hear the anger and fear simmering underneath the calm. "And I don't know."

I watch in the rearview mirror as Atlanta's eyes narrow. "Guess," she suggests in a low voice.

"Why are you trying to get to Prague?" I interrupt. If Prague has something to do with their assignment here on Earth, it's a good bet their "destin" has something to do with sabotaging the International Alliance, which has its headquarters there.

Atlanta's eyes flick toward me, then up to meet my gaze in the mirror. "You fooling? You think we're gonna tell you all our plans now, like we're friends? You're prisoners—shut up and drive."

Dex clears his throat. "Slow it, Peaches," he says softly.

Atlanta whirls on him. "Stop calling me that." In this moment she looks as sulky as any human teenager, and the effect is chilling. "Not in front of the protos."

I unbuckle my seat belt and turn to lean against the door so I can see both of the aliens in the backseat. The strangeness of it all is starting to get to me—I can feel a giddy sort of semi-hysterical amusement bubbling up, and I press my head back against the cool window until it passes.

"We're out now," Dex is saying. "Let's shift by ourselves. No one will believe them if they try to warn anyone—they didn't believe them when we were sitting right there in that cell."

"We can't drive the car," Atlanta retorts. "We wouldn't have known where to look for the car in the first place. And what do we say to the men in the little house there? I know your Earth geography is sirsly shaky, but we can't walk to Prague and get there before—" She glances at me. "In time."

"I can't drive there either," I say, raising my voice. I can see where Atlanta's heading, and I do *not* like it. "Those men in the little house? That's the border crossing. None of us have papers, and we're probably wanted criminals at this point anyway, *and* we're in a car somebody's bound to report as stolen at any moment, if they haven't already."

Atlanta considers this, then glances at Dex, who just shrugs as if to concede defeat. "They're resourceful, like you said," she says finally, raising a defiant eyebrow at Dex. "They'll find a way."

She's turning something over and over in her hands, and as something metallic catches the light, I realize she's got a Swiss Army knife. She must have found it in the seat-back pocket, or else in the first car that turned out to be too fancy to hotwire. It's not exactly a deadly weapon, not like Dex's gun, but as she examines attachment after attachment with interest, suddenly that miniature corkscrew seems a lot scarier than it ever has before.

Dex draws breath to reply, but before he can speak, Jules's voice breaks in.

"We need rest first," he says firmly. "We can't drive through the border right now, we don't have the right documents. If we leave the car here and try it on foot, we can't rely on just managing to steal a third car in one night. If we stay here, we can blend in with the others who are spending the night here while they figure out what to do. We might as well stop for a while too, until we have a plan."

I'm about to protest, to remind him that every minute we waste brings the International Alliance that much closer to tracking us down, but he catches my eye and I fall silent. I know that look—I've *given* him that look. That *shut up, I've got this* look.

So I shut up.

Atlanta glares at him, and then at me, and then at Dex. She glares a lot, I've found. Finally, she speaks. "Beno. I'm gonna put the knife away, for now. But both of you, think on this: You run, we'll find you. We're stronger, we're faster. And if I gotta waste time tracking you, I *will* kill you when I find you."

*When.* Not *if.*

My legs are shaking when I step out of the car, and I lean heavily against the door while Jules circles round to my side. I don't doubt Atlanta's telling the truth.

The two Undying move away a few steps, ostensibly to examine the tree we're parked by, but they're conversing in low voices. I can't help but notice, though, that even while he's talking to Atlanta, Dex is running his fingers down the bark slowly, wonderingly, studying the tree like . . . well, I guess it *is* the first one he's ever had a chance to look at up close.

I keep my body relaxed, leaning against the car, and my voice low. "If we get back in the car and lock the doors, I think I could get it started before they think to break a window. We can't outrun them on foot, but we could drive away."

Jules turns to lean against the car next to me. "We have to go with them," he says softly.

I stiffen in spite of myself and turn to stare at him. "Are you crazy? Has your brain finally just collapsed under its own weight?"

His gaze is serious. "What alternative do you propose? The world is ending, Mia, and we're the only ones who know about it. We have to find out more. We're learning more and more about these Undying every second we're with them, and at some point, one of them will slip."

"How do you know?" I wish I could stop my voice shaking.

"Because someone always *does*," Jules counters. "No one is that good."

"They're not *someones*." Even though Atlanta's turned away, I can still feel the cold, unwavering intensity of her stare. The way she never seems to blink. The predatory fluidity of her movements. "We have no idea what they can do."

Jules keeps his voice low, but his eyebrows lift to emphasize his words. "That's exactly my point. We have no idea. But Mia, they've *already* slipped. Remember when Atlanta said they only need a few people on the surface?"

I certainly remember the coldness of her voice as she said it. "So?"

"Well, you can't take over a whole planet with just a few shuttles. Just like you can't take over a whole planet with just one ship. But it's *not* just one ship, is it?"

My mouth opens, and I blink at him, my surprise briefly eclipsed by the reminder of just how quickly Jules thinks, how beautifully his mind works. "It's a Trojan Horse. A ship full of portals."

"And if they can somehow do that here, build portals on the surface . . ."

". . . then they won't need more than a few," I breathe, finishing the thought for him. "Holy shit, Jules. You're right."

Jules leans closer to me. "We've already tried letting the IA sort it out. Maybe they still will—I hope they do. Maybe someone will actually look at those DNA samples back there, and the word will get out, but we haven't gotten very far on maybes and hopes. On the ship, they were talking about this 'Prime-One destin' like it was one of the most important parts of the invasion—and we're going to figure it out. We have to. And maybe if we can figure out how they're building the portals, or where, we'll stop what's happening. But we have to stay with them to do that."

My eyes sting, and I know I'm tired if the mere thought of attempting Jules's plan makes me want to cry. "They're crazy," I whisper. "She is, anyway. Did you see her with that knife? She's going to snap and straight-up murder us, Jules."

"She won't." Jules *sounds* confident. "Dex won't let her."

I groan. "Even if you're right and Dex *is* somehow on our side, I don't know if you've noticed, but she doesn't exactly seem to listen to him."

"She does, though." Jules sounds surprised, and when I glance his way he's looking at me with his eyebrows up. "She might be giving us all these orders, but haven't you noticed that whenever Dex does speak up, she changes her mind? They're like twins. She might seem like the more dominant one, but she listens to him, even though she doesn't act like it."

I have to admit that he has a point, though he's got a lot more faith in Dex than I have. "When did you turn into the expert on alien behavior?"

"I think some things must be universal." Jules's lips twitch. "Besides, I have a little experience being given orders by a . . . very decisive partner."

He's amused, his eyes gleaming at me, but the words still hurt, a little twinge of self-consciousness plucking at my heart. "Then you propose we don't try to get away? We just take them to Prague?"

"We let them think we're doing as they ask, for now. We don't fight, we don't argue—they already think we're weaker than they are just because they're some superior alien race. We let them think they've won."

"And if we get to Prague and still don't know how to stop them, then what?"

Jules hesitates. "I don't know," he admits. "But it's going to take us a while to get there. We'll figure it out as we go." A flicker of a smile appears on his face. "Now, where have I heard that before?"

I wish I could find it funny, him using my own style of planning—or lack thereof—against me. But my fear is too heavy.

"How do we even get there? There's what, like, four, five border crossings between here and there?"

Weariness sharpens my voice. Escaping IA custody ought to have been the biggest, most daring, most insane thing we'd have to do to warn our home that it's in danger. Hell, *making it* to IA custody should have been enough. Now, with Jules's half-formed plan stretching out in front of me, the idea that our escape was just the beginning makes me want to lie down in the gravel beneath me and give up.

"Only three, if we go through Germany." Jules shifts his weight like he might reach for my hand, but he stops, his arm dangling awkwardly at his side instead. "I can call my cousin. We know a guy who makes fake IDs for the private school kids—he might be able to make us some passports that would at least hold up for sleepy border guards at quiet crossings. He could bring us some money, maybe a phone."

"You make your cousin sound like some sort of spy."

"I'd bet my life on the fact that he'll know a guy who knows a guy. Don't underestimate the Addison gene pool." He smiles at me, that smile he must know is devastating to my attempts to remain unmoved.

I close my eyes so it can't sway me, drawing a deep breath and trying to focus past my exhaustion. "We can't wait here for him, the IA's bound to catch up to us. We'll have to sneak across the border into France on foot. Keep our heads down, maybe change our appearance in case they put out a BOLO."

Jules's teeth flash in the dark, a quick grin that he stifles immediately. "You sound like an American cop show."

"More like a spy thriller." I eye him sidelong, realizing after a moment that I'm chewing on my lip.

"What is it?" Jules asks, making me curse the fact that we've spent so much time together. I don't like it when anyone can read me, and he doesn't even make it look hard.

"Do you really think I give you orders all the time?" The words tumble out before I can stop them, my voice betraying me with its wistful lift at the end.

His eyebrows go up again, and then he smiles again, softer this time. "My word, yes. You don't?" But before I can object, this time he does stretch his hand out, fingertips brushing mine before he gives them a tentative squeeze. "But I'd be dead if you hadn't started ordering me around. I think you missed the more important part of what I said."

Part of me wants to pull my hand away. He's calling me bossy and overbearing—worse than that—and damned if I'll let him hold my hand while he does. But my skin tingles where it touches his, and it turns out I'm not too tired for my heart to start racing. I stare hard at the gravel at my feet.

When I don't respond, he tilts his head as if to try to catch my downward gaze. "The whole partner part?"

In spite of myself, I glance at him. His face looks like it always does, but for some reason looking at him while he's holding my hand is ten times harder than looking at him while curled up together in an alien ship. There, it was life and death. No time for self-doubt or confusion, and certainly no time to examine our feelings. Here, with the crickets singing and the gentle breeze across the Catalonian countryside, it couldn't be more different. My face heats, and my mind empties of any possible reply.

A distant laugh reminds me that we're not alone, that even aside from Dex and Atlanta—holding their own intense, whispered conversation by the tree—there are other cars parked all around us.

I blink, staring again at the camper van laden with outdoorsy gear. I let go of Jules's hand and straighten, all too glad—and maybe a little disappointed—to have a way out of the conversation. "I've got an idea."

• • •

On our stolen bicycles, it doesn't take long to get far enough from the border crossing station to cut across the grassy valley and into France.

I could've laughed—if I wasn't so freaking terrified—watching Dex and Atlanta try to stay upright on the bicycles, following us in wobbly, faltering, winding zigzags. Of course, their clumsiness only lasted for maybe half an hour before they started to get the hang of riding, and now they're every bit as confident on the bikes as Jules and I.

*Damn alien reflexes. They look more at home on the bikes than we do.*

Sometimes they look more *human* than we do.

On the ship it was easy to notice the differences between us and the tall, blue-blooded Undying—the fact that we were *on their starship* was one major difference—but when it's just two of them they don't look nearly so alien.

Dex has slung over his shoulders the rope-like thing he retrieved from the shuttle before setting it to self-destruct. "Rope" isn't really the right word—it has that strange, semi-metallic, semi-crystalline structure that the portal ship had. It's some piece of Undying technology, that's for sure. Just the sight of it makes me uneasy, but Dex looks so *human* pedaling in a zigzag that I don't know what to think. And while I watch, Dex gives a little whistle and veers left, as if to hit Atlanta, who gives an amused yelp and squeezes the brakes so that he shoots off into the grass, laughing.

They tease each other like friends do.

A glint in the starlight catches my eye. It's the grip of Dex's gun peeking out of his waistband. My throat closes, and I concentrate on pedaling.

Jules was able to wheedle the use of a cell phone out of one of the other travelers stopped by the border, while I went and picked the lock chaining the bicycles to the camper. He didn't get hold of his cousin—not surprising, given it was well past midnight in England and even later here—but he left a message. With no choice but to keep moving, we've just got to hope that the cousin, Neal, checks his messages regularly.

The second call he made was to the club that holds Evie's contract. His face, when he came back to me, was grim—and my heart sank. "They said she didn't show up for work today," he said softly, eyes shadowed. "And she's not in her bunkhouse."

Now, I can't dismiss the idea of my sister in IA custody somewhere, scared and alone, with no idea why she's being held. No idea that she's been taken to use as leverage against her fugitive big sister.

I try to focus on the ground in front of me. The task in front of me. *Save the world first,* I tell myself. *You'll be saving Evie too.*

Eventually we come across a dirt trail, and follow that to a one-lane road that passes a number of dark enclosures. Jules says they're vineyards, but all I see are rows of gnarled wooden roots. It takes us a bit of backtracking to find our way to a larger road, but once we reach it it's only a few minutes before we see lights in the distance. There's a little motel, a few shops with dark windows, and a gas station. They're all closed, even the gas station, but there's a map pasted up on the inside of its doors and a sign that says ENTRER Ç'EST ACHETER.

"'To enter is to buy,'" Jules translates, looking amused. "I guess they got sick of people coming in for directions."

Since we're not exactly sure where we are, it takes a while to locate the town we're in on the map. I leave Jules to it, and with Atlanta's sharp eyes monitoring my every movement, I wander over toward an ancient-looking pay phone. I've only ever seen them in movies, and I reach for the receiver with the oddest feeling—like I've gone back in time, somehow, or like all of this is some strange dream I might wake from at any moment. Though I know the phone's a long shot, and I don't even have any French coins to use, I want to call Evie, to try her cell phone—even though that'd be the first thing the IA would confiscate—and find out if she's okay. I wish I could make sure she's not scared, wherever she is—I'll lie if I have to, if it means she can rest easier for even a few days. Before her big sister gets arrested and thrown into IA detention for the rest of her life.

I can't resist putting the phone to my ear, but there's nothing to hear. Even when I jiggle the metal thing that it hangs on, there's not so much as a click. Clearly, even in this tiny town, no one's got any use for public phones anymore.

Except for a bunch of wanted criminals who don't have cell phones.

Sighing, I hang up the phone and head back toward the others. Atlanta and Dex are still astride their bicycles, and Atlanta's eyes follow me as I pass them.

"I think we're here," Jules murmurs, tapping the glass as I approach. "And we need to head up this road until we can go east, and eventually we'll hit the coast. If we follow the coastline north, we'll reach Montpellier sometime tomorrow morning. I said in my message to Neal that I'd try him again tomorrow, so hopefully he'll have a plan by then."

"You want to bike all night?" I don't add the second half of that thought: *My ass is already killing me.*

"Do we have any choice?" Jules glances over his shoulder. "They don't seem tired at all, and while I'm pretty sure Dex can keep Atlanta from murdering us, I don't know that he can keep her from insisting we keep moving."

"Pretty sure?" I eye him sidelong. "Earlier, you were definitely sure."

"Slip of the tongue."

"Which time, the first time or this time?"

Jules grins at me, then turns to retrieve his bike from the bench it's leaning on. "Let's go."

13

JULES

We're finally on the outskirts of Montpellier. We thought we'd be here by early morning, but it's after lunch now—not that we've eaten.

We hit a point just before dawn when we simply had to rest, so we wheeled our bikes off the road and stretched out in the dew-damp grass behind a row of trees planted long ago as a windbreak. Overhead the stars were fading into the pale gray of the pre-dawn sky, and we watched as a handful seemed to fall from their place in the heavens, streaking across the sky.

"That's a lot of shooting stars," Mia murmured. "I had a good view out in Chicago, but there was never that much."

"They're satellites," Dex supplied, around a yawn, earning himself a sharp nudge from Atlanta, who seems to object to sharing even basic information, on principle as far as I can tell. Good thing she doesn't know we used to eavesdrop on the pair of them, back up on the ship.

"Whole satellites?" Mia asked, lifting her head to look across at them.

I glanced over at Dex, who had the gun from his waistband resting on his stomach, his hand curled loosely around it. For all our voices were quiet, the scene almost idyllic, we were still prisoners—and the Undying team weren't about to let us forget it. Atlanta was the only one not lying down—she kept her eyes on us, not on the sky.

When Dex didn't answer, I drew a slow breath. "Something just showed up where their orbital paths used to be." Mia's head tipped toward me, and though she didn't say anything, I could guess what she was thinking. Just days ago we were on that ship that came through the portal and inserted itself into orbit around Earth.

We were up there, looking down at our home, listening to the impacts of communications satellites and research probes against the hull of the alien ship that had disrupted the delicate dance of tiny manmade moons around our planet. Now, they're being knocked from the sky one by one, Earth's creations falling as the Undying monolith overtakes them.

It feels uncomfortably prophetic.

"We thought you'd come ourways, take a look at the ship," Atlanta said, finally glancing up toward the night sky. "Launch something fast as you could."

The truth is, we probably *are* launching something as fast as we can. But it's not so long ago in our history that we had to use fossil fuels to claw our way up into space, and even now with nuclear reactors powering our shuttles, it takes months to build and ready a space-worthy craft. I have no doubt IA teams are working around the clock to get scouting probes and shuttles ready to head up to the ship, but I'm equally sure it'll be too late by the time they do.

The IA isn't what it once was, in terms of might, or heft, or funding. Their support started to fade away the moment the Centauri mission was lost, and though Gaia was meant to be their triumphant comeback, I suspect this tightened border security in Europe is one of the ways individual countries are asserting their own power once again. Now is the time we should be supporting the IA, coming together. Instead, according to De Luca, we're turning on each other.

I didn't say any of this to Atlanta. There's no need for her to know we're further behind, and more divided than she thinks.

We half dozed for a little before we continued on our way. Mia and I were desperately in need of the rest—I didn't so much lie down on the ground as experience an uncontrolled descent—and even Dex and Atlanta looked willing to sit down on the grass for a while.

The enormity of the journey ahead is beginning to sink in. My thighs are aching, my hands are blistered from the bike's handlebars, and I'm walking like a bowlegged cowboy as I dismount my bike in front of a small café in the outer suburbs of Montpellier. It's isolated—I'd guess that it mostly does lunches for the locals— and it's a good place to check in with Neal again, and pray that he got my message.

I lean my bike against the wall, and I'm about to turn and walk in when Mia reaches out to grab my arm.

"Wait," she says. "You look like . . ." Her lips curve into a small, tired smile. "Well, you look like you've been through what you've been through."

Her hands brush the travel dust from my sleeves and straighten my clothes, and I try not to notice how close she is.

I run a hand over my hopelessly messy curls, and as Dex steps closer to Mia, his hand resting casually near the place his gun is hidden, I take my cue and walk toward the café. I could never leave her anyway, but the unspoken threat—if you run, we've got a weapon on her—leaves me shaking. It's smart, that's for certain. We don't want anyone reporting there were four of us, if they're asked. Alone, I can blend in. But I don't have to like it.

The man behind the counter looks up as the little bell over the door rings. "You look like you're having a bad day," he offers, after just one glance at me.

I remind myself to slip into French, to lean on the *o* sounds, to make my voice a little more musical so I sound like a local speaker, less memorable. "Monsieur, you have no idea. The most recent part of my bad day is that I have a flat tire. Could I please use your phone to call a friend? I'm afraid I don't have any money."

He looks me up and down again, and then he nods, digging in his back pocket to offer it to me.

My hands are shaking as I walk out of earshot, then dial Neal's number and listen to the phone start to ring. *Come on*, I urge him silently. *Come on, Neal, come on.*

And then the ringing stops.

"Neal Addison speaking." His familiar voice crackles down the line, and unbearable pressure wells up behind my eyes.

"Neal, it's me."

"Oh, thank God." I can hear the relief in his voice.

"Where are you?" I ask, too eager to remember to be discreet.

"I'm . . ." He hesitates. "You were circumspect, in your phone call, yesterday. I think I understood the place you were talking about. If I got it right, I'm about an hour away."

I hadn't dared tell him yesterday that if we made it across the border we would be heading for Montpellier. I have no idea if anyone's listening to his phone, but I need to assume the worst, because we can't afford to be caught—the fate of the world may well hang on us making it to Prague. So I made a joke about wading into a pond while on holiday—something that really happened when my family and Neal's once visited Montpellier, on our way to Ambrussum, to study the Gallo-Roman ruins there.

We'd diverted for a picnic lunch in the park, and an eight-year-old Neal convinced a four-year-old me that there were undiscovered ruins hidden at the bottom of the pond in question. So in I went to discover them. It was a soggy—and disappointing—experience, and one I'm fairly sure he won't have forgotten.

"Look," I say. "This might be for nothing, but it might not. There's a chance that you'll be tracked. You should draw cash out of the bank and swap your phone for a new one, before you . . . go to that place."

Neal doesn't even know I've been to Gaia, unless my father told him. All he knows is that I've been out of contact for weeks, and now I've surfaced in France, talking like an international spy. Luckily for me, he doesn't seem to think I've lost my mind. "I'll be there," he says simply.

"And Neal?"

"Yes?"

"There'll be other people with me. One's a girl, Mia, you can trust her. The other two, don't say anything in front of them. I'll explain as soon as I can."

• • •

An hour later, we're wheeling our bikes through the Parc Esplanade Charles-de-Gaulle, approaching a small pond in the middle of the green space—the site of my long-ago and ill-fated exploration.

I can see Neal's familiar figure as soon as we come around the bend in the path. We look fairly similar—the Addison genes are strong in both of us, and we play on the same water polo team, so we share the same build. He's a little taller, a little more broad-shouldered, his skin a little deeper brown, but we look more like brothers than cousins. We *are* more like brothers than cousins.

He's clad in his usual leather jacket and he's got a motorbike, but it's not his—it's the wrong color, navy blue, with a white stripe down the side. It's . . . mehercule, it's a gendarme's bike.

I show up on a rusty bicycle, and my cousin's riding a stolen policeman's motorbike. That's us in a nutshell, really.

His blue-and-white steed is parked under a tree, and he's pacing nervously beside it. He always paces when he's thinking. He turns, spots us, and stares for a moment. Then he breaks into a jog, closing the gap between us.

I'm forced to drop my bicycle, and it clangs to the ground as my cousin throws his arms around me.

"God, Jules." He sounds hoarse, but whatever emotion was coming is abruptly stifled as he lets go of me as quickly as he grabbed me. "Dear God, you smell *unbelievably* bad."

His familiar face, his familiar voice, both part of my life for as long as I can remember—together they bring me a little undone. The tiredness and the hunger catch up with me, and my laugh sounds shaky to my own ears.

"Neal, this is Mia," I say, stepping aside to introduce the others. Usually I'd say something more. *This is Mia, my friend. This is Mia, my classmate.* Something to give him some context. But I hear myself hitch on the end of her name, as if I'm swallowing the rest of that sentence, and I realize in that instant that I have no idea what it would even be.

*This is Mia . . . my girlfriend?*

The word is both completely insufficient for what she is to me, and at the same time, completely presumptuous. But still . . .

She offers her hand to shake, and Neal sketches an elaborate bow over it, lifting her fingers close to his lips, miming the action of kissing them.

"You," he tells her, "do not smell terrible at all. I'm sure you couldn't." He peeks up at her, mischief in his eyes, and though she looks a little like she wants to roll hers, Mia is smiling anyway. Neal has that effect on everyone.

"Atlanta," I say, gesturing to the next of our party.

She glances sidelong at Mia, and then offers her hand, just as my partner did. And Neal, of course, repeats his routine.

"You also smell better than my cousin," he tells her, though he doesn't tease a smile out of her, and something in Neal's expression flickers warily. He knows something's not right.

"And Dex," I say. Dex is already smiling, and for a moment I forget he's an alien. *He's adapting so quickly. They're like chameleons.*

Neal clearly takes that smile as encouragement, and mock-kisses Dex's hand too. "And you," he concludes, "I could positively eat."

Dex's smile flickers, and his expression goes a bit blank—but oddly, he doesn't seem entirely put off by Neal's ebullient friendliness. Instead, he almost looks . . . shy.

*Human. And like he might be blushing.*

"I have a hotel room," Neal says, stepping back. "I couldn't book for all of us. The whole continent's at orange security alert, thanks to you-know-what, up there in the sky." He jabs a finger up.

"What's the word on it?" Atlanta asks, looking up, as if the ship might be visible right now.

"It's all anyone's talking about," Neal replies. "Front page on every site. The IA transported it back from Gaia, and everyone's arguing about who gets the tech that must be aboard."

Mia and I exchange a glance that silently acknowledges everything that's wrong about what he just said, but nobody corrects him. Atlanta and Dex just listen, blank-faced.

"You can actually see it from down here, certain times of day," Neal continues. "Anyway, you can't book into a hotel without a passport right now, but I managed to get a ground floor room with a window, so we shouldn't have much trouble unofficially checking you in."

Dex and Atlanta both look at me again, and I realize a lot of what he's saying probably doesn't scan.

No wonder they took a couple of Earthling hostages with them. They were supposed to land much closer to Prague—they *need* us to get from here to there, despite all their skills.

Though to judge by the speed and ease with which Dex, at least, is adapting, they might not need us for long.

I swallow the icy trickle of fear that thought brings, and try to focus on my cousin as he rummages in his pocket.

"Here," he says, holding out a little plastic package. "A new SIM card for your watch, Jules. I replaced mine, too, after your last call. They won't be able to track either of us now." He casts a longing look over his shoulder at the gendarme's bike, and lets out a sigh. "I suppose Fleur will have to stay behind. I've disabled her tracking chip, but sooner or later someone will find her, and I'd rather be far away when they do."

The rest of us keep our bicycles, and nobody speaks as we wheel them silently out of the park. His hotel is only a few blocks away, and Neal strolls through the front door while we head down the alleyway beside it. A couple of minutes later he's popping open his window with a loud creak of rusty hinges, and helping pull the four of us through.

It's a modest room in a family-run pensione, with two small double beds topped by gaudy, flowery bedspreads, and an emphatic sign littered with incorrectly used quotation marks warning against "smoking" tobacco or "electronic" cigarettes—the sort of sign you know there's a story behind, if it's that large. There's a trio of backpacks on the bed.

*Mehercule, please let there be fresh clothes in there.*

Mia speaks. "Atlanta, Dex, you can shower first."

The two have barely spoken a word since we met Neal, but their unspoken question is obvious now—they look around, their gazes lighting first on the door that leads out of the room, and then the door that leads to the little bathroom.

*Do spacefaring aliens even know what a shower is?*

"Neal, could you show them how the shower works?" I ask.

He shoots me a querying glance that only lasts a beat, then nods smoothly. "Of course," he says, leading the way through into the bathroom. Dex follows without hesitation, but Atlanta halts long enough to eye the two of us speculatively, and then crosses the room to shut the window and latch it. It's an old building, and the window shrieks in its frame—she doesn't have to say a word for us to understand her meaning.

If we try to slip out while they're in the next room, she'll hear. And we'll wish we'd stayed put.

As she turns to join her partner, I crack open one of the complimentary bottles of water on the nightstand and hand it to Mia, then pick up the other for myself. In the bathroom, I can hear Neal passing out towels, showing them how to control the water flow and temperature, and jokingly asking if anyone wants help washing their backs. When he reemerges, Atlanta firmly closes the door behind him.

He looks back over his shoulder, then pulls a face. "Aw, they're staying in together? Boy, did I misread that one."

"No," says Mia. "You didn't. They just have different ideas about modesty. And probably, they want to talk where we can't hear."

"That seems more likely," Neal agrees solemnly. "I'm pretty sure he swings my way, and few can resist my charms."

*Oh, Neal. You've got no idea. I doubt he even swings toward our* species.

"We need to hurry," Mia says quietly, sinking down to sit on the edge of the bed.

I settle behind her, ignoring—mostly—the way my thighs scream a protest at all their recent cycling as I lower myself down.

Neal takes a spot on the other bed, opposite us.

"Neal," I start, "I'm going to tell you about the last few weeks, and I don't have time to convince you I'm not crazy. I need you to just believe me."

The laughter falls away from his eyes, and he nods, instantly serious. "I'll believe anything," he says. "I know where you've been."

That pulls me up short. "You do?"

He nods. "A few weeks ago, I got a request through the IA for a vid conference with your father. He'd been using all his allotted time for you, so I was surprised. When we got on, he started talking about how he needed a hand with some of his equations."

I nod. That was as good a cover as any for speaking to Neal.

My father's mathematics are second to none, but that doesn't mean he's a specialist in every area. As an engineer, Neal goes places my father doesn't, sometimes. And though he's only just graduated from university, first, he's family, and therefore to be trusted, and second, he's an Addison, and therefore brilliant.

"It took a while before I understood what he was getting at, with all his hints and veiled references," Neal admits. "It's a pretty insane realization to come to—that you, of all people, had somehow gotten yourself to Gaia."

I nod. "That's where I've been, and Mia too."

Neal glances back and forth between us, and shakes his head. "From anyone else," he says, "I wouldn't believe it."

"*We* can hardly believe it," Mia replies, and when I glance down at her, her eyes meet mine, and we're sharing a look full of everything we've survived. Nobody else on this planet or any other will ever understand what these past few weeks have been like. Nobody, except Mia. "But if you can hardly believe that," she continues, with one of her grins, "then you're going to love what's coming next."

Together, we run him through the briefest possible version of our adventures. The temple, the puzzles, the scratched Nautilus warnings. The ship—its discovery and its launch. The fact that Charlotte Stapleton, the woman who granted Neal his internship, was really an undercover IA operative conning me onto the surface of Gaia. Neal barely seems to react to that news—probably because we don't give him a chance. Because that brings us to the arrival of the Undying.

To the fact that we've finally found alien life, and, unbelievably, two of them are in our hotel bathroom right now. Looking *almost* as human as the three of us.

Neal is utterly silent through the rest of our story: the shuttle landing, our escape from IA detention, the midnight bike ride across the French countryside.

"And then we reached you," I finish quietly.

His face looks ashen, his hands folded tightly together in his lap. For a wild moment I think he's about to be sick, for I've never seen him look so gutted. We've met with setbacks before, but Neal's always figured out a way through. I remember arriving for polo practice after my father's arrest to hear Neal arguing with the team captain to keep me on despite the scandal surrounding my family. He never even needed to consult me, he just *did* it. And it worked.

Neal *always* has a plan.

Now, Neal's eyes flick toward the bathroom door, the sound of running water drowning out everything else. And when he looks back, I can see him like a mirror, reflecting my own fear back to me.

And then my cousin, the guy who always has a plan, turns to look at me. "What do we do?"

The words are a blow all by themselves. I hadn't dared think it, but part of me believed that once Neal caught up to us, once we told him all that had happened, he'd grin one of those devastating grins and tell us the solution we'd missed, in all our exhaustion and urgency.

Mia saves me by answering. "They think we're their hostages," she says softly, tilting her head toward the bathroom door. "We're playing along partly because we're pretty sure they *could* kill us without breaking a sweat if we ran. But mostly because we think there's a chance of learning more about their plan if we stick close."

*We think*, my mind echoes, the words warming that core of me that Neal's fear left shivering. A few hours ago I was trying to convince Mia I was right. Now, it seems, she believes in the plan. Or in me. I don't much care which. I want to take her hand, but suddenly, in front of Neal, I find myself strangely shy.

"We already know that the plan has something to do with building more portals. Or we think it does." I suck in a deep breath and clear my throat. "That's how they'll get the rest of their army down here, we think, after this first wave sets up the portals on the surface."

Neal's face suddenly mobilizes, and though the shift in expression is minute, his eyes sharpen, and he straightens. "Portals? Like the one that sends ships to Gaia?" When I nod, he leans forward, brows lifting. "Jules—that's what I've been working on with your father."

I blink at him. "With Dad?"

Neal nods, energized once more—even if his eyes are still a bit wild, and he looks like he wishes there was a continent between him and the bathroom containing the Undying aliens. "He's been trying to decode them while he's been in detention, figure out how they work. He must have suspected that if he was right—if the Undying tech was dangerous—that someday we might need a kill switch. A way to shut them all down."

My heart seizes, and I feel a hand grab mine and squeeze tight. Mia, it seems, is not afflicted by shyness. "And?"

Neal glances at the bathroom and back. "And we were making progress. I don't have much of the data—mostly, your dad would send me specs and I'd walk him through them. He's better at maths than I'll ever be, but he's not an engineer. And everything we did had to be coded, pretty cloak-and-dagger stuff—he had limited calls out, you know, and they listened to everything we said."

Mia's breath hitches. "So you *don't* know how to shut them down?"

Neal shakes his head. "But he might."

Pent-up frustration and eagerness make me lurch to my feet. "So we call him, we tell him I'm back, we . . ." I trail off, looking at Neal's face. "What?"

Neal's grim expression makes my heart sink even before he says, quietly, "He never made our last call. We were supposed to talk two days ago, and there was nothing. And when I called the IA switchboard and tried to get to someone in the detention facility, I was locked out."

I sag back down onto the end of the bed, half leaning against Mia, who leans back.

"So we keep following them." My voice sounds exhausted even

to my own ears. "Try to convince someone what's happening. Try not to get arrested."

Neal draws a quavering breath. "You said they're headed for Prague, right?" When I nod, he continues, "Well, that's where your dad is. They might've cut off his phone privileges for some reason, but maybe there's a chance we could get in to see him. Find out in person if he's unraveled the portal riddle."

"They'd never let us see him." Mia's voice is cautious, but there's an energy in it she's lacked for days. And despite the hollowness in my own chest, I feel a flicker of warmth trying to respond. "We're fugitives—they'd ID us on the way in."

"I'm not a fugitive," Neal points out. "And when Jules vanished—buggered off to Gaia—I got visitation rights. They'll have to at least tell us why he's not making phone calls anymore."

The flicker of warmth comes again, stronger this time. "And Prague is where the Undying want us to go anyway—if we can get to my dad and he can figure out how to turn off the portals . . ."

Mia finishes for me when I trail off. "Then the only Undying forces here will be the ones who came in that first wave. Hundreds, rather than thousands, or however many are ready to come pouring through to take over our planet."

For a moment, the three of us just look at each other, all wondering the same thing: *Is it even possible for a couple of fugitives and an engineering student to make their way across Europe without being caught?*

But it's a plan. It's more than we had an hour ago.

Abruptly, the water shuts off, and I remember the aliens in the bathroom.

*Mehercule, there's a sentence I never thought I'd say to myself.*

With a start, I recall the pictures I took on my phone of the results of the cheek swab. If the IA hasn't thought to look at them, I can at least try to gather some proof of my own. "Neal," I whisper, leaning close so that my voice won't carry, "do you know anyone back home studying genetics? Anyone you trust, who could look at some data for us?"

Neal reaches into his back pocket to pull out his phone. "Transfer it to me," he says. "I've got a contact back at Oxford. A postdoctoral student."

I cock a brow.

"Yes," he says, unapologetically. "An ex. But we're on excellent terms. Pun intended." I smile, in spite of myself, and he manages one in return. "Veronica will help us, if she can."

As I finish transferring the pics, the bathroom door opens, steam billowing out.

Without missing a beat, Neal rises smoothly to his feet. "I'm going out to get food," he tells a slightly damp and newly clean Dex and Atlanta. "This hotel isn't large enough to provide room service."

Though it isn't clear either of them understand what *room service* is, they understand *out* and *food*. Atlanta nods, and Dex offers a soft, "Beno, thank you."

He's cut his hair with the nail scissors from the bathroom, or Atlanta has cut it for him. Now it curls close against his head, like mine and Neal's, his braid gone. So far he's only seen Neal and me, who keep our hair short because we spend so much time in the pool, and the IA, who all sport military haircuts. So he's gone short, to blend in with what he's observed.

Neal takes his leave, and then it's the four of us again, just like old times.

"What did you tell him?" Atlanta asks, studying my face.

I feel like she could quite possibly count my pulse rate from watching a vein in my temple, and expertly calculate whether I'm telling the truth. "I told him that I need him to trust me," I say.

After a long moment, she nods.

Mia and I take it in turns to shower. I let her go first, and when she comes out wrapped in a towel and an air of utter bliss, for a long moment I can only stare at her. Her cheeks are rosy from the heat, and her lips are curved in the most satisfied smile I've ever seen. Water droplets flick down her thighs as she makes room for me to move past her into the bathroom. Her wet hair falls over her shoulders and water trails down the slope of her chest toward the towel knotted just over her—I jerk my eyes away, and for a few moments I'm focusing so hard on *not* thinking about Mia about to get dressed in the next room that I barely take any notice of getting into the shower myself.

Until the hot water hits me, at which point I forget everything else and stay there until the water turns cold.

After I've dried off and pulled on some of the fresh clothes from the backpacks Neal brought for us, he returns with a large haul from the supermarket. I can't help but notice how interested the Undying are in every kind of food. I'm thrown back for a moment to their wonder as they felt the breeze, and saw the grass for the first time.

All this must be so new, so overwhelming to them. Nothing could've prepared me for the strangeness of being on Gaia, and I'd brought all my own clothes and food—and there wasn't anyone else there. The culture shock—species shock?—for them must be staggering. I'd admire their ability to remain efficiently on-mission if it weren't that same ability that's going to get us killed, unless we're very lucky.

It's late afternoon by the time we've eaten, and though the sun's not down yet, the four of us are nodding. Dex and Atlanta curl up together on one bed, and Mia and I take the other. Neal, insisting it's no discomfort at all, settles himself down in the small arm-chair, pulling up a book to read on his phone, apparently settling in to read while we sleep.

• • •

When I wake, it's dark. I roll over, disoriented. Beside me, Mia makes a sleepy noise, but she's already struggling to sit up, in response to whatever woke me.

"What the hell?" That's Neal, and I know where I am.

I hear him cross the room in three quick strides, and my eyes sting as he flicks on the light. Another two steps, and he's through the open bathroom door.

When he reemerges, his mouth is tight, face grim. "They're not here," he says. "I don't even remember falling asleep, but I locked the door, and I kept the chair by the window. I don't know how they didn't wake me."

That's when I look across at the other bed.

The rumpled sheets are flat.

Dex and Atlanta are gone.

14

AMELIA

"Good, I'm glad they're gone!" My voice is louder than I intended. Despite my exhaustion, I only slept an hour or two last night. Long enough for Dex and Atlanta to slip away, but not long enough to refresh my tired brain. I couldn't stop my mind turning over, couldn't stop thinking. Every turn we make, our options just get narrower and narrower—and in the darkness, making it to Prague seemed impossible. I told myself that everything would look simpler in the light of morning, but now, staring at the empty bed the Undying teens had occupied, I just want to give up.

Jules stares at me. "How can you say that?"

"We can move that much faster without them, and also not have to worry about getting shot or, you know, being killed in our sleep with a freaking Swiss Army knife! We have a million other things to worry about—I don't think losing the homicidal aliens hounding us should be one of them."

It's just us in the hotel room—Neal's gone out to try and find us some breakfast, since the Undying took the remains of the food he bought last night. That leaves me and Jules to figure out what to do about the missing aliens. I admit that knowing they're out there somewhere instead of where we can keep an eye on them is terrifying—but not nearly as terrifying as having them sleeping a few feet away.

"We need them." Jules expression is rather stony, and I can hear in his voice how thin his patience has gotten. "Even if my dad can neutralize the portals they're setting up—maybe they've got some fallback if they can't land more troops through the portals. We have to learn what the rest of their plan is."

"Screw their plan!" My voice cracks, and I shore it up with an effort. "This is so beyond us it's not even . . . A few weeks ago I was standing on an alien planet *certain* that I was in the middle of the worst, most terrible thing I was ever going to have to go through in my life."

His brown eyes, narrowed with irritation, soften a fraction. I don't know what he felt the first few steps he took on Gaia, but I had plenty of opportunity to see how frightened he was in the days that followed. Because I was frightened too, and that shared experience was beyond anything that could've brought us together here on Earth.

*Maybe that means we never should've been together in the first place. And shouldn't be now.* My heart quails from that thought almost as much as the thought of trekking across Europe as a wanted fugitive.

He doesn't speak, and the silence keeps pulling words from my mouth, my mind too exhausted to stop them.

"But I did it anyway, going to Gaia. Because it'd be worth it, because I'd be saving my sister, and we'd be together. But they've got Evie, Jules, or they're threatening to take her, or she's missing, or—or something. We're rapidly on our way to being labeled international terrorists. And we can't even rent a hotel room for fear we'll be arrested. It feels like years, Jules—it feels like *years* since I've had even a *moment* of feeling safe, like disaster wasn't right around the corner. And it was one thing when we were in an ancient temple on another world, and even in the walls of an alien spaceship—but we're home. We're here, against all odds. We got home despite *knowing* we were going to die. And I just—I can't keep *doing* this, and neither can you. So screw the Undying plan, Jules. I'm done. I'm going to find Evie, and make sure she's safe—it's all I *can* do."

I don't even have the energy to care that there are tears spilling down my cheeks. He's seen me raw before, and I don't have anything left to prove to him anyway.

*Let him see me cry. I'm done.*

His arm moves, like the tears trigger some automatic response— but he doesn't reach for me. His voice is hoarse when he speaks, his own eyes red-rimmed. "What about Earth?"

"What about it?" The words are callous, but in my current state I can't help the wobble in my voice. "I don't mean—it's just, what can we possibly do? This is a problem for world leaders, and armies, and . . . and tanks, and missiles, and bombs the size of houses, Jules. What are we meant to do to help in all of that? Two kids in the middle of a world war to end all wars?"

Jules passes a hand over his eyes, clearing his throat. "But we have to—"

"Have to what?" I interrupt him, wishing an instant later that I hadn't. "Bust into the IA with a list of insane criminal charges behind us both, claiming with no proof that aliens are invading the planet, and we need to see their most notorious prisoner at once?" My heart shrivels, but the words are already there, and I listen to them come out with something almost like horror. "All you're doing now is making things worse for your dad."

In the silence that follows, I can hear the distant sounds of traffic a few blocks away. The thumping bass line from someone's car radio rises and falls. A bird gives a raucous cry as it swoops past the window.

Jules's lips were still parted to speak when I interrupted him— now he closes his mouth, gazing at me from across the double beds. It's not the anger that strikes me, though he is mad, fists clenched at his sides and lips tight. What strikes me, what *guts* me, is the pain there—full of betrayal, disappointment, shock.

Like I'm not who he thought I was.

A tap at the door, followed by the rattle of a keycard, makes me swipe my sleeve across my face and look away. The door opens to admit Neal, like a near-copy of Jules himself, his arms full of cellophane-wrapped vending machine food.

"Bad news, team, we need to . . ." He trails off, glancing between us. Then he clears his throat, moving to dump his armload of junk food on the bed. "Look, normally I'd say I forgot the Doritos and give you guys a sec, but we don't have time."

Jules frowns. "Why? What's going on?"

Neal shrugs as he rummages through the pile of salt and sugar until he comes up with some Kinder chocolate. Not real chocolate, of course—that's been an embargoed luxury for at least a decade. And the chocolate "flavored" substitute is nothing like the real thing. "Some flu or something in Lyon, they're recommending tourists stay away. The news was on the TV in the snack room. Roads and trains are gonna be jammed in just a few hours with people overreacting and changing their travel plans, and we've got to get across the border before then."

Jules glances at me. I meet his eye with an effort, fighting the urge to look away in guilt and shame. Because he's got no right to make me feel this way—to think a few teenagers could somehow do more than an entire international coalition of experts is beyond arrogance, it's downright reckless and irresponsible and dangerous, and not just for us.

We tried. And now we've got to do what we both set out to do: save our families.

"Either way," I say wearily, "we have to get out of France. We don't have time to argue right now."

"Did you bring papers?" Jules turns to Neal, barely acknowledging me.

"Yeah, though I don't have a picture for Mia." Neal goes over to rummage through his backpack and pull out two passports, one of which he hands to his cousin.

Jules flips it open and exhales a somewhat mirthless laugh. "Tyler Hogwood?"

"Hey, don't complain, I had like a day. Mia—can I get your picture real quick?" Neal waves his phone, and, numb, I nod. I'll look exhausted and tear-stained and like I wish I were dead, but that's what most people look like when they're traveling, so it's probably for the best.

Neal snaps my picture, starting to make a lighthearted comment about my suitability as a supermodel—albeit a rather short one—and stopping when he fails to get a smile out of either of us. "Tough room," he mutters, plugging a little portable printer into the power port of his phone. It only takes him a few moments to run the edge of a box-cutter along the lamination of the passport page, slip my photo in over the existing one, and then seal it back down with a touch of glue.

Neal inspects it critically and then shrugs, handing it over to me. "Wouldn't hold up under a real inspection, but we'll just have to hope it's good enough. Maybe the mass exodus of tourists will be cover enough."

"How do we get to Germany?" My voice is quiet, and I don't look at Jules.

"I've got train tickets to Frankfurt for us." Neal pulls a printed confirmation page out of his bag. "We just pick them up at the station. It's only a few minutes from here. The line goes through Lyon, but I called and the guy said the train's still running."

"Let's go, then." Jules scoops up a few things from the vending machine pile without looking, and turns for the window we crawled in through.

I'm about to follow suit when Neal calls, "Hey, wait, don't forget your . . . phone?"

Jules just has his wrist unit, and my phone is still lodged in a stone doorway back on Gaia. But Neal's reaching for something half hidden under the pillows on one of the beds.

It does look like a phone, though it's smaller than most of the smartphones people buy these days. One side of it is a dim screen that brightens as Neal lifts the device; the other side is emblazoned with some sort of symbol, a gentle arc from one corner down toward the other.

"That's not ours." Jules's voice has lost some of its stiffness, his curiosity winning out over everything else, as always. "Let me see?"

Neal hands it over, and the three of us hunch over the thing. The display is minimal, black and white. Curved lines crisscross in a grid-like configuration, intersecting randomly with other, more abstract lines.

"One of them must have left it behind." I poke at the display, but it doesn't respond—either it's not a touch screen like our devices, or it's locked somehow. "Are any of these symbols you know?"

Jules shakes his head absently. "This symbol on the back—it looks like the symbol we saw in the first room of the temple on Gaia, the symbol for the Undying. But none of this is writing. It looks more like . . ." He trails off, eyes a bit distant.

"Like a map." Neal points at the screen. "No roads or countries or anything, but this here, this looks a little like one of the elevation maps we use when we're programming drones."

"Maybe it's to track them. If we can figure out how it works, maybe we could keep tabs on them." Jules is staring at the little screen in his palm, and when he speaks again there's a spark of life in his voice for the first time since we were shouting at each other. Or since I was shouting at him, anyway. "Dex. Dex left it here for us to find before they snuck away."

"The disturbingly hot one?" Neal's flippancy is more than irritating—but then, he wasn't on Gaia. He didn't see the corridors of the ship filled with Undying teens like Dex and Atlanta. He didn't hear the way they spoke about us "protos." And he's our only ally right now.

I let my breath out in a groan. "Look, I don't know. Maybe you're right. But that doesn't change . . ." I trail off, because we're talking in circles, and if I tell him again that there's nothing we can do, he'll tell me again that we can't just give up, and we're both right and we're both wrong, and I can't have this fight again.

"It doesn't change the fact that we have to get out of France." Jules's voice is not exactly conciliatory, but it's not as brittle as it was. "We'll have a few hours on the train to decide what to do next. And we can figure out what this is then." He hefts the little device, and then slips it into his pocket.

Grateful for the reprieve, for his willingness to press pause on our disagreement, I offer him a weary smile. He doesn't smile back, though he does meet my eyes for a moment before turning to gather up the rest of our meager supplies. I wish I could take back what I said about his father—but I also can't dismiss the nagging feeling that what I said was *true*. There's nothing two kids can do to stop a war, if that's what the Undying are doing.

I turn to follow Neal out the window, trying to harden my heart the way I did on Gaia. Evie comes first. At the very least, De Luca and the IA know about her, and at worst, they have her. I can't forget that for an instant. She *always* has to come first.

15

JULES

WE FIND A PLACE TO SIT ON THE TRAIN, CLUSTERED IN A SET OF
four seats around a small table. As Neal digs through his backpack
and hands out little cakes from a packet that says *Madeleines* on it,
I can't help turning over in my hand the device that I'm sure Dex
left behind. It's small, about the size of my palm, with the display
on one side and a hard shell of some unknown alloy on the other.
My fingertips trace the symbol for the Undying embossed there: a
circle with a long tail arcing behind it.

Neal interrupts my thoughts. "You really think he left it for us
to track him on purpose? It couldn't be something he and Atlanta
use to keep track of each other, and it was an accident?"

Mia makes a noise indicating just how likely she thinks that
is, but I don't look up at her. I can't just now. The things she said
are ricocheting around my mind like bullets hunting for a target.
I need a chance to *think*. I need a moment alone. But I'm not going
to get one—at least I hope not, because right now Neal and Mia
are all I have.

"There's more to Dex than we know," I say. "Whatever their plan is, he has doubts. Perhaps he had them to begin with, or perhaps we're just not what he expected."

"My good looks probably did come as a surprise," Neal says modestly, around a mouthful of food. "People rarely expect me to be this clever *and* this handsome."

"He's voiced doubts before," I insist. "And there have been other moments."

"The tattoo?" Mia asks, disbelieving. "It was a galaxy tattoo. Most galaxies *are* spiral shaped."

I shake my head. "He was trying to draw attention to it. And we know someone within the Undying tried to use the Nautilus to warn us not to go near the ship in the first place."

"Well, it couldn't have been Dex," she retorts. "He's our age. Or he looks like it. Either way, he wasn't carving reliefs in a temple fifty thousand years ago. Nothing lives that long."

"It could be some kind of symbol of resistance," I suggest. But even I know it's a stretch. We don't have any real evidence for that.

"The moment in the shuttle, though," she says. "That, I have trouble explaining. I could have sworn he made us."

"He did," I agree. "Some parts, I'm not sure about. I'm still wondering if he helped me out, when I was bluffing us onto the shuttle. He asked if we trained with the Cortes squadron, and I didn't know if he was trying to catch me out, or he thought that might explain why he and Atlanta wouldn't recognize me. But he might have been trying to show me the way out with a leading question. There's an explanation for that, but there's no explanation for him seeing us and keeping it a secret from Atlanta, unless his loyalties are divided."

"What I can't understand," Neal says, "is what those two *are*. How can they possibly look so like us and not be us? I mean, mathematically, the odds on that . . . Are we talking surgical alteration? It wouldn't be a bad move, if you wanted to blend with a society you were infiltrating. They couldn't have known they'd have their cheeks swabbed, though, so those DNA tests . . . that should've sent alarm bells off all over the place. Nothing that bleeds blue is going to look like us on a genetic level."

"That's what we have to learn," I say, still not looking at Mia. "If we know that, we can find a way to make the IA listen. And let us in to see my dad about shutting down the portals."

"Well," Neal says, "if anyone can help us, it's Veronica. She knows her stuff. And whatever the answer, none of it can stop us trying to reveal them to the IA." His determination is there in his voice, but of course he knows nothing of my fight with Mia this morning.

Neither of us replies.

• • •

It's an hour later when, despite our limited supply of cash, I'm starting to seriously wonder if the train has a dining car that might offer something superior to vending machine food. But the overhead speaker crackles to life.

"Chers voyageurs, votre attention s'il vous plaît . . ." it says.

I lean in to translate for the others in a whisper. "'In a few moments, the train will pass through the town of Lyon. As you may be aware, the French government has declared Lyon an emergency area, and imposed a quarantine on the city.'"

Exclamations break out all around us—word of the flu might have spread, but this quarantine is new since Neal saw the news this morning. The speaker continues as I translate.

"'Entering or leaving the city is forbidden; however, our train is permitted as long as it does not stop at any station. We will continue through, and apologize for any inconvenience.'"

Judging by the protests around us, some of our carriage mates had intended on disembarking in Lyon. But my attention's on the view outside the carriage window. We haven't lost any speed, and at first the city flies past—I make out a hospital, a cemetery, and as we come into the more populated area, one of the university campuses.

As we approach the Gare de Lyon-Part-Dieu, where the train

would usually stop, we slow down, rattling along the tracks only a little above walking pace. Now, I can make out people moving around outside—more than I'd expect, given the quarantine—but they're too far away for us to get a good look.

From its place on the table, the device Dex left behind gives the softest of chimes. All our heads turn as one, to see a tiny green dot flicker to life on the screen and then fade again. The chime comes again a few seconds later, and then again, a fraction quicker. I glance up, but Mia and Neal look just as confused as I feel.

Then the train clunks over several street crossings in a row, dragging our attention back to the window. We rumble alongside a small strip of shops, and I can see the street below the tracks properly. It's lined with small shopfronts and runs parallel to the rails. I lean closer to Mia to get a good look at the people, and can't help my sharp intake of breath.

A group of figures come into view, making their way down one of Lyon's cobbled streets. They're moving with a lean, steady determination, but there's something off about them. The way they lift their heads and look around calls to mind a pack of predators on the hunt, and one slaps at the glass window of a shop, hand swiping across the gilt lettering painted there. MARGUERITE PÂTISSERIE, it reads. Though there's no sound through the train window, I can see he's roaring his frustration at the barrier.

I couldn't name any one thing that makes it seem like they're not thinking, not understanding or communicating as humans do, but I'm sure of it. It's in the way they tilt their heads, their every move, the fact that no one's speaking, the blank intensity of their expressions. Something has . . . reduced them.

The notification sound on Dex's device has sped to a constant ticking, like it's approaching some sort of meltdown.

"What in the name of . . ." Neal's voice trails off, and between me and the window, Mia's pressed against the glass, staring silently.

Then she explodes into action, somehow vaulting over me, scrambling past the table, to run toward the back of the carriage.

Neal and I waste a heartbeat on exchanging a startled look, and then we're up from our seats, and running after her. The three of us bolt headlong through two more carriages, Neal and I—much bigger than Mia—bouncing off doors and seats.

When we catch her, she's standing at the very back of the train, looking out through the rear window. Despite the distance we've run, it's been less than thirty seconds, and this final part of the train is only just starting to pass the little row of shops.

"There," she says breathlessly, jabbing a finger down at the street. *"There*, look at them."

I see what she means immediately, and suck in a quick breath. Beside me, Neal has his phone out, and he's filming the street below us, and I hold my tongue—I don't want to believe the evidence of my eyes, and just now I can't bring myself to speak.

Quietly, Neal gives our location, the time, and the date, and he tries to hold the screen steady as we rattle along the tracks, only putting the phone away when we pick up speed once more.

"What did you see?" he asks quietly.

"It can't have been," I whisper.

"It was," Mia insists. And I know she's right.

"There were two Undying back there," I say slowly.

"Isn't the whole problem that they look like humans?" Neal points out. "How can you be sure?"

Mia shakes her head. "I'm *sure*. They have a way of moving—there's a way they walk, and look, these two weren't confused like everybody else around them. They were *talking* to each other, and none of the other victims looked like they were even capable of speech. And if they were healthy, there's no way they'd just be strolling down the street, it wasn't safe out there. They looked . . ." Her lip curls. "They looked pleased."

"She's right," I say. "And they were in a pair, like all the Undying on the ship."

Neal murmurs, "The thing Dex left us—it can detect the Undying somehow. That's why it was beeping." Neal's voice is taut with fear. "The question is, did these two just happen to find themselves in the middle of some kind of outbreak, or is there a connection between their presence and what's happening in Lyon?"

Mia's face is white. I'm probably looking pretty ashen myself—Neal certainly looks like he's about to throw up—but she has that look in her eye that tells me she's had a realization, one that we're not going to like.

"Those people back there are like animals." Her eyes are on the window, her voice trembling. "Like they've . . . *regressed* or something, like they're Neanderthals."

My throat tightens. Perhaps it's the time we've spent working together so closely, or perhaps it's some instinct developed over all the studying I've done on this species—but I know what she's about to say a split second before she says it.

Her eyes leave the window and meet mine, and for a moment Neal's not even there. "It's like they're proto-humans," she whispers.

We stand in silence for a long moment as the beeping from Dex's device begins to slow, fading back into silence, but Lyon has one final offering—one that causes Neal to lift his phone to film with a shaky hand once more.

As the three of us gaze down at the final section of track, a pair comes stumbling out the gate in someone's back fence. It's an old woman, still in her nightdress, and a young child with a huge mop of brown curls, clad only in a pair of shorts.

The old woman's lips part in a silent howl, and the child breaks into a run following us, hands up, fingers curled into claws, as if the train is some kind of threat it has to chase out of its territory.

Behind the child, the old woman tries to shuffle to a run too, but she falls, landing heavily on the tracks.

The child doesn't look back, but keeps chasing us, face twisted in rage and confusion and maybe fear, until it's lost from sight as we round the curve and pick up speed outside the city once more.

16

AMELIA

**IT'S HOURS BEFORE ANY SEMBLANCE OF ORDER RETURNS TO THE TRAIN.**
We're not the only ones who saw the horrifying chaos in Lyon.
Ordinarily you'd get officials walking the aisles, telling everyone
to remain calm and stay in their seats, but when we elbowed our
way past the panicked passengers back to our car, we passed one
of the conductors sitting in an empty seat, head in his hands,
while the passenger next to him fired off a stream of endless,
unanswerable questions.

Even the people in charge here are losing it.

We don't speak much once we're back in our seats. The countryside is beautiful, even idyllic—I've never seen so much grass, such
green, rolling hills. Back home it's all dust and stunted trees. But
I watch the scenery pass with an emptiness in my chest, as if my
mind can't process beauty anymore. Vineyards, rivers, picturesque
towns, fields of solar power arrays . . . I watch it go by like it's a
movie.

Because we left reality back there in Lyon.

The train makes a few stops, and some passengers leave—others stay, clearly wanting nothing more than to put as much distance between them and the afflicted town as possible. Another hour passes and a sign whips by, a message written in a number of languages: WILKOMMEN AUF DEUTSCHLAND! BIENVENUE EN ALLEMAGNE! WELCOME TO GERMANY! The conductor in the seat behind us finally pulls himself together and staggers on up the aisle and into the next car. Jules slowly and methodically shreds an old napkin into ragged confetti.

"I think I should post this." Neal's voice is quiet, but it's been so long since anyone spoke that it thunders in my ears so that I barely understand him.

"What?" I stare at him, numb.

Neal's eyes, so like Jules's, flick between my face and that of his cousin. "The footage. I think I should put it online. The news reports . . . Guys, everyone else thinks whatever's happening in Lyon is some sort of flu. That's not a flu. That's the goddamn end of the world."

Jules stays quiet, so I clear my throat and try to gather my stunned and scattered thoughts together again. "People will panic when they see that."

"Good!" Neal's voice is higher than usual. "They *should* bloody well panic. Panicking is absolutely, one hundred percent, no question about it, *exactly* what they should do."

I shiver and wrap both arms about myself. The air is warm, but the goose bumps all over my skin won't go away. "Maybe."

Neal's staring down at his phone, and though I can't see its screen, I know he's watching the footage he took. "Do we say what we know about those two Undying in the background?"

I chew at my lip. "I don't know. Maybe that'll make people think it's all some kind of hoax." *Like De Luca did.*

"Post it." Jules's voice is hollow and soft, but contradicts me without hesitation. "Post all of it, everything about the two Undying. People might not believe that, but the part about Lyon is undeniably true. Maybe a few people will believe the rest of it."

Neal's gaze lingers on his cousin's face for a while, then flicks over to meet my eyes. He only looks at me for a second, though, before bending his head over his phone to do as Jules said.

The silence stretches, until Jules's voice comes softly: "Mia, what you said this morning . . ."

I steel myself, eyes on Neal's bent head—if anything, he's concentrating even harder on the screen of his phone. Opening my mouth, certain I won't be able to make it through the sentence without cracking, I say, "What I said about your dad, I didn't mean—"

"Not that." Jules's face tightens a little, but he presses on. "You said if the Undying wanted Earth, it'd be a problem for tanks and missiles and armies."

"Yes, and I still think—" I get no further, because his point strikes home with all the chilling force of a winter wind across the desert.

What if the Undying *weren't* in Lyon by accident? What if they never planned on needing tanks at all?

"There are no bombs in Lyon," Jules says, almost inaudible.

"What if . . ." My throat tries to close around the words, and I'm forced to stop, then try again. "What if Lyon was just the beginning?"

• • •

The boys sit opposite each other across the table, heads bent over the Undying tracker that Jules thinks Dex left for us to find. With the realization that the horror we witnessed in Lyon might be part of the Undying's plan to destroy us, Jules is all the more desperate to decipher the tracking device, and he watches with single-minded intensity as Neal tries to figure it out and expand its radius.

I'm sitting next to Jules, but I might as well be on the other side of the ocean for all the attention he pays to me. And I can't blame him—even without what we've seen in Lyon, what I said to him about everything he's doing making things worse for his father . . .

I long for something familiar, lost in this blurry green sea of the German countryside. The urge to pull out my phone and call Evie, to see her face and hear her voice, is so strong I can almost feel the shape of the phone in my pocket, like a phantom limb. Looking at the screen the boys are examining only makes it worse, like I'm an addict watching someone light up a cigarette a few feet away.

Abruptly I get to my feet, making the boys look up at me with twin expressions of expectant surprise. They're so similar in this moment that whatever I'd been about to say vanishes, and I'm left looking between them, bemused.

"Are you okay?" Neal asks, brows lifting.

"I . . . I'm going to see if they've got water or something to drink."

Neal slides out of his seat. "I'll go, I need to stretch my legs anyway. Sit, you guys need the rest." I don't miss the little look Neal shoots Jules as he departs. Some things are universal, I suppose, including that *talk to her, dumbass* look.

Neal tucks his hands into his pockets and wanders on up the aisle toward the front of the dining car and the snack counter while I reluctantly slide into his seat, across from Jules.

He's got his eyes on the screen again, though the ease with which he'd been chatting with his cousin has vanished.

I watch the blurry landscape whizzing by outside the window until I can't stand the silence anymore. Letting my breath out, head dropping, I whisper, "I'm sorry I said that about your dad."

Jules is still for a moment before he sets the tracker aside, screen down. He looks up, and his gaze is as troubled as it's ever been. "You're right, though."

I blink at him. "I'm what?"

"The IA is going to be in chaos trying to solve what's happening in Lyon, which to them is a medical problem, an issue for disease control rather than planetary defense. If we go in there talking about alien invasions, they're going to think we're crazy, and when they find out who I am, it's just going to make them even more sure that my dad's crazy. You're right."

His voice is soft, but there's such a heavy sadness in it that my heart lurches in sympathy, my eyes prickling. I've never heard him sound so utterly defeated.

"Jules—"

"What are we even doing?" Jules grips the edge of the table between us, his knuckles whitening. "I had this vision of getting through to the IA, of telling my dad about the portals, and that he'd handle everything and in the process all our crimes—going to Gaia, stowing away on the ship, escaping IA custody, stealing that car, forging these papers—I imagined everything would just be forgiven, because what's happening with the Undying is so much bigger than us."

I watch him mutely, because though I long to talk him out of this—though hearing him speak this way frightens me more than I'd have imagined—he's not wrong.

"Because it *is* so much bigger than us." Jules lets go of the table and lowers his head into his hands instead. "Maybe it's the end of the world. Maybe it's not. But either way, we're criminals. *I'm* a criminal. And I can't go home again, can I?"

My throat is thick and my eyes are burning. I ought to criticize him for not having thought about that before now, before even going to Gaia in the first place. But he's never broken the law before, not like this. He hasn't led the life I have, where home *is* always being slightly on the wrong side of the rules. And all I can think about is how lost he must feel.

"I'm here." My voice is quiet, as if I'm afraid of anyone else overhearing the promise I'm about to make. "I'm with you. And I'm not leaving you. Wherever we go, we'll go together."

Jules lifts his head to meet my eyes, his own reddened and weary. For a long time we sit that way, in silence—then his lips tremble briefly before he opens his mouth to speak, one of his hands moving toward mine.

But before his fingertips do more than graze my palm, Neal is back, and ungently nudging me sideways so he can join us.

Irritation flares through me at the interruption, but one look at Neal's face flushes all the annoyance out of my system.

"What is it?"

Neal lowers his voice, making an effort to sound normal, though it's thick with tension. "They're coming through the cars testing people for that flu."

Jules frowns. "But no one would show symptoms that fast even if it somehow did get on the train."

"I think they're worried people might have brought it on board somewhere else in France, and I'm guessing Germany doesn't want that happening. They say it's just a precaution." But his face is grim, eyes a bit wild.

I lean sideways and see the ticket checker again come through the doorway from the car in front of us, with a few others behind him. "So? We're not sick."

"No, but we do have fake passports. And those IA officers with them probably won't be fooled as easily as the transit officials. Especially if they've been circulating your descriptions."

My heart seizes, and I look again to see that the people filing into the car behind the ticket checker are wearing the uniform of the International Alliance. "Oh *shit*."

Jules stuffs the screen into his pocket, his movements jerky with sudden alarm. "We've got to get out of here."

"And go where?" Neal's eyes are wild with fear.

"Off the train." My voice sounds steady and certain—probably a good thing, though I wish I felt the same. "We're over the border and into Germany, I saw the sign go by half an hour ago."

Both boys turn to look at me, though only Neal splutters a reply. "You want to jump off a moving train?"

I eye the window. "It's not moving *that* fast." My voice is running out of steady and certain at an alarming rate.

Jules cuts his cousin short. "We've got to hurry."

As casually as we can, the three of us abandon our dining car seats and head through the door toward the next car. No one stops us, though that doesn't mean that the officials didn't see us leave—it just means they assume they'll catch up to us in the next car, because where else would we go?

And when I hit the button that sends the exit door whooshing open, I realize why. Standing in the space between cars, we're jostled all the more as each car sways and bustles independently, and the ground whizzing by is moving so quickly the gravel is just a smooth, gray blur.

*It's not going to feel like a smooth gray blur when we go skidding across it.*

"Hang on." Jules detaches my hand from his sleeve—when did I grab him?—and, before we can stop him, goes back inside the dining car. He's only gone long enough for Neal and me to exchange horrified looks before the train decelerates with a lurch and a terrible screeching of brakes, and we both go slamming together against the wall of the car. There's some kind of alarm blaring, and when Jules returns he's a bit breathless.

"Emergency stop," he explains. "But they saw me pull it, we've got to jump."

"Hang on!" I echo Jules's words with a tiny grin, and head the other direction, into the car behind ours. The place is already in chaos, with people reacting to the emergency alarm and the train's rapid deceleration, so I have to shout at the top of my lungs to be heard.

"Everyone, listen!" I cry, noting with satisfaction the heads turning toward me. "There's a fire a few cars ahead and they've pulled the emergency stop—everybody get off the train!"

And while the entire car abandons their seats, I duck back out. Now, when we do jump, half the train's going to jump off right after us, giving us the cover we need to get away unnoticed.

Neal's got his face pressed to the glass of the dining car door, watching the officials make their way toward us. Jules nods at me, and I nod back, and for a moment we're on the same team again. He reaches for my hand, tangling his warm fingers through mine and squeezing.

The train's still moving along at a pretty good pace, but at least I can actually see the gravel now—*though damn, that does not make jumping any easier*—and we're out of time. In a moment, the occupants of the car behind us will come spilling out after us, and the officials from the dining car will have gotten here too.

Neal turns away from the door and stops at the sight of us. "For the love of—stop making eyes at each other and just bloody *jump* already!"

Jules twitches, glances at me—and as one, the three of us throw ourselves from the train.

JULES

IN THE INSTANT THAT I LEAP, I TRY TO REMIND MYSELF TO ROLL when I hit the ground, because that's what they do in movies. But the impact drives the breath from my lungs, sends a wave of pain through me, and then I'm rolling, rolling, with no idea where my limbs are, which way is up, which way is down, the sky flashing past me over and over as I tumble down the embankment.

I only stop when I run out of momentum. I carefully blink my eyes open and look at the sky, my lungs aching as they try help-lessly to drag in breath after breath. To one side I can hear a string of broken, breathless curses, so I know where Mia is, and that she's alive.

Finally I get enough air in my lungs to push myself up onto my elbows, and look around. Farther up the tracks the train has stopped, and passengers are pouring out onto the embankment—among them I see the officials we were trying so hard to avoid. Neal's on all fours beside me, trying unsuccessfully to climb to his feet, and Mia's already sitting up with a grimace. Deus, she's unstoppable.

That thought pulls me straight back to my disagreement with Mia, of course, but I suck in another breath and force myself to my feet, and Mia pulls Neal to his, despite being half his size. Then, wordlessly, the three of us turn to jog away from the tracks and toward the tree line, to get out of sight as quickly as we can.

Pine needles crunch beneath my feet as we enter the forest, my nose filling with their clean, crisp scent. Straight-backed pines tower above us, and the air grows cooler in their shade.

"What now?" Neal's the first one to break the silence, and while I'm grateful for that, it still strikes something uncomfortable deep within me that he's looking to *us* for a plan.

"We obviously can't take the train all the way to Prague," Mia says, still brushing gravel off her clothes as she walks. "I saw a road from the train just beyond the trees. Maybe we can hitchhike through Germany and across the Czech border."

"And say what to whoever picks us up?" I ask. "Tell them we came from where, to hitch this lift?"

"From the train," Mia says beside me. "Where some crazy person screamed that a fire had broken out. Better yet, make it some armed fugitive. We did what any sensible person would do, and ran for it. No need to mess too much with a story when it's already working."

Neal shoots me an impressed look over her head, with a healthy dose of *you-better-not-mess-this-up* and a side-serving of *any-disagreement-you're-having-is-probably-your-fault-because-she's-amazing*.

But it's not that simple, of course. She's right, and I'm right, and nobody's right, and I've never been less sure of what to do in all my life. Back on the train, she looked into my eyes and told me that wherever we went, we'd go together. I want—I *need*—that promise to be true. Hearing her talk about going to Prague again—knowing she'll go wherever she's going with me—makes me feel like I'm taking my first deep breath of the day. I just wish I knew what Prague holds in store for us.

I follow the others to the road that's busy with traffic, perhaps thanks to the evacuation. Mia, the smallest and least intimidating of us—at least until you get to know her—only takes a few minutes to flag down a car holding a middle-aged German couple, who turn out to be called Gisela and Luisa.

Mia's breathless story about a man with a gun on the train does the trick. The Germans aren't keen to hang about and ask for details when they have no way of knowing whether that imaginary man is still on the train or roaming the countryside.

We all have English as a common language, and Luisa uses it as she pulls back out into traffic. I can see her face in the mirror, and after a moment her eyes flick up to meet mine. But while Gisela is all sympathy, there's an edge in Luisa's eyes—something darker, a suspicion, perhaps—that makes me uneasy.

"We should take them to the police," she tells her wife. "But I'm not sure where. The train has come from France, ja? The gunman will be French?"

"The border is behind us," says Gisela absently, while looking at something on a tablet. I can barely see over her shoulder from where the three of us are crammed in the backseat. The cramped quarters are giving me flashbacks to my time in orbit, only this time Neal is shoved in on the other side of Mia.

"And we don't want to go back to France," Mia blurts quickly, her voice wavering. Her fear sounds real to me—I can see her white-knuckled grip on the edge of the seat and I'm not sure she's pretending at all. "The train went through—through Lyon."

Gisela looks up from the tablet, eyebrows lifting. "I am just reading that they no longer evacuate Lyon," she says quietly. "They quarantine the city."

"*What?*" Luisa nearly swerves into the next lane. "There are over a million people in Lyon!"

"And now," says Gisela, eyes on the screen, "that is where they will stay." She twists around in her seat to look back at the three of us, perhaps taking in properly for the first time how dusty and dirty we are. "Was it bad, what you saw there?"

"Yes," I say, because there's no point in lying.

She must read something of the truth in my face, for hers grows more solemn, and she hesitates a long moment before nodding. "I am guessing all your luggage is on that train." She glances across at Luisa, who has her eyes on the road, then continues. "I know you should go to the police, make a statement, but I don't think this is a good area to be in for much longer. This illness in Lyon . . ."

Luisa glances across at her for a moment, wary, switching to German, which she's no doubt assuming none of us will understand. "Was machst du, Schatz?" *What are you doing, darling?*

Gisela shoots her a quelling look, then continues in English: "We are driving across the country to our home, it is near Dresden, do you know it?"

I can feel Mia hesitate at my side, and I'm quick to jump in. "That's where we were going next, that's where we were hoping to get a flight home."

"I think you should come with us. Usually it is about seven hours, it might be a little longer with this traffic. We will take you to the station, or the airport, and you can arrange to go home."

Luisa shoots her another look, glances at me in the rearview mirror—clearly not sold on us—and then accelerates a little more aggressively into the next lane over.

"Sie sind nur Kinder," Gisela says, and though I certainly don't feel like a kid, not after everything we've been through, I'll take the excuse. No matter what we decide to do next, the fact that we're "just kids" won't help us if we end up back at the French border, talking to the police.

I look sideways at Mia, and she nods a fraction. Neal does the same. "Thank you," I say. "Today has been so frightening. We just want to go somewhere we can catch a plane back home to our parents. This was meant to be a safe holiday. We won't be any trouble, you won't even know we're in the backseat."

Luisa softens for that, and shoots her wife a long-suffering look. Then she's watching me again, suspicion warring with something familiar that I can't quite place. "Of course," she says finally— and once she says the words, she doesn't examine me in the mirror again.

Gisela maintains the peace by switching the radio to a local music station, and that precludes any chance of further conversation for the next hour. The countryside flashes by, and I try to press myself against the window to give Mia a little room—she's crammed between two lanky, long-legged water polo players like the meat in a very cramped sandwich.

My back's starting to really protest—funny how as soon as your life's not in immediate danger, you find time to notice other things—when my daydreams are shattered by a violent bang from somewhere up ahead.

Luisa abruptly yanks the wheel to the right, sending the car out onto the shoulder of the road with a scream of brakes and the crunch of gravel, dust and stones flying in every direction.

My seat belt locks into place, sending a bolt of pain through my collarbone as it keeps me from crashing into the back of Gisela's seat, and beside me I can hear Mia gasping for breath, wheezing helplessly as her lungs refuse to cooperate.

Out on the road in front of us is a white minivan lying on its side, blocking both lanes, windows smashed, trails of glass strewn over the road. It's as if someone just yanked the wheel to one side as the thing was going full speed.

*And oh, Deus, that's a day care center's logo on the door.*

Luisa's already scrambling out of the car, and the rest of us are quick to follow—we practically fall out as the doors open, and I can feel my legs shaking as I get my feet underneath me and stumble toward the van. I'm dimly aware that other cars are pulling up behind us, a series of bangs telling me some aren't managing to stop in time, but my focus is completely on the van, and the children I'm terrified are inside.

Luisa and Neal were on the side closest to the accident, and they're running with me on their heels—the underside of the van faces us, one of the wheels still spinning. The driver's side door faces skyward, and a bloodied woman comes bursting through the shattered window, snarling and clawing at the air like a wild animal.

I slam into Neal's broad back as he stops, and Mia slams into mine as we pile up like the cars behind us, and the woman sniffs the air, then starts trying to climb through the window, growling her displeasure at the tight fit. She must have hit her head, because she—

"Watch out!" Mia screams the warning behind me, and I whirl in time to see her grab Gisela, yanking her away from a pair of bloodied, blank-faced small children who have crawled out the broken back window of the minivan, and are stumbling toward her. One has blond hair in two long braids, the ends whipping back and forth as she staggers to one side.

We've seen blank faces like this before. We've seen—

"They're from Lyon!" Neal snaps, grabbing at Luisa's arm to keep her from stepping forward. "They're infected!"

His voice is loud enough that I immediately hear shouts from behind us, hear the news spread back down through the backed-up traffic, but I can't take my eyes off the mindless stare of the woman trying to escape from the minivan's window.

"We have to go," I hear myself say. "We have to go, we can't catch this from them. We have to get away."

My heart's breaking inside my chest, and my mind's all too ready to imagine—this woman must have tried to get the children out when the flu started showing up, she must have . . . She's a good person. *She tried.*

But now she's almost an animal, and so are they, and if this happens to us, then Earth loses the last people who know this is connected to the Undying. Who might be able to stop this thing from happening on a global scale.

We have to go.

And yet we all hesitate for one collective moment, desperately searching for something, anything, we can do. Then the woman snarls again, and as if a spell's been broken, we're freed from our paralysis, and we throw ourselves back into our own car.

There are more children now, climbing out of the broken windows of the van, and Gisela's sobbing as Luisa throws our car into reverse, the tires grinding against the gravel in her haste to get away. As she puts the car into drive I'm suddenly aware of the blast of horns behind us—of people who still have no idea what's happening here—and then everything's drowned out by the scream of metal as my side of the car drags along the safety barrier, and Luisa shoves us through the gap between the barriers and the back of the minivan.

And then we're accelerating, and nobody's speaking, and I can still hear Gisela crying over the soft sound of the radio as she dials the emergency number and reports what happened. She doesn't say anything about the three hitchhikers in her backseat.

After that, we're quiet. I don't doubt each of the others is doing exactly the same thing as me, replaying the crash over and over in their minds, wondering if there's anything we could have done for that woman, those children.

It's about half an hour later when Luisa speaks in a shaky voice. "That was what you saw in Lyon? Their minds gone?"

"Yes," Mia says quietly.

"The whole city?"

"We don't know," Mia admits. "But if they've quarantined them, then maybe. Soon, if not now."

Luisa slowly shakes her head. "By tomorrow, that city will be chaos," she murmurs. "I am . . . an electrician, you would say in

English. Lyon's power comes from their solar array, their power plant. Do you know what happens if the workers are too sick to run the plant? There is no power, almost immediately. This means no lights, no TV, no internet. No news, once the phone batteries run out. Electricity is needed to pump water, so nobody can drink. No traffic lights, so the town is in gridlock, and nobody can communicate to fix it. There is no way to process payment without electricity, so looting begins. If you take away power and then quarantine a city, whoever has not lost their minds inside it . . ."

"We must hope the government works quickly, finds the cure," Gisela says, reaching across to squeeze her wife's hand, voice still thick with tears.

Neal, Mia, and I exchange a long look, filled with all our exhaustion, and all our fear. Because the government doesn't know what they're up against, and they don't stand a chance.

Not long after, Luisa turns the wheel to the right, pulling off the road and into a service lane. My body's instantly back on high alert, and I feel Mia tense beside me, but a moment later, we're both breathing out. Up ahead is a service station—fuel, food, other conveniences all clustered together, with tired holidaymakers filling up the parking lot and hurrying in to restock before they continue their journeys. Oblivious to the disaster behind them.

"We must eat—time for lunch, I think," Luisa says, as she gives up on finding a proper parking space, and simply drives up onto a mostly dead, rather sad little grassy area. "We will return here in half an hour, ja? Do you Kinder have money?"

We mumble *yes* and *thank you* as we tumble out of the car and stretch our legs, and look around to get our bearings. All down the side of the car the doors are scratched and gouged from where Luisa forced us past the safety barrier.

I halfway wonder if Mia would've rather us pretend we *didn't* have money, in the hope of preserving our meager stash—but one look at her face tells me she has no more desire to bilk these people than I do. Not after what's just happened to all of us.

"Not to sound mistrustful," Neal says as we scan our surroundings, "but let's eat somewhere we can see the car, so we can conveniently turn up if it looks like they're going to change their minds and bolt. And somewhere cheap, this cash isn't going to last forever."

And so we end up in a little diner that has a booth against the glass wall between it and the parking lot, keeping one eye on our ride out of here while we do our best to find something edible on the menu. Which still seems an easier task than speaking freely, now we're alone.

I glance at Neal, hoping to signal him to break the silence, because I have no idea what to say myself. But his eyes are glued to his phone, giving me a flicker of indignation—the SIM card he brought me doesn't have any data left, so I can't use my watch to get to the internet without Wi-Fi. Which, judging from the state of this diner, is not something they've got on offer.

So instead, I mumble something about going up to place our order, and head up to the counter. German isn't my best language—I can understand and speak it fine, but I can never get the accent exactly right. The lady behind the counter, a stout, middle-aged waitress with deeply etched frown lines and her hair in a severe bun, nevertheless smiles a warm, friendly smile when I order our sandwiches in my accented German. She bustles off to deliver the order to the kitchen, leaving me alone at the counter.

My whole body tingles, torn between ravenous hunger at the smell of food, and horror still singing through me from the crash and its aftermath. But we have to eat, as Luisa pointed out.

I linger as long as I can, making a show of inspecting the case of desserts while I pull myself together. It'd be foolish to waste our money on junk, especially after living off of vending machine snacks for the last day, but I can't help but gaze longingly at the Käsekuchen and Bienenstich. The latter has the perfect layer of caramelized nuts on top, and I can just imagine the way the custard and almond cake taste.

With a sigh, I turn back—and see that Mia's migrated to Neal's side of the table, and that they're sitting with their heads together, practically in each other's laps. My throat closes for an instant, my heart doing a strange, staggering flip-flop in my chest. It doesn't matter that it can't possibly be what it looks like—even after I spy the phone in Neal's hand, the reason they're both bent over like that, my heart's still lurching by the time I slide back into my seat.

"Jules." Mia looks up, her eyes as wide as I've ever seen them. My lurching heart lurches harder, some nameless apprehension seizing me—but then I see her eyes are more awed than afraid. "Jules, you aren't going to believe this. The video Neal posted—it's got over half a million views already."

"What?" Stunned, I start to reach out for the phone, but Mia shakes her head.

"That's not even the best part. There's a whole group of people here on our side. They're commenting on the video, sharing the info they've seen, linking back to forums . . . Jules, there's an entire website devoted to people who believe your dad is right about the Undying."

The words flit about my ears without really sinking in, leaving me staring at the two of them. Mia's face has hope in it for what feels like the first time in weeks, and Neal's solemn expression is cracking around the edges, pleasure in his eyes and at the corners of his mouth as he tries not to smile.

Mia hands me Neal's phone. "That's the video. Then look at the other tab he's got open."

I switch between the video player and the browser, still feeling as opaque and numb as a block of ice—and it's true.

#IBelieveInAddison, the website reads at the top. There are articles—painstakingly sourced, from reputable newspapers and magazines—and forums and even a bloody *resources* page. When I tap on that, there are links to different translations of the Undying broadcast, transcripts of interviews my father gave leading up to his "freak-out" on TV, and—my heart seizes.

Are the undying already here? Only credible accounts please—check your sources! Baseless speculation will NOT be tolerated, and your posts will be removed!

The link goes to another page under the same domain. And on that page . . .

My poor heart gives up on calm entirely, and I swipe through the feed with shaking fingers. This is no crazy conspiracy-theory group—everything is meticulously researched, and as a scholar I don't use that phrase lightly. And they know, collectively, *almost* as much as we do. More, in some cases.

There's a section devoted to the "UFO" crash De Luca mentioned back at IA Headquarters, the Undying shuttle that was never recovered and dismissed as a hoax. There's a section in which experts—real experts, names I even *recognize* from the field, names I thought had abandoned my father after his televised outburst—try to construct theories about a potential invasion.

There's even one article that comes alarmingly close to the truth, put together by someone whose name I don't even recognize—a teenager, it turns out, younger even than Mia and me. The article suggests that the Undying wouldn't try to take Earth in an all-out war, but that the evidence so far—and this kid has gathered an unbelievable amount of evidence, gleaned from article after article, all listed at the end—suggests a stealth operation of some kind.

These people are organized and determined. There's a section indicating the site has been shut down several times already—by the IA, they claim, and I doubt they're wrong—and assuring forum participants that all data has been saved, and will be re-uploaded in under an hour at a new location.

*The harder they try to stamp us out,* it says, *the louder we'll shout our truth.*

And beneath all these stories, all this news, there's an addition with today's date to the end of the article: a link to Neal's video, and a single sentence: If mankind is reduced to mindless beasts concerned only with survival, the Undying won't need an army.

I look up to meet Mia's gaze. She's been watching my face rather than my hands as I navigate the site, and her eyes are red-rimmed with emotion. "You and your dad aren't alone," she whispers, eyes glimmering with unshed tears. "You never were. They *believe* him."

*She's crying because she knows how much it means to me,* I realize, an instant before my own eyes spill over and I have to set the phone down and swipe at my cheeks.

There are thousands of members in the #IBelieveInAddison forum. Hundreds of articles and links posted. There's nothing official about any of it—from the Harvard head of xenobiology we used to host for dinner, right on down to the teenager gathering news articles after school, they're just people. No one gave them permission to do this. No one asked it of them. They're just people who saw an educator, a scientist, a father, speaking with the voice of knowledge and passion, be silenced—and they decided not to let that voice disappear. People who decided truth was more important than power.

I never forgave the world after it ruined my father. Before that, I'd always believed that right would prevail, that fear and hatred weren't powerful enough to stop the spread of understanding, and that ignorance would always, *always*, fall before truth.

That one open mind could change the world.

And then I saw my father, a gentle, kind man who wears moth-eaten sweaters and never remembers to finish his tea before it goes cold, dragged off a news set by men holding guns. And not only did the world I thought I knew let it happen, they went on to humiliate him over and over on the internet, turning a photo of him being dragged away into a meme saying *GTFO,* auto-tuning his impassioned speech over a beat, and holding him up as an example of why "intellectuals" ought to be ridiculed.

Some part of me saw the world I'd believed in destroyed, and replaced with this mistrustful, apathetic, ignorant planet that made it *easy* to strike out for a new one.

The articles on this site aren't enough to free my father. They're probably not even enough to convince the IA to listen to us if—*when*, I correct myself—we get to Prague. But there are thousands of people out there, probably tens of thousands if you take into account those who read but don't post, who are our allies, even though they don't know it yet.

We're not alone.

A touch on my palm draws me back to myself, and I realize Mia's wrapped both her hands around mine. Either she's forgotten about Neal—who's watching with the widest grin I've ever seen—or she doesn't care. In that moment none of the fights we've had or hurts we've caused each other exist. She's just holding my hand while my world shudders and quakes and slips along its fault lines and forms something new. Something stronger.

That phone, resting quietly on the table between us, has just shown me the one thing I've wanted most, wanted so badly I could feel it in my bones, ever since the IA took my father from me. I'd believed that if I could find something he missed, even the tiniest scrap of proof, it'd be enough to convince them that my father was right. That he'd be released and come home to me.

But I'm realizing now that it wasn't just about bringing him home—it was about saving the world. *My* world, the one I wanted to live in. It's why I went to Gaia, it's the whole reason I abandoned my academic future to become a criminal, it's what I was willing to sacrifice everything for.

This is what I was willing to die for.

Maybe my revelation on the train was true. Maybe I can't go home, back to how it was before. But maybe wherever we're headed can be better.

18

AMELIA

THE SOUNDS OF WHEELS CRUNCHING ON GRAVEL WAKES ME. DISORIENTED, all my senses grope for something recognizable—the only thing they come up with is a scent I'd recognize anywhere, more familiar to me than the desert winds of Chicago. I lift my head from Jules's chest to find him sitting next to me, head flung back over the edge of the backseat, totally passed out. I have to fight the urge to laugh, before I remember where we are.

Tension wakes me the rest of the way. The last thing I remember was Gisela putting on some intensely boring orchestra music that nonetheless seemed to delight Jules. *Of course he'd like classical music,* I'd thought, rolling my eyes but secretly rather charmed. It had been mid-afternoon then, an hour or two after we'd stopped for lunch.

It's dark outside now. Gisela and Luisa are still in the front seats, little more than silhouettes—though I can see that Luisa's got one arm stretched out, and her fingers are curled around her wife's hand as she drives. Neal's on my other side, slumped forward, with his head pressed awkwardly against the seat back in front of him, mouth hanging open. Both boys are contorted into what look like horrifically uncomfortable positions—but then, they're used to being tall in a world designed for shorter people.

I ought to have stayed awake, because right now, I don't trust *anyone*. But if this couple had wanted to bring us to the police or dump us somewhere, they'd have had ample time during the hours we were asleep.

Jules sucks in a deeper breath and then lets it out in the tiniest of snores, like a puppy chasing rabbits in his sleep—and in spite of myself I start to laugh. I try to stifle it, but my shaking body is still in the crook of his arm, and it jars him awake.

From the front seat, Luisa says with only a tiny bit of her usual edge, "Are you now awake?"

"Arggh," says Neal on my other side. He sits up with another creaking groan, staring blankly at the seat back his face was pressed against. After a moment, he swipes his sleeve at what I'm guessing is a patch of drool left behind.

"We are now in our town, very close to Dresden." Gisela's voice is much friendlier than her wife's. "But it is late. Our house is not large, but we often invite our friends to visit us, and we have a little guest cottage. If you would like you can sleep there, and Luisa will drive you on to Dresden in the morning."

Jules is still sleepy—he never did wake up very fast, even on Gaia—and manages to get as far as remembering his arm's around me, and giving me a squeeze. I interpret that as a yes, but the couple's seemingly selfless gesture triggers my silent alarm, the hairs on the back of my neck lifting.

"Um," I say, before coughing to clear the gravel from my voice. "Thanks, but we really need to keep moving."

Jules sits up straighter and looks at me. Even in the darkness I can see his furrowed brow. "Hang on," he says softly. "We're exhausted. We can't, uh, we can't get tickets back to London in the middle of the night."

I eye him, hoping he can see some of the edge in my look.

"We've depended upon these two for too much already." I'm hoping, with the stress in my voice, that he'll understand: Why would two perfect strangers allow us to stay with them when we have no money, no way to repay them, nothing to offer at all except more trouble for them to go to?

In the front seat, the couple are conversing in low voices, ostensibly discussing plans for making us comfortable—but in reality, providing cover for us to speak a little more privately.

Jules watches me, brow still furrowed. "What makes you think we can't trust them?" he whispers.

"What makes you think we *can?*" I retort. If I'd been them, and seen what we saw after that car crash, I wouldn't be taking *any* risks. They could have heard or seen some sort of bulletin about us while we were asleep, and be planning to call the authorities once they get us settled in that guest cottage.

The furrow in Jules's brow eases, and I see his lips twitch into one of those wry smiles that tells me he's about to score a point. "Instinct," he replies, lifting the arm around me to smooth back a bit of hair from my eyes.

*Instinct.* The word I used to convince him to jump through the portal back in the heart of that Gaian temple. Of course, I kissed him too, which might've had something to do with his decision to follow me through. From the gleam in his eye, he's remembering both.

My nerves are still jangling, and I close my eyes a moment. I'm trying to think, to figure out whether my unease is because I don't trust *them* or because I never trust anyone. I honestly can't tell which it is.

"All right," I say, once there's a lull in the quiet conversation between the couple in the front of the car. "That's really nice of you. I guess we could use some real sleep."

Their house is small, a single story with one bedroom and an open-plan living space and kitchen. The cottage out back is even tinier, with a little twin bed and a cramped half bathroom, but everything about it is so cozy that by the time Gisela uncovers fresh sheets for the bed and Luisa brings in a couple granola bars and some apples, my misgivings about trusting the kindness of strangers have all but vanished.

Neal, who'd been in the kitchen in the main house helping Luisa cut up the apples, sticks his head into the cottage and gives a quick laugh. "Yeah, um, can I sleep on the couch in there?" He jerks a thumb over his shoulder at the main house. "This thing is not big enough for three."

Luisa opens her mouth to reply, looking a little stern, but Gisela beats her to it. "Of course! I should have thought of this. We will get sheets."

Neal grins. "I'll help."

"Wait—" I reach out, a sudden flare of panic making me bold, and grab Neal by the arm. "You should stay out here. You're tall like Jules, you'll fit better on the bed. I'm small, I'll take the couch."

Neal snorts, rolling his eyes toward his cousin, whose face is unreadable as he watches us. "Bugger that. Last time Jules and I bunked together, I woke up with a fat lip. You can't put two people this tall in a bed that size. Way too many elbows." Gently but firmly, Neal detaches my hand from his arm. "Most nights I end up sleeping on the couch in my dorm anyway. Night, guys."

And he's gone, leaving me and Jules alone in the little house.

We spent so much time alone on Gaia, on the ship, you'd think we'd be used to it. But so much has happened, and now there's silence, I find I have no idea where to start any of the conversations we should have.

I'm brisk as I turn for the low dresser where they've left the granola bars and apples. "Well, tomorrow's probably going to be insane, trying to get across the border into the Czech Republic, so it's probably a good thing we've got a place to sleep."

Jules sits down on the end of the bed, the only real place to sit in the little cottage. "What's wrong?"

I shake my head, inspecting the wrapper of the granola bar

like I can make any sense of the German ingredients list. "I don't know."

"If you want I can take some blankets and sleep on the floor."

That makes me look over at him, surprise momentarily eclipsing my unease. "What? No, that's—that's stupid." Except that he's managed to zero in on exactly what's making me want to cry. I know I'm exhausted, I know my emotions right now are probably not to be trusted. But the very fact that I'm so tired means I can barely fight the things that want to come out. The same things— the same insecurities—that have always stood between us.

"We've slept together—I mean, you know, actually *slept*—tons of times. On Gaia in the temple, in the ship at the Junction . . . Is it Gisela and Luisa? You still think—"

"That was on Gaia," I interrupt. "And on the ship. This is different."

"Different how?" Jules's voice is patient, *too* patient—it makes me want to snap, just to make him crack like me.

"Different because—because we were going to die there together on Gaia. And on that ship. Because there, our differences weren't so . . . We were more alike there, the things that separated us didn't matter because we were surrounded by everything alien. Here, it's . . . it's *different*."

"You only kissed me because you thought we were going to die?"

I turn to find Jules still sitting on the foot of the bed, his hands clasped in his lap, watching me. His face is calm, but his eyes are wounded, and my throat tightens.

"No, of course not." I swallow. "Maybe. God, Jules—what do you think is going to happen, really? I'd say we were just being teenagers, just hormones and fooling around and it's no big deal, but that's not *true*. I know that, you know that." I pause, a sudden fear seizing me. "Right?"

A little of the hurt in his gaze fades, the lamplight catching in his curly hair, frizzy from sleeping in the car. "So why is that a bad thing?"

"Because it's impossible now." I tell myself it's the exhaustion making my voice wobble. "Even if everything works out, even if Neal can get in to see your father, and he shuts down the portals and stops the Undying and we're somehow forgiven for all our crimes . . . We live on separate continents. I can barely afford to feed myself, and every spare penny goes to Evie—it's not like I can fly to London and see you. And you've got your school, and your dad, and your life, you can't just drop everything and come visit me while I go back to my life of petty thievery. I mean, what do you think is going to happen when all this is over?"

A muscle stands out along Jules's jaw as he clenches it, and he drops his eyes for a moment. When he looks up, that hurt is back, and with it a flicker of anger. "I guess I thought we'd both try to fight for it. For whatever this is."

Frustration sings through me as I toss the granola bar back onto the dresser and turn the rest of the way to face him. "Do you have any idea how naïve that sounds?" I blurt. "You don't know anything about me—you've lived your whole life in your sheltered Oxford bubble. Things *aren't* going to work out. Odds are, if we survive this, I'm going to jail. I'll be a *felon*, Jules. Do you really want a relationship based on a ten-minute phone call once a week from prison?"

The hands clasped in his lap tighten, his knuckles whitening, and then he gets slowly to his feet. There's nowhere to go in the tiny place, though, so he just stands there, lips tight. "So you don't even want to try? I thought . . . I thought you felt the same way I did."

"You don't get it." I stare at him helplessly. "One way or another, I'm going to lose you. When all this is over, I'm going to *lose* you. And that's what I think about every time you touch me, every time I want to—to kiss you, every time I *look* at you. I remember I'm going to lose you."

Something clears in Jules's eyes, their warm brown softening as understanding spreads across his face. "Because everything is different now."

Throat too tight for speech, I nod, feeling a tear slide down past my nose.

Jules steps forward until we're close, but not touching. He doesn't try to take my hand, or kiss me, or even wipe away the tear that his eyes track down my cheek. "I'm not going to let that happen." He's as serious, as intent, as he's ever been. More so even than he was on Gaia, fixated on his mission. "And neither are you. You're not giving either of us enough credit."

"But—"

"Mia, we've been to the other side of the universe and back. We traveled to the heart of an ancient alien temple, we survived pitfalls and scavenger attacks and double-crossing secret agents, and we're about to save the world. Do you honestly think an ocean is going to stop us?"

My mind scrambles to dismiss what he's saying, despite how much I long to be convinced. "It's not the same thing—I was doing it for Evie. And you were doing it for your dad. Everything we've managed to do, we were doing it for people we—"

I stop abruptly, the word sticking in my throat, my whole body freezing.

Jules waits, but when I don't go on, he suggests, "For people we love?"

I'm still frozen, my eyes fixed on his chin rather than his face, too afraid to look up to see his eyes.

Jules takes a slow breath, close enough that it stirs my hair when he lets it out again. "We haven't known each other very long. But we know each other *well*. And yes, it breaks pretty much every rule there is when it comes to what makes sense, what's logical." He ducks his head until he can catch my eye, reluctant though I am to let him. "But you're *Amelia Radcliffe*. When have you ever given a toss about the rules?"

His face is so familiar, so earnestly kind, that my fears and my pain slip away, as tangible and fleeting as the tear about to drop off my cheek. Something settles, deep in my mind—a truth I've been ignoring, denying, even fighting.

Whatever it is, Jules sees it in my face. His eyebrows lift. "Do you want me to sleep on the floor?" There's no guile there, no attempt to guilt me one way or the other. It's gentle, that offer.

Swallowing hard, I shake my head.

His mouth curves a little, and the warmth in his gaze sharpens as it drops a little past my eyes. "Then can I kiss you now?" he asks, watching my lips.

*Rules be damned.*

"Hell yes."

## 19

## JULES

**MY HAND'S SHAKING AS I RAISE IT TO CURVE MY PALM AROUND THE** back of Mia's neck, brushing my thumb across her cheek to erase the gleaming track the tear left behind. And then one of us makes a sound—me, I think—and I'm leaning into her, every part of me utterly alive.

A shock and a shiver run through me as our lips meet, and a piece of me is noticing how soft her lips are, while the rest of me spins out slowly. I've wanted this so badly, and now, as her hands come to rest on my chest, I'm perfectly aware of the thump of my heart, the press of her fingers through my shirt, the warmth of her skin.

I haven't kissed that many girls before, and I've never been that sure of myself, but this is effortless. Mia's hands press harder against my chest, and I take a step back until I'm leaning against the wall. Then her hands slide up to curl around my neck, and mine are at the curve of her hips, and she's lifting up on her toes to chase a deeper, hungrier kiss.

She's perfect, this girl in my arms. This is nothing like the hurried kisses we've shared before, in the moments before risking our lives. Now, I lose myself in her, my fingers finding a sliver of skin at the hem of her shirt, sliding in beneath the fabric so my fingertips can trace up her spine.

I don't know how much time passes before we stop, both breathing quickly, our eyes meeting. I know I'm wearing a foolish smile, and hers isn't so very far behind mine, and I want to gaze at her forever.

"Hi," I murmur, because I've forgotten all the other words except that one.

"Hi," she murmurs back, and then we gaze at each other for just a little longer, as she slowly comes down from her toes to rest on the flats of her feet once more.

"We should go to bed," I say quietly, and the instant the words are out, I hear them again, and my eyes widen, and I splutter a noise that doesn't appear in any language I've ever learned. "Deus, I mean we should go to *sleep*, it's been a long day, and we have another in the morning, and—"

Mia saves me from myself by lifting her hand to cover my mouth. "Quit while you're ahead, Oxford," she suggests, a smile playing across her lips. "I'm with you. One step at a time is fine by me. Let's go to sleep."

"We should be rested, in case we want to try this again in the morning," I say, trying for gravity and falling short.

"Count on it," she replies, tugging me toward the bed.

• • •

In the end, though, I can't sleep. Mia lies in my arms, her slow, even breathing marking out the tempo I should be following. We had a couple of false starts in the going-to-sleep business, but eventually we conquered distraction long enough for her to pass out, and I wish I could do the same.

My heart won't let me, though. I know it was just a kiss, only a kiss, but it wasn't *just* anything. There's not an ounce of *only* in a moment like that.

It was everything.

*She's* my everything, my safe place. Tomorrow, we'll have to rise and face the world once more, face border crossings and the IA and the knowledge that the Undying are on the verge of invading, and that my father's behind endless layers of security, and wonder when our luck will run out.

But tonight, Mia lies here in my arms, and I know we're making a promise to each other. This moment, as I hold her, I'm echoing back the promise to me that she made on the train.

*Amelia Radcliffe, I'm with you. And I'm not leaving you. Wherever we go, we'll go together.*

## 20

### AMELIA

GISELA SENDS US OFF IN THE MORNING WITH A MASSIVE BREAKFAST of eggs and thick slices of spicy sausage, freshly baked rolls with marmalade and honey, and coffee strong enough to strip the enamel from our teeth. Neal eyes us speculatively over his roll, and I know I'm probably blushing, but Jules just grins at him and tucks into his breakfast.

The day is bright and sunny, and once we're off the gravel road again, I curl up in my seat behind Neal. Luisa's driving us, since Gisela has work, so we're not all crammed in the backseat like before. I'm still basking a little in the warmth of last night, and I lean back in my seat with a sigh.

Neal's half turned around in his seat so he and Jules can exchange barbs and teases—they act the way I imagine brothers would act, and I feel a pang as I watch them. The world can't support siblings anymore, not with the resources Earth has. My parents broke the law by having Evie, but she's always been everything in the world that's important to me. I can't imagine my life without her.

It's easy to say the single-child rules are unfair. Easy to know Evie and I are right to stick together. But so much of the world is starving—for food, for medicine, for electricity, for education—that indiscriminately bringing more kids into a world that can't feed them . . . that can't be right either. Jules and Neal are proof that close bonds exist outside of sibling relationships. And true, they *are* family—but at this point, Jules and I are family too. Even if our world can't support large biological families anymore, maybe there's something to be said for found families. Chosen ones.

I watch out the window, my thoughts meandering lazily, and I'm breathing more easily than I have in a long time. In the distance I can see Dresden, past the highway and across the river. Even this far away, I can see it's an astonishingly beautiful city—I'm ashamed to admit even to myself that I'd never heard of it, and imagined some dinky, forgettable place. But there are graceful domed buildings, and towers that look like something out of an ancient fairy tale, and a stone bridge with archways for river boats to pass beneath. I find myself wishing we really *were* going there as tourists, so we could just take it all in.

*Except . . . we* aren't *going there, are we?*

I sit up, blinking. The city's in the distance, vanishing behind us, and we're on a highway.

Heading away.

"Jules." I grab for his arm, and something about my tone makes him stop mid-sentence and look at me. "The city's behind us."

Jules leans across me, craning his head to look out the window. Ease and humor vanished, he demands, "Where are you driving us?"

Luisa is silent, her eyes on the road ahead of her.

Panic sears through me, and I'm half a breath away from fumbling at the door handle, despite the idiocy of leaving a moving car speeding down the highway. "Stop the car!" I harden my voice. "Let us out, we'll hitch from here."

Neal levels a hard stare at Luisa. "You said you were driving us to Dresden."

*I was right. They did recognize us. They had us stay so they could contact the authorities, and now she's driving us to the police. De Luca or Captain Abrantes is going to be waiting for us, and we'll be shoved back into a cell, and we'll never get to Jules's dad, and the world will end. . . .*

Luisa draws in a breath. Her hands are tight on the steering wheel, knuckles showing white. "We are now a half hour from the border with Tschechien—with the Czech Republic. You wish I would turn the car around?"

That stops us all short. I end up staring at Jules, who gazes back at me with equal confusion before looking over at Neal, who just shrugs, looking baffled and petrified all at once.

Not once did we ever mention we were trying to get to Prague. We'd planned on hitchhiking from Dresden if we couldn't find bicycles, because it wasn't that far to the border, and that way Luisa and Gisela would have nothing to tell the authorities about where we went even *if* the IA managed to connect us to them.

Abruptly, Neal rummages in his bag, and as he moves aside a hoodie, I hear the sound that made him start hunting—a faint chiming. Luisa glances across at him, but evidently dismisses the sound as a notification from his phone. I watch from my place in the backseat as he pulls out the electronic device Dex left on the pillow back in Montpellier, and checks the screen before wordlessly turning it so we can see. It's faint, at the edge of the screen, and even as we watch, the little green blip flickers out and the chiming stops.

There are Undying in Dresden, too. Like there were in Lyon, when the flu broke out.

I look at Jules, whose hands curls tightly around mine. We can't go there—we can't warn them, because no one would believe us. We don't know how the Undying are connected to the disease spreading across Europe, only that they *are* connected.

The only thing we can do is get to Dr. Addison and give him what he needs to shut down the portals and stop the Undying.

Luisa is still driving in tense silence. Jules squeezes my fingers, as much to comfort himself as to comfort me, and I try to calm the anxiety roiling around in my stomach. Instead I just feel like throwing up.

The border is crowded. I have no basis for comparison, but judging from the frazzled looks on the faces of travelers and officials alike, I'm guessing the heightened security across Europe is slowing everything down.

Luisa pulls the car into an empty space some distance from the crossing itself. She leaves the motor running, but puts it into park and then passes a hand over her face.

"I hope you have . . . gefälscht? Das Wort ist . . . *fake?* I hope you have fake papers. I do not know how you will cross, I do not want to know. But I know your face from the Zeitung. From the newspaper." She looks up at the rearview mirror, watching Jules.

Jules's hand tightens around mine. "Have you told anyone else about us?"

"My wife, even she does not know." Luisa retrieves her handbag from under her seat and pulls out a thick envelope, which she then clutches in one hand as she turns in her seat to look at all of us. Her face is still troubled, still suspicious, still rather severe, as she regards us. "I do not know whether I should stop you, but I think you are good Kinder. These times, they are . . ." She stops to hunt for the word. "Frightening. You go to find your father, ja?"

I hold my breath, my eyes on Jules. He swallows, quiet for a long time. Then, he says simply, "Yes."

Luisa hands the envelope to Neal, who opens it enough to show a stack of euro notes before he closes it and looks up, wide-eyed.

Suddenly, unable to hold it in anymore, I blurt: "Don't go back to Dresden." The innocent chime of the Undying locator is ringing in my ears. "Take Gisela and go somewhere safe—somewhere away from the city."

Luisa's looking at me now in the mirror, and though she hesitates, she nods after a long moment. "I will. Go, I do not want someone to see you in my Auto."

Confused, torn between suspicion and gratitude, we all fumble with our seat belts and the door handles. My legs feel wobbly, and the heat of the sun reflecting off the pavement feels like an oven despite the cool morning air. We all stand there beside the car, unmoving, staring at each other—until Luisa rolls down the passenger's side window.

"When you see your father," she says, just before she shifts the car back into drive and pulls away, "tell him I believe in Addison."

My heart's still racing as we stand there, watching her car vanish back over the slight rise in the road. I find my gaze pulled toward Jules, whose face is nearly unreadable—but only *nearly*. I can see his lips a fraction tighter than normal, the slight drawing in of his brows, the tiny flare of his nostrils as he struggles to breathe normally. It was one thing to see anonymous avatars online in support of his father—another to stumble upon one in real life.

Luisa's suspicion toward us, at least in comparison with her wife, makes sense now. If she'd recognized Jules as Addison's son, it would've made everything real for her too. Using a hashtag or posting a comment in a forum is easy. Breaking the rules and choosing a side and fighting for what you believe is far harder.

I reach for Jules's hand, a tiny part of me worried that he won't want that support just now, or that it'll make him crack and cry, or—but his fingers curl around mine without hesitation.

Neal lets out his breath in an audible whoosh, and scrubs his hands over his close-cropped hair. "I guess we'd better try our luck at the border."

The lines of cars at the gatehouses stretch far back beyond the border itself, but the booth for hikers and cyclists has far fewer people waiting. It's not until we fall into step at the end of the line, though, that we see why there are lines at all.

A dozen uniformed IA security officers are conducting searches of travelers' belongings, asking them questions, and conducting random inspections of documentation.

Neal shifts his weight from one foot to the other, trying not to look nervous. "Should we duck out of line, try to sneak across somewhere else like in France?"

"I don't think we can," I murmur, anxiety sharpening my voice a little. "If we go now, after seeing the security officers, it'll be a dead giveaway that we've got something to hide."

Jules's eyes are scanning the people currently being questioned at the crossing. "They're looking at everyone—I don't think they're looking for us specifically. We've still got our fake passports."

"And they're only doing close inspections at random." My voice sounds far more confident than I feel. "Odds are they won't look twice at our passports, and we've got nothing incriminating in our bags."

"Except this." Jules pulls out Dex's tracker from his pocket. "But given that they didn't believe us when we were standing next to an Undying landing craft, I doubt anyone's going to think this is strange."

Neal draws in a breath, brows furrowed. "Then we act like everything's normal, and hope we don't get stopped."

The line drags itself forward, and with each shuffling step my heart rate speeds up, and we come closer to the IA officers ahead. I put myself in between Jules and Neal, so that we're clearly a group—if one of us gets stopped, we might be able to pull the *but I've got to stick with my boyfriend* trick and follow—because I bluff better than either of them.

We make sure we've all got our passports ready and our bags open, so that we'll spend as little time in front of the officers as possible. And I murmur to them not to try to avert their faces, to meet the eyes of the inspection crew for a second, smile faintly, and then break eye contact—not enough for them to really remember us, but enough that it doesn't seem like we're avoiding them.

Jules's backpack is mostly vending machine junk food and dirty laundry, and he gets a little eyebrow lift from the officer inspecting it once we reach the front of the line. He shrugs—I told him to speak as little as possible, just in case the British accent somehow cues them to his identity—and smiles at her, and she hands it back with a roll of her eyes.

"Wait until you're in your thirties," she murmurs wistfully. She speaks English with only the slightest trace of an accent. The IA trains their agents well. "You won't be able to eat like this, that's for sure. Now, I've just got another couple of questions. First, can you count down from one hundred for me, in increments of seven?"

Jules blinks at her, but after an encouraging nod from the official, he begins.

"One hundred, ninety-three, eighty-six, seventy-nine, seventy-two . . ."

"Thank you," she says, glancing down at her screen and hitting a button.

Neal leans down so he can speak to me in a whisper. "That's a question from the Mini-Mental State Exam, I did it in a psychology class at uni. They're checking for deterioration in cognitive function."

"Lyon," I murmur, as the woman lets Jules through. They're looking for people in the early stages of infection.

Another of the IA officials finishes with his traveler, but I'm quick to head for the woman who let Jules through. She was friendly, at least, and that might be helpful. Let Neal—with his valid passport and lack of criminal record—head for the unknown quantity.

"I keep telling him the same thing about eating all that crap in his backpack," I say conspiratorially to the IA officer when I hand over my bag. My heart is going a thousand beats per second, and my palms are sweaty, but I summon an air of bored patience, the exact sort of stereotypical teenaged apathy that makes most people not bother thinking twice about me.

The guard smiles briefly at me, and looks through the odds and ends in my bag, which aren't much better than Jules's. "Kids," she says dismissively, but with a bit of humor in her gaze. She reaches under her table, pulling out a protein bar and set of headphones, holding both up for me to see. "Can you name these, please?"

"That's a protein bar, and those are headphones," I say, making sure I look baffled. "Um, do I need to know about those in the Czech Republic?"

She offers a quick, reassuring smile. "Just a new procedure from International Alliance HQ, nothing to worry about. Enjoy your time in the Czech Republic."

Relief sweeps across me, making me dizzy as I grope for my bag, mumble a thank-you, and hurry my steps toward where Jules waits with an exaggerated air of nonchalance that would make me laugh, if I weren't so unraveled myself.

The other officer hands Neal his bag and his papers, and he turns toward us with an inimitable grin, slinging it back over his shoulder.

But he doesn't get two steps before the officer he'd been speaking to calls, "Hang on a second."

Neal stops, flashing us a brief look of panic, before turning back to the officer. The man scans his features with a frown. "You look familiar. Step this way, please."

*Shit. Shit shit shit.*

Of course, Neal isn't wanted for anything—not as far as we know. But the last name on his passport *is* Addison, and while that's not exactly a unique name, it wouldn't be hard to make a case that he'd know something about one of the fugitives from IA custody.

The officer brings Neal over to the booth, tapping at the window and asking some question of someone inside. Neal flashes us another look, this one far more grave and fearful—and then I realize why. The official's given a printout by someone inside the little office, and though I can't see what it is from here, I do see a pair of photos at the top.

It's a wanted bulletin.

"He looks like me," Jules whispers. "Maybe our official hadn't seen the bulletin or something—but Neal's getting stopped because we look alike."

I bite at my lip, my thoughts paralyzed. "We've got to just go. They'll see he's not you, and they'll let him go, but we can't be around for them to—"

"Excuse me, would you two please come this way?" One of the regular immigration officials gestures us over. "You're traveling together, right?"

Two more IA officers have joined the one detaining Neal.

"No," I lie, "we just met in line. We've got to go if we're going to stick to our hiking schedule. . . ."

The first officer glances our way, and then his puzzled expression vanishes, replaced with surprise and a hint of grim satisfaction. "That's them. This one—maybe he's related, I don't know, but look, isn't that them?"

Jules's hand grabs for mine and squeezes. Somehow, I recognize from his grip what he wants to do—and just now I've got no better ideas. If we run, there's a chance we could make it past the parked cars on the other side of the crossing, and down the embankment on the far side of the highway before anyone could organize a chase.

The officers have guns—but they wouldn't fire on a couple of teenagers. Especially since it's not like we're wanted for murder or armed robbery. But then, I haven't seen whatever wanted bulletin went out. I don't know what the IA is saying about us. I don't *know*.

And seeing a line of IA uniformed officers, all with rifles slung over their backs, makes my legs feel weak and rubbery.

I squeeze back, holding for a while, and then release. "I'm not sure what you're talking about," I say aloud. For Jules, I squeeze his hand once, twice—I ready myself to run, and tighten my hand a third time.

"Hold your questions," a crisp, authoritative voice calls. A woman in an IA Intelligence uniform strides past us. "I'll take it from here."

"Intelligence has no authority at border crossings," protests the officer detaining Neal. "This is a directive from international security to detain and question those two."

The woman retrieves Neal from the officer holding his arm. "Call De Luca's office yourself if you want an explanation. But I outrank you, Officer, and I had breakfast with De Luca this morning, and I don't owe you anything."

Neal, baffled, stumbles along as the woman steers him toward us. I don't blame him for his confusion—I'm confused myself, and Jules's hand in mine has gone lax with shock.

The woman ushering Neal toward us, and gesturing for us to come with her, is Mink.

21

JULES

"LET'S GO," MINK SAYS TIGHTLY, AND MIA AND I EXCHANGE A glance that contains a whole conversation.

*What's she doing here?*

*I don't know.*

*Can we trust her?*

*When have we ever been able to trust her?*

*Do we have a choice?*

*I don't know.*

As if sensing our doubts, Mink speaks in a low voice. "I said, let's go. Unless you want a bullet in the back, you'll shut up and come with me without making a fuss."

My breath catches in my throat, my whole body responding to the threat.

I don't doubt she's capable of shooting us. We've seen her do it before, and she's got a gun holstered at her waist.

Before I have a chance to reply, or even to think, the IA officials have caught up with us once more, all protesting volubly.

With an exasperated look at the crew of genuinely innocent civilians waiting for their own border-crossing inspection—all of whom are straining their ears to figure out what's going on with this sudden burst of activity—she opens the door to the guard-house and marches inside, all of us following her like a confused, terrified, and in some cases outraged, parade.

Mink points at what looks like the guards' break room. "You three, in there." *The adults need to talk* is the unspoken corollary to that.

We do as we're told, and I leave the door carefully ajar so we can overhear the territorial dispute happening outside. I hover by the crack for a few moments, straining my ears.

A man's voice is speaking, loud and strident. "With respect, ma'am, nobody is taking anybody anywhere until I've scanned your ID."

Mia's already on the far side of the room, and my eyes widen as I realize she's stuffing the jacket of an IA uniform inside her backpack.

"What are you doing?" I hiss, despite the fact that the answer is bloody obvious.

"What I can," she replies, shoving the fabric down and cinching the bag closed. "I don't know what's coming next, but let's be ready as we can be."

"There's an ID in this locker," Neal says, pulling out a card on a lanyard, and tossing it across the room to Mia, then closing the door of the locker beside him.

With a nod, she shoves it in her bag.

Deus, they're two of a kind.

My attention's yanked back to the door when a series of piercing beeps emanates from some kind of machine. I hear the man's voice again.

"This identification has been suspended."

Mink's voice is rich with scorn. "Bullshit, it was working just fine when Director De Luca sent me to pick them up."

*De Luca. Have they made their peace, or is she just throwing his name around for authority?*

"Nevertheless," the man insists. "We can't just hand them over to you."

"You were going to send them to Prague anyway, weren't you?" she asks, frosty now. "That's exactly where I'm going."

"And yet I still cannot simply give you the prisoners."

I ease away from the door to speak to Mia and Neal in a low voice. "They're fighting over who takes us to IA Headquarters in Prague," I report. "It's about an hour's drive. We might have a chance to get away during the trip, or when we arrive."

"If we don't, then we're locked up for good," Mia says, grim. "With Dex and Atlanta already arrived, or on their way."

Neal digs around in his bag until he can pull out the Undying device. It's silent now, and he fiddles with it while Mia finishes stuffing her bag full of whatever she can find that might be useful.

Then Neal lets out a startled oath. From where I stand, all I can see is the back of the device, emblazoned with the arcing meteorite that is the Undying's symbol for themselves.

"What is it?" I whisper.

"It zooms out." Neal crosses toward us so that we can all bend our heads over the little screen. "If you touch here like this, and then tilt the whole thing up and down . . ." He demonstrates, and the display's grid lines and terrain map jump and wobble dizzyingly. A little blip flashes by—the Undying in Dresden that we drove past.

As Neal starts to get the hang of navigating the thing, another little blip shows up near the first. For a moment I think it must be Lyon, except that when he zooms out further, I can see the sharp shift in terrain that marks the Alps. This dot is much closer—in Nuremburg, perhaps, or Stuttgart.

Another dot joins the first two. And another, and another. Munich. Berlin. Paris. London.

The terrain lines vanish into the sea as Neal's shaking hands tilt the screen all the way back.

New York City. Bogotá. Nairobi. Sydney. Hong Kong. Mumbai. And at least a hundred other dots in between, until the entire world is freckled with green.

I can hear Mia's breathing next to me, quickening, her voice coming out ragged and frightened. "They're already everywhere."

I take the device from Neal's unresisting hands and tilt it back in. My heart sinks, even though I already knew what I was going to see. "They're in Prague."

"Do you think it's Dex and Atlanta?" Mia's face is white.

"I don't know. Probably." My head's spinning. They'll be able to spread the Lyon disease everywhere, and the Undying will have the ability to transport troops instantly between cities—they could destroy St. Petersburg one day and invade Los Angeles the next. They'd have a way to bring instant reinforcements, no matter what damage our armies could do—assuming the world's governments could even muster an army quickly enough to counter the Undying's movements.

"We've got to try and convince someone you guys are telling the truth." Neal's voice is soft. "They're taking us right to where Uncle Elliott is being held, and if he's figured out how to shut down the portals, maybe we'll all still have a chance. But only if we can get in to see him."

My reply is cut off when the door swings open to reveal Mink, and a sweaty man standing behind her. Neal casually takes the device back and tucks it into his pocket, like it's just his phone and not a forecast of the end of humanity.

Mink glances at him and then actually snaps her fingers at us. "Let's go."

"*We* are transporting you to Prague," the man says. "The agent here will travel with us."

So the answer to the question of which one of them is our

captor has been answered: both of them, but perhaps him slightly more than her.

There's nothing to do but acquiesce, especially since they're taking us where we want to go—so long as we can convince someone of the truth before we're dumped in a cell and forgotten. We let them bind our wrists with bright blue zip ties, and with our bags clutched in our bound hands, we file out of the room under armed guard.

The vehicle that's waiting is a small truck with a covered back, two benches facing each other in its rear. The driver climbs into the cabin, and the three of us climb into the back, along with Mink and an IA soldier.

All five of us sit in silence as the dark green countryside slips by, and we hum along with the flow of traffic. I know we should try and convince Mink we're right about the Undying, but I can't even think where to begin. What argument can we make that we haven't already tried?

Is she our ally, because she helped Mia and me out of detention the first time? Though now I can't help but wonder if we were never meant to escape at all the first time, but just escape De Luca, and run straight into her arms instead.

Back when I thought she was Charlotte Stapleton, when I thought she was recruiting me for a private expedition to Gaia, this woman and I spent hours in London cafés, talking about the importance of exploration. Of discovery. Of what can be achieved when we think beyond the immediate, and seek out ways to exceed ourselves. I saw in her a kindred spirit then, a mind as devoted to understanding our universe as my own.

But as Mink, as the head of the covert IA operation that tracked me to the heart of the Undying temple . . . she manipulated me from moment one, perfectly willing to let me die in the process of trying to unravel the Undying's mysteries and extract the ancient ship from the Gaian ice cap. Mia and I watched as she shot an expendable operative in the head.

I worked until my eyes nearly gave out to get the ancient ship operational while she held a gun to Mia's temple. She stood unmoved as we pleaded with her to listen to us, to believe us when we told her that the ship was dangerous and that the future of our entire planet could very well hang in the balance if she went ahead with her plan to send the ship through the portal back to Earth.

But she did it anyway. I couldn't get her to listen to me then.

"Mink, we have to talk." It's an instant before I realize the voice raised over the sound of the motor is mine.

Her gaze swings around, glacial. "We really don't," she says simply.

"Well, then I'll talk, you listen," I say, lifting my zip-tied hands in supplication. "You're not incompetent—you *know* the two we had with us in Catalonia weren't scavvers you hired. You know they came from somewhere else."

Mia leans in to rest her shoulder against mine in support, and raises her voice too. "You *have* to believe us. What we saw in Lyon? Just the beginning."

Mink's gaze is flat, and completely unmoved. She studies first me and then Mia, ignoring Neal—the boy she spent hours with, pretending to hire him to convince me her company was real—and ignoring the soldier who sits clutching his rifle beside her.

"Think of the consequences," I urge. "If we're right and nobody listens, we could be wiped out. If we're wrong, what do you lose by looking into it?"

"Mr. Addison." My hopes shrivel and die under the weight of that tone. "Let me be clear. My IA status has been suspended. Director De Luca is under the impression I was involved in your escape in Catalonia a few days ago. My only way back into the fold is with the two of you in my custody."

"Does that include me?" Neal asks, all charm, with no hint of the anger he must feel for this woman. He wasn't on the poster. Perhaps he can still get to my father somehow. "You can just forget about me if you like. I mean, usually I'm the popular cousin, but—"

"Enough," she snaps.

"Can you at least take a message to my dad?" I'm pleading now, my voice cracking. Even if nobody listens to us, perhaps when they finally realize we were right, he can do something. "Tell him to finish his work on closing down the portals. Tell him that's what he'll need to do."

"Mr. Addison," she snaps. The soldier at her side shifts his grip on the gun, responding to her tone. But Mink glances at the guard, as if she's about ready to take the soldier's gun and sort me out herself. "Be silent."

And so we all are. I'm exhausted, and my eyes are hot and aching, and beside me Mia's slumped, her head in her tightly bound hands.

Slowly, eventually, the trees sliding by outside the truck give way to the outer suburbs of the city, and then to the city itself. Prague is a mish-mash of historical buildings with cobblestone streets, and sleek, modern construction.

Almost at walking pace, the truck begins to climb a hill. Neal's the closest to the back, and he's looking out, watching the streets go by. I can see the tension in his body—we've played sports together for years, and I know when he's considering a move. But he can't, not with the armed soldier right there, and Mink's gun at her hip.

We edge past a pair of black wrought iron gates, the curls of metal ornamented with gilded highlights, and pull in to the side of the road, the engine shifting tone as the driver sets it to idle. Beyond the gates is a large courtyard, teeming with guards in IA uniform, and a long, snaking line of what I realize are tourists waiting for admission. On the far side of the courtyard is an ornate, U-shaped building several stories high, bordering the courtyard on three sides.

It's Prague Castle—International Alliance Headquarters—a sprawling complex made up of old and new, public and deeply classified. The place from which the IA sets the course of humanity—or used to, when they had the full support of the entire world behind them.

The driver climbs out, and Mink leaves her place opposite me to jump down from the back of the truck. She turns to meet our eyes one by one, her hand resting on the pistol at her hip.

"Stay here," she says, fixing me with a long stare, before she moves on to Mia. "Are we clear? *Stay here.*"

And with that, she moves around to join the driver, and presumably argue with the gate guards about her ID, or let them know who she's bringing in.

Mia, however, is staring straight past me, out at the crowds. "Wow, there's a lot of tourists here," she says suddenly.

I blink, but follow her gaze, looking out to the milling throng making their way along the streets. "Yes," I agree, bewildered, but waiting to see where she's taking it.

"You could really get lost here," she says, leaning forward to get a look past me. "I can barely see half a block."

*Ah.* And there it is. I'm about to fall headfirst into one of Mia's on-the-spot plans.

In fairness, they work far more often than I expect them to.

And our alternative is a cell.

"You're right," I say, nudging Neal with my foot. "Talk about busy."

Neal shoots me a quick, confused glance, but when I tap his boot with mine again, he falls in line, joining in without understanding why. "What a place," he says cheerfully, leaning his head out the back of the truck to look around.

*That* mobilizes the soldier. "Sit back," he snaps, gesturing with his rifle.

"Easy, mate," Neal says peaceably, holding up his bound hands to remind our captor that he's restrained. He's holding on to his bag, which is how I know that he understands we're up to something. "I'm just having a look. Pretty sure I'm about to be locked up for the rest of my natural life, so this might be my last chance to see the sights of Prague. What's that building over there?"

As he's talking, monopolizing the guard's attention, Mia's

twisting around, turning her back on me. For a moment I'm lost, and then she subtly wiggles her hips. I look down, and a surge goes through me as I see the outline of her multi-tool pressed against her pocket.

Without giving myself time to think, I pull it free and flick out the blade. Quietly, quickly, we take turns removing each other's bonds while Neal continues irritating the guard. There's no way to cut the ties around his wrists without being spotted—he's just going to have to run with them tied.

The guard has a gun. But it's a rifle, not a handgun—not as easy to aim and fire in close quarters. He won't be able to aim it at any of us for a few seconds, and by then, we'll have to be in the crowd of tourists. We'll have to be among so many other bodies that it's impossible to hit us.

I turn around with what I hope is a sheepish smile, but is probably a terrified rictus, and meet Neal's eyes. There's a question in his gaze as I pick up my bag, and ever so slowly, I incline my head.

Neal doesn't hesitate.

He hurls himself at the door just as Mia uses her newly freed hands to unlatch it. He spills out onto the cobblestones, and I scramble after him, catching him by the elbow as he stumbles, his hands still bound. Mia's nimble, throwing herself out behind me, shoving her way past two men with cameras to clear a path for us.

"Stop!" It's a sharp shout behind us, but I don't look back. We've made it half a dozen steps, and the soldier will be out of the car by now.

Mia grabs a woman by the shoulders, pushing her out of the way, and I duck through after her, Neal by my side.

My whole spine is tingling, the place between my shoulder blades twitching, expecting a bullet with every instant that passes. We're nearly at the edge of the square.

I glance back just once, as we round the corner. Mink and the soldier are after us, Mink's face intent and driven in a way that's hauntingly familiar—and then I realize.

In this moment, she looks exactly like Atlanta. I don't look back again.

Mia has the lead, and the three of us race through the crowds of shoppers, twisting and turning, taking corners. We pause for just an instant, so she can cut the ties from Neal's wrists—he looks like a prisoner on the run with them held out in front of him. We have a head start on our pursuers, and if we can stay out of sight for long enough, they'll lose track of us.

Eventually Mia grabs at my hand and gasps Neal's name, and we slow to a walk, turning the corner again and mingling with the people walking down the street. "Slow," she pants. "Speed gets you distance, but it leaves a trail to follow."

We ease into the crowd, which is large—it might be a weekend, in fact. I have no idea what day it is.

"Did we lose them?" I ask, breath still coming quickly.

"I think so," Mia says, looking back. "Though let's keep moving."

Neal has his phone out, and I rest a hand on his shoulder to stop him crashing into anyone as he swipes quickly at the screen.

"There's a youth hostel five minutes from here," he says. "We could get a room, get off the street."

"Get the directions," Mia says grimly, "then take the chip out of your phone. I know you both replaced them, but I can't think of another way she could have found us at the border. She must have figured out where Neal bought the new ones, and tracked those."

She's right, and I pull off my watch, and eject the chip, dropping it onto the cobblestones and grinding it to pieces with my heel. My image library is saved to the device itself—everything we found on Gaia, and everything after.

I look over to make sure Neal's doing the same, but instead he's staring down at his phone, brow furrowed. "Come on," I murmur, jogging his elbow with mine. I doubt anyone could move fast enough to have a trace on our phones already, but the last thing I want to do is underestimate Mink.

"Hang on," Neal replies. Something in his voice raises the hairs on the back of my neck. Mia hears it too—she turns back toward us, shooting me a questioning glance.

"Is that the video you posted?" I lean in over Neal's shoulder.

"It's got over six million views," Neal replies, voice hushed. "And look at the comments, there are people who believe us. The #IBelieveInAddison people are going nuts. They've latched on to my username, and at least some of them have figured out I *am* an Addison. They're asking me to come to the forums, to tell them more, to share what we know."

My eye catches on something, and I grab Neal's sleeve. "Hang on, go back—what's that sidebar link?"

It's in the "You May Also Like" clickbait parade, but when Neal scrolls back up and taps the link, my stomach tightens.

"Apparently your friend Director De Luca had to give a press conference after the Lyon video went viral," Neal reports. "They're saying it's not a flu at all anymore, but they think it's something in the water there. Damn, but that feels good—we made him have to face what was going on and tell at least part of the truth."

I want to join in Neal's raptures about the satisfaction of forcing power to tell the truth, but I can't. I can't even pause to dwell on the fact that the "flu" isn't a rampaging contagion that'll kill us all. Because my eyes are on the picture from the press conference that first grabbed my attention. I reach over Neal's shoulder to take the phone from him, ignoring his protests.

I pinch-zoom in on the picture of De Luca standing behind a podium with the IA seal on it, and my heart sinks. I glance at Mia, debating for a moment whether I should even show her what I've seen—but when she sees my face, her own drains of color and she reaches out in wordless demand for me to pass the phone to her.

I hand it over and then rub my thumb and forefinger against my eyelids, trying to dismiss the image from my mind. Among the various officials and nameless civilians gathered behind De Luca in the picture was a young woman. A girl, really. Dressed professionally, but the sleek lines of her jacket didn't hide the fact that she's younger than the rest by at least a decade.

And though I've never met her—I knew her instantly.

She has Mia's eyes, her chin, even the way her hair parts—she doesn't have nearly as many freckles, and her face is a little rounder, but the resemblance is unmistakable.

*Evie.*

I squeeze Mia's shoulders, but they stay rigid under my hands—and I don't blame her.

De Luca's sending us a warning, loud and clear. He's got someone we care about—someone Mia already volunteered to give her life for, when she went to Gaia. And if we do anything that displeases him, if we threaten to drop a match on his powder keg, well. Then he's got Evie, and we don't.

I can't help but think something must have changed, something to make him think we're connected with what's happening. After all our warnings about the end of the world, perhaps he's starting to look around and wonder.

"Pull up the directions," Mia says finally, handing the phone back to Neal. "And ditch the SIM card."

Her voice is thick and heavy, and I want to wrap my arms around her there in the street. The last time she saw her sister's face, it was on the dying screen of her phone, half a universe away on the surface of an alien planet, when she decided to share the last of our oxygen with me rather than make it to her rendezvous point and her way home. It was when she chose me over her sister.

It wouldn't matter if I told her that that wasn't the choice she made—that she chose hope, chose some other answer that we hadn't found yet. That it was faith, not betrayal. But right now, I know the only thing she's thinking about is the girl in that picture, standing a few feet away from the man trying to hunt us down.

• • •

Half an hour later we're installed in a small room with white-painted walls and tatty curtains, containing two sets of bunk beds, with thin blankets folded across the foot of each thin mattress. We've paid for all four beds, closed the door firmly behind us, and we're sifting through my vending machine stash in search of the most edible options.

"Okay," says Neal. "So after that stuff at the border crossing, they'll have added me to the bulletin about you. If I try to see Uncle Elliott, I'll just be arrested."

"Right," I agree, glad Neal was willing to break the silence. "And there's no reason to think they'll listen to us two any more than De Luca did. We might get lucky, but . . ."

Mia, whose face is still pinched with frustration and worry for her sister, huffs a soft breath of sour laughter. I can't blame her—it feels like our last shreds of luck ran out long ago.

"We still need to get to Uncle Elliott," Neal says. "We've got the locations of the Undying on this tracker Dex left—and we know the portals are key to their plan. We've got to get that info to him so he can shut them all down."

The silence from Mia is deafening—this is where she'd be in her element, coming up with harebrained schemes and rushing off half-cocked to scare the life out of me with some daring feat or another. But she's just sitting there, head bowed, elbows on her knees.

We've all been thinking of the people we care about. Neal's parents—my uncle and aunt—are back in England. Our friends are at Oxford. I think my mother's in Switzerland, and though we haven't spoken much since she left dad and me, I still love her. She's my mum, and I can't even wholly blame her for leaving my dad. His theories made him sound mad—the whole world thought so.

We can't contact any of them, for fear the IA is listening and will trace the call—and perhaps for fear they wouldn't believe our warnings if we tried—but I know we've all been thinking of the warning Mia gave to Luisa, and wishing we could do the same for those we love.

But for all those thoughts that have sat with us during long car journeys, and during the night, neither Neal nor I have had a moment like Mia just did. To see Evie there, standing behind De Luca, when she's devoted her entire life to keeping her sister safe, when she's *risked* her life to keep her sister safe . . . I can't imagine.

"So let's think about what we have on our side," Neal says, following my gaze to Mia's slouched form.

"An IA jacket, and an ID we can maybe modify," I say.

"Languages," Neal says. "You could pass as being from a lot of different places."

"Mia's brain," I add, and that's enough to make her lift her head and shoot me a surprised look. "What?" I say. "You're the quickest person I've ever met in a tight spot. You always think of something."

"We have the people online," she says slowly. "The #IBelieveIn Addison people. I don't know what use they can be yet, but Luisa showed us they're real, and at least some of them will help us."

"We should decide if we want to participate in that conversation," Neal says. "You have a lot of pictures you could add."

"Maybe," I say, but I can feel myself sitting a little straighter just at the thought of that community out there, refusing to accept what they're told, asking questions and demanding proof.

Mia lets out her breath slowly. "We're still going to have to try to get in to see Dr. Addison. We stick to the original plan—it's just harder, now we can't use Neal." Her voice is quiet, her brow furrowed with concentration. "Whole sections of the castle are museum now, right? Open to tourists?"

*You wanted a harebrained scheme that would get us all killed, Jules.*

I stifle that thought. "They'd catch us before we got halfway to him."

"Maybe." Mia's still thinking. "Probably. But what else have we got left to try? At least if we're arrested and questioned, we can warn them that Atlanta and Dex are here—if we can't convince them that they're aliens, maybe we can convince them that they're bioterrorists or something. That they're connected to the Lyon disease. If nothing else, maybe we can stop them taking over IA Headquarters. Or whatever they're doing here."

My heartbeat's starting to quicken, the thought of trying to infiltrate the IA—once the world's most sophisticated government headquarters—nearly as frightening as being caught by Mink on the streets of Prague. But Mia's sitting up, talking, being *herself* again for the first time since seeing Evie on Neal's phone, and I can't help but be carried along with her. "We do have the ID badge and the IA uniform jacket," I say.

"And we have an advantage they're not prepared for," Mia adds. When I raise an eyebrow in query, she flickers a tiny smile at us. "We're just a handful of kids. What trouble could we possibly be?"

Neal's been quiet a while, his head bent over his phone. Without the SIM card, he's limited to using the hostel Wi-Fi, so it's been taking him a while to look up whatever he's searching for. But just then, he lets out a muffled exclamation.

He looks up, wild-eyed, to find Mia and me looking at him, and even as I watch, his face goes a bit ashen.

"What is it?" My stomach's sinking—I don't think I've ever seen Neal look so scared.

"Veronica replied," he whispers. "My geneticist friend at Oxford. She answered us about the samples we sent."

My heart leaps. With hard proof that Atlanta and Dex are some unknown alien species, we won't *have* to sneak into the IA. We could walk straight in, announcing our identities, and *hand* them proof that the invasion of Earth is happening right now.

I cross to my cousin's side and take the phone from his unresisting hand. I'm reading the email, my eyes taking in phrases like *highly unusual microarray* and *long strings of homozygosity* without digesting them. Because at the bottom of each result is a standard label in bold.

"Human DNA Microarray," I whisper.

Mia lurches to her feet. "Human? But they bleed blue!"

Neal's pallor makes sense now. He'd expected to open an email full of exclamations of wonder and amazement, disbelief from the first geneticist to analyze the DNA of an alien race.

Instead he found a mildly intrigued old friend talking about various random genetic markers—but *human* genetic markers.

"They're humans." My voice sounds like poured concrete, thick and slow. "Whatever we saw, whatever we *thought* we saw . . . it's not just a mask on the surface. They're *humans*."

**22**

**AMELIA**

"IT DOESN'T REALLY LOOK LIKE A CASTLE," I MUTTER, NOT bothering to hide the disappointment in my voice. Prague "Castle," home of the International Alliance, is more like a collection of vaguely old stone buildings than the soaring structure I'd imagined. The first floor of the main building is a museum, with a little bit of history of the castle and the city, and a *lot* of the history of the IA.

Jules eyes me sidelong, a smile hovering about his lips. "Were you imagining something out of a fairy tale?"

"Shut up. If you can't trust Hollywood, who can you trust?" Getting into this part of the castle was easy—cursory bag checks at the entrance, not even any ID required. The rent-a-guards at the door barely gave our faces a second glance.

Life is just continuing here as normal, and despite our attempts at jokes, it feels like the three of us are just swimming through it. The Undying are here in Prague. The Undying are . . . My mind still shies away from the word, too bewildered to know how to respond. *Human?*

Last night, while Neal went out to source us food and buy a couple of burner phones with almost the last of our cash, Jules helped me change my hair. Pink and blue streaks are not exactly low profile, after all. We've been through so much—so close to certain death for so long—that dyeing and cutting off my hair ought to have barely registered. And yet as Jules snipped away, I found to my horror that there were tears falling among the locks of damp hair littering the porcelain of the bathtub.

Somehow, it was like seeing the last little piece of myself, of who I was before all of this, cut away.

Jules tossed the scissors aside once he'd finished the task and leaned forward to wrap his arms around me from behind, pulling me in against his chest and pressing his lips to my temple. He didn't speak, but then, neither did I. He just held me until Neal came back, and we could come out of the bathroom dry-eyed.

Now, I'm sporting a short red bob and fringe that makes me look startlingly different, and I have to admit I don't entirely hate the effect.

There's nothing we can do about Jules and Neal and their distinctive height, but there's so many people that no one looks at them twice. Tourists are everywhere. Crowds aren't usually my thing, but today they're a comfort—in the press of bodies, there's no possible way for us to stand out.

After reading Veronica's email, we're back to trying to find a way to reach Dr. Addison. We have no idea what to make of her results, no idea how to begin to grapple with what they might mean, but it doesn't change our mission. The Undying are still here. They're still building portals. And Jules's dad is the only one who'll know how to shut them down.

IA Headquarters, aside from its museum exhibits, is an administrative building, not a prison. Addison was kept here largely to quiet the human rights activists claiming you couldn't imprison him indefinitely without a trial—here, they can claim he's simply being *detained*. There are parts of the castle off-limits to the public, offices and whatnot—and a large underground security complex.

That's where we have to go. Through the exhibits, and down through the secured part of the building. Without getting caught. The thought makes even *me* quail, and we all slow down once we're inside. It'll take us a while to get the lay of the area, see if there's any pattern to the guards' movements, figure out which doors are least heavily monitored.

So when Jules's steps veer toward one of the exhibits, I don't protest. This might be our last real moment of freedom. Of peace, before we're arrested. And here, surrounded by other teens, and families, and tourists of all descriptions, life almost feels normal.

At the nearest exhibit, a kid is pressing a button over and over that triggers an audio recording. There's not much to hear, just oddly rhythmic static, but Jules veers over toward it like it's a dog whistle and he's an obedient Labrador.

"It's the broadcast," Jules explains under his breath. "The original Undying broadcast."

I listen, but it still just sounds like noise. But a picture on one of the exhibit standees grabs my eye, and I tug at Jules's sleeve. "Look—your dad."

Neal starts reading aloud, covering up the fact that Jules has gone very quiet. "Though scientists were quick to recognize that the signal had an artificial structure that suggested intelligence, it took one of the world's leading experts in mathematics and linguistics to decode the message. Dr. Elliott Addison, despite his later disgrace—um, never mind." Neal's quick to turn toward the next set of standees, conveniently coming between Jules and the rest of the summary of his father's contribution to the International Alliance.

We stroll backward along the time line, until Neal lets out a bleat of excitement. "Oh, *awesome*, they've got a scale model of the

Centauri ship!" Forgetting us entirely, he lurches forward to inspect the sprawling, bird's-eye-view model of the ship.

The decision to leave Earth in search of an answer to the world's overpopulation was what led to the formation of the International Alliance. We're all taught about it in school: a series of meaningless dates and names to memorize, how various world leaders settled on an international charter of basic laws, the voting process, all of it. But here, looking at the ship that was built as a result of that global collaboration, all those old lessons come to life.

Neal's in engineering heaven, inspecting a replica of one of the engines in cross section. My eyes linger on the model of the ship, on the star map of the Alpha Centauri star system, on a terrain map of the planet in orbit around Proxima Centauri that was to be humanity's second home.

Jules is still quiet, and I know his mind's on the one-paragraph description of his father, a man who changed history and is remembered only for the tirade that ended his career. I reach for his hand and give it a squeeze. "You know, this exhibit is actually pretty cool."

"Hmm?" Jules blinks and looks from me to the ship model. "Yeah, I suppose it is."

"I mean it." I move until I'm standing in front of a glass case containing a uniform from the Centauri mission. One leg of the uniform has been cut away, revealing a cross section of its complex structure, with different layers of insulating gel, armored fabric, and electronics. A masterpiece of design, from a time when all of humanity worked as one.

I can see myself in the glass, and when I stand on my toes it almost looks like my reflection is wearing the uniform. "I mean, in school we know how the story ends before we know anything else. We already know the mission fails, and everybody dies, and the IA sort of falls apart and turns into just another bureaucracy, and they're just remembered for messing up and killing a bunch of people."

Jules snorts. "What a legacy."

"No, listen to me." I tug his hand until he's standing alongside me in front of the case. "When you know how the story ends you kind of don't care about what happens. But look at all this, Jules. When you really look at the ship and the uniforms and the map and all of it . . . look at what we can *do*. When we stop fighting each other and look outside ourselves."

I'm lost here, because the inspirational speeches are Jules's territory, but the *feeling* is there, and I'm desperate for him to see it. "I mean, did you know we could do this? People did all this. It's incredible."

"And history will remember them as a failure." Jules's gaze is remote. He's not talking about the IA.

"Who gives a shit about history?" I abandon my attempt at speechifying, and turn to look at him, intent. "Right now, I'm saying *I* think it's amazing."

Jules glances at me, then does a double take, lips twitching. "You're irresistible when you're scowling."

Beyond him is the long memorial wall, covered with the names of those who died in pursuit of the Centauri mission, but I keep him turned toward me. "I was trying to distract you by pointing out the noble appeal of all mankind looking toward the stars for a united common purpose greater than any we'd shared before, but I'll settle for making out inappropriately in the middle of a public exhibit."

Jules laughs in spite of himself, and reaches up to tweak a lock of my newly dyed red hair. He starts to speak, but something's nagging at me, something off.

My eyes go past him again to that memorial wall, and for a long moment I don't see anything. Then I catch a glimpse of something—Neal? But Neal's still over at the engine, in the middle of a dozen eight-year-old school kids, pushing buttons and exclaiming when bits of the engine light up in response.

Not Neal. But someone tall. Two someones.

"Oh my God." My voice is strangled and thin.

Jules, who'd been ducking his head toward mine, freezes. "What? You said we could make out, I was just—"

"No—look. They're here."

I ought to warn him not to stare, not to make our observation obvious, but I'm too floored. Jules turns, and I feel it when he spots them.

Dex and Atlanta, dressed not all that differently than we are, doing their best to blend in with the crowd. Atlanta's examining the names on the memorial wall, evidently trying to look interested in the exhibit, and Dex is casually scanning the crowd.

His eyes swing our way without warning, and before I can try to pull Jules somewhere less obvious, his gaze halts on us.

For a long moment we stare at each other across the sea of tourists. Then he's turning toward Atlanta. My heart seizes, and I scan the exits, certain I'm going to see them both charging our way when I look back. But instead, Atlanta's turned away and is moving off, and Dex is coming toward us.

Jules's hand is so tight around mine my bones creak, but I don't mind—in this moment, it's the only thing keeping my own fear in check.

Dex, with an air of studied casualness, meanders toward us and nods. "Pretty cool exhibit, huh?" He says "cool" the way our orphanage director used to say it, like she was trying to be young and hip.

Jules is staring at him, his face rigid—my mind is scrambling too, but I'm used to speaking when my ideas are still only half-formed.

"What are you doing here?" I whisper. "Did you leave us that tracker?"

"Yeh. Stop staring." Dex is not looking at us, his eyes on the placard next to the Centauri mission uniform. "I told Atlanta to check the security on the staircases, I don't have a lot of time." He might not have our slang right yet, but in every other way he's sounding smoother. He's been learning to blend in more ways than one, changing the way he talks.

"Why are you helping us?" Jules's voice comes out in a croak.

"Stop asking questions, I don't have time to answer them, compren?" Dex slips his hands into his pockets, and though the movement is casual, I can see muscles standing out in his arms. Behind him, I spot Neal look up from the engine display, his eyes widening when he sees us. "You need to compren something if you're going to stop this: It's all about the portals. If you can stop us using the portals you can stop the occupation."

We were right about the portals—they *are* the key to everything. But then the rest of what he says catches up with me. "Occupation?" I repeat, fear creeping into my gut.

"The Undying occupation of Earth. Once most of you are regressed, we'll be in custody of the planet." Dex glances from me to Jules. "You're here for your father, yeh?"

I can feel Jules's shock through our joined hands. A moment later his fingers go lax, slipping from mine. "How do you know who my—"

Dex cuts him off. "Are you fooling? Sirsly, the first thing we did when we got here, the *very* first thing, we figured what you knew about us. How would that *not* be the first thing we look for? It's all over your internet, your television broadcasts, your books and newspapers and podcasts."

Neal's moving toward us, carefully. I catch his eye, and when he lifts his brows, I shrug. *I don't know if we're in trouble or not.* What Neal would be able to do about it, I don't know, but at this point I don't think it's going to help if he sneaks up behind Dex and tackles him to the ground.

"Of course we looked up what you knew about the race of mysterious aliens who led you to Gaia." Dex is still talking, sounding so much more like us than he did a few days ago, his eyes intent on Jules. I might as well be invisible, but it just means I can scan for Atlanta, for some sign that Dex is trying to trick us. But his body language, reflected in the glass uniform case, is urgent rather than aggressive.

"Why wouldn't we memorize every lecture Elliott Addison ever gave about the Undying, check every paper and book he ever published on us, every video of his meltdown on your TV?"

Jules's jaw clenches, but he manages to keep himself under control.

Dex shifts his weight from foot to foot. "That's how we knew we could win. When we saw the way they treated Addison when he tried to tell the truth, that was when we *knew* we could win." His eyes are shadowed, expression grave. He glances over his shoulder, but there's no sign of Atlanta. Instead he sees Neal, who gives him an awkward little wave, like he wasn't considering trying to attack him thirty seconds ago.

When Dex turns back to Jules, he lets his breath out in a sigh. "That day in the landing pod, when you guys shifted planetside with us, I know you saw me look at you. You saw me recognize you."

Jules says nothing. I could burst with pride that he's learned to keep his mouth shut and not volunteer or confirm anything he doesn't have to, except that I'm pretty sure he's just silent because he's standing there in some stunned combination of shock and fury.

Dex shakes his head. "But it wasn't that I realized you were from Earth, that you were a proto. I realized you were Jules Addison."

That shatters Jules's stillness, and he raises a hand to gesture in a way that's so like how he speaks when he's correcting me on history or language that I fight the insane, fleeting urge to laugh. "Hold on, you couldn't possibly have—"

"Your voice sounds like his," Dex interrupts without missing a beat.

Jules, floundering, is silent again.

"You said, 'Onward, if you dare,'" Dex presses. "His words, his voice. You're here for your father. Yeh?"

Jules's eyes flick toward me. But at this point, I'm out of my depth. No amount of quick thinking or understanding of human nature is going to help us here. I lift one shoulder, gazing helplessly back at him. In the glass of the case, Dex's reflection is wearing the Centauri uniform now, and it steals my gaze. A few moments ago I was thinking about what our species can accomplish when we remember we're not actually all that different. And now that symbol of unity is superimposed on a human from outer space.

"Yeh?" Dex's voice cuts through my thoughts, and Jules's too, his urgency obvious.

"Yeh," Jules says finally.

"So are we."

The words hit hard enough to knock the wind from me, and from Jules's stunned face, I know he's half a heartbeat from total breakdown.

"You've got to get to him before we do. Prime-One, it isn't just about IA Headquarters. Our destin is to kill the one man with the know-how to stop us. Unless someone else gets there first." Dex's hand comes out of his pocket, this time holding a small electronic device, which he hands to Jules. "Take it. We got backups on backups when it comes to infiltrating this place. Atlanta will get us inwards even if it turns out I forgot to pack the code breaker. I can slow her down, but I can't do anything if we reach him before you do."

Jules stares at the device, which is about the size of a drinks coaster, blankly. "You're here to kill him?" he whispers.

Impatient, Dex jostles his shoulder. "This thing—it unscrambles door codes. You can get to the secured underground wing where prisoners are kept before we do."

Those words seem to shatter whatever spell is holding Jules, because he reaches out as if to take Dex's sleeve and blurts, "Wait—wait, we need you. We've got too many questions. . . . Who are you? *How* are you human? Why are you trying to take Earth, and how did you even get into space so long ago to begin with? Why all the elaborate lies and puzzles and—"

"I don't have *time* to answer." Dex's voice lifts a little in irritation, but he gets himself under control. Neal has crept up alongside us, and he's watching the Undying teenager with an unreadable expression. "I'm not fooling, I can't, not right now. I've gotta shift."

Jules's arm moves again, though he still doesn't actually take hold of Dex. But instead of a torrent of questions, this time he just asks one. "Why are you helping us?"

Dex's gaze swings over toward my face, then Neal's, where it lingers for a moment before flicking back to Jules. His lashes lower for a long moment, and then he says softly, "Because you sound like your father. I really gotta shift. Good luck."

Then he's moving away, back into the crowd. But I'm still staring at the uniform case, my mind still seizing like it did before, like I've seen something wrong and I just don't know what it is yet.

"Jules," I murmur, a rising confusion and certainty prompting me.

"Just . . . just give me a second." Jules's voice is taut with feeling.

The Centauri uniforms are a deep blue, emblazoned on the right breast pocket with the flag of the International Alliance and the logo for the Centauri mission, a landing craft streaking across the trinary star system that was their destination.

"Jules—" I try again. I can feel Neal straightening next to me, sensing the urgency in my tone.

"They watched videos of my father being mocked," Jules mutters to himself, clearly oblivious to me and to his cousin, "and *that's* when they knew they could beat us and take Earth?"

My eyes stick on the Centauri logo. On the cutout of the uniform's leg, and the layers inside the suit. "Jules!" I shout, not caring that a few people nearby turn to stare at us and then move away, slowly.

Jules blinks and looks up. "What?" His voice is sharp with irritation.

"Look." My finger's quivering as it points toward the case.

We all grew up knowing the Centauri mission logo. But it's history, a thing long gone, so far in the past that it's become background noise. All it is to us is a symbol of failure. But now it snaps into focus as if it's brand-new. It's the first time either of us would've had reason to look at the logo since we've been to Gaia.

Jules is silent, his eyes wide, his lips parted. Beside us, slowly, Neal pulls out the tracking device Dex left behind for us, and turns it over to look at the back. Etched into the casing is the Undying symbol, the one we saw in the temple on Gaia. A meteorite, streaking across the sky, we always thought.

Or a colony ship, streaking through a star system.

"How is this possible?" Neal whispers.

"It isn't." Jules's words are dismissive, but he can't stop staring at the uniform. "It isn't possible, okay? The temple on Gaia is fifty thousand years old. The Centauri mission left Earth only sixty years ago."

"And even if the ship itself wasn't destroyed like the IA thought, they only had resources for . . ." Neal's frowning, and abandons his mental calculations. "There's no way they could still be alive today even if they weren't immediately destroyed when the IA lost contact with them."

"But they're human." I'm remembering Atlanta, how she stood there scanning the names on the wall of Centauri mission casualties. "They're human, and look—the leg of the suit. The insulating gel—it's blue, isn't it? The Undying guy on the ship who was injured was wearing a suit. I mean, different from this one, obviously, but . . . what if it's the same technology?"

"So it looked like blue blood when the uniform got cut." Jules's voice is stunned and slow.

"Maybe they faked the temple somehow." Neal is watching Jules with something almost like apprehension, like he's waiting for an explosion to occur. "Maybe it's not as old as we thought."

"Geologists and archaeologists dated the temple carvings with a margin of error less than 0.08 percent." Jules's voice is faint, falling back on his scholarly roots like I'd crawl beneath a familiar, warm blanket. "They couldn't have faked it."

I reach for Jules's arm, which moves without resistance, and retrieve the device Dex gave us. Jules doesn't even seem to notice.

"Guys, they're going to kill Jules's dad. We have to get moving, *now.*"

The device Dex handed me activates at the touch of a button, a display screen showing a ten-digit number that flips backward through each digit until it shows zeroes across the board. I'm trying to ignore the sheer panic flooding my system at the mere thought of what lies ahead.

Jules's lips press together, hard enough to thin them into a line, and then release. "Mia's right," he says softly. "We're out of time— let's go."

• • •

"Maybe they're time travelers." Neal speaks in a low voice, but not a whisper. Jules is used to following my instructions when it comes to acting like you belong, but Neal's a novice, and it's taken him twenty minutes to stop acting like a conspirator in a spy thriller. "Like maybe they're coming back from the future to get revenge on us for sending their ancestors to Centauri in the first place."

"Time travel's not possible," Jules mutters. "It breaks all the laws of physics, it's just a fantasy." But just now, in the face of all we've seen, that denial is sounding a little thin. And from the look in his eye, he knows it.

"Even if it were possible, why wouldn't they just travel back to a point before the mission left, and warn someone not to send them?" I reach up to smooth back a lock of hair. I'm still not used to its color, and I keep seeing my bangs out of the corner of my eye. But what with the surprisingly decent haircut, and our pilfered IA jacket, I look like a professional—albeit rather short—IA security officer.

The boys, whose clothes aren't quite as informal as mine, can pass for wearing business casual, and Jules has the stolen IA badge clipped to his pocket. Together we look like coworkers strolling through the underground corridors.

*I hope.*

Still, my skin prickles at every sound, every shift of the still, heavy air around us. I haven't forgotten that Atlanta and Dex are here too. Dex just told us he won't be able to stop Atlanta killing Dr. Addison if they get there first. If we meet, I don't know if he could stop her from trying to kill us too.

Neal sighs. "And if they could travel in time, why would they even need the Lyon disease? They'd be basically gods, they could wipe out the IA and all our planetary defenses just by going back in time to before they existed." Frustrated at disproving his own theory, he shoves his hands into his pockets.

"Heads up." My voice is low and casual, but it stops all conversation—a woman in a navy blue suit emerges from an intersecting corridor, nods absently at us, and continues on her way.

The secured part of the castle had enough entrances that we could use Dex's code breaker out of sight. Which was good, considering it took us a good ten minutes to figure out how to operate it. But once inside, it's been surprisingly easy to pass unnoticed. People see what they expect to see, and most of the rooms we've passed since we got down beneath the exhibit floor have been offices. These people aren't highly trained operatives or security agents, they're just office workers.

"We've got to figure out where they'd be holding my dad," Jules says, once the woman's out of earshot again. "We can't wander around here forever, we'll get caught."

My pulse hitches up a notch as a thought comes to me. "Hang on. I've got an idea. Stay here."

I turn and jog back toward the woman in the suit, calling out, "Hey, excuse me!" I can almost feel the twin expressions of horror Neal and Jules must be wearing, but neither of them try to chase me down.

The woman pauses, looking over her shoulder, and then turns when she sees me approaching. "Is everything okay, ma'am?" She has big, luminous brown eyes and a moderate accent, consonants and vowels pronounced with care.

Remembering I'm wearing the jacket of a security officer, I flash her a reassuring smile. "Yeah, I just need to ask—do you know where they're actually holding Addison? I just transferred from the Catalan branch, and I'm completely lost."

The woman's eyes warm, amusement in her face. "It is a maze, right? I started last year and I still get lost. But I'm just an accountant, I don't know anything about the Addison thing, and I don't have clearance to discuss it anyway."

I skate past that, sighing and making a frustrated sound in my throat. "Even just a general direction would be a big help."

The woman's brows draw in. "Why are you looking for Addison anyway? Aren't his guards part of a separate unit?"

I step to the side and gesture behind me. One glance shows me that Neal looks absolutely panicked, already halfway around the corner—but Jules is still where I left him, watching and listening. Tense, but waiting.

"See that kid?" I've found that being dismissive of people my own age sometimes makes others see me as older. Hopefully between that and my uniform, this woman won't realize I'm no older than the "kid" I'm talking about. "That's his son."

The woman's eyes widen. "Dr. Addison's son? He does look like him. Isn't he wanted for arrest?"

I grin at her. "How do you think he got here? We scooped him up yesterday, the plan is to use him as leverage against his dad. De Luca sent me to escort him down here."

Her eyes narrow again. "*You* report to De Luca?" Suspicion clouds her features, and she looks me over a second time.

"Sure do," I reply. "I'm just in my first year, but I was the only one with clearance for this level close at hand." The woman glances over my shoulder again at Jules, hesitant. In a low, conspiratorial voice, I add, "Look, between you and me, I'm in way over my head. I'm terrified to ask someone in charge, because they'll just tell De Luca I couldn't do my job. I need this promotion."

The woman sighs. "Well, I don't know exactly," she says finally. "But there's a wing beyond the situation room at the end of the hall whose doors use a different code—none of us ever go in there. If I had to guess where they're keeping Dr. Addison, that's where I'd look."

I flash her a smile. "Thank you *so* much. Seriously—what's your name? If I get this promotion maybe I can return the favor."

"Iveta," she replies after a pause. "Iveta Nováková."

"Got it." I nod firmly, despite the fact that I'm not sure I could repeat that name a second time. "Thanks again. Take care!"

I turn and hurry back toward the others. Jules's lips are twitching, and he meets my eyes with an approving grin.

Neal, watching from the corner, is wide-eyed. "Bloody hell, she's got ovaries of steel." He reemerges from the corridor after checking that Iveta's moved on.

"Told you." Jules reaches out as if to take my hand, then thinks better of it, given the cover story I've just laid out. "Let's go."

The coded door Iveta mentioned leads to another hallway, although there's a muffling quiet in this area that immediately puts me on edge. There's a security room just inside, and while there aren't any monitors—clearly, they're not foolish enough to put all their secrets on display—there are duty shift rosters in a folder, and a fire exit map on the back of the door. Between these, we can trace a route to what can only be Dr. Addison's cell, although he's never referred to by name in the duty rosters.

This time we get more than a few looks as we make our way down the corridor. No one stops us, but I can feel their suspicion the way a seasoned detective can detect deceit, and by the time we're at the cell, my skin is crawling.

Neal's got the code breaker, and he doesn't wait for prompting to start it working on the code to the door.

"Hurry," I hiss, before I can stop myself—there's nothing Neal can do to go any faster, after all. But here, in a wing full of guards who've probably interacted with Addison on a daily basis, the odds they'll recognize Jules have skyrocketed. And these guys will *know* I'm not here to add Jules to their list of prisoners.

Jules is still, standing at my side and staring blankly at the door with his face gone ashen. He hasn't seen his father since his arrest, and I can't imagine what's going through his mind. Evie and I were taken from our parents so young that she doesn't even remember them, and to me they're just distant figures of warmth and safety. I can't imagine what it's like to have a parent you love as much as Jules loves his dad.

Finally, after what seems like an eternity and a half, the numbers on the display of Dex's code breaker stabilize, and the door gives a click and a little whoosh of air. The door slides open a crack, and Jules's steadfastness shatters instantly.

Bolting forward, he shoves the door aside with a gulping gasp for air, blurting, "Dad?"

Neal and I hurry after him, but I'm only a few steps inside before I come to an abrupt halt. Something's wrong.

The cell is covered with books and papers. Complex calculations are taped up along the walls, along with diagrams and sketches, and long pages of text. Some of the walls have even been written on directly, black magic marker in a slanted scrawl that reminds me eerily of Jules's handwriting.

But though it looks more like the hideout of a conspiracy theorist madman than the prison cell of a brilliant scholar, that's not what stops me.

What stops me is that the cell is empty.

Addison's not here.

23

JULES

"What?" Neal's voice is pretty much a panicked shriek. "Where is he?"

"Dex and Atlanta?" Mia's spinning in a quick circle, as if we might've missed my dad on first glance. "They got here before us and . . ." She trails off, not looking at me.

"No." I barely recognize my own voice, hoarse and harsh, the words choking out as my throat tightens. "No, no, they can't . . ."

I drop to a crouch as my legs seem to give out, planting one hand against the floor to support myself. I can feel my father here, his presence as strong as if he were beside me. This is his place—with all the work he's pinned up to the walls, the equations, the signs of a creative frenzy.

I might almost be back at Oxford, standing in his study, and with an overwhelming wave of homesickness, I desperately wish I were. Surrounded by his things, I could be in a tent on an archaeological dig, or a wide-eyed visitor to any one of the shabby apartments he's used as makeshift offices around the world. In this instant, I'm a thousand versions of me, all staring up at the boards of evidence, artifacts, and equations he's built over the years.

But he's not here. Maybe he's not anywhere anymore. A roaring rises in my ears.

Then Mia's crouching in front of me, fingers under my chin, lifting my gaze to meet hers. "Hey," she says quietly. "Jules, I know. I *know*. I'm so sorry, and I wish I could tell you he's okay, and I wish we had time to stop and think about this, but we don't. And I'm *so* sorry for that."

I try for a slower breath, keeping my gaze locked on hers, willing the rest of the world away as I let her anchor me.

"We have to keep going," she says quietly. "I need you to look around. He's covered every centimeter of this place, but maybe he's left a sign, some way for us to know which part of it's important."

Then there's a big hand squeezing my shoulder, and Neal's crouching beside me, his own voice shaky when he speaks. "Jules, mate, I don't want to sound morbid, but there's no reason Atlanta and Dex would escort Uncle Elliott out of here and kill him somewhere else. Someone would notice them moving him. They'd kill him and leave his body in this room, and it's not here. So maybe . . ."

They're both right. Maybe the Undying got to him ahead of us, and maybe he's dead. Maybe he's not. Either way, we have to keep going. So, legs shaking, I push to my feet and make myself look at the walls. Pretend I'm just in the study back at home, and there's a lesson here for me somewhere.

In my mind, I can hear my own, younger voice asking, *What does it all mean, Dad?*

In response, I hear his gentle answer. *Well, what do you see, Jules?* And then . . . I *see.*

My birthday jumps out at me from among a series of frequency notations tacked up on the wall. It's a call to me, of that I'm sure.

My heart speeds up to hummingbird levels.

It's not over yet. My father *did* leave something for me. I just have to find it.

My eyes fly around the room, searching for the message I know will be there. It only takes a few moments to find one word, written in capital letters and underlined twice, scrawled up on the wall above the door frame.

<u>VEGAS</u>, it says. Nobody else would know what that means.

Over the years, my father and I have been away on plenty of digs my mother never would have approved of, chasing half-baked clues her scientific mind told her weren't viable. So whenever we needed to talk about one of those trips, we'd joke about going to Las Vegas. It was silly, because it was one place neither my father nor I could ever imagine ourselves. It *is* an archaeological site these days, the ruins of gold and neon lying abandoned in the middle of a desert where the water finally ran out, but it's not the sort of place we focus on, even if it was fun to kid about finding a lost jackpot that would fund our next expedition.

Now, I know that one word is code for *this is a plan I can't speak out loud.*

Whatever he wants me to know, it will be here, but it will be encoded. I might not know where he is, or if he's okay, but I'm absolutely certain he's left me what I need.

"Here," I say, staring up at the strings of figures above the door. "This is the bit that matters."

Neal parks himself beside me, softly whispering to himself as he searches for meaning in the equations. "Are you sure?" he says, after half a minute. "These don't make sense, and they don't follow any of the codes he used with me on our phone calls."

I know the answer almost before I say it. "Use my birthday. That's the cipher. Push every letter and number forward twelve, then take the four for the month, April, and—"

"Got it," he says, completely locked on to the scribblings in front of him now.

"Do you recognize anything from the work you were doing with him?" Mia joins Neal, gazing up at the message, her voice barely daring to hope. "Could this be a way to shut down the portals?"

"Think it through," I say, willing him silently to hurry, but trying to keep my voice calm. "Make sure you have it right."

"I think . . ." I can hear the strain in his voice, and I can only imagine the mental calculations he's performing. "I think it's a frequency. It's a microwave frequency. This would fit with our idea that the portals needed an activation signal. The ship will broadcast it via a satellite relay around Earth."

"Great, so we need to get *back* to the ship?" Mia's voice is like lead.

"No, we just need to stop the portals receiving the signal. A frequency jammer. Or maybe jammers, all around the world, in each city where there's a portal."

"So we jam the signal," Mia says, "and the portals don't open? No toxin. No flu. No invasion."

Then a new voice speaks from the doorway. "Beno," says Atlanta, her tone subzero. "You're not so dumb."

My veins turn to ice as I drop my gaze, to find Atlanta and Dex standing side by side in the open doorway. She's holding an IA pistol, hefting it in her grip.

But though I freeze in place, Mia's instincts are completely different.

She darts forward, making a grab for the gun, wrapping her hand around Atlanta's as she tries to get her finger on the trigger, already twisting it around to point it at the Undying girl.

Seeming to almost *flow*, moving with impossible speed, Atlanta wrests it away from Mia, turning the weapon to point it straight at her head, forcing her to stumble back to join Neal and me.

"You protos," she says, her voice rich with disdain. "You protos and your weapons. You think they'll keep you safe, but look how easy they're turned yourways. Where is Elliott Addison?"

Despite the sheer terror that comes with having a gun pointed at your face, something in me releases just a fraction. *They didn't kill him.*

Quietly, Dex rests a hand on his partner's shoulder. "Easy, Peaches," he says softly. All his love for her is in those two words.

Just as it was every moment I listened to them in their quarters, through the wall of their ship. I know that wherever they grew up, these two grew up together. Their ties go deeper than I can possibly understand.

"Enough," she snaps. "It's one thing to feel sorry for them, Dex, but they keep popping up—if there's any chance they'll interfere, it's better to just kill them now."

Mia's breath hitches sharply, but I'm watching Dex, whose eyes go from the three of us beyond the barrel of Atlanta's gun, to her profile. In that moment he looks so stricken, so sad, that my heart gives a sympathetic lurch.

*Only too human after all.*

"No," he says finally, taking a step past Atlanta to put himself between us and the gun.

"What?" Atlanta snaps, jerking her gun away and taking a step back, as if even pointing the gun in his direction is unthinkable. "You fooling? It's so not the time."

But Dex's face is grave, no sign of humor there. "Our people— we were wrong to come here like this," he says quietly. "Our home has been the stars for centuries now—not this planet, not if it means genocide. Tell me you see that, A, deep down. That none of this is right."

"Of course it's right," Atlanta retorts with confusion. "They've had their chance with this planet—we're the ones who can save it from them."

"Maybe." Dex's voice is still quiet. "But not like this."

"Nothing has changed." Atlanta's lips quiver, her eyes anguished. "Dex, we grew up training for this, our whole lives. This one big push, and then all our people can come home."

Dex draws a long breath, and though his features are calm, there's a fight going on behind his eyes. "You're right," he says softly. "I *have* been training for this my whole life. I'm not who you think, Peaches."

"Stop *calling* me that!" Atlanta gestures with the gun, swinging it briefly toward Dex, who lifts his hands. For a long moment, she stares at him, uncomprehending. Then the barrel of the gun lowers, and her eyes widen. "You mean—all those stories. Dissenters, traitors among us working against us, to *help* these protos? Those stories—they're true?"

"The Nautilus is real." Dex is still speaking softly.

My pulse quickens, a jolt of excitement drowning out the fear for just a moment. *I was right.* The symbols scratched all over the Gaian temples and embedded in the deepest layers of code in the original Undying broadcast—not only were they a real warning, but I've got living proof right here that not all of the Undying want to wrest our planet from us by force.

Atlanta's shaking her head. "You're not one of them. I've known you since before I can remember. I'd *know.* You're not a traitor."

"Lower the gun," he pleads, soft, gentle, unmoving. "This isn't who we are. It's not who we have to be."

A shudder goes through her, as though she can't contain her response. She's heaving for breath.

His words are so soft I almost miss them. "I love you, Peaches. I pledge, you're my best friend. But I'm not going to let you kill them. It's not too late to stop what we're doing."

"Don't do this," she whispers. She lifts the gun, this time to aim it back at her partner again, its barrel wobbling and wavering. Her whole body—which had once seemed so alien in its deliberate movements and strength—is shaking. "Please, Dex. It's not too late for *you* either."

Dex is shaking too, but he doesn't move. He stands between her and us, the barrel of the gun pointed at his chest. He says nothing, but I can imagine the pain on his face. Whatever side he's chosen, he loves his partner, and this is killing him.

My heart thumps. Once, twice, three times.

Atlanta's finger tightens on the trigger a fraction, and she draws a few quick breaths, trying to force herself to act. But as a tear escapes her reddened eyes and tracks its way down her cheek, she cracks, lowering the gun to her side. She takes a single step back through the doorway, then slams her hand over the button just beside the door frame.

The door slides closed at lightning speed, and a red light springs to life beside it. All four of us lunge forward, tangling together as we scrabble for the controls, but we're an instant too late.

The door's firmly sealed, Atlanta's gone, and we're locked inside.

24

AMELIA

"QUICK," JULES SAYS, STEPPING BACK TO MAKE WAY FOR DEX.
"The code breaker, open the door!"

But Dex doesn't move a muscle, simply staring down at the
blinking light. "It only works when a lock's able to be unlocked,"
he says quietly. "This one isn't designed to unlock from the inside."

"So . . ." Jules's voice trails away.

"So we're stuck here," I say. "Until someone comes along and
finds us."

"But we know how to block the portals," he protests, voice rising. "We know how, we can't just—"

"We know how," Neal says. "But we don't know *how*. We don't
have any way to broadcast a jamming frequency worldwide. And
there's no way we can travel around the world to a hundred cities
to jam them each one by one, even if we could get out of this cell.
*And* we still don't have any way to make the IA believe us. What are
we going to do, point to Dex when they show up and find us here,

him with his completely human DNA, and insist he came from a spaceship?"

"Because that worked so well last time," I mutter.

All the faces around me are grim. "Mia's right," Jules says. "There's nobody out there who'll believe us. Deus, this is almost worse than it was before. We know how to save our people, and nobody's going to listen."

"Not true." That's Dex, from his place by the door. He's speaking slowly and thoughtfully, as if he's working through an idea. He's still staring at the door, as if Atlanta might come back through it. "That's not true. There are some people who believe you. And they're all over the world, yeh? I've been watching them since we landed."

It takes me a long moment to understand what he means, and I see it dawn on the others' faces.

He's right.

We might be trapped in here, but we have allies out there. They're the friends and colleagues of Elliott Addison, even his competitors. They're the people online who refuse to believe what they're told without being shown the facts behind it. They are Luisa, in Dresden. They are everywhere.

They believe in Addison.

But will they be enough?

All we can do is hope.

"I'm posting what we know to the forums," Neal says, pulling out his phone, and backing over to his uncle's desk to sink down into his chair. "Before someone finds us here and confiscates my phone. The folks on those forums told me they wanted to hear from me, they invited me to come tell them what's happening. Maybe they'll pick this up. Maybe they can build jammers, save their own cities. Save as many as they can."

We fall silent as he works furiously, occasionally glancing back at the codes his uncle left scrawled above the door. Jules is watching the door, and I'm watching Dex, who's still hardly moved.

We might have sixty seconds until someone shows up to discover us. Or, if they all think Dr. Addison is somewhere else, if the IA moved him to a new location, then it could be a *very* long time before anyone looks in here.

However long we have, I don't want to waste it. I want answers. I have hundreds of questions burning through my mind—questions with impossible answers—and Dex is the only one who can unravel everything that's happened to us. Jules begins to pace as Neal types, and I find myself walking laps of the little prison-cell-turned-office in the opposite direction, passing him twice every circuit. *Like caged animals*, my brain supplies.

After a few minutes Neal lowers his phone, cradling it in one hand. "I've done my best," he says. "I've given them the specs. Now we have to hope they understand us. That they're the sort of people prepared to pull apart their microwaves and start modifying them, given sufficient proof of what's going on."

"That's what all this has been about," Jules says softly. "Truth."

I want to soak up the sound of his voice, drink in every second I can stare at him, because when they come and find us here, I probably won't see him again for . . . well. I probably won't see him again. Or Evie.

But despite this, I find my gaze twitching across to Dex, taking in his lean height, the dark hair, the skin a shade somewhere between mine and Jules's, and the droop of his shoulders where he stands. *I'm in a room with a member of a race that's trying to wipe out humanity.*

It was a lot easier to just hate him when I thought he was an alien. Now, knowing he's as human as I am . . . somehow, it makes everything worse. Complex and nuanced, Jules would say. *Messy*, say my own thoughts.

"Thank you for helping us." Neal, surprising me with his gravity, is watching Dex with his eyes full of sympathy. "I could see she meant a lot to you."

"She's my other half." Dex clenches his jaw, and a tear streaks down one cheek as he turns his face away. "We grew up together. We've been partners since before we could read and write."

"What kind of partners?" Neal rummages through his pockets until he produces a mangled, crushed plastic packet of tissues. He rises to his feet and walks over to Dex, offering them to him. Trying to understand this boy who's suddenly in our midst.

Dex looks between him and the tissues, a trickle of confusion momentarily eclipsing his misery.

"For when your nose starts running," Neal provides helpfully. "Or your eyes."

Dex, brow furrowed, takes the packet and extracts one of the tissues, then carefully wipes at his face. He looks up to meet Neal's eyes briefly, and though he doesn't smile, there's a shift around his eyes. "Thanks. We're . . . I don't know how to describe it. We're supposed to be together. We always are." And, judging by his tone, it hurts right now that they're not.

"What *is* with the partners thing anyway?" I ask, making Dex twitch and look my way. "On the ship, in Lyon, you and Atlanta . . . why do you all go around in twos?"

Dex lifts a shoulder. "All of us on the retrieval team have partners. A partner keeps you focused, has your back, isn't afraid to challenge you, comprens your thinking and your capabilities better than you compren yourself. And if you ever start to doubt your convictions . . ." Dex's eyes go distant again. "Then a partner keeps you on track."

"Retrieval team?" Jules echoes. "Retrieval of what?"

Dex's eyes flicker toward Jules and stay there. "Of our home."

Gently, carefully, each word like a cautious step through a minefield, Jules speaks into the quiet. "Your people are from the Centauri mission."

Though there's no lift at the end of his sentence, the words are a question anyway. Dex watches him, hints of anguish showing about his eyes and lips, and then drops his head.

When Jules looks my way, I can only lift my shoulders helplessly. If Dex doesn't want to answer our questions, we can't force him. We're not killers or torturers, and anyway, he helped us. But this could be our last chance to understand everything that's happened.

The silence stretches until Neal turns to retrieve his uncle's chair, wheeling it across the room and offering it to Dex, then sinking down to sit on the floor. "Are you regretting what you did? Stopping her from killing us?"

Dex's tight lips relax a fraction, and then he ducks his head. "I should've tried harder to shift her. I should've explained somehow—I should've . . ." He makes a strange, swooping gesture that, while utterly foreign to me, conveys an all-encompassing helplessness that makes my own heart ping with unexpected sympathy.

"Of course you regret hurting your partner." Neal's voice is gentle. "But do you regret the choice you made?"

Dex just sinks down slowly into the chair. "I chose what I chose." He's quiet and still for a few seconds longer, and then he draws his shoulders back and takes a long, bracing breath. The tissue's still clutched in his hand as it curls into a fist. "And yeh. My ancestors were the crew and colonists on the Centauri mission."

"But how?" The words spill out of me before I can stop them. "Your tech is so much more advanced than ours, and the ship only left Earth like sixty years ago, and the temple on Gaia's a zillion years old, not to mention a zillion light-years away, and . . ."

I'm braced for my torrent of questions to send Dex back into lockdown, but he's just watching me, an odd almost-warmth in his eyes, like some part of him is amused. "Looking at it yourways, the ship did leave only sixty years ago. But ourways, it's been over three centuries."

Jules pushes off from where he's been leaning against his father's desk, sending a stack of papers fluttering violently to the floor. "Time travel?" he blurts, his skin going several shades darker, his own hands clenched into fists. "All this time we've been trying to figure out this absurd riddle with no answer, and all this time it was something that's—that's—impossible! Time travel isn't possible. It isn't."

Every face in the room turns toward him, shocked by his uncharacteristic outburst. Standing there with fists clenched, lungs heaving, face flooded with ire and eyes blazing, he looks like he's ready to fight someone.

*If ever there was something Jules would be ready to knock someone down over, it'd be an academic discussion about abstract concepts of quantum astro-whatever . . .*

Despite myself, I burst into helpless laughter.

This time all eyes in the room go to me, including Jules, his fists relaxing in surprise. I lift my head to explain what was so funny, that he's objecting to the concept of time travel while sitting in a detention cell in Prague with an ancient time-traveling space-human turncoat-alien whose people want to steal our planet. I want to tell Jules I'm fine, but I can't stop laughing, my whole body seizing and quaking, spots forming before my eyes as my lungs struggle to get enough air. I reach for the wall behind me and slide down onto the ground, shaking.

As soon as I realize I can't stop, my brain short-circuits. It's not funny anymore, but I'm still laughing, like the wires have gotten crossed and I want to cry or scream or explode into bits all over the inside of the room, but all I know how to do is keep laughing.

Jules is on the floor next to me in seconds, wrapping his arms around me as I gasp, tears running from my eyes. He draws me in against him, one hand cradling the back of my head. For some reason it's the feel of his fingers running through my newly cut hair that reminds me that my body's a thing I can control, and with his arm around me, I take a long, shuddering breath.

When I can look around again, the other boys are staring at me. I cough, twinges of embarrassment rising up now that the panic-laughter, whatever it was, is fading. I cough, and try to draw a breath, and it *snorks* through my clogged nose and makes me realize I must have snot just absolutely *everywhere*.

The light shifts, and when I look up, Dex is there crouched in front of me, the squashy packet of tissues held out flat on both palms, like an offering of tribute. His expression is grave, and he makes such a *human* tableau despite not knowing how to hand someone a tissue.

Another tiny little laugh escapes, like an aftershock reminding me that the tectonic plates of my abused psyche aren't done shifting around yet. My fingers are shaking as they reach for the tissue packet. Weakly, I smile at Dex. "Thanks."

He smiles back, and because I'm looking at him, I can see the moment when the strangeness, the *familiarity*, of that human connection hits him. The Undying must have expected us to be as unfeeling and alien as we thought they were. A shadow crosses his features, and he returns to the chair Neal offered him.

"We're not time travelers," he says softly as he sits. He looks across at us, and when I nod—*I'm okay, go ahead*—he takes another of those smooth, bracing breaths. "Though yeh, we have shifted in time. Eight years into the journey to the Alpha Centauri system, something went wrong with the ship. A design flaw during construction. We sent a distress call Earthward, but after waiting weeks for it to reach them, the only reply was that they couldn't help us. We were abandoned."

"They didn't have another ship," Neal murmurs. "They *couldn't* have helped. The colonists knew that."

"Maybe." Dex's expression is grave—he obviously has no desire to debate whose fault the failure of the mission was. "But while we were trying to patch the ship, an unidentified anomaly appeared, and caught up the ship, drawing it into uncharted space. We call it the Storm—and that's the easiest way to compren it. Imagine you're in a boat on the ocean—" He pauses and looks around. "Does Earth still have boats, do you compren what that is?"

I blink, momentarily meeting Neal's eyes before looking back. "Um, yes, we know what boats are."

Dex's mouth twists, a hint of wry humor there. "It's not a lixo question. For us, everything about Earth is ancient history. I mean, do you people know off the top of your head whether the ancient Egyptians knew about . . . antibiotics?"

"Um," I say again, "actually, yeah, pretty much everyone in the world knows ancient Egyptians were way before antibiotics. That's not the best example you could have picked."

Jules's arm around me squeezes, and he whispers in my ear, "The ancient Egyptians actually did know about antibiotics. They, um, used a kind of medicinal beer." The words are apologetic. The gleam in his eye when I turn to glower at him isn't.

From the look on Dex's face, his sharp ears picked up on Jules's whisper. But when he grins at me, for the first time I feel warmer for seeing him smile, rather than disturbed by how an alien could seem so human. "So yeh. Boats. Imagine a boat on the ocean, and a storm shows up and gives you hassle. Once you're at the mercy of the weather, you don't know where you'll have shifted once the storm passes. You could be kilometers off course."

"Or centuries," Jules murmurs.

"Or millennia." Dex's grin has vanished again. "Though we didn't compren at first that we'd been shifted in time as well as space, because nothing around them was familiar. Without any reference points you could be dropped anyways, any*when*, in the universe and have no idea."

"So it took you fifty thousand years back, the temple's age on Gaia?" I ask.

"Not that first time, that came much later. After the Storm, the Centauri crew were stranded with no help, and only enough supplies to reach their original destination—so only a few years' worth of food. This is actually my favorite historical era," he adds shyly, as if confessing a guilty pleasure, though the pride in his expression says otherwise. "The resilience of our ancestors, their ingenuity, the dozens of ways they worked out to extend, preserve, and sirsly, even *grow* their own food in those early decades is staggering. There's a whole trilogy of movies about it."

"You have movies?" Neal's eyebrows shoot up.

Dex blinks at him. "Are you fooling? Of course we have movies. It's not like we can build massive interstellar spaceships but somehow not compren a video camera. Our movies are like your . . . what'd they call it? Virtual reality? They're kind of interactive, yeh? You can watch, or you can pick a role in the story and be *in* the movie, and the characters are all programmed to react spontaneously according to their personalities."

Neal's cheeks flush a little, but he chuckles anyway, looking only mildly embarrassed. "I'd like to see those movies about the crew right after the Storm."

"They're beno." Dex studies Neal out of the corner of his eye, measuring, thoughtful.

Jules clears his throat. "So the Centauri crew figured out how to extend their rations . . . ?"

Dex blinks, looking back toward us. "Yeh. And they discovered that the Storm was not a unique phenomenon, that there were these anomalies all over the place. That probably, they created the one that pulled them in when they were trying to get their broken ship to shift, trying all kinds of lixo ideas. They shifted through every one they could find, hoping to get lucky and get sent someways Earthward, someways with star patterns they could recognize. But that was when their astronavigators comprenned why all their calculations were giving them so much hassle—that the Storm they were traveling through was shifting them in time as well as space, yeh? The probability of finding a hole in space that just *happens* to bring you anywhere Earthward is so tiny that it was actually pretty foolish of them to even try. But when you add in time as a variable . . . to get close to Earth *and* come out at a time when they could actually get help, a time when humans were spacefaring?"

Neal hisses through his teeth. "Yeah, that's pretty grim, mate."

"Sirsly grim."

When Dex falls silent, I realize that my heart's pounding—in spite of everything, despite the fear and hatred I have for this race of invaders, I desperately want him to continue the story. Because suddenly, it's stopped being the story of the Undying—a remote, alien race—and become *our* story. The story of people just like us, trying to survive. "What did you do when you realized you'd probably never get home?" My voice is hushed.

He glances at me. "We became the Undying," he replies simply. "We abandoned the idea of returning to Earth—remember these were all still the original colonists, and they'd been beno with never seeing Earth again anyways. We decided to find a new home. We started searching for star systems instead of entry points to the Storm, for habitable planets instead of astronomical reference points."

"How long did it take you to find someplace?" Jules is as riveted as I am—his arm has gone lax around me, so fixated is he on Dex's story.

"Well, at first we concentrated on things like asteroids and moons and planetoids with dense mineral deposits, so we could get the materials to build more ships, faster ships. We poured every last resource we had, after what we needed to survive, into scientific research. Every new child born was raised to question, to explore, to try and compren things outside the boundaries of what we believed was possible. Our ancestors knew we could survive— but that we wouldn't, unless we pushed at the limits of human resilience and creativity."

A little finger of dread creeps down my spine, and I echo Jules. "How long were you lost in space before you found a place to live?"

Dex's expression is calm, but there's an endless depth to his gaze and I already know what he's going to say. "We didn't."

Neal's breath catches. "What do you mean you didn't?"

"The universe is a big place," Dex replies mildly. "Planets and stars and nebulas and everything you can see from planetside—all of that makes up a tiny, tiny fraction of what's out there, and the spaces in between are almost endless. There are definitely habitable planets out there—thousands of them, probably millions. But the scale of just one galaxy, let alone the universe . . . Our brains sirsly can't compren how far apart everything is. Even with countless places to enter the Storm, your odds of emerging anywhere near a star system with habitable planets are vanishingly, impossibly low. And we never have."

"So . . ." Jules speaks slowly, quietly. "In all that time, everywhere you went using all the Storm anomalies, across the universe and back . . . ?"

Dex nods. "In three hundred years of searching, we never found a planet that could support life." His lashes drop, and he gazes at the floor. "Earth is all we have. It's all any of us have."

My throat is tight, and I'm grateful for Jules at my side, because without him I'd feel so tiny, so insignificant and alone, that I'd curl up and cry. As if he can sense my thoughts, Jules arm tightens around me again.

"We did compren one thing, though." Dex's eyes are still on the floor, though the faded blue-gray carpet—with its myriad, unidentifiable stains—can't be holding his attention. "All that time trying to use the Storm anomalies to travel, we comprenned how to harness them for our own use. How to create them."

Neal leans toward him, a sudden spark igniting his excitement. "The portals."

"The portals," Dex confirms. "It wasn't like we could just tell a portal 'Take us Earthward!' or anything, it had to be a link between two known places. Two artificial portals are linked to each other through the aether—the space between space, the space inside the Storm. It meant, though, that we could spread out—we could shift from ship to ship, the whole fleet staying together even when we were light-years apart. We could specialize. Mining ships, plantation ships, ships dedicated as schools and universities, hospital ships . . . We built a civilization. Wherever we were, *whenever*, we could visit another ship from our own time instantly."

"It sounds like your people basically figured out how to live without a planet at all." Neal's voice is gently impressed. "So why did you all still want to come back to Earth?"

Dex glances at Neal sidelong. "Not all of us did."

Jules leans forward. "What do you mean?"

Dex sighs. "If it were me? I'd be happy to live on the ship where I was born, among the stars, never shifting planetwards except to explore. And I'm not the only one. But most of us . . . humans aren't built that way. People want a home, a place that's theirs, and you have to understand . . . we all grew up thinking that had been taken from us forever, unless we could go *home*. Our real home."

"And Gaia?" Jules reveals very little in his voice. He's so different from the boy he was. He's cautious now. He's driven in a way he wasn't before, even when flying halfway across the universe to search an alien planet for his father's freedom.

Dex lifts his head, meeting Jules's gaze unflinchingly. "A little less than a hundred years before I was born, a woman named Verna Glasgow, an artist by trade, had an idea. The only thing stopping us from using the portals to shift homeward was that there was no matching portal on Earth. But if there was a way to make mankind *bring* a portal Earthward . . ."

My mind reels, trying to grasp all the pieces and assemble them, but every time I make one connection, three others seem to vanish like smoke. "So . . . but . . . why all the riddles? Why not just explain all this in the broadcast?"

"Because there was another problem, yeh? We were a race of thousands by then. We were centuries beyond protos—Earth humans—in technology. If we just went home, there'd be no place for us. Not among a people who abandoned us when our ancestors' ship first broke down."

"But they *didn't* abandon you," Jules says, though the protest is gentle. "That was always the understanding—we put all our eggs in one basket. We bet everything on the Centauri ship. There was no second ship to send."

"That's not how our story goes," Dex replies. "Our history says we called, and nobody came. And now, after all this time, we'd be shifting to a dying planet with no power to stop what was happening. We couldn't just shift home. We had to *take* our world back, as the rightful stewards of this paradise you don't even realize you have."

Neal says softly, "You had to save the world."

Dex clears his throat. His fingers are twined tightly together in his lap. "At that point my people existed in a time about fifty thousand years before this present. That's where they'd shifted through their most recent portals. The temples, the broadcast, the portal ship . . . it took decades to put together. By that time Verna Glasgow was in her late fifties. And as she watched her idea grow, and mutate, and grow again, and seed itself, and change into something she didn't compren anymore, she realized she'd been wrong. That we'd survived for hundreds of years alone in space—that we didn't just survive, we *thrived*. That we didn't need to take Earth, we didn't need to destroy our Earth counterparts so that we might live."

Jules's body has gone rigid next to me, but it isn't until he speaks that I understand why. "She saw what she'd created, and changed her mind. She tried to warn them."

"And she was dismissed as a sentimental fool talking a pile of lixo, causing hassle." Dex knows why Jules's voice has changed. The Undying know everything about Elliott Addison, after all. "An artist, after all, not a leader. They let her contribute to the murals and decoration of the temples, but when she refused and made a public appeal to all the ships in the fleet, she was shouted down. All she could do was pass along her misgivings to her children. Teach them that there was room in this universe for all of us. That what we were planning was murder and deception. That even if we saved the world, we'd be dooming ourselves."

*Artists and scientists*, I think to myself. *No one wants to believe either.*

Jules is squeezing my hand, hard. I ease free, and curl my fingers through his instead. The gesture seems to restore him somewhat, and he takes an audible breath as Dex continues.

"Her children found others who were uncertain. Who didn't accept this universally proclaimed truth that we were the superior, evolved version of humanity. Who didn't want to destroy billions of lives for the sake of thousands. And some who simply didn't want to give up life in the stars for life on the dirt." His eyes lift. "It became a secret society, yeh? An underground resistance. Waiting until the day the Undying would return to take Earth, so that maybe they could stop what was happening from within. Just in case the warnings left by Verna Glasgow when she was decorating the temple weren't enough."

A strangled sound comes from Jules at my side, and when I look over at him, his eyes are wide with understanding and accusation both. Stricken, he sits unmoving as Dex gets slowly to his feet and unbuttons his shirt, peeling it down to reveal his bare shoulder.

Swirling around the joint, its arms outstretched to curl around the edge of his shoulder blade, alive with translucent gold and purple and deepest indigo, is the spiral galaxy.

"We call ourselves the Nautilus."

**25**

**JULES**

I'M CLINGING TO MIA NOW, AS THOUGH SHE'S THE ONLY THING THAT might stop me from floating away. As if her weight beside me on the floor will somehow prevent me from breaking free of the Earth's gravity and spinning away into space.

And why shouldn't I fly free of the Earth's grasp? Every other rule has been broken. Why not this one too?

"This is so elaborate." My voice is husky, strained, the pressure my mind is under reflected in my body. "It's just *so* elaborate. Your language didn't evolve into something unrecognizable in three hundred years. That doesn't happen."

"No," says Dex, his dark eyes on my face as he watches me work toward the conclusion.

"You created the glyphs to convince us you weren't human," I say quietly.

"Yeh."

"And you built a temple you never used."

"Yeh."

"And you sent a signal, pretending to be a dead alien species, all so you could lure us to Gaia, through the temple, and to your ship?"

"Yeh."

My voice is cracking, now. "Because we're *so* awful, so untrustworthy, that going to all that trouble, undertaking these herculean tasks, seemed a better bet to you than simply contacting us and asking for our help in building a portal to help you come home?"

His whisper is deathly soft. "Yeh. You gotta compren, after centuries of being taught about the greed and wastefulness and selfishness of the humans who abandoned us, who trashed a planet that was unique in all the universe, not one of us would have ever thought a plea for help would've been answered this time."

"You banked on our greed," Mia says. "You banked on the fact that if you told us there was treasure on the line, we'd go through anything to find it."

"Well," says Neal, as Dex buttons his shirt and sits, "in their defense, they were right."

Perhaps Neal wants to divert us away from this talk of blame, because he leans against a desk, facing Dex.

"Tell me more about the portals," he says. "I've been working on them with Uncle Elliott—with Dr. Addison—these last few weeks. We've only ever seen manufactured portals, but the way you talk about the naturally occurring portals, they sound to me like they work differently. They sound wild, unpredictable."

"They are different," Dex agrees. "That difference is why we needed you. The naturally occurring portals, like the one the first Centauri ship was lost through, they lead through the aether to a set time and place, and you can't change it. No matter when you enter the portal on one side, on the other, you'll emerge on a specific day, at a specific time."

"But that's not how our portal works," Mia says, beside me. "The portal between Earth and Gaia, it always leads to the same *place*, but it doesn't lead to the same *time*. Otherwise, every expedition, from the first one through to ours, would all have shown up on the same day. But we didn't. We arrived just a moment after we left. The same distance apart."

"That's right," Dex agrees. "That's the difference between a naturally occurring portal, and one that's constructed. And it's why we needed your help. When you received our transmission, you built a portal between Earth and Gaia. A manufactured portal. We knew it had to be after our ancestors left, or they never would have left, and none of us would exist, yeh?"

"The grandfather rule," I breathe. *The paradox that explains why time travel could never work, even if it* didn't *violate the laws of physics.*

Mia leans in against me. "That's the one about how, if you go back to before you were born, you might accidentally stop yourself being born?" she asks.

"Right. The Undying needed a portal back to Earth after the Centauri expedition left, to make sure they didn't accidentally prevent their ancestors from leaving, and prevent themselves from being born."

"Yes," Dex replies. "So even if we could have found it again, we couldn't have just gone back through that very first Storm portal to reach Earth. We'd have arrived in the same instant our ancestors left, and we might have prevented them leaving at all. What we could do, though, was send a signal out into the aether."

"Oh, I see," Neal breathes, as soft as a prayer. "You send a signal into the aether, and it emerges from every portal it can find, doesn't it? Including that first Storm portal. That's how you knew your signal would reach Earth at the right time to set us to work building the portal you needed. Your ancestors would just miss it."

"Yeh." Dex nods. "But we weren't sure where in time we were—we hoped we were in the past, but it could have been thousands of years until you showed up on Gaia. But as soon as you took the ship through the portal to Earth, you activated all the internal portals on the ship, and we knew it was time to send our teams through."

He's sounding a little better, and he's speaking mostly to Neal—I think Neal's steady gaze genuinely helps, even if he's no Atlanta. Neal's presence helps most people, I've noticed.

"Right," Mia says, and her tone of voice tells me she's working toward a conclusion she doesn't like one bit. "So you get the signal, you know the ship's reached Earth, and you start sending through your teams. And they head down to Earth, posing as bits of space junk, but really . . ."

Dex nods, as if she's finished her sentence, dropping his head. "But really, they're building portals planetside, preparing for the arrival of the reclamation teams," he says quietly.

"After most of Earth's humans have lost their minds," I murmur, trying to ignore the sick feeling growing in the pit of my stomach. "Since the test in Lyon was a resounding success."

Dex leans forward, burying his face in his hands. "It's not going to matter much longer," he says, muffled. "They're all scheduled to activate a couple days from now, but there's no way Atlanta won't speed up her plans. It'll be hours, not days—and Prague will be just like that town, only millions more will be affected."

I'm struggling for breath, and beside me, Mia makes a sound like someone's struck her.

*Hours.*

We had even less time than we'd imagined.

"Will anyone survive?" Neal whispers.

Dex lifts his head again, his gaze distant. "Well, we will, for a while. No running water in here. But unless someone lets us out before the toxin takes over . . ."

"Then we'll die of dehydration." Mia's voice is tiny. Scared. After all we've been through, I can't blame her—we passed up a dozen deaths preferable to dying of thirst, forgotten in a basement while the world burns.

"Maybe people who live somewhere small will survive for a while," Dex says. "Somewhere high. Maybe in the mountains, upstreamward, where the water won't come from somewhere infected. All the big cities will be gone. Or rather, there'll be olders in charge, Undying stewards. The portal teams are all our age—we were trained on planets with Earth-equivalent gravity, to prepare us. No air or life on our training planets, not places we could call home, but enough to make sure we'd be able to handle being planetside when the time came. The stewards will find it harder going, down here, but they'll make the sacrifice and take the hassle, to run the cities."

Mia's voice is thin and small as she asks, "But what about all the people who do drink the toxin? They'll be like animals, dangerous ones, and there'll be millions of them, everywhere."

Dex swallows, looking nearly as sick as I feel. "The toxin makes most people infertile," he says quietly. "Yeh, they're dangerous. But all we'll have to do is wait."

*For humanity to die out.*

Everyone's quiet for a long moment, and it's Neal who breaks the silence. He's staring at his phone again. "We have another problem," he says, soft and solemn. "The people on the forum are picking up what we're saying, but only about half the targeted cities have anyone who's on the ground, and knows what they're doing, and says they're building a jammer."

"Half?" Mia lifts her head, stricken. "That's still hundreds of millions—maybe billions, I don't know—of people who are still going to turn into . . . turn into those things we saw in Lyon."

We're all silent, reeling from this new gut punch. The flicker of hope that even if we didn't make it, some places might—it was something to hold on to. But though the Undying may not be able to take over the planet in the next few days, they'll be able to take a lot of it if they can wipe out dozens of cities in one night. Earth will certainly never be the same.

My mind feels sluggish, and with a wrenching effort I force myself to focus. There must be some way we can increase the reach of our message, find new allies—but I can't see it.

Dex rises slowly to his feet, scanning our weary faces. "The first thing we saw, when we arrived," he begins slowly, "was the power of your media."

"I doubt we've got supporters at any local news stations," I mutter.

Dex raises an eyebrow. "I mean the pictures, the videos, everything that floods your networks—sirsly, when one video is seen enough times, it reaches a kind of critical mass and suddenly millions are watching."

Mia's eyes widen. "You're saying we need a video, something people will watch, and tell their friends to watch—something that gets attention and proves what's going on somehow."

Dex nods. "And I can think of someone the world would watch—they watched his father, after all, a million times over."

All eyes swivel toward me, and a bolt of sheer terror stiffens my spine. "No," I whisper, almost inaudible even to myself.

"The Addison speech," Mia murmurs beside me. "Part two."

26

AMELIA

Jules's eyes fix on me, and the hint of pain and accusation in them hits like a blow. "What good would it do for me to be the one on camera?" he blurts. "If anything, the world's *less* likely to believe me, given that they don't believe my father."

"But the point Dex is making is that the first problem is getting people to watch the video at all. We need them to tune in. The second part, the *believing us* part—that comes later."

"Mia," he says simply, his gaze saying the rest. His father's fall from grace—the mocking, the memes of his impassioned plea, the repetition of the injuries over and over—it was almost too much for Jules to bear the first time. And now we're asking him to put himself in the middle of it again, with—he believes—little chance of success.

"I know," I whisper, twisting my body in to face his, shutting out everything else. "But there's no other choice, Jules. They could find us locked in here any minute, and we'll lose our last chance to spread the warning. This time, it will be different." There's a ferociousness in my voice that startles me, and I realize that I really believe that I'm saying. "This time, they've seen Lyon. This time, there's an army of supporters out there just waiting to help spread the word, and you'll be broadcasting from inside the IA, right in front of your father's work. This time, they'll listen, like they should have listened to him. Nobody's going to look at you and doubt you, Jules. They never could."

I can see the pulse at his neck, quick and delicate and so, so fast, as he tries to steady himself. And then he closes his eyes, and lets out a breath. "There's no other choice," he echoes. And I'm not sure if it's resignation, or a leap of faith, but I know he'll do it.

"Neal, can you get some sort of livestream hosting site up?" I have only the vaguest idea what I'm talking about, but Neal nods like I'm speaking his language. I squeeze Jules's hands as I continue. "And a countdown. Dex, when are the portals activating?"

"They can be turned on manually," Dex replies, "but they're not scheduled for mass deployment for another fifty-two hours and eight minutes."

Neal's lips twitch. "You're not big on precision, are you?"

Dex blinks owlishly. "Seven minutes and forty-eight seconds now."

Neal laughs, but his amusement doesn't last long. "You think anyone apart from Atlanta will turn theirs on early?"

"I don't know," Dex admits. "It's possible, if they see the broadcast. But there wasn't a plan for it, and we're a big network. Even after we started chasing Jules and Mia around our ship, it took us two days to accelerate the launch schedule—we don't change course quickly. Planetside, we all operate independently, and there's no system for communicating a change of plan. Nobody anticipated any real proto resistance, to be honest. No offense."

Neal snickers, and abruptly I realize that his joking, lighthearted nature doesn't irritate me the way it once did. Then, it seemed like he didn't understand the weight of what Jules and I had to accomplish. Or that it was all some big game, a bunch of kids playing at international spydom. But the warmth in his face is real, and now I can't not see it. His face looks so much like Jules's when he's being sincere, and whenever he speaks Jules looks just the tiniest bit lighter. And when Jules is lighter, my own mind feels freer.

I don't think we'd have gotten this far without Neal. And not just because of the passports he brought us.

"All right." I clear my throat, just enough to get their attention back on me. "Then we need to do this now, before someone finds us and takes the phone, and hope it spreads."

Jules finally speaks again, still holding my hand, his voice almost steady. "It's good timing. It's noon here, so it'd be eleven a.m. in England," he says. "Six a.m. on the east coast of the US. A lot of people will be awake to see it."

My brows lift, focus derailed the tiniest bit. "You just know that off the top of your head?"

Jules lifts his eyebrows right back at me, and now his gaze is steady. "I looked it up. I had a compelling reason to learn what the time difference would be between, say, Oxford and a suitably anonymous town on the east coast of America."

He doesn't add *when this is all over*. But it's there in his eyes, in the determined set of his jaw. I haven't forgotten the promise I made him—that we're in this together, from now on, no matter what—and for the first time, I wonder if it could really turn out that way.

So I don't try to hide the smile those words spark, and I don't suppress the flutter of excitement that he'd been looking up our time differences, and I don't turn away to hide my blush.

"We'll have everyone on the #IBelieveInAddison forums to help spread the word," Neal says, head down, already fiddling with his phone. "And my followers."

"You have followers?" I ask.

"Many. He posts pictures of the Oxford water polo team," Jules says beside me, dry. "Our uniform doesn't involve shirts."

I blink slowly, and just give my brain a minute. It's been through a lot lately, and that's quite an image.

Neal is logging in to his accounts and setting up a stream, while explaining to Jules the information he'll need to give about building a frequency jammer—once he's convinced everyone he's for real.

Jules is nodding, brain working overtime as he memorizes it, expression dubious. "I'm going to convincingly tell them we can stop the portals opening and save the world with a secondhand microwave and some duct tape?" he asks. "Why don't I just throw in some chewing gum and a shoelace?"

"If you like," Neal replies. "As long as you look a lot less disbelieving when you say it."

"And," Dex says, from where he's studying Dr. Addison's equations, "you gotta do it quickly, before someone realizes we're here and imprisons us. Jules, if you can convince enough people, it *will* work. My people gotta have the portals to shift the virus planetside, distribute it to the cities. There's not enough of us trained in Earth gravity to invade head-on, and all our shuttles are already down on the surface, most of them self-destructed by now."

"And what're the odds they'll just drop a rain of bombs on our heads or something out of petty vengeance?"

Dex's eyebrows rise. "And destroy the only habitable planet we've ever known?" He shakes his head. "Without the portals, I don't think they'll have any choice but to leave, or negotiate some kind of peace."

*Peace.*

A week ago I would have scoffed, pointing out the sheer inhumanity of the invaders at our doorstep, and claiming there was no possible way this would end peacefully. But Dex—and the rest of his unseen Nautilus operatives—have reminded me that even enemies can be complex. Even enemies can become allies.

Jules starts muttering his script to himself, head down, as Neal positions the camera. I spin away to pace, and stop short when I abruptly realize there's someone staring back at me through the observation window in our locked cell door.

His perfect black hair is still perfectly in place, and his perfectly shaped eyebrows are lifted just a little, but there's something a little wild about Director De Luca's eyes.

"Guys," I say, and the warning in my tone grabs everyone's attention, so that a second later, the only sound in the cell is the soft hum of the door as De Luca opens it.

"No," he says, turning his head to speak to someone outside, and I catch a glimpse of an armed soldier. "Stay outside. Close the door behind me."

"Director, I—"

De Luca silences the protest with one raised hand. "You don't have security clearance for this conversation," he says, and steps into the room.

A moment later, the door hums closed behind him. And then it's the five of us.

The silence stretches as we all face the man in the doorway, trying to get his measure. His eyes sweep across us, coming to rest upon Dex.

He breaks the silence with one question, voice low. "Is there a cure?"

I'm glancing at Dex before I have time to register the implications of that question. The Undying boy draws a quaking breath and shakes his head. "For Lyon? No."

De Luca's face tightens, and this time I can see the fear in his eyes as he gazes at Dex. "Your people," he says, and then pauses for a few long heartbeats, struggling with the question he's about to ask. "Are they human?"

My heart seizes, and I glance at Jules. His eyes are waiting for mine, kindling with a tiny flash of hope.

*De Luca knows.*

Dex looks rather fearful himself. It's one thing to be found out by a handful of teenagers, and quite another to be the sole captive of the man responsible for the security of the whole continent. "Yes, sir," he replies. "We're the descendants of the Centauri settlers, lost in space and time."

De Luca's shoulders sag a little and he steps back until he's got the support of the cell wall at his back.

"You believe us now," Jules says quietly. There's anger in his voice, and I can't blame him. If De Luca had believed us earlier, we wouldn't be in this position. The world would've had time to prepare for the invasion. Maybe they could have even stopped Lyon. But when I look at Jules, his body is rigid with control.

He's angry, but he's not going to blow this last chance to win ourselves an ally.

De Luca's face is troubled, his habitual mask of superiority and disinterest cracking and mixing with fear and confusion. "I don't know what I believe," he says slowly. "But I know our researchers have shown that the disease in Lyon has come from an artificially engineered toxin, and that it's far more sophisticated than anything we've seen before. I know that the shuttle we were assembling to send a team of astronauts up to the ship in orbit was sabotaged, using technology our engineers haven't manage to decode yet. And I know—" His eyes flicker across toward Jules and me. "I know *you* believe it."

It's not an apology. I don't think we'll ever *get* an apology from a man like De Luca. But he's changed his mind. And that's all we need.

"You have to let us out," I say, trying to keep my voice even and suppress the urgency in my heart.

Both De Luca's eyebrows shoot up. "Are you insane? I have to question you. All of you. If any of what you've been saying is true—and," he admits with reluctance, "clearly some of it is—then the fate of the world rests on what you know."

Helplessness wants to take over again, but I ball my fists at my sides, summoning strength to speak up to this man with the power to keep us locked up indefinitely. "Maybe if you'd questioned us a few days ago," I reply. "But we don't have time for that now."

Jules nods, adding, "One of the operatives—the girl you had in custody with us in Catalonia—she's headed for the portal here in Prague as we speak. You've got to let us stop her."

De Luca eyes each of us, clearly taken aback. But either his comeuppance has shattered his composure more than I thought, or he's more *frightened* than I thought, because for the first time since we encountered him, he looks uncertain. "You're asking me to leave the fate of this city, and quite possibly the world, in the hands of a group of teenagers."

"Believe me," Jules says wryly, "we *tried* to hand off responsibility to the grown-ups half a dozen times. Now, we've got no other option."

"I'll gather some troops to send with you," De Luca says finally. "Give me a few hours to put the orders through."

"We don't have a couple of hours." Dex straightens, a hint of impatience in his stance. "And troops will just make her fight. I've got to try to talk her down, or a lot of people are going to get hurt."

De Luca shifts his weight from foot to foot, the reality of the situation contradicting every procedure and rule he knows. "I can't just let you all go. I can't just wait to see what happens."

"You have to." Jules's voice is quiet. He's been quiet since he agreed to do the Addison speech reprise. If De Luca lets us out, we might be able to stop Atlanta and then broadcast the video afterward—the rest of the world has a couple of days, but Prague has hours at best. Jules isn't off the hook yet. He'll still have to stand exactly where his father did.

Suddenly, an idea hits me with all the force of a freight train. "You know what you can do?" I interject, talking over the start of De Luca's reply to Jules. "Put out a statement of support. Tell the world that the IA has changed its stance on the warnings of Dr. Addison. Tell them to listen to his supporters online, and to pay attention to what we're asking of them, and—and most of all? Tell them to bloody well listen to his son when he goes live after we've stopped Atlanta."

De Luca takes a step back, boot heel thudding against the wall at his back. His gaze flickers between me and Jules, every nuance of his body language screaming discomfort. His jaw tightens, and for a moment I think I've blown it—that he'll lock us up after all, just out of petty vengeance and embarrassment.

But then he lifts a hand and raps on the door at his side. A few moments later, the soldier outside opens it. De Luca steps through and then holds the door out with one arm, eyeing the four of us. "I will."

I exhale, some of my tension draining away, and sneak a glance back at Jules. He's watching me, stunned, and when we all move toward the cell door, he steps close to me and whispers, "Thank you."

De Luca clears his throat, a gesture of hesitation that he's clearly unused to. "I'll send backup as soon as I can. Where do you think this Atlanta will be?"

"In the old waterways below the city," Dex replies, with utter certainty.

"I'm in the uncomfortable position of realizing nobody's going to believe me any more than I believed you. I'm not sure how quickly I'd be able to get an official force together. But if I can't help you, I think I know someone who can."

• • •

The underground of Prague is . . . not what I expected. I'm not sure what I was picturing—something like a sewer system in an American city, or tiny dirty tunnels—but instead it's like there's an entire second city below the streets of Prague.

Getting in was easy enough. Getting here was hard. I would have thought running from the police would be far less terrifying than hiding away on an alien spaceship. Instead, every second of our trip through the city was torture. Once we were out on the street again, every siren, every shout, every car that turned unexpectedly or pedestrian who happened to walk our way made me certain we were about to be attacked, either by the Undying or by IA forces who didn't know De Luca had changed his mind.

A shriek as we passed a street vendor drew out a tiny, answering yelp from my throat as I whirled around—but the sound came from a child being handed an ice cream cone. With the torrent of pulse-pounding anxiety flooding my system I couldn't tell the difference between delight and terror.

Once we reached our destination, though, it turned out there were Prague underground tours offered all around the city, and tagging along the end of one—and slipping away at the first opportunity—was child's play.

Now, as we emerge from a brick-lined tunnel into a vast underground courtyard with vaulted ceilings and intricate stonework, I can't help but stop short, my mouth open as I stare.

"Beautiful," Jules whispers, his eyes shining. "This looks like—what, thirteenth century?"

"Hmm, I'd say so, look at the stonework. Definitely from the twelve hundreds." I answer like I know what the frak he's talking about, and for once it makes him laugh—after a moment of hesitation where he forgot he was the only archaeologist among us.

"What is this place?" Neal asks. Our voices echo, but in a muffled way, since the spaces aren't that tall.

Jules is all too happy to reply, shining his flashlight—handily provided by the tour company—around the place. "Back then, the city was built lower than it is today. They raised the street levels so they wouldn't flood, so the new buildings just got built right on top of the old ones. Some of the underground city is basements and storage rooms, but a lot of it is like this—abandoned."

"A whole city below a city," I whisper, fascinated in spite of myself, in spite of what we're here to do.

"We should keep shifting." Dex is uneasy. "Up here there's a shaft to the cistern—we'll have to climb downwards."

The corridors and tunnels twist and turn, some small enough to require us to crawl on hands and knees, others looking exactly like alleyways, complete with rough-hewn doors on either side like decrepit old houses.

One of the tiny corridors—more like a big pipe, I realize—emerges into a much larger area, and the moment my head emerges from the tunnel I feel how different the air is. This is where Atlanta cut her way through to the old waterways, and though it's hard to see the detail in the torchlight, it's almost as though she melted her way through the rock. I guess, after all their years of exploration, it's not so far-fetched that the Undying would have the technology for that.

Dex, leading the way, offers me his hand to clamber out of the pipe, followed by Jules and Neal. At our feet is a neat round hole in the ground, its cover already heaved up and out of the way.

*Atlanta.*

"Is there any way she knows we're coming?" I ask in a whisper.

"We got no way of tracking you," Dex replies. "She won't know. She wouldn't believe we could have got out of the cell."

"And the portal? Could she move it, just in case?"

"No," he says, holding out his hand. "The tracker I left you at the hotel, do you still have it?"

Neal pulls it from his bag, offering it to Dex.

"Here," Dex says, tapping the screen, and zooming in. "Look, same place."

"We thought that was tracking Undying teams," I say, leaning in to look at the display, shoulder to shoulder with Jules.

"Close," he says. "You remember the cables I pulled out of the shuttle before we blew it?"

I nod, my mind conjuring up a picture of Dex with a coil of what looked like rope slung across his chest as we rode through France.

"That's what we need for the portal construction," he says. "That's what it's tracking. They give off a unique energy signature, even when dormant."

We all gather around the uncovered manhole, gazing down-ward, where a rope has already been anchored to the edge and left to dangle. Twenty or thirty meters below us is an inky expanse. The plink of water drips here and there, echoing in the distance.

"The old waterway." Jules sounds breathless, and I know he'd be in scholarly heaven if he allowed himself to be distracted.

Suddenly, I feel like we're back on Gaia, surveying that first great room inside the spiral temple. Nothing could ever match the strangeness of that moment, but something about being here with Jules, when his eyes are lit with that inquisitive fire, surrounded by ancient stone, facing a near-impossible task . . . it feels familiar.

*God, when did* this *become my normal and familiar?*

I duck my head and ease it into the hole to look at what's below, keeping my movements slow and steady. Most likely, Atlanta's already down there, deep in preparation to get her portal up and running. If she sees my face instead of Dex's, I'm sure she won't hesitate to shoot.

I wait, blinking slowly, giving my eyes all the time they want to adjust, but there's not a trace of light down there. I click on my flashlight, keeping it mostly muffled with my fingers, and ease my way back to take another look. Slowly—keeping it as far from me as I can, in case she aims a shot at the source of the light—I uncover it.

The expanse of water at the bottom doesn't look deep—the level isn't high enough to reach most of the pipes leading away from the reservoir. But one pipe's bricks have been crumbled away, leaving only the tiniest heap of rubble to dam the water from gush-ing away.

"Thatways is where the water's meant to go, and join up to the city supply," Dex murmurs, after he and the others have joined me on their bellies around the shaft. "Which means . . ."

Slowly, he traces the beam of his own flashlight back along the walkway against the far wall. Then, like some nightmarish creature looming out of the shadows, it's suddenly *there*—the portal, squatting in the darkness. Inert for now, but alien nonetheless. In this watery, ancient cathedral of stone, it looks deadly.

"Why isn't she here?" Jules whispers, and Dex is silent a long moment.

"I . . ." He clears his throat softly, tries again. "I don't know. I was sure she'd try and start the portal, complete the mission in case we sent anyone after her. I don't know why she'd set it up and leave it. But maybe it was too much."

I can hear the strain in his voice, and I know the others can too. Whatever his moral convictions, this is the person he loves most in the world he's talking about. And he's broken her.

Question is, does that make her more or less dangerous now?

"Well," I whisper, "just because she's not here doesn't mean she's not coming. We should try the broadcast from here. There couldn't be a better backdrop than the portal. That thing would convince me, that's for sure."

"You're right," Jules murmurs. "Let's go."

I glance at the others, who look as daunted as I feel. And then, without a word, we begin the long climb down to reach the reservoir, and at its end, the Undying portal.

27

JULES

**DESPITE THE COOL AIR DOWN HERE, MY PALMS ARE SWEATING AS DEX** sets up the camera—just one of our new burner phones, mounted on a chunk of rock, with Neal's backpack underneath it to give it a little grip. Mia stands beside him, studying the image of me over his shoulder, gesturing for me to shuffle a little to one side so I'm framed properly.

Neal's sending out the news on all his social networks and urging the forum members to help spread the word—*Jules Addison answers his father's critics with the truth about the ship in orbit, live at the top of the hour, you don't want to miss this, pass it on.*

Neal finishes his work, flipping his phone around and propping it next to mine, but facing me, so I can see the streaming feed and make sure I stay in shot.

I want to keep the portal in it, as well. It's mounted against the high wall behind me, just above the surface of the water. I can see the long, rope-like strings of circuitry Dex rescued from the landing shuttle before he blew it up, fixed into the stone itself. And spreading out from the curve of the rope, glimmering in the beam of our flashlights, is the kind of crystalline rock we saw all over the temple on Gaia. It's as if the Undying tech is leaching out of the framework Dex and Atlanta brought here, and making itself part of the stone of the waterways.

The others are talking quietly, but their words are mostly a buzz in the background.

I'm scared. I'm scared, and I'm so tired. I want to find somewhere dark and safe, and hide there until this is all over. It feels impossible, standing up to speak the truth when I know how many people are out there, just waiting to take apart my every word. To do to me what they did to my father.

And if they do—if I fail—whole cities will fall.

"Jules, we're ready," Neal says quietly. "And . . . wow, do we have a lot of viewers. Maybe De Luca came good and told people to watch."

*They're coming to see a car crash,* my terrified heart insists. *They want something new to auto-tune. To mock. It's going to be just like last time. You're going to be a joke, and they won't hear what you need them to hear, and—*

"Hey, Oxford." It's Mia's voice, calm, breaking into the trickle of rising panic.

And when I look across at her, she's smiling. A small, private smile, just for me, playing across her lips like we know something the world doesn't.

And I know that whatever happens, it's not going to be like last time. Because she promised we'd stick together.

"I'm ready," I say quietly.

Neal leans down to swipe at the screen and start the broadcast, and nods at me to begin.

I take a deep breath, and look down the lens of the camera.

"My name is Jules Addison," I say. "And I don't have long, but I want to tell you a story. To find the start of it, we have to go back sixty years. The Earth's climate was failing. The deserts were growing, the weather becoming more and more unpredictable and violent. The future looked grim, but humankind managed to set aside its differences, and through the formation of the International Alliance we came together to reach further than we ever had before. We founded the Centauri mission. We dreamed of a new world, and a new future.

"But we all know how that part of the story ends—or at least, we think we do. Their ship failed. They called for help, and we had no second ship with which to answer. And then they vanished, falling silent forever, and we lost more than a colony ship. We lost more than the hundreds of people on it. We lost hope. We lost our future. But though we've always ended the story there, it turns out there were many more chapters to come."

My eyes on the camera, I speak about the way the Centauri settlers fought for survival, tossed about through space and time, searching for another planet like Earth. I speak about their failure to find one, no matter how far they traveled, how hard they looked.

"When I first heard that," I say, ignoring the viewer count on the phone that's facing me, though I can tell it's ticking up and up and up, "I felt small. I felt infinitely small. Our planet is an insignificant speck, when set against the scale of our galaxy. But the fact that we are tiny, and alone, and yet we survive—that does not make us insignificant. It makes us *magnificent*.

"That wasn't the story the Centauri told, though. They only remembered, as centuries passed for them—centuries spent far in our future, far into our past—that they called for help, and we did not come. They remembered that we had a precious planet, and we seemed determined to destroy it. When they hunted for us with their transmission, it never occurred to them that we might offer help. Not a wasteful, heartless people like us. So they called themselves the Undying, and they baited their hook by telling us about our own misdeeds.

" '*Ours is a story of greed and destruction,*' they said. Those are the words of the Undying transmission my father translated. '*Of a people not ready for the treasure they guarded. Our end came not from the stars but from within. . . . We were not, and never had been, worthy of what had been given to us.'"*

I let the words echo a moment, let them soak in, before I continue. "They have returned to us now, and they are our enemies. And a part of me isn't even sure we have the right to protest that. They want to take our planet from us—they started in Lyon, with the outbreak you've all seen by now thanks to that video that leaked out.

"These portals"—I point up over my shoulder now, and one of my companions shines a light onto the glimmering arch—"are like the portal we used to travel to Gaia. Soon, they will open to let through teams of Undying in every major city on the planet, here to spread the toxin that caused the disaster in Lyon. This is their plan, because they never thought it would be worth asking us for help. They didn't believe we'd answer.

"We have to stop them, but we don't have to do it with missiles—in fact, we can't. We need your help, no matter where you are in the world. We're putting links up on the screen as I speak. We need you to build these transmitters, to jam the signals they need to operate the portals. We need you to get to work, and to broadcast on this frequency as soon as you can."

This was where I planned to end my speech, with a plea to the citizens watching to help fend off the enemy. But I'm not done. Not done talking, not done understanding, and not done fighting. I know that now.

"We need to stop them from doing this," I continue. "And then we need to prove ourselves. We can't strike back against them. We mustn't. Meeting force with force is not the answer. We have to prove that we're more than they believe of us—that we *are* worthy of what has been given to us. They finished their broadcast to us with these words, which were meant to be bait. But I say they are a challenge that we should accept.

*"So choose. Choose the stars or the void; choose hope or despair; choose light or the undying dark of space. Choose—and travel onward, if you dare."*

Blood's pounding through my veins as I look down the camera for my final words, but I'm oddly calm. "What if we offer our hands to those who don't believe in us? What if we travel onward together?"

As the echoes of my words die away, I finally look away from the screen, to find the others standing behind it. Neal is watching the feed, his face full of hope. Dex's eyes are shining with tears. Mia's gaze is waiting to meet mine.

And then, abruptly, her face is illuminated, a bright light shining from behind me. A cold hand curls around my heart as I slowly turn.

The portal is powering up, flickers of light running along the arch of it. Then the rock within it shimmers, turning liquid and oily, a rainbow rippling across the surface.

Atlanta steps out through it, and lifts her hand.

She's holding a gun.

Her eyes meet mine, and we both hold still for an interminable instant.

And then something strikes me in the shoulder—an odd sensation, like a kick.

And then the pain comes, burning down my arm, spreading across my chest.

And then I look down, and see the blood soaking my shirt.

28

AMELIA

THE GUNSHOT'S ECHO IN THE CAVERN IS A VISCERAL, GUTTING BLOW. And in its wake I am deafened, numbed, frozen.

Jules turns slowly toward me as he looks down, blood blossoming against his shirt like a rose pinned to his chest. Behind him the portal ripples, blurry vague shapes coming through to stand with the blurry vague shape that shot Jules. Somewhere nearby someone is shouting, and one of the blurry shapes shouts back. And water drips from the ceiling, ticking like a clock, each droplet falling slower than the last.

When Jules looks up, his eyes meet mine. His brows are drawn together, lips parted, his expression one of gentle disbelief and confusion—and *apology*. He tries to speak, and though I can't hear the shouts erupting all around me, I can hear the sound that gurgles from Jules's throat.

He staggers and then crumples to the ground.

I only become aware I'm moving when a pair of arms wraps around me and drags me backward. Someone's telling me something, ordering me to do something, a dim, buzzing annoyance in my ear. I struggle against my captor, clawing at the arms, jamming my heels down against their feet, and finally jab my elbow back as hard as I can until I hear a crunch, and the arms loosen—just enough.

I break free and run. Behind me someone shouts a curse, and footsteps come after me, but I've never moved so fast in my life, and I throw myself down just as another shot cracks against the backdrop of noise. Something whizzes past me and bits of stone fall in a shower behind me. I reach Jules's side on my knees.

There's blood everywhere now—the rose is a garden, a sea of red. I rip off my jacket and press it against his chest, pushing as hard as I can to try to stem the flow of blood. Jules moans and coughs, and my heart quakes.

*Still alive.*

Fragments of what's happening around me reach my brain. Dex's voice nearby, shouting, pleading. Another voice, inhuman and cold, a monster's voice, shouting back with tears choking her. Booted feet running, a muffled exclamation of surprise from Neal. More voices, human voices. The click of readied weapons.

"Look at me," I beg him, bending low.

Jules's wide eyes blink, and shift toward my face. His features, twisted with pain, relax the tiniest bit, and he clutches at my arm with a hand sticky with his own blood. "Did it work?" he whispers.

A sound, some mix of laugh and agony, escapes my lips. "Yes," I tell him, gathering him up onto my lap. "Yes, it worked. Millions of people saw. You did it. You saved us."

Gunfire erupts in the background, and then more gunfire, the echoes making it impossible to tell its origins. Jules stiffens, his eyes widening in fear. "What's—"

"It's nothing," I interrupt, cupping my hand against his cheek, trying to keep his focus on me. "It doesn't matter."

His eyes are still rolled sideways, though, and that look of bewilderment is back. "Is that *Mink?*" he mumbles.

I don't want to take my eyes from his face, but I lift my head just a moment. It *is* Mink, and a handful of others in secret-ops black, already shooting as more of them come rappelling down from the opening overhead. The Undying are shooting back, and stone is flying every which way, and Dex is shouting, and Neal is pressed against the stone, one hand to his face, where his nose is streaming blood.

"De Luca must have asked her to back us up," Jules murmurs vaguely. "They ended up on the same side."

"Jules—look at me." I stroke his face, and his eyes swing back toward mine. "Stay with me, okay?"

His eyelashes dip—and my heart drops too—and then lift in a slow, weary blink. "Are we on Gaia?" he mumbles, confusion furrowing his brow.

I gulp back a sob and pull him against me. Something about keeping the wound elevated above his heart. Something about keeping him close to my own heart. "No, we're home." I drop my head, pressing my forehead to his. "We're home now."

"My dad's going to love you." Jules's voice is thin and soft.

I lift my head, and water keeps dripping down, down from the ceiling, down from my face, down from the corners of Jules's eyes. "I can't wait to meet him," I manage, trying to sound happy, trying to sound warm. Trying to sound like I'm not watching Jules die.

His eyes close again, and I tap at his cheek until they open and fix, with some effort, on me. "Tomorrow we'll be the first people ever to set foot in this temple. . . ."

I try to smile at him. "You picked me up and whirled me around in the air. I had no idea I could feel that way until I met you." I stroke his cheek, wiping his tears and mine from his skin. "That kind of wonder. That kind of hope."

More gunfire, more shouting, more cracking of stone and splashing of water. Battle rages all around. No one's aiming for me. With one bullet, Atlanta destroyed us both.

I shift my grip, arm aching from pressing the cloth against his wound. I trail my fingers over his jaw until his eyes soften.

"I love you," I tell him.

His cracked lips curve, and a little glint dances there in his eyes. "I know that."

The air in my lungs escapes, laughter and horror, and I give him a little shake. "Don't try to play it cool. You love me back."

The glint softens, and the smile fades, and his brown eyes meet mine with such a sudden clarity, clear of the fog of pain and blood loss, clear of everything but certainty. "I know that too."

It's getting harder to hold him, his body growing limper, his head heavier against my arm.

He sighs. "Mia," he whispers. And then his eyes roll away from me, and his head drops back.

I can't let go of him. My arms are frozen around him, his heavier weight pinning me down with him. I'll just stay here with him until it's over.

*When all this is over.*

Those words echo in my mind, again and again and again. *When all this is over . . .* We'll be together. We'll figure it out. We'll find a way to love each other. We'll have a chance to see what we're like when we're not fighting for our lives. We'll start over. We'll be together.

*When all this is over.*

My hands sticky with Jules's blood, my every muscle screaming protest, I lift my head.

The two sides are facing off against each other, the Undying in cover around the portal, and Mink's people shielding themselves around the mouth of the tunnel. There's no sign of Neal—I hope he's behind cover somewhere, out of harm's way—and Dex is still talking, trying to appeal to Atlanta.

Atlanta, who's only a few yards away from me, still near the portal, her shoulder against the stone, gun trained in the direction of her opposition.

Gently, I ease Jules down onto the stone, smoothing the edge of his shirt back into place, drying the last few tears still left on his face. He looks like he's asleep. He looks peaceful.

Then I get to my feet and walk toward the girl who murdered Jules.

I'm in her blind spot, flanking the Undying. The others will see me, and Atlanta might even hear me, but not before it's too late. She's dismissed me—she destroyed me, after all.

And I may be destroyed. But I can still take her with me.

I break into a run at the last moment, so that when I reach her I collide with her and knock her to the ground. Her grunt of surprise and pain nearly drowns out the clatter of the handgun skittering on the stone. Her hand stretches out, but I have a rock in my hand, and I smash it at her face, and then dive for the gun myself.

By the time I'm on my feet again, Atlanta's on her knees, blood pouring from a new gash across her cheek—but she freezes when I swing the weapon around to point at her.

This time, I stand far enough back that she can't do what she did at IA Headquarters. This time, I make sure the safety's off. This time, my hand is steady.

"See how easily it's turned yourways?" I say softly.

Atlanta's comrades have stopped shooting, and I hear Mink's voice shouting at her own forces to hold their fire.

Atlanta's eyes are red-rimmed, her face puffy with emotion, but I have none to spare for her. She could have stayed with her partner. She could have trusted him. She chose this outcome—who am I to change the fate that comes from that choice?

"He wanted peace," I choke out, the gun pointed at her face, its grip still warm from her hand. "We would have *welcomed* you if you'd just asked. But I figured out why you hate us so much."

"Because you've treated this planet like lixo," Atlanta spits. "Because you're not fit to live here. Because you're sub-human."

"No." I gesture with the gun, and she presses her lips together. "You hate us because we're a mirror. You see in us the worst of yourselves. Every fear, every failed promise. So you try to make us into monsters, beasts to be slain or corralled. But you *are* us. You're *us,* just on a different road. The whole reason you exist is because we did come together, once, and set out for the stars. That you exist—it's a miracle, Atlanta. What you accomplished. That you survived. Your existence is proof of what humanity can do. Proof that there's nothing we *can't* do."

There are tears on Atlanta's face, and her gaze shifts, just a moment, to the side. Toward where Dex stands, frozen, watching.

"You could have come here in peace, and your survival, your technology, your inspiration—your story—would have changed the entire world. You could have proven that we are *more* than— than this." My voice is raw with crying, and my shattered heart gives way. I don't have anything left.

"You want to know the funny thing?" I whisper. "If it had been me you shot—if it was Jules standing here now, holding this gun—you wouldn't be in any danger at all. He would never, not for anything, pull this trigger."

Atlanta doesn't speak. She just looks up at me, and in her eyes I see a certainty settling into place. My finger curls around the trigger. Distantly, like a memory from some other life, I remember being in the halls of the Undying portal ship, standing over a guard, saved from having to shoot her by Javier's intervention. I'd said I would do it, though looking back, I know I couldn't have.

Now, I know that girl's gone.

My heart empty, I say, "But I'm not Jules."

I draw a breath.

"Mia?" The voice is soft, frightened. And so familiar, so unexpectedly *home* that I freeze, the heart I thought had stopped starting to pound as I turn my head.

Two figures are standing by the ropes dangling from the opening overhead. One a tall man with an oddly familiar stoop to his shoulders and a haggard look on his face. The other, a girl, her face white, her eyes round with horror.

A mirror of myself. Of the old Mia. The one not covered in

Jules's blood, the one not ready to blow Atlanta from the face of the earth.

"Evie." The name slips out like a moan, and as if my voice were some sort of cue, the rest of my body starts to tremble.

"I told you two to stay in the safe house," snaps Mink, who's half hidden behind a fallen column, her rifle still trained on the Undying soldiers.

"And we chose to leave," says the man at Evie's side. His voice, the British accent, the tilt of his head as he speaks—even if he weren't one of the most recognizable faces in the world right now, I would know him anywhere. Then his eyes move toward the motionless form of his son behind me.

And then it turns out I'm not empty at all, but so full of grief and fear and pain that the dam can't hold it back. I'm weeping, staggering back. Dimly I'm aware of Mink's forces moving quickly, overtaking the Undying troops who dropped their weapons when I took Atlanta's gun.

Of Dex, bursting from behind his cover to run to Atlanta's side, his arms around her. Of Neal, who wasn't in hiding at all, but carefully making his way around the perimeter of the room to reach his cousin's body.

And of Evie, who comes straight for me, and as my legs buckle she catches me, and we sink to the stone together. She holds me as I cry, murmuring in my ear, so like our mother used to do when I was tiny, when she was a baby, though she doesn't remember our mother at all.

I don't even ask how she's here. Distantly I know it must have been Mink. That she listened, when we tried to tell her in the truck that we needed Addison to finish his work on the portals. That she must have got to him, got him out of his cell, that she must have picked up Evie so the IA couldn't use her against me. And probably a dozen other things we'll never know about, maneuvering behind the scenes.

I want to focus on Evie and not Jules dead on the ground. I want to focus on the face I thought I'd never see again when I was on Gaia, when I was on the Undying ship.

When *we* were . . .

I gasp for breath, a fresh wave of pain sweeping over me.

"Help me up," I whisper to Evie. For once she doesn't argue with me, and lets me lean on her as my shaking legs threaten to give way.

The song of distant sirens, indistinct echoing shouts, steps running—help must have already been on the way. The phone, I realize, is still propped up on the rocks. Still pointed toward us. Recording—and broadcasting—everything. The view counter is frozen on ninety-nine million viewers. The app doesn't have the capability to display anything higher.

The time that had slowed while I held Jules, while I held the gun, comes rushing back. Mink's talking with the Undying, and Dex is disabling the portal while Atlanta watches, weeping. And Jules is . . . he's lying there on the ground, EMTs gathering around him to transfer his still form to a stretcher.

I stagger forward, my heart suddenly squeezing so hard it hurts. I can't let them take him away, not without me.

A uniformed officer grabs hold of me just as I reach the stretcher. "Stay back, miss," he says in thickly accented English.

Dr. Addison turns a red-rimmed gaze on me. "Let her through," he says in a voice that's somehow gentle and authoritative all at once.

The officer frowns, but lets go of my arm. When I reach Jules's dad, he looks down to see the confusion on my face. I find myself stammering, babbling. "Jules wasn't able to talk to you since—how do you know who I am?"

Dr. Addison shakes his head. "I saw what you did for him. How you looked at him." He pauses, and then adds, "And I've seen the wanted posters with you together."

His eyes are so much like his son's.

"I'm Mia," I whisper. "And I'm in love with your son."

I can't say *was*. I *was* in love. I can't do it.

A hand creeps into mine, and I curl my fingers through Evie's.

"Time to move," says one of the EMTs. "Sir, you can come with us. Everyone else has to stay back."

Dr. Addison speaks before I get a chance. "They're coming too," he informs them, his low, gentle voice soft and aching with sadness. "They're family."

29

AMELIA

It's raining as the car pulls up to Dr. Addison's cottage, droplets running down the windows and dressing the world beyond in gray. The driver offers to escort me to the door with an umbrella, but I wave it away. The water is bracing, and strangely alien at the same time. If I didn't know I was in another world from the neatly manicured lawn, the healthy, soaring oak trees lining the streets, or the hired car that arrived at my hotel to bring me here today, the rain would do the trick.

Evie's back at the hotel. She offered to come with me, to hold my hand if I needed it or just offer moral support, but I wanted to come alone.

He always told me I'd fit right in here. That his dad would love me. That it wouldn't matter that I was a thief and a liar and a criminal. But now, trudging up the front walk by myself, I'm not so sure. Maybe it was just that I'd fit with *him*, wherever he went, as long as we went together.

I swallow hard, coming to a stop before the door, abruptly

wishing I *had* taken up the offer of the umbrella. My hair's plastered to my forehead, and my careful attempts at makeup are no doubt dripping down my face. But I raise a hand to knock anyway.

The door opens before I can.

Dr. Addison is there on the other side, and for a moment I'm so struck by the similarities between him and his son that my heart seizes painfully, and I'm robbed of speech.

"Mia," he says softly, his eyes warm. If he notices my apprehension, he gives no sign—he just steps out onto the rainy walk and wraps me in a hug.

*I'm Mia.* The first words I ever spoke to this man, in that dark, bloodstained cavern in the underground of Prague, were all he needed to hear. *And I'm in love with your son.*

He was the one who arranged for Evie and me to come back with him to Oxford. He got us our hotel room, hired the driver, made sure we had everything we could want, like fresh clothes and room service.

But for all I would've once thought I'd died and gone to heaven in such luxury, without Jules it all feels . . . hollow.

Dr. Addison ushers me inside, showing me where I can take off my wet shoes, and offering me a warm sweater when he notices me shivering a little in the damp. The hoodie he returns with is filled with a familiar scent, if a little faded. It's one of Jules's, no doubt.

My throat closes as I clutch it close to me.

We talk a little—he asks about the hotel, and after my sister, and shares the news that not only has the IA dissolved Evie's contract, they actually raided the club that had her, liberating half a dozen other underage girls.

His is an old cottage-style house, and though it's not spacious, there are little touches here and there that give it a strange sort of grandeur. Portraits hang at random intervals all over the walls—some are paintings, faded with age, and others are photographs, more recent. The staircase is old and winding, with an ancient carved wooden banister thicker than my waist.

Dr. Addison sees me looking at it, and offers a tiny smile. "He broke his collarbone sliding down that banister when he was seven," he tells me, eyes crinkling with the memory.

When I first met Jules, I never would've thought him capable of sliding down a banister. Now, I can picture it with perfect clarity.

His father's watching me, and when I look up, he tilts his head to the side with obvious understanding. "Here's me talking your ear off, when that's not why you came. I hope you'll come often, Mia—you'll always be welcome here, no matter what. But for now—would you like to see him?"

Wordlessly, I nod, my heart stuttering. Reliving the moment on the way up to the streets of Prague, when one of the EMTs suddenly lifted her head, eyes wide.

I can still hear her voice: "He's got a pulse!"

Dr. Addison leads me through the house, explaining that Jules's bedroom was upstairs, but that it seemed impractical to get him up there, so they made a place for him in the parlor. Whatever a parlor is.

We arrive at a room with long, curtained windows lining one wall, a piano in one corner, and a bed at the far end. Once my eyes see that, they fix there. Dimly, I hear Dr. Addison say, "I'll give you some time," as he closes the door gently behind me.

Heart pounding, I let my feet take me closer. His eyes are closed, his face still and calm. I reach out, fingertips brushing the linens on the bed, courage failing me for a long moment.

"If you are trying to watch me sleep," comes a familiar voice in the quiet, "then we're going to have to have a long talk about what constitutes appropriate behavior."

In spite of myself, I laugh, the tension and fear falling away like the rain falling outside. "Your dad made me promise I'd do as little to disturb you as possible," I protest. "Like seeing me might make you relapse or something."

Jules opens his eyes, finding my face as his lips curve in a hint of a smile. "He's being rather overprotective." Carefully, he plants his hands on the bed's surface and pulls himself upright a few more degrees, propped against his pillows. As I start to protest, he throws me a sharp look. "Not you too."

I eye him sidelong. "Both of us had to watch you lie there bleeding in that cavern." I meant the words to be light, joking, in keeping with the tone he chose. But my voice wobbles, and betrays me. "You don't get to complain if we're overprotective."

Jules lifts one hand in an eloquent gesture of helplessness, and props himself up a little more. The bandages hide some of his chest and one shoulder, but he's not wearing a shirt, and the rest of him is bare. He notices the little grin on my face before I do, and has both eyebrows lifted by the time my eyes go back to his face.

"Appropriate behavior," he reminds me primly.

"Mm-hmm," I reply absently, still grinning.

"Come here," he suggests, with the air of someone who knows he's pushing his luck.

I glance at the door, which is still closed.

Jules lets out a sigh. "The cat's out of the bag, Mia," he points out. "I think my dad knows about us."

"Yeah, well," I retort, defensive, "I was given strict instructions not to upset you when I came. I'm pretty sure that extends to other forms of excitement."

Jules makes a sulky face, and settles for claiming my hand instead. I let him take it, ignoring the faint stab of regret that he doesn't keep trying to get me to kiss him.

"So that's why my dad won't tell me anything about what's been going on."

I raise an eyebrow. "Really? You'd think he'd know you well enough to know that *not* knowing would make you far crazier than anything the truth could do."

"Never underestimate the power of denial for an Addison," Jules replies airily.

I squeeze his hand. "I'll sneak you a few articles if you promise not to tell him I gave them to you."

Jules laughs. "Deal. How's Evie?"

"In absolute heaven." I grin at him. "Our hotel room's got streaming movies and chicken wings—I don't think she's ever going to leave. De Luca pulled some strings and got the club shut down—she's free."

I've never said those words aloud. Now, I find my throat closing, eyes burning. Jules is watching my face, and leans his head back against the headboard with a warm smile.

"You kept your promise to her," he says softly.

I clear my throat, focusing on the thread pattern of his comforter rather than his face. "What else . . . well, you know your dad's on the reintegration committees, finding placement for the Undying who want to return to Earth. There's way fewer of them than you'd think, though. Dex definitely wasn't the only one who, deep down, felt that his home was a spaceship."

"I haven't seen Neal—I got the impression from Dad that he and Dex . . ."

I'm grinning again. "And then some. I guess the Addisons can be pretty charming when they want to be." I wink at him, just to see him smile. "Though to be honest, I think part of why they've gotten so close so fast is because Dex misses having a partner. Neal's never going to be what Atlanta was, and he isn't trying to be. But having someone with him, I think, makes Dex feel a little less lonely."

"So there's still no sign of her?" Jules's voice is quiet.

"None. Technically, the IA people know where she is, they know where all the Undying agents are. All the ones who turned themselves in, I mean. But her reintegration destination is secret, like all of them. Dex hasn't heard from her."

Jules inspects my hand in his, idly stroking his thumb across my finger. "I don't blame her, you know," he says with a sigh. "She was doing what she was trained to do. She was a foot soldier."

"Yeah," I say. Because I don't blame her either. And I'll be grateful for the rest of my life that Evie's voice reminded me who I was, stopped me following Atlanta down that path.

"Poor Dex," Jules murmurs.

"Well, he and Neal are keeping busy, anyway. It's going to take a long time to unravel the intricacies of Undying technology even with their help, and even longer to reproduce it and implement it in all the cities and towns that need that power, but in a couple of years the world is going to look completely different. Clean power, clean water, all across the globe . . . it's hard to imagine."

Jules exhales a long sigh. "Mehercule. It doesn't seem real, does it?"

"Well, it's not all sunshine and rainbows," I point out. "There's still half a dozen Undying operatives unaccounted for, who clearly don't like the idea of the peace accords. And as many countries who refuse to allow Undying to immigrate, out of fear. There've been anti-Undying protests all over the place, including London, and there are plenty of people who think we should've blown the ship out of orbit."

Jules waves his empty hand in a dismissive gesture. "People are idiots," he says simply. "Nothing's going to change that. But I think as soon as the lights start coming on, thanks to the Undying tech they're sharing with us, people are going to come around."

"I hope so."

Jules watches me for a few moments, head tilted, as if studying me. "So how do you like it here?"

"Oxford?" I blink, considering my answer. "It's . . . very different. Wet, for one thing."

"I meant here, this house."

I blink again, and look down at him. "To be honest, I barely paid much attention. I was a bit focused on seeing you. But it's nice. Big. Nice banisters on the stairs, seems like you could really get some speed up."

Though I say the words lightly, Jules laughs regardless and mutters, "He's such a tattletale." His laughter fades in favor of a keen-eyed, penetrating look. "But you like it?"

"Yeah, I like it."

"I was thinking once my dad lets me go up and down stairs, this could be your room."

"My—" Voice cracking, words failing me, I splutter to a halt and stare at him. "My—?"

"Your room," Jules echoes firmly. "Dad thinks it's a great idea. We can't afford to keep you in the hotel indefinitely, or get you your own place, but we've got more room than we need. Evie could stay here too, although my dad thinks he can get her into that school in London that we were talking about, and they've got housing. He's got a lot of clout these days."

Head spinning, I stagger to my feet, hand pulling away from Jules so that I can move—my legs feel like they're full of bees. "You want me to live with you?"

"Well, yeah, if you want to. Look, it's weird, I know it's weird. It wouldn't be like . . . it's not like I'm asking you to move *in* with me." Jules takes a long, careful breath, watching me as I pace back and forth. "But if you wanted to stay . . . there's a place for you here."

I glance back at him, and he holds my gaze for a long moment before I manage to look away again. "You kept saying that."

"And I meant it."

I keep moving, aware that I'm tangling my fingers together and fidgeting like a child, and not caring. "Jules—don't you think you should wait? Think about it? You're still recovering . . . You haven't gotten back to your normal life yet. Oxford and classes and . . . and your dad, and everything. How do you know you'll want me here when your real life starts up again?"

Jules doesn't answer for a long, long time, not until I stop to look back at him and find his gaze waiting for mine, one eyebrow raised. "For one of the smartest people I know," he says gently, "you can be unbelievably stupid."

That startles a little huff of laughter from my lips. I don't know which word surprised me more: *smartest* or *stupid*. I shake my head, my throat too tight to speak.

"Mia," he says softly. "We've been to the other side of the universe and back. I told you we wouldn't let an ocean defeat us. A few classes and some work with my dad won't, either. Unless you've changed your mind"—and his voice is very careful now, very even and quiet—"and you'd rather go back."

His eyes, even at this distance, halfway across the room, catch and hold mine. There's a question there, an uncertainty that belies his firm words. For a moment I think maybe he's not sure about this after all, that he does actually have doubts about whether I'd fit in here in his world.

And then he blinks, lips quivering, and I realize: *He's not sure if I want to stay. If I want him.*

Abruptly I'm moving, my restlessness vanished, the tension in my body vanished. I drop down onto the edge of the bed and reach not for his hand, but for his cheek, leaning close until I can rest my forehead against his. "I want to stay with you," I blurt, dimly aware of a tear clinging to my lashes. "Idiot."

Jules laughs, but it's quick, because in another instant he's tipping his face toward mine and curling his hand around the back of my neck. Before I can protest on account of his injury, he's kissing me, and for a moment I forget he was ever shot.

After a time, I lift my head reluctantly, gathering my wits with some difficulty. "Do you smell something?" I ask, blinking, my stomach stirring and reminding me that I was too nervous to eat this morning before I left to come here.

Jules looks up too, considering, one hand still resting at my waist. "That would be Dad making lunch," he says. "Chicken and lime with porcini mushrooms, if I'm not mistaken." I draw back enough to stare at him, and he grins. "Where do you think I learned to cook?"

# 30

## DEX

## SIX MONTHS LATER

THE FAREWELL SESSIONS ARE IN A LARGE, WHITE ROOM WITH A LOW
ceiling. It's a pristine, antiseptic environment, a nod to the quar-
antines they used to observe before the old astronaut launches.
There's nothing sterile about this place, though. The room is filled
with talk and laughter.

There are dozens of tables spread around the place, laid out like
we're all about to participate in some kind of formal banquet with
terrible catering. I've learned a lot about large-scale catering over
the last six months, attending functions and negotiation sessions
and planning meetings. And though I used to joke with Atlanta
that we'd be ruined once we'd tasted real food planetside, the truth
is that our stuff—*sponge food*, Neal calls it—beats out a watery faux-
chicken cutlet any day. Good thing too, given how many sponges
lie in my future.

But even as my lips quirk at the thought, I know I'm focusing
on food to prevent myself from thinking about who's at the table

with us now, gathered around as if we're about to begin a meal . . . and who's not.

Jules and Mia sit side by side across from us, his arm around her shoulders, her hand on his leg underneath the table. They're almost always touching, I've noticed, when they're together. And when they're not, they always know exactly where the other one is. Neal and I are only a few steps down the road to . . . what did he call it the other day? *Our own personal demonstration of intercultural diplomacy.*

But I sirsly hope one day we can be something like Jules and Mia.

We've got a long time ahead of us to see if we can.

Jules has his head together with Neal, and though Neal's bigger frame is clad in his blue-and-white uniform, and Jules is in civvies, they look like brothers.

"I'm just saying," Jules is insisting, "that if I were you, I'd be checking the cargo hold twice. They changed the crew manifest just this morning. Are you sure they've packed everything you need?"

Neal snorts. "Yeh, I'm not listening to you when it comes to packing, dear cousin. The way Mia tells it, you showed up on Gaia toting enough stuff for a party of six."

"I was told there would be—"

"—transport available," Neal and Mia finish for him, laughing.

Behind them I can see Dr. Addison standing with his brother and his sister-in-law—Neal's parents—letting us have these last moments.

Mink is standing with De Luca, the pair of them scanning the room—more similar than they want to admit—on the lookout for hassle.

Mink—I've adopted Jules and Mia's name for her, and in truth, I think she likes it—is always scanning the room, no matter where she is. She's always watching, always assessing. Sometimes I suspect that by the time we shift back Earthwards, she'll be running the planet. In the first, vital hour of the first, vital meeting, she was the one who faced down the Undying leaders, and made them see that engineering a cure for the people of Lyon was more than a good diplomatic move—their future depended on it.

I'm pretty sure Mink can do anything, and for sure, she's not done with us all yet. That story isn't over.

But for now, Evie's in school, and Mia's as in-school as you can be, when you're one half of the most recognizable couple on the planet. She passed her high school certification last week after finishing her private tutoring. And Mink's been watching her, in particular—I suspect there's a future in covert ops in store for Mia.

For now, she's laughing again as Neal rattles off what he swears was a young Jules's packing list for family holidays, over the splutters of his cousin. And the sound of their laughter fills up my heart.

But as fast as I can fill it, that happiness quietly drains out a hole in the bottom. The empty place at my side feels like a missing limb—like a missing heartbeat. I don't know why, but some part of me thought maybe she'd come to see me off. To say goodbye. To let me hug her one last time.

In ten minutes, we'll all part ways to head for the launch ceremony. Neal and I will be onstage with representatives of the rest of our crew, and they'll be in the audience, listening to the speeches that outline our hopes for the future.

Our ship, the *Unity*, is on a ten-year mission. We won't shift back Earthward more than a handful of times over the next decade, and by the time we're done, nearly a hundred more ships will have joined the search with us.

The *Unity* is only the first step of a journey all parts of humanity—no matter where we've spent the last few centuries—will take together. We'll head for Centauri once more, and we'll go far beyond. None of us knows what we'll find out there. I mean, just because we haven't found an Earth-like planet yet doesn't mean we won't one day. As the boy across the table from me reminded us all just half a year ago, space is big, but we are magnificent. And we are stronger together.

Our crew will be a mix of the best and brightest humans ("and us," Neal always says) from all backgrounds—Earthborn or Undying. At least at the beginning, those from our fleet will be young, trained for the gravity our Earth counterparts need. That youth will be an advantage, I think. Our minds haven't grown closed, yet. Or most of them haven't.

Others of my people will remain here on Earth, to share our technology or to learn, to travel or to make their homes, some among the other humans, some apart.

Atlanta is one of those who will remain on Earth. I compren that's for the best, because it's what she wants. But these last six months, I've been torn in two, pulled in both directions by the future that's calling to me, and the past that's so completely tangled up in my heart that I can't begin to separate myself from it.

It's like there's a non-stop babble of voices in my head, calling me to hunt for her, to stay with my friends, to try one more time to get in contact, to push her from my mind and kiss Neal, to wonder if she got my messages, to focus on my next *Unity* briefing.

I never thought I'd shift apart from her like this. But then again, I never thought I'd betray her. All the soldiers who followed orders that day have been pardoned, but that's only the official part of it. Forgiving ourselves, forgiving each other, that's much more complicated. I still have no idea if she'll ever forgive me. I never thought she'd need to.

I never thought I'd step aboard a ship and leave her behind.

But she's finally planetside, with all the things she wanted. She can feel the breeze every day. She can learn to swim. She can run on grass and sleep in the shade of a tree. Though I miss her desperately, I hope that this place will be everything she dreamed.

As if he's sensing the feeling welling up inside me, Neal reaches for my hand under the table, giving it a quick squeeze, even as he shoots a retort back at his cousin.

A soft chime rings through the room, and all around us, conversation stills. It's the signal we need to wrap up our farewells. And suddenly, with the pressure of making our last words something meaningful, everyone's tongue-tied.

"Look," I say, honestly not sure as I begin it how my sentence is going to end. "These last six months—"

But I get no further. Mia interrupts me. "Dex," she gasps, looking over my shoulder.

Beside her, Jules goes still. I can't think what it could possibly be, and I twist around to—

All thought dies. The constant static, the babble in my head, is abruptly silenced for the first time in half a year.

Because Atlanta stands in the doorway, clad in the blue-and-white uniform of the *Unity* mission. The same uniform as me.

I gulp for air, like I'm a ten-year-old on my first assisted mission, glued to the spot until Neal firmly plants a hand between my shoulder blades, and pushes. Then I rise from my chair, legs unsteady, and half stumble the first few steps toward her.

Her lips curve into her usual, achingly familiar smirk, one brow lifting, as if to say, *Really, you forgot how to walk?* And for that, I remember how to *run*, dodging bodies and swerving around tables, shifting at the speed of light to fling myself into her open arms, our bodies smacking together.

"What are you doing here?" It's a stupid question—she's wearing the uniform. But I won't believe it, I *can't* believe it, until she says it.

"I'm going home," she says quietly, arms still wrapped around me, head resting on my shoulder, cheek pressed to mine.

"But you *are* home," I murmur. "We've spent our whole lives getting here, back to Earth."

"No," she says, finally easing back, dropping her hands to take hold of mine. "I finally figured out what you knew all along." She's looking over my shoulder, and when I glance back, there's Neal—he must have run to keep up with me—shooting her one of his gentle, welcoming smiles. Jules and Mia have nearly reached us.

"I don't understand," I admit.

"*You* are my home," she says quietly. "I thought it was here, this planet, the place we came from, but I was wrong. You're my home, Dex, you always have been." She pauses, flicking her gaze to Neal, and wrinkling her nose. "Though I pledge, if you think I'm sharing a room with you two, you're heading for ten kinds of hassle."

I don't have any kind of comeback, and Neal's just laughing at her. "We already decorated," he informs her. "You're safe."

"You made the crew list?" That's Jules, and he doesn't seem completely surprised. Nor, now I turn my head to look at the pair of them, does Mia.

"Yeh, approved about ten minutes ago," Atlanta says. "Plenty of time to spare. It helps that my partner was already a crew member."

The chime sounds again, and Neal turns away to pull Jules in for a hug, as I lean down to gather up Mia for the same. Neal's parents close in now, and the Addison family, born and chosen, are one big tangle of limbs, clinging together for just a moment more.

"We'll send you a vid first chance we get," I promise, as we all step back.

"Keep an eye on the place for us," Neal adds, tugging his uniform straight. "I may have dreamed about this my whole life, but that doesn't mean I don't want to come back someday."

And then it's time to go.

It's so sunny outside that as we head for the wide doors that lead out to the stage and the speeches, I can't make out a thing that's waiting for us.

But that's all right. With Neal on one side of me and Atlanta on the other, I'm ready.

Together, we walk toward the light.

## ACKNOWLEDGMENTS

It's been many years now, and we still pinch ourselves every day that we're able to tell stories together for a living. We don't ever plan to stop, and we're so grateful for the people who helped us with this one.

To the readers, librarians and booksellers who help us share our stories, thank you from the bottom of our hearts. Without your support, none of this would be possible. Word of mouth is real—every time you tell someone to read one of our books, you're doing us an immeasurable kindness. So thank you!

To the incredible team at Adams Literary—Josh and Tracey Adams and Cathy Kendrick, as well as to our fantastic film agent, Stephen Moore, and the many international agents who've helped these books find homes overseas, a thousand times thank you. We are grateful for you every day.

To the fantastic team at Hyperion—Laura Schreiber, Mary Mudd, Emily Meehan, and Cassie McGinty, to everyone in sales and marketing, publicity, production, managing editorial, and everywhere in between, thank you for taking such great care of these books!

In Australia, a huge thank-you to Anna McFarlane, Jess Seaborn, Radhiah Chowdhury and all the wonderful Allen & Unwin team for your incredible support.

To the team at Listening Library, particularly the wonderful Nick Martorelli and Fred Sanders, and our incredible narrators Alex McKenna and Steve West—thank you so much for bringing Jules and Mia to life!

We owe the experts who helped us with our research a huge debt of gratitude—as always, everything we get right is down to them, and everything we get wrong is on us. Many thanks to Ellen Kushner for intel on French vending machines, Josh Hale for genetics advice, Marguerite Syvertson for space smarts, Howard Jones for defending the Earth while armed with nothing but a microwave, Jana and Vanessa for checking our German, Léane our French, and Albert Ubeda our Catalan. Many thanks to Soraya Een Hajji for the Latin cursing, and to Dr. Kate Irving for devising yet another way to wipe people out. We're very grateful her Hippocratic oath doesn't apply to fictional people.

We are so grateful for the many wonderful friends who support us as we wreak fictional havoc—much love to Marie Lu, Stephanie Perkins, Jay Kristoff, Leigh Bardugo, Kiersten White, Michelle Dennis, CS Pacat, Eliza Tiernan, PM Freestone, Alex Bracken, Sooz Dennard, Sarah Marsh, Kylie Irvin, Erin Bowman, Nic Crowhurst, Kacey Smith, Soraya Een Hajji, Liz Barr, Ryan Graudin, Kate Armstrong, the Roti Boti Gang, the House of Progress, and the Asheville crew.

And finally, of course, our families—you are unfailing in your support, and we are more grateful to you thank we know how to say. To the Spooners, Kaufmans, Cousinses, McElroys, Miskes and Mr. Wolf, thank you, and we love you. To Brendan, a thank-you and *I love you* from Amie for being the world's best husband.

Thank you *all* for following us through two series so far—we're off to get back to work, and can't wait to share our next world with you!